Praise for Curtis White

"Curtis White is a one-man band, a whirling dervish, a devil who speaks in tongues, a master of bewitchments, parodies, and dazzling tropes."–Paul Auster

"Curtis White writes out of an admirable intellectual sophistication combined with viscerality, pain, and humor."–John Barth

"Curtis White's fiction presents a scintillant, ironic surface, one that is barely able to contain the bleakness of American *fin-de-siècle* exhaustion, which latter is his essential theme."–Gilbert Sorrentino

"Witheringly smart, grotesquely funny, grimly comprehensive, and so moving as to be wrenching."–David Foster Wallace

Other books by Curtis White

Memories of My Father Watching TV
Monstrous Possibility: An Invitation to Literary Politics
Anarcho-Hindu
The Idea of Home
Metaphysics in the Midwest
Heretical Songs

R E Q U I E M

Curtis White

Dalkey Archive Press

Portions of this book have appeared in the following publications:
Alt-X, Cyber Corpse, NY Press, and *McSweeney's.*

Library of Congress Cataloging-in-Publication Data:

White, Curtis, 1951-
    Requiem / Curtis White.– 1st ed.
    p. cm.
    ISBN 1-56478-308-1 (acid-free paper)
    1. Dystopias–Fiction. 2. Pornography–Fiction. I. Title.

PS3573.H4575 R47 2001
813'.54–dc21

                                        2001028785

Partially funded by a grant from the Illinois Arts Council, a state agency.

Dalkey Archive Press books are published by the Center for Book Culture, a nonprofit
organization with offices in Chicago and Normal, Illinois.

www.dalkeyarchive.com

Printed on permanent/durable acid-free paper and bound in the
United States of America.

In Memoriam: Earl E. White 1927-2001

Contents

Dies Irae

Kyrie Eleison

Lacrimosa

Requiescant in Pace

"Life takes more from one than death does."
–Johannes Brahms

Prefatory Midrash (Genesis 22)

To my son, a.k.a. The Modern Prophet

Let's think this thing through. You and me. Father and son. Abe and Ike.

You have wondered what it means to be a regular human-type man and I am happy to respond. I am happy to help you understand, but you will have to try hard. I fear, though, that this silly business about The Prophet is not going to help. Son, the age at which it was appropriate and maybe even cute for you to say "I am Zorro" or "I am Superman" has passed. Long passed. But now you say that you are a Prophet of some kind, although what kind is not entirely clear to me. A "Modern Prophet" you say, as if that clarified something, but I say, okay, I can accept that at face value. For what it's worth. Coin of the realm, as far as I'm concerned. Your mother is another matter. You are killing her with your "antics," as she says. Frankly, I think she and your sisters have concluded that you're just out of your mind. And none of this even touches on the very private and personal things about our family that you divulge to God-knows-who in your little "prophesies." But I won't dwell on either antics or the whoppers you tell. I won't even dwell on the stunning whopper you've been spreading about me and the asphalt sealer on the driveway! Where the hell did that one come from? But I'll be honest, in your mother's eyes I've been guilty of a few "antics" myself over the years. And a few whoppers to boot!

Our first problem here is that, as a non-regular human-type person, you can have nearly no hope of understanding what I mean when I say normal, even though I am very willing to try to use your "special" language here and there, a language I am not likely to use well precisely because as non-special and regular I have never used this language before and have no idea what I'm doing, really.

But let me first try to say something, not about my regularness, but about your specialness. Your specialness consists mostly in two things. First, this terrifyingly complicated language you use. It crawls everywhere, doesn't it? It is horrible to imagine what the inside of your head is like. Terrifying. I think of ancient cities with wandering streets up- and down-hill, beneath which are layers of cities centuries old, winding and twisting deeply, without a single straight boulevard. It is a city made all of alleys, Son. Your brain. Which I am visiting now. There are no main streets here, at least not as I know them. A main street is a big wide easy street. The Easy Street, Son. Have you heard of it? I'm on Easy Street, or was until you turned up with your new name, and new language and big questions. But you see that Easy Chair over there? I'm going back. Eventually, I'm going back. I'm going to sit in it. I'm going to sit in the Easy Chair on Easy Street. Then I'm going to watch TV with your mother. And I won't have a stinking care in the world.

The second thing your specialness consists of is desire. You want something. But what is it? That's what I ask and, if you're honest, what you ask. The idea that you could think of accomplishing this "desire" with this hideous, frightening language is hideous and frightening to a much higher degree. It is a tortured thought that I can compare only to the thoughts I had when I tried to think about the leaders of those countries with whom we once made war. And I asked myself, what do they think? Hitler. What does he want? How does he explain this to himself? (Oh, I know, now you're asking yourself in that special introspectroverted way of yours, "My father says I'm like Hitler," and my answer is, yes, you are in some ways like Hitler for me. But please don't take that in the wrong sense.) And now you ask *me* to enter this language, so that I can explain to you something you can only—you believe—understand in this language, but it is exactly the language that will keep you from understanding, Son, when what I want to do is just hand you a brick, a brick from a garden chipped here and there, with some greenish moss against the red of the brick and some mud too. Feel it. It's cold, isn't it? Bricks *are* cold. I used to press them against my cheek. And that was pleasurable. But if I did that, you'd look at me with that pained look you use and so I am trying, Son, I'm really trying, I'm putting these words on, I'm pulling the night down over my own head. Your night. Hitler's night. I'm not happy about any of this, but I do it for you. Out of my love for you. *Love,* Son. Is that word a part of your language? I don't see it, although I haven't looked everywhere. It's a simple word, really.

The other night I watched some old home movies that your uncle made when you were very small and, while most of the film was not of you (strange as that might seem to you), there was one moment in which you stood by your baby sister in her carriage and you were only two years old yourself and you were posing but not for a *moving* picture, Son, and I went over to you and your sister and I took your little immature arms, arms like toys made from sticks from our old dead American Elm, and I waved them, flapped them up and down as if you kids might be chubby birds. We wanted motion–your uncle with his new home camera *really* wanted *motion* or what was the point?– and you kids just sat there. Ha! But I could see in this brief moment from our long ago past that when I bent down and took your little hands I should have known (but this is something I could have known only if I were you, if I were "special," if I lived in your language, there's an irony there, isn't there? and how I hate that notion, *irony,* as if the world was designed destructible, all for pulling the rug out from under and nothing more) should have known, Son, that these were hands that would never touch a brick. That would never put the cool-ness of the brick against a cheek. I should have felt what I can only see now, your aura, your eyes, the sacrificial son, looking into the cam-era, puzzled, asking little ill-shaped questions, but ill-shaped and im-mature or not they are exactly the questions your father would never ask and never want to ask.

So, I should have stopped it there, Son, should have done us both a favor. When I saw this difference and was convinced of it for the first time. You inhabiting the wrong language. And it was not forbidden that I knew of. But no means presented itself to me. Not even a brick! And besides your uncle was watching and catching it all on film, me and you and your sister, trying to get you dummies to move.

There! Do you see it? I've clearly said it, what you want to know. No?

All right. We'll do this the hard way.

Okay. This is who you are, I believe, though it hurts to say. You're cleaning the sink in your new old Victorian home that you and your skinny wife are so proud of. You have a cloth in your hand. A tea leaf presents itself. You wipe at it. But the cloth is contaminated with other tea leaves from earlier wiping. You wipe up the one but leave a half-dozen leaves behind. You wipe again. The old leaf returns, sticking to the wet surface and two or three of the new cling as well. A flare goes off inside your brain. You realize your hand is damp and cold. You hate that. Then a fierce itch catches your nose. Suddenly you realize you have to urinate. You might just pee on the floor. You wipe at your nose with the hand holding the cloth with which you tried to clean the sink. You smell the nasty smell of mold, rubber, rotting rubber, and sink-muck, including tea leaves. All this evidence begins to accumulate in your brain. You reach a conclusion: life is a failure. My conclusion is somewhat different: you are the sort of person who can be beaten by tea leaves.

An attempt to clean the sink has moved you through distinct stages to a desire to kill yourself. Am I accurate? This is your life that I am describing, I believe. Even your skinny wife, watching this "spectacle" (as your mother would call it) from the kitchen door, is very rightly appalled and amazed. At *you,* you goofy kid!

Don't cry, Son. Please. I still don't like that. It still hurts me and I want to do something about it. You were always a weepy boy. It makes me reluctant to do what has to be done. But there's nothing to be done. Only explained. And even that, I wish you'd let me stop.

And *my* life? Kansas. Dirt. Roads. Things made of wood. Women in dresses. Women curiously far away. Like silhouettes. But I did hear them laughing. And I always heard them calling me to dinner! My mother would call, "Carl, can you help me read-up the table." "Read-up!" That's how she said set the table! You know, she had her own special language. But it was the special language of Kansas. Oh, Kansas! Oh, tables! And mothers in dresses! Chipped beef on toast! And out the window all dusty dirt and some trees waiting for me. If an airplane flew overhead, we cheered in surprise and clapped our hands. The marvel!

I've been meaning to talk with you about something, Son. When I make something, when I make a house, for instance, don't tell me that because, say, it has vinyl siding that it is somehow "self-shattering." I don't know what this can mean, this word. It's an idea, isn't it? That's what you'd call it. And you probably got it from a book, if I'm not mistaken. But I'm *happy* with the home I've built, even with the low-maintenance vinyl that you despise. *You* try making a damned house, Son! But you say the word "self-shattering" and I get confused. I can't stop thinking that word. It comes back and back like an airplane flying overhead again and again. And after a while you stop cheering and marveling and start wondering when the plane will stop flying overhead. Because it's making a hell of a racket.

This hurts. You are killing me. And isn't that strange? After all my forbearance, it's me that gets it. After all the not-putting-an-end-to-it back then, it's me. Oh, look up, Son. Raise your chin. There you go. I do love you. What does that mean? Love? I'm committed to you like dirt and rocks. Listen to this:

"Then opening her fertile womb, the earth brings forth at God's command unnumbered living creatures, in perfect form and fully-grown. Ferocious, roaring, leaping, proudly grazing for their food, spreading fleecy and gentle, like dust, arising in swarms, assembling, the hosts of insects. Then in long dimension, creeps, with sinuous trace, the worm."

That's a quote. I memorized it for you. It's from the Bible. This quote shows what a father's love is like, Son, my only son. I like that bit about the worm. Worms can talk, you know. Sometimes they talk right inside your head. Hey, look at this. What's in the dirt there? Yes, that's a brick all right. But what's inside the brick? Imbedded, if you will? Here, I'll get it. Ha! It's a marble, old one, too. Now, how'd that get in a brick? A miracle! A simple miracle! The sort of simple thing that calls us back to the things of the world. The dusty things of this world of ours. Or the sticky little green leaves that you see in spring-time. We called this a cat's-eye when I was a boy. Look at that green, would you. What do you think? It's a nice green, eh, Son? Son? What have you got to say for yourself? Say something prophetic, why don't you.

"My words, the words of Chris, son of Carl, of a priestly family in the American suburbs, came to me from the Lord who said to me, 'Before I formed you in the womb I knew you.' Then the Lord extended his hand and touched my mouth."

Requiem Aeternam

The Human Condition (1)

And then he was overboard and in the cold ocean water. He was only five miles from Ocean Beach and the Pacific Coast Highway, but it might as well have been a thousand. The tide was going out and it was evening. Not even he knew exactly how it happened. Tripped? A tricky current? One too many Anchor Steams (which was the bravado behind the folly of this joy-cruise on a spring evening in spite of small craft advisories)? Or the dogs? Probably the dogs. Basset hounds. Sweet but deadly dumb. Really, he had no idea. Here's what it was most like. It was most like: it's time for you to be in the water. It was just time for this, clear and simple.

Once he'd gotten his heavy, sodden jacket, pants and shoes off (which helped nothing with the hypothermia, you can believe, or the icy panic), he was able to see the boat circling to the left, the rudder stuck hard to the right. And he could see the dogs, Harvard and Holofernes, paws up on the edge of the little craft, barking and wagging their tails, enjoying this game and wondering if they were supposed to jump in too. Now a little anxious about it. Some dim doggy corpuscle aware that this was no game.

The boat was in fact making a very tight circle about him, little could he tell. For him, the damned boat and the yapping dogs barely stayed on the horizon. It was obviously futile to swim straight for the boat. It would always flee him. Besides, he was not a very strong swimmer, in spite of his many years of sailing. No, he had just one chance. But how to exercise it? The question was, how to know what the right geometry and math would be. The boat's on this tack at X speed (allow for incoming wind [+20 mph] if heading in); the man's swim-

ming at Y speed (allow for out-going tide if in-going swimming, opposite in opposite event). How many degrees should the man attempt to
lead the boat by? If he was in the center (and damned if he wasn't
pretty close), each radial arm contained a different, very profound,
and very secret answer. To know the answer to that math was, it occurred to him in that his last moment, to know God. To know the
answer to the question—by how many degrees should I lead my little
boat, with my lovingly dopey dogs, which circles around me now like
a sacred riddle—was to know God. If he hadn't been on the verge of
panic in that moment, he would have been calmly dumbstruck by the
incredible beauty of this understanding. But, then, he always had been
perhaps overly impressed by the ability of the "smart kids" to do those
hard math problems. Believe me, in this moment, he wished he'd
spent more time with those equations instead of running for the har-
bor. He'd just throw the old textbooks in the back of the truck. Little
could he imagine this moment when the boats and the math books
would have so much to do with each other.

And God, too, thrown into the bargain!

"Hell, I might as well stay where I am and wait for the damn thing
to run over me."

He actually thought that! Sitting out there in the middle of the
Pacific with a little dinghy and two basset hounds circling him absurdly if not unkindly, he had that thought. This was evidence that he
was getting beyond the panic and into a certain calm. But perhaps the
cold was getting to him. It had been about ten minutes now and he
was starting to shut down.

Then a strange thing happened. I'm assuming that this "shutting
down" was, at another level, a sort of "letting go." He saw the boat
now, not moving one bit, quite calm, just a few yards from him. The
dogs had their feet up on the edge of the boat. They weren't barking
or whining or bouncing anxiously. They were watching him quietly.
It was as if they were observing him. As if this were some sort of test
he was undergoing and they were his judges. Imagine that! When you
die, animals judge you! He had to admit, it made a lot of sense (oh, in

the extremity of the moment, to be sure, that explains a lot of it, these crazy thoughts). Who better to judge humans than these creatures or beasts upon whom humans had been visiting death for centuries in holocausts, blood sacrifices, jungle pogroms, in search of a meal or a pelt, the bear penis and the rhinoceros horn, animal death endless and oceanic.

But wait a minute, these were his pets! Good old Harvard! Sweet Holofernes! Here boy! Catch! Wanna go for a walk?

So, if that was the case, why were they so sober now? Like long-eared angels of the God of Abraham and Isaac. They stared at him. Evaluating. Reading like the most careful exegetes his every response. Perhaps that meant that there was still time for him. Perhaps he could still make a good impression.

Yes, if he made a good impression on his own dogs he could go to heaven.

Something like that. If he had a little more time, he could refine this theology.

So the two basset hounds, his pets, stood with their little stubby legs, their barrel chests, their saggy jowls and ears like regal drapery, looking down on him in final judgement. Then, hard as it was to believe, he saw them muttering to each other, exchanging stern comments, from the side of their mouths. They never took their dispassionate brown eyes from him.

What could they be saying? Were they recalling the time he'd dislocated puppy Holofernes's shoulder slamming him into the soggy patch of carpet where he'd peed? Was that it? Was this righteous revenge? Or maybe they were remembering the time he'd literally knocked his little lovebird unconscious because it put the death grip on his finger. Would these canine patriarchs take up the cause for pet birds?

He could see their bizarre lips move articulately, as if memorializing his every worst act. With great, deep precision.

Well, that was it. Really. Quite enough. Something in those lips. The way they perfectly captured the essence of his life. And he surrendered.

"I'm sorry. Forgive me. I am willing to die."

And he began to sink. And as he sank he could just see his dogs come to full alert, peering over the edge of the boat, understanding everything, absolutely everything about this moment for their pal, the owner, the master, the human. And there was sincerity and sorrow in their eyes.

Jezebel Shall Be Like Dung (1)

(A visualization exercise on modern death.)

Bad as it is (and I think it is mostly pretty awful), you can still learn something from TV. For instance, I saw a docutainment about the death of Marilyn Monroe.

I noticed when I was a boy that Marilyn Monroe was always trying, but never quite succeeding, to let me see her breasts. I mean, I saw parts of her breasts that allowed me to imagine that there was more, but she never managed to contrive a means of allowing me to see the whole, the all-in-all of her breasts. But boy did I want to! I think if she had lived longer she would have gotten there. It really did seem pretty important to her. That thought consoles me to a degree. It is kind of women all over the Internet–especially hotcampussbabes– to very quickly get to the point and show me all of their breasts. But there's something sad and insufficient about them. For most North Americans, the infinity of breasts available to them as pornography merely supplements the absence of Marilyn's ultimate breasts. Marilyn's breasts are the ur-breasts, the "raw" breasts, the Genesis of breasts, and hence the only real breasts in all of human history. Even when she leaned way over that famous Academy Award table, laughing, her gown cut low in front, nearly to her ankles, you couldn't quite see. What the hell is the matter with cameras, anyway? Can cameras fail or refuse to see what is revealed? Is it like the snapshot of God that you rush to the 24-hour developer booth only to see that the whole roll is overexposed!? She was never quite able to reveal the "artifice of eternity."

Now, I know that Marilyn had sex with both John and Robert

Kennedy. So they surely saw her breasts. Which is the reason they had to die, according to Yahwist sources. It was sort of like when the people of Sodom came to Lot demanding that he let them fuck the Angels of God. This people was so fallen that they not only fucked everybody else (except, apparently, Lot, his wife and daughters—and what was wrong with them?), but they demanded the right to fuck the heavenly beings sent to kill them. It's a funny last wish, no? "We want to fuck those guys!" "But those guys were sent to kill you!" "We don't care about that. Send them out here!"

Brief Inter-Jezebellum Divagation

I hope that the myths about your life "passing before your eyes" in your last moment are not true. No wonder people are afraid of dying! We shouldn't have to go through this stuff twice. I hope that what really happens is that your entire record collection, all of it, rock, jazz and classical, and your favorite Stevens and Yeats poems, get fast-forwarded, or dubbed, or downloaded before you head off for the Great Wringer. 'Cause that's why they put you through the Great Wringer again. It's a machine like those old clothes washers, only a lot bigger. All of that earthly beauty and wisdom gets left behind, enriching infinite space. If heaven is in fact good, this is why: the residue of our happiest experiences of beauty are there. Imagine this accumulation over centuries! Think of all the people who have ever loved Mozart's *Requiem* re-hearing that beauty in the Beyond, how subtle and rich (how "faithful," as audiophiles say) that music becomes over the eons.

Which is why TV is evil. It threatens to pollute heaven. When prime-time viewers go through the Great Wringer, a viscous, black, oily substance is left behind. A thick, tenacious goo. It's the *Exxon Valdez* on a cosmic scale. It is an incredibly sad thing for God who has to *live* up there, after all.

So, anyway, Marilyn had sex with John and Robert (Bobby). I've seen pornographic movies where a woman blows two men at once. This notion inevitably occurs, but it is really just a distraction. Pay it no heed. I know you've seen the same damned thing, or can imagine having seen the same damned thing, which is the same damned thing, but in this circumstance pay it no heed. It's like in Zen practice where you're supposed to be just breathing. Not thinking. Until you're pure breath. The thought of Marilyn and John and Bobby in a pornographic scenario is just a mean distraction. Don't think about it.

Stop it!

I remember once reading a story in *Life* magazine about the charmed circle of the Kennedys. The Camelot crapola. And this article reported that one day John F. Kennedy was walking past the White House kitchen and for no reason at all, except his unbelievable kindness, he poked his head in the door (I'll bet it was a swinging door and painted white) and said, "What's the soup, Cookie?"

"What's the soup, Cookie?" he said. Just like that.

He was a "king" who cared about his little people, even the people called Cookie. *Life* magazine made me love the President with that one narrative aside. Now, however, I'm troubled by the idea that the name "Cookie" was just a generic name for a cook. (And a diminutive at that.) John Kennedy didn't know this person's name. He had never poked his head through this door before. He didn't even know it was the fucking kitchen. He was extemporizing for the reporter. Ad-libbing in his usual inspired way. This is how doubt and cynicism infiltrate and contaminate faith.

We do not know what the soup was on that day. Corn chowder? Something New England, no doubt. It's stupid to speculate. One way or the other, this is a long-gone soup. Nothing of this soup remains, regardless of the skill and care of the chef, Mr. Cookie. Even if there were, say, a photograph of the soup, we could only look at it and say, "Surely, this soup is dead. This is a dead soup."

Marilyn. John. Bobby. This so-called "docutainment" concentrated on the absolute lowest aspects of their drama, making it very difficult to absorb (I think that's the right word) the beauty and wisdom. We are told that she wished to be the First Lady. She would dance around her little house and sing, "I'm the First Lady" to the tune of "I Feel Pretty." Being a celebrity wasn't enough. Being the Goddess of Breasts wasn't enough. When she was First Lady, people would take her "seriously." (Which was a very silly thing to want. As an acolyte to previously mentioned mammary mysteries, I can say that I took her very seriously and there were many more like me, brothers and sisters!) But Jimmy Hoffa began bugging the Peter Lawford home where the Kennedys and Marilyn would meet for their fun and games. Hoffa was gathering evidence that he could one day use against them in order to save racketeering in America. Another noble pursuit.

(So, think about it. Hoffa may actually have had at least an audio version of our above-speculated pornographic scenario. Think what that would bring at an eBay auction! Interesting but threatening to meditative equipoise.)

One day, the Kennedys began to feel that Marilyn was a potential liability. John quit her. Bobby tried to maintain the relationship (as who wouldn't!), but Marilyn began drinking and drugging. The First Lady fantasy was getting difficult to maintain. She was receiving threatening phone calls (from whom?!) and being shadowed by the mob. Everything she touched felt "bugged." The entire world was one large invasion of her sense of self. She felt contaminated, polluted. She was being raped. By bugs! Only the idea that at least *one* of the Kennedys still loved her kept alive the hope of some kind of happiness.

"What's the soup, Cookie?"

Well, finally even Bobby had to say enough is enough. So one day when he was in L.A. and didn't want to have to deal with Marilyn, he asked his buddies Lawford and Frank Sinatra to pretty please take her out of town up to Lake Tahoe and the Cal-Neva Lodge, which Sinatra owned. Just keep her out of the way, wouldja? Forty-eight hours. No biggee. She's a grown-up, you're her friends, so it's not really kidnapping. (Just like all those bugs weren't really raping her.)

But she wasn't that dumb. She figured out what was going on. She was essentially a prisoner. So she said, okay, just give me some drugs and I'll get through this weekend or die, which ever comes first. She was fucking disgustingly smashed on pills and booze. Just ask the airplane pilot who took them out there. Bloated. Near unconscious. Probably drooling. To see her breasts in that moment would have ruined everything.

Saturday night they went to dinner to see Frank's show. He was up there singing, "Let's fly away, let's fly, let's fly away." Oh fuck that son of a bitch hypocrite! Fly this up your ass, you mob gofer. Then there was Peter Lawford smiling his ass off. Just that smile in itself is something to hold against a guy like that. The world is going to shit (just ask Marilyn; Marilyn?; Honey, wake up!) and this joker is smiling. Then there was Lawford's wife, the Kennedy, John and Bobby's sister.

Now, really, if we concentrate on this one detail intensely enough—a young woman of the Kennedy family would marry this smiley, vain, celebrity joker—we should see the utter dysfunction of the family, the horror of the future, and the reason why God once got so depressed that he said, "I am sorry that I made them" (Genesis 6:6).

Like why he made the smiley fuck Lawford.

But there are more details here. Sinatra also invited his pal Sam Giancona to this little dinner show. So there you've got the infinitely cynical Sinatra, for whom "friends" are "friends" (never mind that they're Kennedys and Mafia), you've got the sister and the lover of the Attorney General out to break this same Giancona and his mob, and Giancona himself sitting there thinking, "I'm gonna kill your boyfriend. I'm gonna fuck you, movie star. Tits. No, I'm gonna find someone else to fuck you, because I hate drunk women. Even if their boobs are mystical. Hoffa will fuck you. That guy's an animal. He's got a stronger stomach than I do. I'm too delicate. And I'm gonna kill your brother" (he gestures with his little martini glass at Mrs. Lawford née Kennedy) "and any other Kennedy goombah who fucks with me. Then I'll personally fuck you, unless you're more like this blonde bimbo than you seem. But no, you're one of these icy Kennedy babes. That's why you can even sit at this table as I consider the death of your brothers, and the rest of you smiley fucks, especially you, Lawford, who are not only a drunken smiley fuck but talentless as well. As for Frank, well, he's *paisan,* country, and homestyle. He's the true master of this situation. And that ain't no smile on his face. That's showbiz. That's professional. I respect that. Therefore, he's no smiley fuck who deserves to die. No. In the end, I like Frank. He's the kind of guy who gets to live a long time."

But then Mr. Giancona scowled and looked back at Marilyn in her boozy slump. And his last thought: "Okay, let's see them tits then, you blowsy souse, cuz I'm sick of them Kennedys lording them over me."

No, I don't know that this is what Giancona thought, but he was there (just watch the docutainment that I saw on TV) and he must have had *some* thoughts and how could he not think of sex and murder while sitting with Marilyn and a Kennedy?

Trust me on this one.

So, one more visualization exercise. This is how we make history real. It has been "Revealed" (faith comes from belief in or confidence in Revelation) that on the night of her death a murderer visited Marilyn. But who? A representative of the Kennedys? (At that moment, Bobby was playing touch football on a hillside to the east of San Francisco. In my opinion, that's trying too hard to be too innocent.) A mob hit man? You choose. But what we have to imagine is the moment in which this murderer inserted a barbiturate suppository in Marilyn's ass. There is a Shakespearean and unimaginable hardness here in the thought of the human being that could be this cruel, this sacrilegious. "I cannot draw a cart, nor eat dried oats; if it be man's work, I'll do it." And off goes the innocent and lovely Cordelia into the Great Wringer and it's still a century before Mozart can offer some comfort. Same thing here. Hoffa says, "Gus, I got a little job for you in L.A." Next thing, ol' Gus has got a gun to Marilyn's head and with his other hand he's sticking an overdose in her ass. God that sounds bad.

I'm sorry, this is a severe thing I'm asking of you, I know, but if you are to realize the truth of this murderous World-Unto-Death you must visualize the bulky fingers, the slippery suppository, the gentle push, now a little harder against the resistance of her sphincter.

See it?

The Life of Chris (1)

Things were going pretty regular at first. Chris was just another twelve-year-old boy. He liked Willie Mays and the San Francisco Giants. Then one of his friends, Dave, asked if Chris would like to go to Sunday school with him. Chris said yes because the friend was a friend he liked and because Dave's dad had a 1950 Bel Aire with old dusty fabric on the seats that smelled exciting and sad, although Chris would not have known to put it in those terms at the time. But from the first he was different that way. He was one of those boys who could smell time. He also liked Dave's father's hat that was made of straw and made Chris think that he was being driven around by Sam Snead.

Sam Snead the golfer.

They went to the Oakland Interdenominational Neighborhood Church out by the Granny Goose Potato Chip factory in Oakland. The factory walls had a huge cutout relief, painted in brilliant colors of a Mother Goose (complete with bonnet and basket) and her numerous gosling progeny. For Chris, church and huge cartoon geese were inevitably, permanently, inextricably and happily connected. Thinking of Christ's willingness to thrive essentially in the shadow of the Great Granny Goose and her potato chip factory made Chris very tolerant of other aspects of this Sunday school business. Like the prohibition on dancing.

At any rate, from his family's perspective the whole Sunday-morning-go-to-Granny-Goose-church-with-the-friend-and-Sam-Snead-in-the-handsome-'50-Chevy-thing was harmless, although Chris's dad had to wonder what was so all powerful interesting about church if it meant missing John Brodie and the Niners and Y. A. Tittle and the

N.Y. Giants on TV. His dad suspected that girls were involved but, after all, a grown-up guy who looked like the golfer Sam Snead was taking him there and back in a very orderly way, for crying out loud, so where did the girls and all that kind of trouble come in?

But then one Sunday, Chris brought home a little plaque (a prize for perfect attendance) that he hanged on the wall over his bed. It read: "Teach me to do Thy will."

"Okay," Dad thought, "first no Y. A. Tittle, now this. I gotta look at this dumb plaque every time I go in his room." But he forbore. He was actually good at forbearing, Chris's dad. Then Mom got her little shock.

One day Chris came in and sat next to her at the kitchen table as she shucked peas (to tell the truth, Mom never saw a pea that wasn't in a can, but we don't know what the hell she might have really been doing, so shucking peas it is, and besides this is about Chris and the weird thing he was about to say and not really at all about what his mom did or didn't do at the kitchen table).

And he said, "Mom, I don't understand Johannine doctrine. It's confusing to me. Can you explain it?"

"What dear?" She didn't even look up from the pea shucking.

"Johannine doctrine. The Church teachings running parallel to Paul that began in the gospel of John and continued in the Epistles in John 1."

"What about it? Or them?"

"Well, I'm just confused by his logic. I mean, I'd like to like John because Paul I think, from what I can tell, is probably where my Sunday school teacher got his 'no dancing' crap."

"Chris, your language, please."

"Sorry. But John, whoever he was, has this argument. He says, in chapter 2, 'Hello, people. I'm writing to you so that you won't sin. But if you do sin, remember, Christ died for us and he'll be an advocate for us with God!'"

"That was nice of him, dear." Shuck, shuck.

"Yeah, but it goes on. John says that in order for us to have Jesus on our side in talking to God that we have to 'know' him. And the way to 'know' him is to follow the Ten Commandments."

"And?"

"Well, anyway, it seems to me that there's a logical problem here."

"Logic? I didn't know you knew about logic already."

"Right, Mom. I'm not dumb, you know."

"I didn't say you were dumb. I just said I didn't know you knew about logic." The pea shells were piling up greenly before her.

"Well, here's how I see it. If in order for Jesus to intercede for your sins you have to know him, and in order to know him you have to follow the Commandments, what's the point? If you follow the Commandments, how can you sin? And if you can't sin, what's the use in knowing Jesus? I don't think this plan really gives Him much to do. Lot of hanging around in Heaven waiting for a follower of the Ten Commandments to sin is what I see. And the guys who don't follow the Commandments don't give Him anything to do either. From Jesus' point of view, they can just kiss off. Because he doesn't 'know' them. Anyhow, I don't get it and it's really bugging me."

His Mom finally actually looked at him. "I can see it's bugging you. Are you sure you read this part correctly?"

"Oh great, Mom, first you say I don't know about logic, now I can't even read."

"Calm down, please, and don't raise your voice with your mother. I think this is called a problem of interpretation. Can you show me the passage?"

"Sure, it's right here." He pushed an open Bible toward her. He'd been holding it on his lap, his finger keeping the page.

"I see. You've even marked it in red. Do you think you should write in the Bible, dear?"

"Why not? Is writing in the Bible bad? How would I know? Is this something Jesus could help me with?"

His mother was paying more attention to the passage than to this question. "Hmmm," she said. She read. She read again. She frowned. She read once more, employing her finger this time. Finally, she looked up from the text and at her son. There was fear and trembling in her eyes.

"Mom? Are you okay?"

Murder Mystery (1): The Crime

They found the corpse at dawn the day after a big snow tornado. It was fairly well intact, being frozen, and it couldn't have been dead for long. Finding it so quickly should have aided the investigation.

Typically, in the aftermath of tornadic snow, nearby communities would cooperate in cleanup. Sometimes this meant a downed building or barn, more often it meant mountains of pigs marooned and frozen to death by the sudden ferocity of the Canadian twisters. Farmers would pile the little pink, stiff-legged corpses by the roadside, and then the big shovels and harvest trucks would come by, collect the damned, dead beasts, and haul them off to the rendering facility next to the state penitentiary in Pontiac.

At any rate, one such load of pink bundles was being dumped before the giant shredders. There were some people hanging around, watching neutrally. Something about the way the little stiff legs poked out seemed to hold a nearly endless fascination for certain locals. An enormous dredger bucket was gobbling up a new mouthful of the pathetic, enigmatic creatures. The engineer manipulated the familiar grips and throttled the roaring behemoth. The foreman, perched atop a slick hillock of flesh, sipped a cup of coffee, a glazed donut in his other hand. The bucket was making its way through the pile. The foreman spit. Seagulls spiraled overhead. It was a regular day. Suddenly, a man on a nearby wooden pier began waving his arms and shouting to the engineer, telling him to stop.

"There's someone in the bucket! Someone's lying in the bucket!"

The annoyed engineer looked at the man then back to the bucket. The bucket swung in mid-air, its cargo all bloated pinkness and poking legs. "What the hell is the matter?"

Then the foreman saw what the man had seen. Two naked, chubby legs. Human. Childish. Amazing that he was able to see them at all, the pink blended so perfectly with the frozen pigginess. But without question, there were two legs sticking out of the mass of pork. The socks (though dirty and tattered) were the big giveaway.

The engineer swung the bucket over to the side, onto some cold, muddy ground, and the foreman and a couple of spectators helped to pull the little body from the pile. Somebody threw a bucket of water over the corpse, washing away mud and unidentifiable gore. The little, naked legs seemed to shine. They looked almost glazed or candied.

The boy was naked from the waist down except for the socks. His legs immediately struck observers as perfectly shaped. Astonishing that legs like these could be on something dead. He wore a thin, white T-shirt, stained with blood, which seemed strange since his body was unmarked. He had no pubic hair yet. His face was slightly swollen. His hair was medium-length and messy with small clumps of something that looked like breakfast all stuck within it.

It was hard not to assume that his hair had always looked more or less like this, even before he was the dead body of a young boy lying among pigs.

Isolation (1)

Dear Editor:

I am repeatedly struck by how often the letters people write to you affirm the presence of God in our lives. And it has occurred to me that living in Normal, Illinois, in this moment in time is very much like living in the Bible of Moses and Aaron and Joshua, when the Lord talked to his people and told them how they were to behave. When people die on the busy interstate system that passes our little town, when their sports utility vehicles pile into concrete embankments or into trucks or other sports utility vehicles, I no longer think of it as tragic. I do not wonder how God could allow a family of five to perish on the side of the road on Christmas Eve. I am not confused by bad things happening to good people. Rather, these deaths affirm for me the idea that God has his elbow in the punch bowl, as my mother used to say, and that he has something big planned for us. The people of our little town are in for some big and very profitable surprises soon! I cannot say what these surprises might be, but if you doubt me, please, consider these parallels.

In the Bible, before the Israelites could inhabit the Promised Land, *all of them had to die.* True! None that exited Egypt with old Moses arrived. None! God smote them himself. Or he had them smoted. He submitted his people to defeats at the hands of their enemies.

Of course, when God's will strikes close to home, it is much harder to accept, though accept it we must. Well, his will has struck close to home for me this last holiday season. It is my husband. My husband Roy, who has been my loyal husband and our family's principal breadwinner for thirty-five years. Well, something is wrong with his head. I think the best description of it is that it has come loose. It may be that the muscles in his neck have simply been stretched by some inexplicable force to a degree where they no longer work to hold his head in place.

I had never realized before how heavy a head is! I would estimate (given my experience with my husband's head) that they weigh about ten pounds. The connection to his body is now so stretchy that I was actually able to pretty much just put the head on our bathroom scale.

This all began Christmas morning after opening gifts. This is why I know that his condition has to do with God's divine will realizing itself on earth. Roy got tools for his shop in the basement. Large tools that required clamps. I think clamps may have something to do with this. Well, he went off to install them and I began to cook the cinnamon rolls. Then, around 10:30, he came up from the basement with the most awful grimace on his face. He clutched his head in his hands. I didn't realize it at that moment, but he was actually holding his head in place. This is where the clamps could be relevant.

Have you or your readers ever played with that toy that has a wooden ball with a hole in it attached by a string to a stick? And you flip the ball in the air and catch it with the stick? I believe that is the sort of relationship Roy has developed with his head.

Well, my question is this: can you tell me what has happened to my husband's head? And do you have an opinion about whether or not this is one of the strange ways that the Lord our God works in?

Sincerely,

Edna Mayfair
Normal

Mozart's *Requiem*

It is reported that, shortly before his death, upon hearing the Lacrimosa of his *Requiem,* Mozart fell into tears. He wept at the beauty of his own successful representation of universal tears. He succeeded in making those old tears, the tears of eternity, present again, as if for the first time. What we must here wonder is what it means about history, what it means to be human *then* and what it means to be human *now,* that you could gather all the cold children of these United States together and play Mozart's short eight bar Lacrimosa and every eye would be dry. Uncomprehending. Dead, in a certain way.

One of the marvels of the coincidence of Mozart's *Requiem* and his own death (for the two are inseparable for everyone except those we should rightly want to call *spoilsports!*) is the large number of tales that have grown up around the *Requiem,* like so many leitmotifs, like a Wagnerian re-scoring of the whole thing.

For instance:

Mozart was killed by Masons.

Why? Well, Mozart was a very enthusiastic member of a local lodge ("Beneficence" or Δ), as was Haydn and even Haydn's patron, Prince Esterházy. Freemasonry flourished in Austria not least because of the initial enthusiasm of people at the very top of the Austro-Hungarian Empire (for instance, Francis Stephen, Duke of Lorraine and husband of the Archduchess Maria Theresa). So strong, in fact, were Freemasonry's political connections in the Empire that Emperor Charles VI suppressed the Papal Bull of 1738 condemning Freemasonry. What business was it of the Pope? Why should he care if some privileged characters got together to make up an eclectic religion out of the tatters of Egypt-tinted occultism, Christianity and political libertarianism? They were just like kids playing a fun game. The name of the game was World History.

The growth of the Lodges was mostly confined to Vienna and there were never large numbers of people involved, but they were very prominent people—members of the nobility, wealthy businessmen, and art celebrities like Mozart—all mingling freely and exchanging secret symbols and rituals. But we're not talking adolescent Trekkies here. The true purpose of these secret societies, and there were a lot of them, was to allow for a privileged, exclusive and secret context for business. These secret societies were the original Rotary Club, Knights of Columbus, business networks! Capitalism was being invented there! That secret handshake was the cost-benefits-analysis handshake, and don't let 'em tell you any different! It was the invention of insider trading. See? Insider trading doesn't seem so insidious or unfair, seems downright logical, if you think of capitalism's origins not in factories but in secret societies, unnatural unions of burghers and barons. The original merger. And as for the criminality of insider cheating, that's just one brother lodge member helping another. As for those outside the club, *tant pis!*

Personally, for Mozart, his status as a Master Mason was also business. He needed wealthy subscribers to his concerts. He was his own one-man entrepreneurial operation. He also frequently borrowed money from one Johann Michael von Puchberg, a merchant. After obliging incredible groveling from Mozart, in letters in which Mozart depicted the most extreme suffering of his wife and children, Puchberg would send him twenty bucks. Tiny sums so that Mozart could go to the store, you understand. (Of course, from our perspective, the only decent thing that made Puchberg's life worthy of mention is exactly these pathetic sums which he sent to the impecunious Mozart. Would that he'd sent a thousand!) My point is, I don't think Mozart really *got* the Masons. I don't think he realized that everyone was taking the mumbo jumbo of it all seriously. Mozart was, as ever, just playing, although his play was also, as ever, serious.

As I've indicated, in some ways, everyone was taking it seriously. That's why they eventually got in trouble. First, you've got the nobility talking to merchants who then talked to artists. Such a cross-fertilization was bound to produce a hybrid (i.e., a revolutionary worldview). This was precisely what Joseph II and the Austrian secret police thought was going on. And they weren't wrong. Many Masonic orders *were* involved with Jacobism and the ideals of the French Revolution. The American revolutionaries Franklin, Washington and Jefferson were influenced by Masonry in the Declaration of Independence. Now, we might reasonably protest that the aristocrats in Vienna's orders would not have had regicide in mind (being who they were), but as the people in France discovered, Ideas have a life of their own. And so thought Joseph II and his secret police . . . *another* interesting invention that we owe to Masonry!

But what I'm trying to tell you is the story concerning Mozart's death at the hands of the Masons. That is the story of *The Magic Flute.* As H. C. Robbins Landon tells it in his book *1791: Mozart's Last Year*:

"When the first printed libretto of *The Magic Flute* appeared . . . readers who opened it saw an engraved frontispiece. . . . To the uninitiated this sheet would have looked like . . . an archaeological excavation in Egypt. . . . Many people would have thought they were seeing some abstruse Oriental vision. . . . But some of the audience knew that the symbolism referred through a whole series of unmistakable hints to the Ancient and Venerable Order of Free Masons. . . . Having been uneasily prepared for something vaguely connected with the Masonic ritual, many Brothers in the audience of 1791 would have had even more of a shock when, in the middle of the Overture, they heard the music come to a stop and, after a pause, continue in very slow tempo with three-times-three chords in the following rhythm:

Part of the Masonic ritual is the use of a knocking rhythm three times in succession."

In short, the stupefying truth is that in this famous opera one symbol after another is derived from the Order. And what's stupefying is that Mozart made a vow of silence in joining the order. It's a *secret* society, Wolfgang! In fact, Mozart would have said in the *responsorum* to the "Examination upon Entrance into the Lodge":

"I Hear and Conceal, under the Penalty of having my Throat cut, or my Tongue pulled out of my Head."

That's a pretty picture. But who knows, Mozart may have laughed afterwards. It's hard to imagine him taking this threat seriously.

Whatever the case, Mozart went to Prague and unveiled the opera during the coronation celebrations for the new Emperor. He returned home the same unreasonably enthusiastic musical genius he was before. Then six weeks later, he was implausibly dead.

They didn't pull his tongue out, but, nonetheless, it was some kind of ugly death: burning with fever, his limbs swollen with water to the point that he couldn't even roll over in bed, smelling already of an internal disintegration. Thus the final destiny of the composer of the immortal Jupiter Symphony and the String Quartets to Haydn. Done in by the sinister society with whose secret laws he'd run afoul. The Masons.

According to his sister-in-law, Sophie Haibel, "His last movement was an attempt to express with his mouth the drum passages in the *Requiem.* That I can still hear." This drum passage imitates the ritual rhythms of the Masons. This is no different from a murdered man whispering the name of his murderer with his last breath.

Salieri Poisoned Him

Salieri was the Chapel Master to the Emperor and the most influential musician in Austria. Old Salieri denied any act against Mozart in no uncertain terms, but Salieri on the verge of death–and in a Kafkaesque frame of mind–confessed to the whole thing. This one's been told ad nauseam by Peter Schaeffer in his vapid play *Amadeus.* The movie is even more vapid. Mozart's wife, Constanze, knew perfectly how wrong were any such suspicions of mayhem and said so often and publicly.

But look how Constanze is treated by Schaeffer. All tits and giggles. She's a warning of what happens to anyone who tries to get in the way of a good story.

A Messenger From the Beyond

Of course, everyone's favorite story is the one about how a messenger from the beyond, a strange man on horse, came to Mozart's door claiming to represent a "powerful connoisseur" and requested that Mozart write a requiem to honor the death of someone much loved. He would not say who this patron was. He asked Mozart to name his price and paid it on the spot.

As he composes, rapidly, with increasing intensity, enthusiasm and interest, Mozart is pursued by the idea that he is in fact creating a requiem for his own death. He has two contradictory impulses.

Impulse one: if I don't actually write it, I won't die. Constanze Mozart, in fact, insists that he stop working on it because he's working himself to death. In that sense, the *Requiem was* the cause of his death. Did Mozart imagine that if he *never* wrote a requiem he would be immortal?

(There are other stories like this one in the lives of the great composers. Mahler, for instance, was afraid to write his ninth symphony because he knew that Beethoven died after his ninth. So he wrote *Das Lied von der Erde* as his ninth not-symphony after which ruse he felt safe to write the ninth as if You-Know-Who couldn't count. But the fact remains, he left his tenth symphony unfinished.)

Impulse two: if the *Requiem* was to be his last work, then it must be his crowning glory, written with utter clarity and vigor in spite of fever, swollen extremities, failing kidneys, whatever. This was the course he took.

Ultimately, the world learned that the messenger had been sent not by Mr. Death but by one Count Walsegg, a ludicrous penny-boy in spite of his wealth, who liked to have works composed for him and then pretend he had written them himself. He wasn't really kidding anybody, though, he just liked being humored by his house musicians, who were by their own testimony happy to do it, count their wages, and laugh about it over *weisen bier.*

I don't mind this debunking of the Walsegg legend so much because the "true" story is itself a good one, a Shandian kind of story about an "original" and his hobbyhorse. There are probably more stories about this Count Walsegg character and, frankly, I wish I knew some of them. Alas, the only one that has come down to us has come down to us because it was attached to the great Mozart like a fluffy bit of lint caught on one of Mozart's fabulous frock coats. (Mozart really was a sort of dandy. When he died he had nine fancy frock coats in his armoire.)

Killjoys

What we ought perhaps to wonder about is what to do with killjoys like H. C. Robbins Landon in his *1791: Mozart's Last Year.* Landon loved Mozart's music, and loved the idea of the man as an actual man. He found Mozart's very real and tragic death at age thirty-five very sad. But he also felt this curious need to blot out all the myths and legends—all the stories which emerged from the glottis of the vox populi over the years. Landon wanted to correct the record. In fact, his last chapter is a "vindication" of Constanze.

Now, there's something funny here. This Constanze lived a long human life, much longer than Mozart's, and she's been dead for over a century and a half. For the sake of what does Landon defend her? From *what* does he defend her? Well, first he defends her from the representation of her as all tits and giggles in *Amadeus.* And, to a lesser degree, he defends her from Mozart's own complaint that she let actors tie things about her calves at after-hours cast parties. (By the way, Mozart must have been naive. She was a "theater major," so to speak! Anyone who's ever had the opportunity to hang with the theater majors knows what I'm talking about. As Othello said, "Goats and monkeys!")

'Nuther thing: the story of Constanze's indelicacy has always appealed to me because it's so typical of the erotic libertinage of the age (á la *Don Giovanni* and Mozart's librettist, the notorious Lorenzo Da Ponte, who was kicked out of Venice for adultery). What has always been very clear to me is the fact that sex was *dangerous* in the 18th century, in part because of disease and in part because people murdered each other over it. Mozart himself would have little to do with sex (outside his relationship with Constanze). As he wrote his father, "I have too much horror and disgust, too much dread and fear."

What I don't think Landon gets is the fact that his "true" story does nothing to get rid of the more scandalous stories. They're still good stories. We probably always suspected they were false, and now we know. So what? In fact, Landon's version of the story of Mozart's death is little more than just another story among many. It has no particular superiority, unless you would claim superiority for narrative squeamishness. In fact, it even has its own *pornography*. The pornography of the really real. Like the chapter in which he goes into the most God-awful grisly detail about exactly how Mozart died. The lubricity of the medical gaze:

"[Dr. Closset] reasonably suspected that Mozart had a growth within his brain. . . . In my view, Closset was puzzled by the recent symptoms of fever, painful joint swellings and skin rash. . . . Mozart died from the following: streptococcal infection–Schonlein-Henoch Syndrome–renal failure–venesections–cerebral haemorrhage–terminal broncho-pneumonia." (Davies, quoted in Landon, *1791.* . . .)

Mozart's. . . . *BODY.*

Story of a Cell

The story that doesn't get told is one suggested by Dr. Davies. He proposes that Mozart "contracted his final illness during his attendance at the Masonic Lodge on 18 November 1791 (there was an epidemic in Vienna at that time)."

Happy Mozart. Triumphant composer of *The Magic Flute.* But carrying like a death sentence in his back pocket two already damaged kidneys. He's among his Masonic brothers in the modestly bizarre circumstances I've already discussed. He's about to be named Chapel Master to the Church of St. Stephens, although he doesn't know it. So, he may be hinting to Puchberg that he'll be hitting him up again soon, because in spite of his celebrity he's broke. But one of his lodge brothers doesn't feel well. Or he'll soon not feel well. One of his brothers is exfoliating, is shedding dangerous strep spoors, bacteri, whatever, in the air. Or on his hands. In those Secret Handshakes!

Oh, Mozart! our collective Love!, you who bring us to our knees two hundred years later, you imp, that Secret Handshake was with Mr. Bones.

And now he wipes his mouth. Indiscreet. Like a little boy.

And now the little cell-your-death is on its way. Feel it? It is a little dark stranger.

This is all very adagio, by the way.

Coda

What *was* in the air in that Masonic lodge?

The day after Mozart died, a lodge-brother, Franz Hofdemel, husband to one of Mozart's piano students, Magdalena, accused her of having an affair with little fastidious Wolfgang. (Of course, he didn't know of Mozart's very reasonable "horror and disgust" on that score. The sex score, that is.) Hofdemel maimed his wife, cut her on the face, hands and throat with a razor, and then killed himself.

This is a true story that came to pass because of a contemporary legend about Mozart's amorous exploits. Mozart was, after all, the composer of *Don Giovanni*. But the brilliant libretto was the creation of Lorenzo Da Ponte who based it in part on legend and in part on what he had really done with a friend's wife in Venice. These facts belong together, but the syntax is wrong. Magdalena's husband should have suspected her of fucking Da Ponte, not poor Wolfie. But he didn't know Da Ponte. Still, he could smell him through Mozart's music, and on his wife. Goats and monkeys. Rotting mushrooms. Spirochetes. Viral spirals worming their way along.

Contrition (1)

What pleases me most is the silent applause.

—W.A. Mozart

CAST OF CHARACTERS

CONSTANZE, wife to Mozart
SÜSSMAYER, assistant to Mozart
SALIERI, court composer and rival to Mozart
PAPAGENO, a character in Mozart's *The Magic Flute*
PUCHBERG, a wealthy businessman, Mason and benefactor to Mozart
OFFICIAL, nameless official to the court of Leopold II

SCENE: *An anteroom in the palace of Emperor Leopold II. The room is empty except for six chairs, one of which is vacant. In the other five sit* CONSTANZE, SÜSSMAYER, SALIERI, PAPAGENO, *and* PUCHBERG.

TIME: *The period after the death of Mozart. All are dressed in mourning, except* PAPAGENO, *who is dressed like a bird. A big yellow bird.*

ACTORS: *All should be C students in a mediocre Midwestern university theater department. The only qualification for the roles is that they be "goats and monkeys." That is, they all seek to bed the girlfriends and wives of fiction writers because 1) they want to; 2) they know fiction writers feel it all, "nothing is lost on them"; 3) they think it will help give the work of the fiction writer(s) more depth (they equate human pain with depth, the more raw, unexpected and arbitrary the deeper); and 4) they're goats and monkeys.*

Enter OFFICIAL

OFFICIAL: [*Seating himself and shuffling some papers on which he has notes*]
Well, this is a cheerful little gathering. And I won't keep you any
longer than is necessary, but it is the case that the Emperor is concerned with the number and severity, I might say the extremity, of
the rumors circulating regarding our dear departed Herr Mozart.
Above all, the Emperor desires that there should be an end to the
suffering you and the court endure.

PAPAGENO: Kind sir, can you tell me why I am here? I never had the
pleasure of knowing Herr Mozart. I am a person who catches wild
singing birds for the pleasure of the Queen of the Night.

OFFICIAL: Please, Herr Papageno, if you can hold your concerns and
questions until later, perhaps we will all be clearer about this situation when we have finished talking. [*Consults his papers*] Now, what
His Majesty finds most curious and troubling is not the existence
of rumors and scandals surrounding the life of Herr Mozart. *That*
he is quite used to and comes under the disposable heading of
"court intrigue." He knows what to do with all that. What has come
to trouble him is the idea that you all have personal concerns about
your conduct toward Mozart. You have expressed feelings of guilt
and worthlessness in relation to him that go far beyond even what
has been rumored and these feelings, irrational though they may
be, are worrisome precisely because they threaten *you*. Perhaps,
Frau Mozart, you could begin.

CONSTANZE: Well, to say that I am unhappy says very little. I have
tried to think that my thoughts and my confessions are just part of
my grieving and that soon they will pass. But as you point out,
there is something disturbing, or unreasonable, about some of my
feelings.

OFFICIAL: Yes. Certainly. Go on.

CONSTANZE: I feel as if all my own worth has left with my husband.
And as I give thanks to him and to God for having given him to
me, I simultaneously feel this great loathing for myself. I feel de-

filed. And all my life seems colored by it. I feel compelled to confess things. Awful things. For example, I have told many people of the time that, when I was a young girl of nine or ten years, I once hung my naked bottom out a window so that my cousin and his friends could see my private parts. And I remember howling and laughing as if I were possessed. And this story is true! And I know that one part of my mind—a very strong part—thinks that it was an *essential* moment for me. That that moment catches who I am. Sordid and unworthy.

PAPAGENO: [*In shameless glee*] You really did this? How I wish I had been one of your cousin's friends! Or your cousin! I have never seen anything like this! For though I lack nothing for desire, I am one of those poor souls who live perpetually deprived.

OFFICIAL: Herr Papageno, please. You will have an opportunity to speak later.

PAPAGENO: But she has really caused me to see this scene. It's very clear in my mind. I'm very happy about it.

OFFICIAL: Frau Mozart. Would you like to continue?

CONSTANZE: Yes. I have not only confessed to this childish act; I have also confessed to more adult acts. For instance, my dear husband once scolded me for allowing a handsome and celebrated actor to slip a garter onto my leg at a party while he was out of town. What I didn't tell him is that later, after the party, the actor returned, to retrieve his lover's garter, he claimed. He didn't want her to think he'd lost it. And I said to him, "Yes, why don't you take her garter," and I offered him my leg. But of course his hand didn't stop at the garter but proceeded until it had found my most private parts. And he stroked me there until I dissolved in his arms. [*Anyone interested in an actual image of this moment may see it painted on Papageno's "Magic Bell Box" in Ingmar Bergman's movie version of* The Magic Flute *(1975) now widely available on videocassette.*]

OFFICIAL: Hmmm. Yes, this is very serious.

CONSTANZE: And I have confessed this thing to our friends and dear Mozart's benefactors: his brothers in the Temple, and really anyone who would listen. But it's not true. I never did this thing. But I feel like I should do it now, that and much more.

PAPAGENO: Do you really?

CONSTANZE: [*She considers*] Yes, I believe I say this in all seriousness. Perhaps if I were to repeat the act with someone (as a way of affirming or assuring myself that I did in fact do it the first time), then perhaps I would actually be punished for my wickedness. I feel like I desire punishment as companion for my sense of defilement.

PAPAGENO: My dear lady, I am but a humble fowler, but if there is ever anything. . . .

OFFICIAL: Herr Papageno, please! May I interrupt you? I begin to sense that you really have very little self-control, especially over your tongue.

PAPAGENO: Sir, as I said, I have spent most of my life in the company of birds. Birds sing when they will. And is there any part of a person more birdlike, more trilling, than the tongue? I have a bird in my mouth, sir, and he will sing when he will.

OFFICIAL: Your presence here has also been "willed" at a level whose thinking is inaccessible to me. It is my feeling, though, that I cannot help these people if you are constantly interrupting. Especially in the *way* you interrupt. I fail to see how your comments can help these people.

PAPAGENO: I'll tell you what. Henceforth, I'll interrupt only when I feel like it.

OFFICIAL: And how is that an improvement?

PAPAGENO: I could interrupt at every opportunity. I have known many a bird that would. There are birds which so abhor silence that even the spaces between notes are intolerable. Hence the rolling song of a canary, for example.

OFFICIAL: Well, do you others have anything to say to Frau Mozart?

SÜSSMAYER: Yes, I do. I have been listening to this wonderful woman and I am very deeply moved. I understand what she means very personally, as I will explain later. But as for her own conduct, I have virtually lived with this virtuous woman and loyal wife for some time now. As Herr Mozart's assistant, I am constantly at their home. And I can assure anyone who would wish to know that she was always loyal. No, "loyal" doesn't say enough. She loved her husband ardently. And it pains me deeply to see her abuse herself with these false thoughts which are surely the result of some mental disturbance which comes with her grief.

CONSTANZE: Thank you, Herr Süssmayer.

PAPAGENO: [*Laughter*]

OFFICIAL: [*Annoyed*] Papageno, stop that puerile laughing. This is not the moment for it. Your conduct becomes increasingly offensive.

PAPAGENO: Excuse me, sir, but something funny just popped into my mind. I don't know where it came from. It was just a little phrase. Bing! And there it was. Like a berry in the bush of my mind. Very bright. The phrase was "fatuous ass." Isn't that funny?

CONSTANZE: [*Coloring*] Oh dear. How could he know that?

SÜSSMAYER: [*Crestfallen*] Don't think I don't understand what you mean, Constanze. I know how the maestro thought of me and my small talents.

PAPAGENO: Really!? You mean, I've hit on something?

CONSTANZE: [*Pleading*] Oh, my dear Süssmayer, please believe that my husband had the deepest affection for you. Because he did. This is so even if, on occasion. . . .

PAPAGENO: He would call him a fatuous ass?

SÜSSMAYER: This is very depressing.

PAPAGENO: I think you need to look at it as others do: you took the single most beautiful work of the most beautiful creator of music in human history, the *Requiem,* and made a pedestrian wreck of it. You even left out whole sections, like the Lacrimosa, for which Mozart had left perfectly coherent sketches.

SÜSSMAYER: [*Groaning*] The worst of it is that as soon as Mozart was gone, I fled to the camp of his rival, Herr Salieri.

CONSTANZE: I have to admit, I was disappointed. That hurt.

SÜSSMAYER: But I did it only to survive! Had Mozart lived, I would surely have stayed on with him. If for no other reason than to see what came next from that head. Do I need to feel so guilty about being what I am, about wanting to survive? Should I kill myself because I'm mediocre?

PAPAGENO: Deeply mediocre, Herr Süssmayer. [*Laughing quietly to himself*] "Fatuous ass." Very funny.

SALIERI: [*Stands suddenly, head bowed*] When it comes to guilt, none has a burden greater than mine, as Herr Süssmayer has only begun to indicate.

OFFICIAL: What do you mean, maestro?

SALIERI: I mean that I killed Mozart.

CONSTANZE: Oh, not this again. It's absurd.

OFFICIAL: Maestro, you have tried to confess to his murder before and no one will believe you. You have been affected by the false rumors vicious people have spread. But you don't have to believe them! The Emperor doesn't believe them. It pains him to see his loyal servant in this mad remorse.

SALIERI: But I remember it very clearly. I poisoned him.

CONSTANZE: You rarely even met with Mozart. How could you have done this?

SALIERI: I slipped it into his drink. That's how I did it.

PAPAGENO: Really!? That's awful. What kind of poison was it?

SALIERI: A brew given me by demons. Acqua toffana, I believe it was.

PAPAGENO: How operatic! Demons!

OFFICIAL: Salieri. Listen to me. You are a favorite of the court and have been for many years. Herr Mozart was a young man of great genius and ambition and if he had lived longer eventually he would have gained the prosperity and respect that he longed for. He too wanted the support and the money provided by the court. It is natural that he was a threat to you. It is natural that you should have responded in ways which protected your high position, even if your response was not always generous or kind. You did intrigue against him. But you did not kill him.

SALIERI: Still, the poison could not have helped matters.

CONSTANZE: Herr Salieri. My husband was not unaware that you were his rival. But he also respected you. In fact, he wrote me from Salzburg just before his last illness about how pleased you were with *The Magic Flute*. Believe me, he was happy to know that at heart you enjoyed his work.

PAPAGENO: [*Rising and passing before* SALIERI, *his hands behind his back like a lawyer making final remarks*] Herr Salieri, I would like to see you punished. I would like for you to hang your bony haunches out some window (as Frau Mozart has described) so that the citizens of Vienna can come by and take a good whack at you with whatever is at hand. Musicians first, whacking you with their instruments, the timpanist raising his mallets overhead to whack you with, the baker using his rolling pin, women whacking you with their children. [*Pause*] But, really, isn't it punishment enough to now that for decades you produced music whose only virtue was soporific? And you, Süssmayer, you couldn't even bore people properly!

SALIERI: [*Sitting*] I killed him and I'd kill him again. I'd kill him into infinity. I want to suffer and be forgiven. Again and again.

PAPAGENO: Hahaha! That's very funny! It really is. Punished into infinity. This little party has been far more entertaining than I ever imagined. For I can see on my left an infinity of windows with the haunches of the guilty Salieri and on my right an infinity of windows with the sweet buttery buttocks of Frau Constanze, ooh!, and me running up the middle of this street, kicking Süssmayer like a rolling hedgehog before me, whacking Salieri's old behind with whatever came to hand, then over to this dear lady's smelliferous bottom for encouragement and sustenance and stamina and just, you know, the will to go on with the kicking and the whacking. With such an occupation I do believe I could quite abandon my birds.

OFFICIAL: [*Defeated, chin in hand*] Papageno, are you done?

PAPAGENO: [*Considering*] I think so, yes.

OFFICIAL: Because we wouldn't want to hurry you or interrupt.

PAPAGENO: Oh, don't worry about me. I'll let you know when I have something to say.

OFFICIAL: Thank you. Now, Herr von Puchberg. Many thanks for your patience. We have yet to hear from you. But we have learned that you have been distraught and depressed since Mozart's death. Can you say why? The court would like to help.

PUCHBERG: My thanks to the Emperor for his concern. I am a simple businessman. I have managed the textile firm of Michael Salliet for many years. After Herr Salliet's death in 1780, I married his widow.

PAPAGENO: Well, Lord, that was a clever thing to do, you old swindler. You're filthy with loot then, aren't you? And all you had to do was hold your nose and cuddle to that old, used, smelly thing.

PUCHBERG: Beginning around 1788, after I had met Herr Mozart in the Masonic Lodge, he began writing what have been called "begging" letters to me, asking for money.

PAPAGENO: *Called* begging letters?? Even the stupid animals in my woods know that he groveled at your boots. He would have licked them if you'd laid off kicking him. He was ready to credit you with starving his children if you didn't send him ten bucks. "If you, dearest friend and Brother, abandon me now, I am lost, wretched as I am, together with my poor sick wife and my child, and through no fault of mine." Suck up! He was a leech!

PUCHBERG: The truth is that Mozart operated in a world where his work was stolen or paid for on the cheap. It was the least I could do to help such a great genius.

OFFICIAL: Why, then, do you feel so bad about it?

CONSTANZE: In truth, dear friend, you often helped us.

PUCHBERG: Well, Mozart would ask for very particular sums, sometimes large, sometimes small. But I never once gave him all that he asked for. It was as if on the one hand I honored his talent by giving him money, but on the other, I always held something back. I refused to acknowledge his full need. The part of the money I didn't lend him was, I now realize, a form of my wish that he should die. I wanted him dead, just as most musicians in Vienna wanted him dead, but for my own reasons. He had a daily beauty that made me and my textiles and my money ugly. I would think of his music and want to help. I would take the guldens in my hand. I would look at them. They would look like shit in my hand. But that was all I had to offer. It was all I was. So in despair and self-loathing, I would take some of the guldens (be they shit or not-shit) and return them to my pocket. I would give him only enough to keep him minimally alive. Just alive enough that he could come back to me the next day and ask for more.

CONSTANZE: [*Head in hand*] Dear God!

SÜSSMAYER: How awful.

SALIERI: Herr Puchberg, these were my very thoughts.

OFFICIAL: Again, this is merely your grief speaking. Let us be reasonable, friends. Let me provide you with a healthier perspective. One that I am sure you will adopt in time, when you're feeling better.

PAPAGENO: Excuse me, sir. May I ask a question?

OFFICIAL: Could I stop you?

PAPAGENO: If you put a lock on my mouth. If you have one. The Queen of the Night has one.

OFFICIAL: Lucky her. Go ahead.

PAPAGENO: My question is this: Herr Puchberg, did you have more money? Could you have afforded to fully support the Mozart family?

PUCHBERG: Yes. Easily. Of course.

PAPAGENO: So, on the one hand there is the magic of the Jupiter Symphony and the Quartets to Haydn and on the other there are the stacks of caca which you hoard and which genius needs some poor part of to fill its belly while it prepares the next access to the sublime for mere mortals like you, who could never in a bazillion years get to the sublime on your own. And you refuse the Beautiful your Caca? Is that about the size of it?

PUCHBERG: Yes. I suppose so.

PAPAGENO: Well, that's disgusting. *He,* sir, should be punished.

OFFICIAL: He will not be punished. He is a fine member of this community. He is prosperous and he helps to create the prosperity of all.

PAPAGENO: He will not give Caca for Beauty! I think this failure to offer appropriate tribute to the true God merits plagues, or dismemberment, or at least a good stoning out beyond the city wall.

OFFICIAL: [*Getting up, gathering his papers*] I think you misunderstand the purpose of this gathering. We've accomplished about as much as we're going to today. Which is to say, nothing. And I will report as much to His Majesty. And you, Herr Papageno, can expect a visit from a representative of the court.

SÜSSMAYER: Well, wait a minute, now. I believe that Papageno has a good point. He has quite persuaded me. He's on to something.

SALIERI: It is disgusting, isn't it? Worse than my poisoning by a long shot. He insulted God, in essence. Isn't that your argument, Herr Papageno? I say the rich man should die. It is easier for a needle to pass through a camel's eye, or something.

PUCHBERG: Good Lord. Look, I thought this was an opportunity for sharing. Therapy. Mutual support.

PAPAGENO: [*Kneeling in front of* CONSTANZE, *kneading the hem of her dress, perhaps slipping a hand up her shapely leg*] And you, Madame? What is your verdict on this son of Moloch?

[CONSTANZE, *raising her head from her lap where she has been weeping*]

PAPAGENO: Look, she's been crying! [*to* PUCHBERG] You've made her cry! On top of your other calumnies!

[OFFICIAL *goes to door and signals for guards*]

CONSTANZE: Herr Puchberg, I have long considered you a benefactor. But these confessions of yours have stoned my heart. We only asked for more of your money which was nothing more to you than . . . what it has been called here.

PAPAGENO: Shit! You denied them your shit!

PUCHBERG: It's easy to hate a rich man.

PAPAGENO: [*Strikes* PUCHBERG *with his fist; others rise to join him*] Death to the man whose world is made of money!

49

Treachery (1)

This story also comes under the heading "Life on God's Green Earth, As We Find It, Right Here, Right Now."

According to George Fisher of the Johns Hopkins University, we have the following requirements for sustaining life on Earth:

"The Earth must be close enough to the Sun that its temperature is in the range of liquid water. Its gravity field must be strong enough to retain an atmosphere that gives a surface pressure in the field of liquid water (unlike Mars, or the Moon). Its daily rotation be fast enough that diurnal temperature variations are not too extreme (unlike the Moon). It must have a crust light enough to form large continental masses, but thin enough to permit plate tectonics to operate (unlike Mars)."

For you and me, these facts lead us to conclude that we all ought to wear slippers when we go outside, and we ought to walk very gently. And no more loud noises!

Unhappily, not everyone responds as we do. Consider the following case history of base treachery:

A landlord in my little hometown was sentenced to jail for repeatedly fighting with his tenants. Well, these things happen, you say.

But let me continue. This local character, let's call him S, received his stiff sentence after failing to abide by the terms of his previous conviction for intimidation. S argued his defense by shouting obscenities at the judge, Elizabeth R. So that added to his burden a count of contempt of court.

Amazingly, a new assault charge was added *during his incarceration* when S spit in the face of a guard. According to S himself, "I spit in my captor's face, and it was a damned good shot."

But let's return to the criminal moment itself. In the summer of 1999, S was arrested three times in five days after police responded to disputes between S and his tenants. In the last incident, S was discovered in the basement of his building stabbing a pile of laundry (owned by a tenant) with a long knife. According to police, S commented, "I told her and told her, clean the lint drawer out before starting a new load. But does she listen? No! Well okay then. That leaves it pretty much up to me, doesn't it?"

When the arresting officer requested that S put the knife down, S waved it from side to side as he had seen people do in movies and started toward the officer. Naturally, the officer drew his gun. S responded by saying, "Go ahead and shoot me." I think he actually felt that if he were shot that would further vindicate his rage.

The only defense made for S's conduct came from his sister, who argued that he was struck by a train some eighteen years earlier which left him with permanent brain damage and an inability to control his temper.

S's only coherent request was that he be allowed to "disappear from America." (Oh, they're gonna disappear you, dude, that's what states are good at.)

Meanwhile, the aggrieved tenants at S's building were themselves arrested for burglarizing S's apartment while he was in jail. The brother of one of the tenants in question was already serving jail time for "criminal damage" consequent to breaking into S's apartment and dismantling his wheelchair. (It's interesting that the convicted brother to the charged tenants "dismantled" the wheelchair, according to media reports. This implies an intriguing "care" in the so-called "destruction of property." He must not have "dismantled" it very well, though.)

So, I ask in conclusion, given the fragile state of our geological context (as provided by Fisher), what hope have we, given the presence of characters like Mr. S?

Slim to none?

Two more things:

1. According to Fisher, "Because we are among the youngest of the mammals . . . we obviously are not essential to the existence of life on earth. Aside from a few bacteria, viruses, and parasites that have learned to live at our expense and some domestic species that we have bred into dependence, few of our fellow creatures would miss us if we were to disappear."

2. Mr. S and his angry ilk (and that includes congressional representatives and real-estate developers) owe somebody or something a big apology. Before it's too late. They need to ask for forgiveness. Otherwise, there will be an awful lot of happy mollusks when we're gone.

And you wonder why God wonders why he made us?!

Confutatis Maledictus

The Soul in Paraphrase (1)

To: Honeycomb@teenslut.com
From: Tom@english.nwfsu.edu
Subject: your awesome site!

Dear Honeycomb:

Where to start? I am so revved by your site which I have just visited for the first time that I swear I'm too excited to know where to begin.

First, this is the first time I've ever had the guts to send fan e-mail to a site before. I mean, this whole big world of online, virtual sex with cyber-sluts (as I believe you are called, correct?) is new to me. Believe it or not, I find participating in this world even scarier than going into a porn shop or a topless place, *neither of which I've ever done!* Again, believe it or not! Of course, I could excuse myself by saying that here in Topiary, Florida, there are no porn shops—and I would be telling the truth—but the larger truth is that those places scare me to death. Once, I admit, I began to go into one when I was over in Talla-hassee at a Writing Across the Curriculum Conference (I'll explain what that is another time when there's room for a whole lot of bore-dom in your life). I was just about to go up the steps when two other men went in just ahead of me.

(By the way, have you noticed that more and more often porn shops are opening in ornate Victorian houses and that they are really doing a swell job of keeping up architectural details and thus the his-toric value of the buildings? We used to have to depend on funeral parlors for this important civic function. But they seem to be passing the torch on to porn shops. I don't know why I should expect you to know, but what does this mean? Is it a metaphor? It always seemed appropriate that the keepers of the dead should be responsible for the preservation of the past, but what am I to think of this idea that the purveyors of smut are now to . . . to what? . . . care for the dead and the past the dead are a part of? Is that Eros's new job?)

Anyway, these men I speak of wore muddy boots and Levis that hung down over their hips and had their wallets chained conspicuously to a belt loop (by the way, what's in those wallets? crown jewels?) and jean jackets over torn, hooded sweatshirts and beards and farmer hats and, frankly, "dirty" expressions on their faces. And I couldn't help imagining that they had big penises, too, and hands that are frightening to shake. Like, what does this man do to get hands like this? Nothing that has anything to do with porn shops, I'll bet. Although what they do do with their hands that does have something to do with porn shops can't be more pleasant because of the other things that they do to give them the hands that they have. If that makes sense. At any rate, boy, did I ever change my mind. I just walked on by and around the corner where I had a little anxiety attack in private.

Sorry. My point is that I'm easily scared by such things, I have too much horror and disgust, but—strangely—in spite of the apparent privacy of the Net, I have always found online porn just as scary. You know what I mean? Probably not. Well, I think it has to do with the weird public/private nature of the whole thing. It's deceiving, right? You feel alone. You're in your own office or home or whatever. You're alone. But if you push a button that sends information (your e-mail address for example) "out there," well, you really have no idea what you've done in that moment. Perhaps you've stimulated the guidance systems for a network of military satellites which provide coordinates to Stealth fighter-bombers and Apache helicopters and that these enormously destructive weapons have now discreetly focused their laser guidance devices on your own home, zeroing in on you through your digital cable pickup. Believe me, as I sit here typing this ardent fan mail to you I'm very much wondering whether I'll have the courage to click on that send button. Because once you click on that button it's like you've invited the whole world into your machine, your office or home, or into your *head*. Yes, that's how it really seems to me. When you click on that button, you've invited the whole world into your dirty head. How much less "private" can you get? So there's a weird totally private/totally public vacillation that goes on that scares me as much as the men I see at porn shops who are probably the kind of men who in another time could take a shit in the middle of the dusty street and kick some dirt on it and then just walk away! Sturdy, natural fellows. And appalling. But what makes the Net worse is that interfacing with it, sending a message to it, this opening of an avenue or vein or (!) circuit in my own machine is to open up an avenue or vein or (!) circuit in my *brain* where anyone may see that there is shit (my shit!) all over the Goddamn dusty street. And at that point, I collapse. I collapse in shame and horror and a weird sort of pain. I don't know how to describe this pain that I associate with being able to look inside one of the veins inside my head and seeing what's there, but I'd like to be able to describe it and then feel okay about it instead of feeling like I'm going to be punished for this. Some all-seeing God has noted how the inside of my brain violates a huge percentage of his 236 commandments that He piled on top of the Big Ten.

Maybe you can help me with this. Your beautiful site suggests to me that you can. It suggests to me that if you saw inside the plaque and simple sin of my interior avenues/veins/circuits, you'd not judge me harshly. You'd find some compassion.

And maybe you'd even help me to DO some of that dirty/plaquey stuff inside my head, even if only virtually, which is what this is all about, right?

Whoops! I think I hear my wife's little Chevy Nova pulling into the drive. I gotta go. I didn't even remotely say what I wanted to say, so I'll have to write back. In the meantime, I hope you'll have time to write me just to say hi and that you got my message. Assuming of course that I click on Send rather than Quit when I'm done here.

Okay, here I go. It's Send or Quit and it's. . . .

To: Tom@english.nwfsu.edu
From: webmaster@teenslut.com
Subject: your fan mail @ Honeycomb

We at teenslut.com are happy to provide our paid-in-full members many exclusive services. When you become a member, you get access to the member's club of the most intimate photos of our girls, as well as video clips (for Java-ready computers only), talk rooms, biographical information and private e-mail lines as well.

When you join, you will receive a code name that will open the world of Teenslut© to you, to your mind and imagination, right in the privacy of your own home or office and all without having to visit your local porn shop. Say goodbye to that! Say goodbye to those dirty, scary, boon companions!

Teenslut.com accepts all major credit cards over its secure, encrypted lines. Even your e-mail address is secure. Or, if you wish, you may send a monthly check for $19.95 to Teenslut, Box 707, Austin, TX, 78767.

Thank you for your interest. The girls at Teenslut await your return to our site. By the way, our monthly update with new photos of all the girls has just been installed. There are some new and innovative interactive features, too, which we are proud to be pioneering for our customers.

Sincerely,

Webmaster
Teenslut.com, where a world of illegal minors is virtually yours.

To: Honeycomb@teenslut.com
From: Tom@english.nwfsu.edu
Subject: my disappointment

I have joined, that is, I have sent a money order for $19.95 to the address in Austin simply so that I could convey to you how starkly angry I was to receive a response from your webmaster. All of my worst fears come true! The webmaster–if he's anything like the snotty, pustulous nerd employed in my academic department at NWFSU–is a young man all of whose enthusiasms are soiled and adolescent. I understood that e-mail correspondence was to be private! I feel violated!

Well, you won't be hearing from me again and you've certainly received your last money order from the Topiary, FL, postmaster.

To: Tom@english.nwfsu.edu
From: Honeycomb@teenslut.com
Subject: e-mail #742319

Dear Tom:

I am in fact very happy to receive e-mail from you. Please understand that the message you received from our webmaster is an automatic response sent to all e-mail accounts not on our members list. There are no soiled boys, or whatever you said, for you to be worried about.

I understand that you are hurt, scared and angry. But you are now a member and we can communicate. I'd like to communicate. Please use your members' password to access our members-only club. There are photos there you haven't seen. My understanding is that they are more explicit. I can only imagine what they mean by that. *You* could actually tell me . . . if you only would!

Waiting,

Honeycomb

I Have Taken My Good Papa in Plaster

Mozart is easy. Even a superficial person can get Mozart while reading the newspaper. You can get Mozart while reading *People* magazine! And "people" regularly do! Hence the absurd popularity of moronic CDs like "Mozart for the Morning," "Mozart for Quiet Times," "Mozart for the Comatose." These CDs are related to Mozart in the same way that Pringles are related to potatoes. They're pre-chewed, reconstituted and altogether fraudulent. Mozart as Muzak. It is now (thanks to these products) impossible to listen to the opening of "Eine Kleine Nachtmusik" without feeling keen despair. I taught the damned thing to my cockatiel, and even he whistles it contemptuously.

But my point is that Mozart assaults you with the forcefulness and clarity of his ideas. Youth, energy, cleverness. Haydn, on the other hand, you actually have to listen to. I have this theory that you can't really listen to Haydn without headphones. He's too subtle. If you listen to him as you listen to the child Mozart, while reading *People,* you won't hear a damned thing. It will seem all manner. Listening to Haydn while walking around the house or talking on the phone, he's just this frenzied laying on of violins in a galloping or waltzing manner. Automatic patter. Or the affect of the *galant.* But for us, he's a *galant* with bad breath. An old man with gray hairs in his nose. You don't want him in your house. That's Haydn in our present moment. The strange thing is that my largely unlearned and naive assessment of Haydn has in fact been the dominant perspective on his music since the early 19th century when E. T. A. Hoffman among others (like Haydn's student Beethoven) condemned him to aesthetic and cultural irrelevance. In the words of Hodgson, Haydn was "the benign, bewigged old gentleman who used to compose dainty little symphonies." Even the astute Robert Schumann wrote of Haydn, "He is like a familiar friend of the house whom all greet with pleasure and with esteem but who has ceased to arouse any particular interest."

But if you actually listen carefully to Haydn (and no simple thing that! who remembers how to listen? it's as lost as seeing!), you discover that Haydn is . . . always thinking. The texture of his music produces a sense of thoughtful speech. It's pure argument in time, the medium for philosophical and moral contemplation. In fact, Haydn is still thinking. He's dead, but his work is still thinking. Dead Haydn is more thoughtful than any live person I know. No wonder we don't like him! "Thoughtful speech" is something we're not capable of. Try telling your Windows 98® system to produce some thoughtful speech for you. See what you get. You'll get what you deserve.

And Haydn is patient in a way Mozart couldn't even imagine let alone perform. Here's a secret: Mozart is afraid you won't like him! He's neurotic! Blame his overbearing dad if you want; I don't care what the cause was, the effect is unmistakable. So he has to rush to a good part. Then another. He's like the crazed lover who imagines that if he can keep his lover rocking with orgasm she won't leave him. (But of course she says, "Thanks for the rocket, lover. Seven! In a row! You're something. By the way, I'm moving to New Jersey. Daddy found me a job in the advertising business.") Only when Mozart knew he was dying did he calm down a little bit.

Okay, enough. Listen to "The Seven Last Words." This is the string quartet version. It's a requiem of sorts. Haydn's requiem for Christ and human suffering in general.

The Seven Last Words of Christ (1)

1. *"Father, forgive them, for they know not what they do."* (adagio)

Statement

The story of Joseph Haydn's life is one that he himself thought would be of little interest to anyone. Haydn lived for most of his productive professional life in the countryside, as the music director and court composer for various princes Esterházy at Einstadt Castle and Esterháza on the other side of the Danube from Vienna. He was responsible for directing and maintaining the court orchestra and for writing music to be performed by the orchestra.

Argument

In 1732, the year of Haydn's birth, peasants under Prince Esterházy could not leave the land, could not marry without permission, had to work as forced labor for a certain part of the year, and then had to tithe both the church and the prince. Haydn was born into this peasant class.

Development

He came to the notice of the Court Chapel Meister one day when a school rector found five-year-old Joseph pretending to perform music on the street with his parents by sawing at his left arm with a stick as if he were accompanying on the violin.

Restatement

When Haydn himself became Chapel Meister in 1761, he remained a peasant in the form of a "house officer" and was under "permanent obligation to compose such pieces of music as his Serene Princely Highness may command." Many of Haydn's compositions are the product of forced labor.

2. *"Verily, I say unto thee, today wilt thou be with me in paradise."* (grave e cantabile)

Statement

Elements of this theme are retrieved in the next movement in which we discover that the demand on Haydn to compose, to create, was not simply arbitrary or willed because it could be willed in the place of "majesty" where "willing and doing are one." There was some "reasonable self-interest" (if you will) involved, at least for the Prince. For Prince Nicholas also enjoined Haydn "to apply himself to composition more diligently than heretofore, and especially to write such pieces as can be played on the baryton."

Prince Nicholas was virtually the only (not very good) barytonist in Austria.

Argument

According to Robbins Landon, the pressure of work in those early years caused such a strain on Haydn that, in 1763, he consumed "a steady stream of laxatives, purgative medicines, medicines for wind in the stomach, and Electuarium (a mixture of various medicines with prunes, and sometimes honey, used as a strong laxative)."

Development

Haydn secretly taught himself to play the obscure baryton and within six months was a far better performer than the Prince. He surprised the Prince with a concert of new music on the baryton, hoping to please his Majesty. Prince Nicolas's only response, however, was, "You are supposed to know about such things, Haydn!" There was more than a touch of passive aggression to Haydn's obsessive efforts to master the difficult baryton. But after this performance, he never touched the instrument again. The degree to which the Prince had the last word may be measured by the fact that during this period of fourteen years at Esterháza, Haydn composed one hundred sixty baryton trios. With a smile.

Haydn's digestive problems continued unabated until 1775 when, to everyone's relief, the Prince abandoned the instrument.

Restatement

Very late in life, after his triumph in England, Haydn returned to the court of Esterházy under the young know-nothing Prince Nicholas II. One day, during an orchestral rehearsal, the Prince entered the room and made a criticism of the music. Haydn turned to him and said, "Your Highness, that is my business."

During the same period, the young Beethoven, who had studied counterpoint briefly at Haydn's knee, said to the old master, "I never learned anything from you."

In these two anecdotes, Haydn brilliantly and economically figures both the Great Revolutions of the 1790s and the Reign of Terror.

Isolation (2)

Dear Editor:

I read with great interest the letter from the woman whose husband's head had come loose. I think I can help her. This is not exactly a secret, but still some people don't know.

It has come to my attention that someone is spraying us with chemicals. Most people with whom I have discussed this matter believe it is the military. In the wake of these "chemtrails" people come down with flu-like symptoms which sometimes develop into pneumonia. I believe this may be related to this "loose head" business.

Reports on the spraying have come in from forty states. Pilots and policemen have made some of the reports. Thousands of photographs and videos have been taken. Springfield, Illinois, is on the list of cities. Therefore, this is a local matter.

We need to get to the truth here for the sake of the poor woman and her husband and for all of us.

What I want to know is: are we being sprayed? And what's the name of the chemical?

William Thomas,
Rural Normal

Murder Mystery (2): The Detective

Chief Inspector Hume was awakened at 6:30 in the morning by a phone call informing him of the investigation.

"Hume?"

"Of course this is Hume. I'm at home. I'm in bed. I'm trying to sleep."

"Barocco."

"What do you want, Detective?" There was a heavy taste of lead in his mouth.

"They've found the body of a little boy in among some frozen pigs."

That was the beginning of it. Hume replaced the phone in its cradle and lowered himself carefully from the bed, trying not to wake his still-sleeping wife, Grenda, who was sunk like a great, brown lump in the mattress. Hume thought of most things in his home as "brown" and "lumpish," but his wife in particular–her name seemed to invite it–was always the great, brown lump to him. What sort of name was this, anyway, Grenda? Was his name Thorvald? It was one of the fundamental riddles that life offered to Hume but which he never seemed to have the energy to answer. This is to say nothing of the question of how he'd come to marry this woman. There was probably some logical cause and effect, but Hume could not remember it.

As soon as Hume put his feet on the floor, Grenda was up with a grunt.

"What's happened? Where are you going?"

"Same as always. I got a call."

His wife rubbed at her forehead. "I didn't hear it."

"That doesn't change much. And I've got to go."

"I'll get up and make you some oatmeal."

"No, please, just stay in bed. I don't eat breakfast and I hate oatmeal."

"It's good for you."

"I don't like oatmeal. You know that. It's not a complicated thing."

Five minutes later, Hume was finishing a tepid cup of Rapid Fire® tea, made from the hot water tap as he ran by the sink. It was an essential herbal concoction of natural and plausible synthetic herbs which simulated the physiological effects of Methedrine in a soothing mint context. A very popular drink in the 21st century, even if most people actually boiled the water before they made it. The "mint context" always seemed to dominate for Hume. He never felt more energetic. It didn't work for him. Nothing worked for him. Or perhaps it was just the fact that his wife always pursued him into the kitchen and out of the house before he had finished his cup. "Why do you always have to hurry?" she would complain. "Why can't we just sit and talk while you finish your tea? Let's be civil. We're husband and wife. We should talk. That old body won't get any deader."

"That old body is a little boy, my dear."

"Oh."

Hume abhorred the idea of sitting with his wife in the morning. His stomach wasn't strong enough for it at that hour. Any hour, to tell the truth. No, abhor was not too strong a term for it. Poor thing. It wasn't her fault. It was her bathrobe. It was brown and heavy and made her look like a small hill. Clumps of food stuff massed in the terry cloth like matted hair on a dog. He tried to be generous, but it was so painful to be generous at that hour. It took a lot of effort to be generous. He couldn't help wondering, "*What* has she eaten in this robe? And *how* has she eaten it?" He'd feel the gorge rise and he'd sprint from the house, overcoat flashing behind, saying, "I have to catch the train."

We might say that Hume had an unhappy marriage, but that would be superficial. The unhappiness of his marriage was just the beginning of it.

Who Cannot Weep May Learn from Thee (1)

MURDERER: I would prefer not to speak of this at all. I think I have already said something to that effect. What you know, you know, but that's it.

PROPHET: You will not be allowed silence. Whatever you have said in the darkness will be heard in the light.

MURDERER: And what I have whispered behind closed doors will be shouted from the housetops. Don't even bother with that little game. Look, I'll speak as long as it's clear that I feel no need to speak. I feel no need to confess in either the religious or legal sense. And certainly not the psychoanalytic sense.

PROPHET: We're indifferent to your needs.

MURDERER: And you already know what happened. You know exactly what happened. There's no secret and nothing to confess. Technically, I *have* confessed. Ask my lawyer. I "pled." What's the point? I killed them. When I looked my lawyer in the eye and said, "I did it and I'm going to confess to the whole thing," he wasn't at all surprised. He just said, "Fine, I can make this work to your benefit." Whatever!

But what's your story? You call yourself a prophet? You read the Bible? Check out Elijah and Elisha. Shit. Elisha waxed forty-two *children,* man, because they called him baldy. Where's that at? I guarantee you that I had that much cause and then some.

Murderers become like angels after their deeds. Some people think that your mind gets confused and panicky–"Oh, I killed someone! How could I do that! Now they're going to catch me." But that's only what people who have never murdered think. The only murderer that I know of that really reacts in that way are the bodybuilders, you know, with the snow banks of muscles built by massive steroid abuse and the tiny shrunken testicles. Now, your bodybuilder truly does go into a nasty panic over the idea that "they" are going to catch him for this misdeed. But that panic is just another symptom of steroid abuse, like the muscles themselves. We've got a whole wing of those clowns here. It's funny to watch them desperately pumping iron and their bodies collapsing around them like deflating balloons. Or like the Wicked Witch of the West, man. "Oh no, I'm melting!"

Now, a person who kills someone in self-defense or in war or something, that person suffers like a son of a bitch. That person grieves and is confused. Hardly understands anything at all. That's because the cloth has not been torn. But in the case of a murderer, everything becomes simple and clear for the first time. The cloth *has* been torn. The covenant binding you to others is broken, you did it deliberately, and you're prepared to take the consequences. You get this incredible calm ability to see things for what they are. It may sound strange to say, but murder is the ultimate enlightenment. You probably didn't know that.

PROPHET: I'm listening.

MURDERER: Yeah, you better be cautious because this new capacity of mine works great with Prophets like you.

PROPHET: Go on.

MURDERER: Well, I just wanted to say that when I told my lawyer that I was guilty as hell—premeditated as a complicated sauce—he looked at me and I looked in his eyes and what I saw in his lawyer soul appalled me. And in that moment I knew that lawyers are worse than murderers. They are wholly without truth, man. Lizards, I think. One goes from a lawyer's eyes directly to the reptilian part of the brain. The white pulpy part attached to the base of the brain that kinda curls down like a parsnip. A parsnip is a fucking bloodless carrot. And that's how I think of lawyers. Anyway, I went right in his eyes straight to the back of his brain, did a quick scan, understood everything about the guy in a moment, with my newfound murderer's calm and clarity, and made my conclusions. I judged him. There is no reality in a "system," in their "justice system." Reality is in what happens and what you can do. I judged that son of a bitch and found him wholly wanting. It made me so mad I wanted to eat his Goddamned leg. Ever done that?

PROPHET: What?

MURDERER: Eat a guy's Goddamned leg.

PROPHET: *(Horrified)* You're kidding.

MURDERER: *(Laughs derisively)*

PROPHET: Okay, you got me. Almost got me.

MURDERER: Almost my ass.

PROPHET: Go on.

MURDERER: The really weird thing about this lawyer was I think he felt me. I think he felt my energy pouring through him, scouring a path, making an audit. And in a moment he went from like "You lame fuck, you went and got caught, didn't you?" to total, silent respect for me. Awe may not be too strong a word for it.

You get guys who say they meet a guy like me, a murderer, and they look in our eyes and are afraid. Baloney. At least in this case baloney. My lawyer was afraid, all right, but not because of anything he saw in me. The only thing that guy saw in me was money and BANNER HEADLINES and more money. No no. That guy *felt* me do my audit. He knew he was known by someone so pure and so precise . . . well, it's scary for anyone to be known like that. Let alone a scumbag lawyer. You know how much those guys cost us humans, in terms of being able to keep faith with universal forces? A lot. I don't know how to quantify it for you, but a lot. Forget about the fucking ozone hole. The problem with our relationship with Being is lawyers. Woe to those scholars of the law, I say. They mess you up without bothering to lay a finger on you. Hypocrites. There's more guys I could name. Like congressmen. That's what I fault myself for. I shoulda killed some lawyers and congressmen. But God's supposed to be taking care of that, so I hear. Or he's going to.

That's why it's scary to meet a murderer. We're like semi-angelic.

It feels great to be so uncomplicated. So clear. It's not exactly purity, but it's like that.

PROPHET: Please don't take this as a criticism, but I think you're stalling. You're deferring what you are obliged to provide. This strategy can't work. You know that.

MURDERER: I just thought you might be interested in my observations. Isn't this some sort of learning experience for you? What's a murderer's mind like? All that phony, liberal bullshit.

PROPHET: I was interested, personally. But that's not what this is about. And I could care less what the inside of your mind is like.

MURDERER: Well, screw you too.

PROPHET: Don't be defensive.

MURDERER: Defensive? Are angels defensive? There's no need for that with us. Angels like me come into town and the people say, "Throw his ass out here. We're going to rape him up one side and down the other." Check it out. Lot, the angels of God and the people of Gomorrah. Unbelievable. And didn't *they* kill a bunch of folks? So when people come on to me like that, I fuck them *first,* brother, and I fuck them good.

PROPHET: You are not an angel of God. If you would just finish your story, you'd understand that.

MURDERER: I didn't say I was an angel. I said I'm *like* an angel. You ever take a poetry class? That's a simile. One thing in the place of another. An overlay. Something to see me through.

PROPHET: Okay, okay. Calm down and continue.

MURDERER: No problem. I don't seem calm to you? You're the dude that's pushing this. I still don't see why you couldn't just read about it in the paper. I thought they did a good job with it. It was pretty accurate.

PROPHET: We're not interested in accuracy.

MURDERER: Really. What are you interested in?

PROPHET: I am a prophet. I am interested in prophecy.

MURDERER: Huh? That's like saying I'm a dogcatcher, I'm interested in dogs. But I'm not a dogcatcher. What kind of prophet are you anyway?

PROPHET: Modern.

MURDERER: Modern. What the hell does that mean? If you were living in biblical times, would you be like one of the eight hundred that Ahab and his wife, ol' Jezebel, whacked? Speaking of whom, I bet that Jezebel was hot. There's this stripper at the Hot Nights Club that goes by Jezebel. And she will *not,* I repeat *not,* reveal her breasts. And yet she's the most popular and profitable stripper there. She just shows you this cleavage and it's like, okay Jack, this is eternity right down here. But it's not for you. And the guys eat it up. The other girls are hanging around flopping their wares on your forehead, but the fellas are going, "Hey, get that shit out of my face. You're distracting me." Ol' Jezebel, man. When I look at that stripper's cleavage, I'm cool. She knows it too. I'm thinkin' of the original Jezebel. What that was like. Her and Ahab. What was sex like after whacking a few prophets? Unbelievable.

PROPHET: I think you have the wrong idea about prophets. Prophets are basically poets. That's what the so-called prophets in the Old Testament were in many cases. Poets. Maybe not the real heavy hitters like Elijah and Isaiah and Jeremiah. But Daniel, for instance, was just an inspired poet. Inspired. God breathed into him.

MURDERER: This is some logic. So what you're telling me is that crazy-ass Jezebel whacked a bunch of poets? Good Lord. So if by prophet you mean poet, then I'm. . . .

PROPHET: Source material.

MURDERER: Oh shit, I get it. You're going to write a book about me. Like *People* magazine or *Frontline* or some fucked-up journalism thing. Well, I'm glad I know that because now I can shut up.

PROPHET: No. I'm not writing a book of that kind. And you will not shut up until we're done here.

MURDERER: *(Ponders)* You're right. I can't just stop, can I? This is really not about what I want to do. This is kind of freaky. I'm not sure I know what's going on.

PROPHET: Don't worry about it. No harm will come to you. Or no more harm than what you've done to yourself. Now, tell me how you met your wife.

MURDERER: How I met my wife. She was British, you know. Born in London. Socially busted but culturally powerful. That's such a funny old story that never quite finishes itself or stops being true. The fucking Brits are social and political losers—and I'm not just talking about after the war, although they sure as hell were the real losers of that one—I'm talking about way back even in the eighteenth century. Let a bunch of ex-cons and ne'er-do-wells kick their asses in 1776. But culturally, you know, they've always got something. They know how to speak. They know which books to read. They always strike me as being poetic in a sort of antique way. Like Tennyson. Which is probably why they're such losers politically. I mean, what the hell do you do with Tennyson these days? *In* fucking *Memoriam.* I don't know one single poem, or even one single line of his poetry. Probably all about death. And yet, when you meet a Brit, no matter how fucked up, they could be heroin addicts or flipping burgers in fucking Denny's, you get this sense that if you asked about old Tennyson they'd get all happy and start quoting the bitch.

Anyway, I was working as a technician at the hospital here in town when we met. She was working in Records. Can you imagine that? A Brit, head full of Tennyson and knowledge about what books children ought to read, clear in a way an American can *never* be clear about why children shouldn't watch TV, not even *Sesame Street* (and I'd like to talk to you about *that* one some time; you've never really watched Sesame Street until you've watched it with the clean sight of a murderer). A Brit like that working in Records: "This one came in with this disease or this broken thing on this date and we did this to him and he owes us this much. This one came in and died and his family owes us this much." Or, "this one's okay now but back then she had some shit in her urethra." What kind of stuff is that for a Brit to have in her head? Right next to Tennyson, too. It makes me sick. It makes me think I did her a big favor. It makes me think I should have killed some other guys. Like the guy who owns the hospital. How do you get to him? I mean, he should know what the spiritual effect on the universe is when you keep all those records. The clutter. Anti-clarity.

PROPHET: That's very sad.

MURDERER: Sad? What's sad? You haven't heard sad yet, pal, although for me sadness is now all taken up in light. Oh the light, man, it's unbelievable.

Back to the beers. So we met at a local place for beers after work. Place called Legends dedicated to dead rock 'n' roll stars like Jimi and Janice and Morrison and Lennon. A smelly dump if you want to know the truth. Brits like to drink, too, at pubs. They have what they call pints of stuff that look like beef broth. Anyway, Joy (that was her name) didn't know about what all's involved in drinking beers in a bar after work in the United States. But I did. The way she used to look. She had a regular thin pretty face. Brit women are not beautiful but they're almost all nice. Nothing you'd want to take a picture of, but nice. She wore her hair straight to her chin with little red bangs. Her hair was red. And she always wore very clean, pressed clothes. Nothing polyester. She was all about natural fibers.

But what Joy obviously didn't understand was that in America you go to a bar so that you can get drunk and then wander home with someone and take off your nice not-polyester clothes. I mean, she was authentically surprised in that inscrutable Brit way when I suggested this to her.

The Soul in Paraphrase (2)

To: Honeycomb@teenslut.com
From: Tom@nwfsu.edu
Subject: Your last

Dear Honeycomb! Okay. As I've tried to explain to you, this is already a very iffy situation for me. I have a horror of being discovered among "porn monkeys." But since you have explained things, to a degree, and you can assure me that no "webmaster" is looking in on our communication, and this *isn't going to any public posting place,* I will return (if for no more than whatever length of time my $19.95 buys).

But I have now had the opportunity to peruse your members-only pages and I was heartened by what I found there. Honeycomb, that's some crotch shot! Actually, that's not what I want to say. I hardly know what I want to say. It's not as if I hadn't seen a crotch shot before. Oh, they've got them posted, tacked up, hung and thumbnailed (whatever that means) everywhere. They've got them blonde to a nearly invisible fineness and they've got them black and coarse as Shakespeare's sonnets. They've got them shaved and rubbed like some master woodworker's been attending to it with ever finer applications of tung oil and 000 steel wool, and they've got them like the proverbial briar patch or some primeval swamp where the ferns grow thick. They've got them cropped like a putting green or like this crotch is joining the Marines, and they've got them braided and bearded. They're out there, they're available, but I don't need to tell *you* about it.

But yours. I don't want to overstate this so I'll pause before saying exactly what I think I saw: yours had an aura. It was angelic. It was like the burst of blinding light that the Bible speaks of. Painful and wonderful. A revelation. Exalted as opposed to trivial or bombastic. That is, what most women have got is no big deal, yet they act as if a guy ought to be willing to trade his jet skis for it. In short, most women are just like several wives I've had. The sad part is, I was willing to trade the jet skis. Right down to the present wife. I can see them all, shaking Miss Thang as they purl in their own wake off on the horizon. Which is why pornography has always seemed such a kindness, and hyperporn available at work or at home, is downright humane. I'm thinking Nobel Peace Prize here. We get to go through the whole arcane and bizarre ritual of desire and theoretical exchange, in which I give everything for very little, but I get to keep my jet skis!

You have, in my view, not only created an ideal erotic website for me (and that was my hunch all along: among the infinity of porn sites out there, one had my initials carved into it), but you have in fact invented new sonorities in the type, in the "genre" *tout court*. You have taken the lax habits of vertical combination and modified them through the rigorous logic of contrapuntal lives (maintaining with equal force the parallel developments of unaccustomed effects: breasts, ass, quim, all proceeding forcefully, independently, with a dexterous and vertiginous inevitability (revelation!)). It is as if I were present at the very first appearance of words! And that extraordinary dark coloring which surrounds the bright stuff. Where in the world did you get it?

Well, I hardly know how to say this, but I was so inspired and excited by the interpenetration of these parallel movements you effected that when at last I quit, as eventually I had to (I could *buy* AOL with the money I've sent scudding through the phone lines searching for Eros), I immediately sat down, put on my Sennheiser 600 stereo headphones (which isolate my poor wife from my music and poor me from my wife), and played Beethoven's "Diabelli Variations." And weren't they just *diabolique!*

Honeycomb, your site has opened up aspects of those trying variations that I had never before suspected. There are lots of "tweaks" in the audiophile world. Spending thousands of dollars on speaker cables is one "tweak." Smoking a bowl of the intense, genetically-enhanced dope that we have these days is another. If you'll allow me a digression, am I wrong in thinking that this modern dope is like hitting an upholstery tack with a pile driver? (i.e., the tack = my poor brain; the pile driver = this cruel dope). No wonder it's illegal. You probably don't remember the old days when we had to put the stuff in shopping bags, burn it in the fireplace, then climb on the roof and breathe deep over the chimney. Worse yet, we then had to listen to the Moody Blues on a stereo system the roommate bought at Sears! But no one has ever mentioned the outstanding possibility that an amateur porn site (unaided by client-supplied auto-erotic manipulation) could generate such a revealing listening experience . . . and to Beethoven, of all things.

So, I'm impressed.

And grateful.

Tom

To: Tom@english.nwfsu.edu
From: Honeycomb@teenslut.com
Subject: Beethoven et. al.

Tom—It was a long shot to begin with and perhaps it's just not to be. My situation is so bewildering in itself that I don't know how to account for it, although I will try. But your letter has added a whole new level of bewilderment, through which I must first move before I can even approach my own awkward incomprehension.

My confusion with your letter is of many kinds. Some of it is reasonable, given the situation (but what *is* the situation?). Other aspects of it are far less reasonable.

Please, Tom, try to pay attention. I know that you must think that everything is funny and that I'm being funny and that this is part of some funny game. But I need your help. That's what's simple here. Help. Help me. I am a suffering human being and I am reaching out to you. This is a cry in the darkness. The darkest imaginable darkness.

First, I was very disturbed by your letter. Beethoven? Drugs? Jet skis? Why are you telling me these things? I don't understand. I just don't understand. Telling me these things doesn't help me at all. What I need is your *help* (I pray you come to understand that simple word) with very basic questions like, where am I? Why am I here? Can I leave? *How* can I leave? *Can you come get me?????*

See? Do you understand now? Do you understand, Tom? Thomas? Is that what your lovely wife calls you?

Second, if I comprehend what you've been saying to me, you have found me in some sort of dirty, pornographic computer game. You have seen *pictures* of me? Naked? With my legs spread?

My God. My God, my God, my God.

Listen. Just listen. My name is not Honeycomb. My name is Wanda. I was born in 1922, in Kansas, a little town called Norcatur. My father was a brick mason. I grew up in a house built by the hands of my father. I was a farm girl and in many ways I am still. During the war, I moved to Washington D.C. and worked in a stenographers pool in the War Department. My whole being was given over to that effort. I never thought of myself, let alone of my body and the sort of base gratification you have been speaking of. I am a deeply religious person. When I wasn't working, I volunteered at the local V.A. hospital, talking to wounded soldiers, or I went to church or I just stayed home.

I met my first and only husband (the only man with whom I ever had sex) at the hospital. After the war, we returned to his hometown outside Cleveland where he worked for the railroad until his death from a heart attack in 1973. I stayed in the Cleveland area for a while, but in 1975 I moved to Chicago in order to be near our only child, Janet, and her family, especially my granddaughter, Sarah.

Part of what bothers me about your last e-mail is the facts that, first, I have never liked sex. I loved and admired my husband (he was a good person and worked hard for the railroad) and I helped him in many ways with a difficult life, but I always understood why they called sex a marital "duty." I did it when I had to, when there was no way to avoid it. And I did it because I wanted to have children. I could find no way around that one. But I never "desired" it (and hardly understand what that idea might mean), and it sure never helped me to understand Beethoven. Happily, Stanley was understanding or perhaps he was just willing not to complain too much, or perhaps we really were "right for each other" because he rarely suggested that we ought to have sex and in fact I think that he may have liked it as little as I did. And why should a person find anything attractive in sex? It requires the total abandonment of any sort of composure or dignity. It's like throwing yourself off the top of a cliff, I think. Or finding the rolling eyes of a madman alluring. Think of where people put their faces, their noses. There's what?, one percent of the people in the world who are sufficiently physically attractive to allow a person to override what is most human and fundamental: disgust and nausea! The truth is that disgust is much more common, much more basic than lust. Isn't that right? And so how do you explain why the same act that is innately disgusting with ninety-nine is some kind of heaven on earth with that one? It never made sense to me, and I was blessed with a hero for a husband.

But his willingness to forgive my lack of desire may also have had something to do with me. I am not a pretty woman. Of course, now I am in my late seventies! But even in my youth, I was plain and a little lumpy to look at. Honest but lumpy. The idea that someone somewhere would get excited looking at a picture of me naked, well, it makes me laugh. But it also makes me a little angry. I have always very firmly kept myself away from such things. Not out of any moral zeal, but, as I have tried to explain, because I personally found it messy, painful and mentally disturbing.

So, Tom, what exactly are you seeing? That's what I don't get. What does this body look like, exactly, because it's hard to believe that it's mine. Aura? Revelation? I don't think so.

Here's the only connection I can think of and it is my second problem. In this place where I find myself, things are very dim. Not completely dark but dim. Complexly dim. Corridors appear lit by some strange light and then it all disappears and another hallway opens on another side. It reminds me of a time when I was a little girl and my parents took me to a museum in a big city. Well, somehow, I got lost. I wandered down colorful, brightly lit halls full of paintings and that was scary enough. They were not the colors of the countryside. I didn't understand these colors. But then I found myself among Egyptian things and then a while later among animals like bears and ducks. To this day, when I see a duck I am afraid. I looked at their waxy bills and feet and stared into their shiny, dead eyes. And so even now a live duck seems like a duck that is hiding what it really is: one of those dead, scary, stuffed ducks at the museum. So when I would cross a duck in the park, or just wherever, I always had to fight the impulse to scream at it, "Liar! You are a liar!" I don't believe I ever did scream this, but on several occasions I said to my husband, in chilly tones, "That duck is a liar! He's hiding the whole thing. He won't be honest about it at all." Needless to say, my husband—dear Stanley—found these moments "pretty spooky," as he used to say.

Shades pass me here, dim figures like the anonymous adults at that museum. They all seem to know where they're going. And they are going somewhere. But I'm not. I'm stationary. I seem to be stuck. I'm not always sure I can feel my feet. And surrounding everything, the constant hiss of . . . I believe they're numbers, infinite as grains of sand. That's what we have for music here, I guess. Futuristic, I suppose. But I can't see much, not even my own body. I do, however, feel things now and then.

I will tell you what I feel. Something is touching me. Something unusually cold and hard. It touches me where I do not wish to be touched. But I do not know how to say "no" to it. What kind of "no" would make sense to this thing, in this place? And why am I convinced that a regular human "no" wouldn't make any sense at all to it?

But the long and short of it is, I believe I am being raped. I am being violated. I can feel these things that I have never liked. Not even with my own husband. So, I have been crying a lot. In this confusion.

Tom. I don't know you. I know you don't know me. But this little channel of communication that has opened between us is the first recognizable thing that has happened to me since I came to this place. I am an old woman and I probably don't have long to live, and no doubt I am not what you're interested in for your little games on the computer. Nonetheless, I'm going to ask you to help me.

Get me out of here. Tell me how I can leave this place, if you can. I'm telling you, I don't like it here. It's scary. I don't like being touched by whatever it is that's touching me. Those hard, hissing fish. You must know something about all this. Can you give me some ideas or hints or instructions? I just want to go home. I have a canary and two lovebirds and I did not ask anyone to feed them for me before I left.

And here's the big one: is it possible for you to come and get me? I have no idea how to tell you to get here because I don't know where I am. But perhaps you will understand. Perhaps I am just an old lady who has outlived the things she can understand. Perhaps this will be no more difficult for you than walking to the corner. Or pressing the right button on your computer.

Please, respond quickly. And consider seriously the things I have told you.

No Comment

I should like to know how a woman's voice managed to interrupt this orgy of male self-absorption.

Something Understood (1)

PROPHET: My God! Look at this place! It's unbelievable.

MADMAN: State of the Art. Of course, it's an old art.

PROPHET: But what is it?

MADMAN: What's it look like?

PROPHET: It looks like those eighteenth-century woodcuts, like Hogarth or something, of a madhouse. House o' Bedlam.

MADMAN: You got it.

PROPHET: Of course. What else could it be? The heavy stone walls, the filthy dirt floors, the bars on every window, the rats, the manacles hanging from the walls, the crappy cots with the leather straps for support, the squalor, the smell. But these places don't exist anymore! Even the modern version of "insane asylum" was gone by the 1970s. And this is a good deal older than that.

MADMAN: You are correct, sir. You are not here.

PROPHET: Stop kidding around. I'm serious. What is this place and why are you here?

MADMAN: Well, it *is* a madhouse. The explanation that was given to me was very simple. I was told that I was "mad"–not mentally ill, as they're supposed to say these days, but "mad"–and that I would have to go to a "madhouse." A House of Bedlam. It feels to me like I'm in a place from roughly the 1830s. Continental, don't you think. Comte de Quelquechose. What would you guess?

PROPHET: That's the one thing that seems wrong here. There is no Bedlam to this House. In fact, it's dead quiet. There isn't anyone else here, is there?

MADMAN: Of course not. This place was reproduced just for me. I actually had some research done and found the original. It's based on the nineteenth-century state mental hospital at Colditz, thirty kilometers southeast of Leipzig. The building was described in one resource as a "forbidding castle, used at various times as a fortress, a prison, a poorhouse and a concentration camp." The second son of Robert Schumann, Ludwig (named after Beethoven), spent most of his life there. Schumann himself visited once, and some biographers feel that it was Colditz that provided Schumann with his intense fear of insane asylums.

PROPHET: Amazing. They must have thought a lot of your madness, because even if it is a nightmare, it's an expensive nightmare. You can't build institutions like this anymore. Union labor alone makes it prohibitive. And those rocks!

MADMAN: Between you and me, I think it's all done with a software package.

PROPHET: Huh? Have you tried kicking any of these walls?

MADMAN: Please try not to be obvious. You and Doctor Johnson. You know what Hegel did with so-called sense certainty. Barely qualifies as human. Low as you can go.

PROPHET: Okay, well, anyway, I'm curious. Tell me your story.

MADMAN: No.

PROPHET: No? Here we go again.

MADMAN: What again?

PROPHET: I have the hardest time getting people to tell me what they must tell me. It's supposed to be easy. It may be that I'm simply not very good at this.

MADMAN: You didn't tell me that I had to tell you. So okay. I'll tell you.

PROPHET: *(Glares)*

MADMAN: I'm just fuckin' witchoo. Remember, I'm supposed to be "mad." Get a sense of humor.

PROPHET: All right. But let's please get on with it.

MADMAN: Why? You in a hurry? More madmen to talk to this afternoon?

PROPHET: Not madmen. Murderers and corporate CEOs, sex offenders and defrocked priests (if that's not redundant), sorry fuck-ups and university administrators (if that's not redundant), logging company execs. I'm in a big hurry with them because the Dalai Lama is in the process of making them all hungry ghosts. The Dalai Lama takes personal offense when a thousand-year-old sequoia is turned into exchange value.

MADMAN: University administrators too? I'm surprised they're lumped in with defrocked priests and logging execs. I didn't know they were so bad.

PROPHET: Ever met one?

MADMAN: Oh a few. I, of all people, shouldn't be surprised. Like, how in the hell do you think I got here?

PROPHET: Well, let me put it to you this way. If Dante had known about college deans, he'd have had them swimming in Satan's snot in the ninth circle. And he'd have thought they deserved worse. Like inside of Satan's snot would be nine more tiny circles, and in the ninth snotty circle of the ninth circle are nine snotty bolgias, and in the ninth bolgia, creaming with the quintessence of snot, you find deans.

MADMAN: Serious. They just seemed to me to be sorry fuck-ups. Anyway, the story here is simply that a year and a half ago, I was an assistant professor of sociology at a public university here in the middle of Illinois. I needed a research project, but nothing sufficiently ambitious occurred to me. I wanted to do something not only big enough to get me tenure at that dump but to get my ass the hell out of there and into a department where two or three people actually had a damned brain. Oh God, it pains me even to think of them. Especially the "distinguished" professors. Old C. P. Snow had it right: "These gentlemen are lucky in their subjects. It must be very nice not to need an original idea."

Then one day I read about this Human Genome Project that those people with very big brains, thank you, were pursuing over at the Beckman Institute a few short miles down the dreary interstate. They were mapping every little tiny genetic hallway and darkened recess.

This is the gene that makes you blink your eyes every few seconds. This is the gene that designs the nerves that make your legs itch. This is the gene that makes designer jeans irresistible whether on the rack or on a very good butt. Like that. The unbelievable, minute wholeness of the knowable. And I asked myself, what's the sociological equivalent of this project? And it came to me. Thus my "Everything That's Said" project. I would map all the nodes *and* the relations among the nodes *and* the fluidity of the whole map because it is a map but only for an instant and then it surges and things change maybe not a whole lot from moment to moment but over time a lot. So I'd need a kick-ass computer capable of fractal modeling of the most advanced kind. Because this was to be a *human,* not just a conceptual representation. I mean, at least genes stand still. Each node would need to be capable of *speaking.* Telling its story in the middle of its endless transforming.

And the audacity of this project just came at me like my girlfriend's breasts used to come at me when we took that homemade Ecstasy my buddy in chemistry cooked up. And I thought, Marxism has been powerful but how absurdly, how comically *crude* it is. Capitalists have these interests and say these things. The proletariat have these grievances and say these things. And this has passed for *complicated? Profound? Earthshaking? This has made the brains of college students hurt?* But I could see that the deployment of the field of forces was in reality thousands of times more rich, intriguing, true and, finally, simply more real than Marx's poor start.

PROPHET: Okay. I think I'm with you. But you're going to have to go slow and explain everything.

MADMAN: Amazing. That's what my dear department chair said to me just before he started having his little discreet lunches with the dean. I thought you weren't like them?

PROPHET: Like who?

MADMAN: Never mind. Let's just say you're one of those befuddled students who can't remember if the proletariat is the rich ones or the poor ones. Fucking hopeless. Why do I have to tell all this to *you?*

Talk about insult to injury.

PROPHET: *(Coloring, offended)*

MADMAN: Okay, okay. Never mind. I'll give it a shot. My best shot, buster. Ready?

Isolation (3)

Dear Editor:

I have only one thing to say to your nitwit readers in Anytown, USA, and if they can't understand it, if it's somehow too *obscure* for them, then they are truly a lost people.

And it is this: AS YOU READ THIS, NEGROES ARE MAKING UP NEW WORDS.

Sincerely,

PAYING ATTENTION

P. S. Anyone wishing to pursue this matter may contact me at PO Box 1664, Trenton, NJ or at covenant@hotmail.com

The Binary God (1)

PROPHET: Okay. Here's your question. Is a person insane who tries to commit suicide by lacerating his wrist with a pretzel? And *how* do you know?

ALPHA: Wow. That's some crazy question. Where do you get questions like that?

BETA: Is it factually based, this question?

PROPHET: Yes, it is factually based. The son of a friend of mine rubbed his wrist with a pretzel until he bled.

BETA: Oh, hear that? Son of a friend of yours! Wasn't a teenager by any chance, was he?

PROPHET: Yes.

BETA: Well, that answers the question in itself. To what can I compare this generation? I think today's teenagers are all possessed by demons. I have one word for you: Littleton. I'm just surprised he wasn't trying to kill his poor teacher with this pretzel. When I see a teenager on the street, boy or girl, I put my hand on my gun butt.

ALPHA: That's about the size of it.

PROPHET: Okay. The question, if you please.

ALPHA: Well, I believe that this question must be approached like any question, even if it is about one of these loony teenagers. So. He's either crazy or not crazy. The pretzel is either a weapon or it's not a weapon. He was either trying to commit suicide or he wasn't. Let's start there.

BETA: Hmmm. Let's start with the pretzel. In my opinion, a pretzel is not a weapon.

ALPHA: Except, perhaps, for one of these loony kids.

BETA: Actually, depending on the kind of pretzel we're talking about, this could be inspired. If it's one of those soft pretzels that people put mustard on, the whole thing is a joke. But you can get these so-called pretzel sticks now, with the huge pieces of rock salt on 'em. And brother, you know, I'm thinking about one of those now and that is probably an aggregate that you could sand a floor with. I mean, one of these determined dumb fucking kids *could* do some damage with a pretzel of that kind.

ALPHA: Unless he was just kidding. Joking around with a pal. That's the other possibility. It's funny. Committing suicide with a pretzel. Kids laugh like crazy about that kind of thing.

BETA: *(Laughing)* You know what this is reminding me of? My own crazy kid. Oh jeez! I'll never forget that one.

PROPHET: What?

ALPHA: Yeah, what?

BETA: Oh Christ, it's too funny. Poor dumb, fucking, loser, dopey kid. God bless 'im.

ALPHA: Just tell us, okay?

BETA: *(Laughing)* He . . . oh man . . . I've got the giggles . . . he . . . he masturbated in the shower using my Lava soap for a Goddamned lubricant. Oh Christ that's funny!

ALPHA: Isn't that the soap with fucking *pumice* in it? Fine volcanic dust for like essentially wearing down the grease and adhesives on a working man's hands?

BETA: That's the stuff!

PROPHET: Even I remember those commercials on TV. "Only one soap gets these hands clean, mister. Lava."

ALPHA: And those hands! Remember those break-your-skinny-little-pencil-neck hands?

BETA: Let me finish this. And so he's in there, in the shower, going to town, probably not paying any attention to what he's doing, like usual. And then he notices something warm and just different in his lubricant. So he looks down and, oh my, the crimson horror!

ALPHA: Ouch.

BETA: He came out of the old bathroom dripping, naked, shocked. His mother screamed. I think she thought he'd whacked it right off there was so much blood. But the poor, miserable, motherfucking look on that little loser's face. Oh man, priceless!

PROPHET: So what did you do?

BETA: Fatherly counsel, of course. "Use the Johnson and Johnson Intensive Care next time, you idiot." Like that.

PROPHET: You weren't very sympathetic.

ALPHA: Here we go again. Remember where this started. Crazy, murderous teenagers and their pretzels. This is nothing to fool around with. You take it easy on these kids and they'll steal your balls.

BETA: You got that right, pal.

The Life of Chris (2)

Good evening, I'm Terry Gross and this is Fresh Air. *My guest tonight is a writer, I guess you'd call it, right?*

Close enough.

A writer named Chris. Just Chris? You also publish under the name Modern Prophet?

I answer to both.

But why a "prophet"? Are you religious?

Yes.

What church do you belong to? What order?

Order?

Yes, which religion?

I went to the Oakland Interdenominational Neighborhood Church out by the Granny Goose Potato Chip factory when I was a boy. In California.

So you're a Christian.

You say so.

What about the "prophet" business?

I was known before I was born. I'm very special. God touched my lips. Actually, it was more my ears. I mostly listen to people.

Really. How interesting.

You know the expression "if you could only hear yourself"? I help people to hear themselves. They learn more that way. Besides, I don't know much, really.

I see.

That's all really.

One of the fascinating things about your career is that although you've published, what, seven novels over a twenty-year period, no one seems to know your work. I didn't know of you until my producer told me that we'd be interviewing you. You're not exactly a household name. Why is that?

My books aren't very popular, I guess. I'm a prophet. No prophet is honored in his own house. Jesus said that.

He did?

Yes.

I've heard that saying before. So, it was Jesus who said that. Interesting.

Yes.

I guess that what I'm wondering is how you managed to persevere. Book after book. Totally ignored. How many books have you sold altogether between the seven?

Not quite a thousand.

So, under two hundred copies per book?

About.

That can't make you very popular with your publisher.

Probably not. But I don't really see eye-to-eye with my publisher. He's very difficult. He has an anger problem.

Do you think that your sales are so low because the books are bad? Or you write poorly?

No.

Indeed. Let's move on to the subjects of your books. Some of your themes. They're very disturbing, aren't they? A blurb from your local congressman on your last book called you "sick." I think he also used the word "disgusting."

He probably did. Sounds like him. There is troubling material in my books.

By my reading of your work, they're violent and sexual and mentally disturbed without being—as with, say, Hollywood movies which use the same themes—at all entertaining.

I don't know about that.

Your books aren't even interesting. I find that a very intriguing approach to writing a novel.

I think they're interesting.

Why?

Because all those things really happened to me.

I see. Well, on that score, one of your favorite themes is masturbation. There are a lot of allusions to masturbation in your books. Did you masturbate a lot when you were young? Do you still masturbate a lot?

Everyone masturbates, I think.

But in your work it seems to be at the very center of your sense of what it means to be alive. Or maybe even awake. Is that true, for you?

You say so.

Also, there are a lot of subtle allusions to a very dark time in your life. I take it that you mean your life. There was a time when you drank a lot. Just how much did you drink?

Quite a bit at one point.

What did you drink?

Beer and whiskey.

I find that very sad.

Why? Sometimes I had a lot of fun. I did stuff when I was drunk that I never would have done sober. That's a plus, I think. From a certain point of view.

Another related and significant theme in your work is degrading, humiliating, shameful sexual relations. When did you have time for this between all the masturbating and drinking?

It wasn't difficult. I had a lot of time.

Many of your most degrading sexual experiences, according to your books, were with the wives and husbands of your closest friends. Why was that?

They were my friends. I liked them. I felt secure with them. They weren't strangers.

But the irony was that, to have secure sex with people you cared about, you had to betray other people that you also cared about. Don't you think?

I didn't care about them as much as the people I was having sex with. Or I didn't care so much about them that I let it get in the way of having sex with their spouses.

I see. Didn't you ever wonder what would happen if they all found out? Weren't you ever afraid of what they'd do?

No. I thought it was funny. Back then. I've had a change of heart now.

Really.

Well, once there was a birthday party for my wife and it occurred to me that I'd had sex with at least one member of every couple we'd invited. In some cases both.

Boy. You must have been pretty uncomfortable.

Not really. Only when more than one of them tried to meet me, like, alone in the bathroom.

What about the role of your mental illness in your stories and novels? You seem to be obsessed with the idea that bugs or lizards or wormlike creatures might be living in your body. Why is that?

I get depressed, that's all. Everyone gets depressed.

But not everyone thinks that their sadness is caused by bugs in their brains.

It seems natural enough to me.

Finally, there is your father. He often provides a very strange sort of comic relief in your work. Painful comic relief. What does he think of your books? One of your books is about him applying a black tar substance, a sealing asphalt, to your driveway. Again and again.

Hundreds of times, Terry. When he wasn't applying the sealing compound, he was watching the driveway for signs of cracks or weathering. He liked it very dark black and shiny. Over time, our driveway built up to be about six inches higher than the sidewalk. Driving over it was like hitting a wall. But he was very proud of it. He always insisted that it was the best driveway in the town. He spent enormous amounts of time just sitting out with it, on Mom's little kitchen stepping stool.

And you had a problem with this hobby of your father's?

Yes.

Because it implied some sort of horrifying abandonment? As if he preferred applying layers of black, sticky sealing compounds to spending quality time with you?

Yes. I think that's it. I make that clear enough in the book.

Well, Chris, all fathers do something like this, don't you think? I know my own father was perhaps excessively concerned with the idea that germs were on our toothbrushes, and he would spend his evenings cleaning and boiling them and shopping for new ones. This didn't harm our family or our feelings of love for our father.

If it's true that all fathers do something like this, then all fathers are morons. Your father sounds like a moron to me.

I beg your pardon.

I apologize.

Well, I won't push you on this subject any more. But on the whole, it's a strange combination of things that you write about, won't you admit? Dysfunctional sex, betrayal, drunkenness, peculiar neuroses, and then blaming it all on your father. Do you think this could have something to do with why your books aren't more widely read and known?

No. I think it's because I'm a prophet and I can't be appreciated in my own house.

Okay, Chris. That's enough. It was very nice meeting you and talking with you. Yours is a fascinating career in certain ways. But I have to say that this one may be, as they say, for the cutting-room floor. We may not be able to use it.

Why not?

Actually, I'm not sure how you got to this point in the Fresh Air *production process. You must have a very good agent.*

I don't have an agent.

Well, something was persuasive for my producer.

I couldn't say.

One last question, off the record. Why do all these horrible people that you talk to in your new book, Requiem, *why are they willing to talk to you? How do you get their trust? One professional to another, here.*

They have to talk to me.

What do you mean?

They don't have a choice.

I'm still not following.

God makes them.

I see.

You have to talk to me too.

I have to talk to you?

97

That's probably why your producer agreed that you'd "talk to me."

How interesting. Ironic too. I mean, who's being interviewed here?

I've never been confused about it. For example, if I were to ask you about your secret website at housewifesluts.com/terry, you would be obliged to answer.

But Chris, I don't have a website, secret or otherwise.

Yes you do. Everybody does. And I know you do, because I have it from a very good source. There's a laptop right here on your desk. I'll prove it to you. Just punch in the address.

No, I won't do that, I don't have a site, and you're wrong to say that everybody does. If someone is using my name out there, it's copyright infringement, invasion of privacy, and libelous.

Whatever. You still have to talk about it.

Okay, this is getting a little weird. I'm going to leave now.

You can't.

Just watch me. Hey, what's the matter with this door? Something's wrong with the lock. Okay, now I'm getting scared. Did you do something to the lock, you disgusting little creep?

Not me. Why don't you just come sit back down. It won't take long.

Have you come to kill me? I know who you are—the Holy One of God!

Oh come on now. Don't get carried away. It's not that bad. Calm yourself. Come on. Sit down and tell me all about it. Just let it out. We all have demons that make us do what maybe we shouldn't. You'll feel better later. I promise. Terry?

Oh shit.

Dies Irae (Day of Wrath)

Isolation (4)

Dear Besotted Editor:

I have it. At last I have it and you will not deny me the pleasure of displaying my discovery any longer.

I now have evidence that Being takes no special joy in Living.

What is this evidence? I have learned (by doing nothing more daring or ambitious than reading a book, something your doubly-besotted readers ought to try) that birds take no joy in flying and that if, all other things being equal, they are given a choice, they will–I don't know if "happily" is the right word here–but they will whether happily or not at least quite willingly abandon flight altogether, allow their wings to atrophy and in what I *think* are extreme cases will even turn to *burrowing,* to living under the ground–and, yes, you could say, like something properly dead and buried! (Let us hope that these are extreme cases, for it is sad beyond all sadness to imagine that they are not extreme but simply the most *advanced,* that is, the most fully realized, of *every* bird's desire.)

And how do I know that birds take no joy in flight and will "happily" return to the ground and even to living under the ground given a choice? As I said, I read a book. That's all it took. And this book described in very clear, unmistakable terms how the so-called flightless birds (like the moa, the flightless cormorant, the emu, the ostrich, etc.) living in some dim, dark, distant era, on isolated, predatorless islands, like the Galapagos, they simply abandoned their capacity to fly. Gave it up as if it were the merest nothing. You should just see the lazy bastard cormorants (safe on those rocky shores that know no foxes, or cats, or even a good sturdy rat as far as I know) wave these puny vestigial wings, weaker than seasoned "buffalo wings" at your corner pub, wave them proudly in some sea breeze for all the Goddamned world to see.

Is this a desire to live?, to thrive?, *as a proper bird!?*

I don't think so.

The people who wrote this book about birds were *scientists,* my friend!

In any event, as I mentioned above, in the most extreme case (that of the kiwi) this "bird" will actually take to living underground as if it were some sort of stinking badger or groundhog. And the kiwi has in fact been heard to *grunt.* By bird watchers! Why a bird watcher would take any interest in a thing that crawls from the ground and sticks its snout in the sand is beyond me. And it grunts! People in New Zealand are so confused that they've given a *fruit* the same name. A bitter-sweet greenish fruit. A kiwi. Now what, I ask you, does *that* mean? Run out of words down under?

Now, the interesting thing is that in spite of the kiwi's indifference to flight (I'm using the kiwi here because, as I said, he is the most extreme and therefore the *truest* instance of what I'm speaking of), the kiwi (degenerate, devolved representative of "birds" in general) still seems to desire to live even if it takes no joy (never mind a bit of species pride) in living. I repeat, it takes no joy in what is most conspicuously joyous about its being.

I mean, if you think wings, do you think flying or just exactly what?

And yet should you approach a kiwi on its isolated New Zealand beach, it will, or so I am assured by aforesaid book, grunt in horror and scurry as fast as its two little bird feet can take it back to its burrow.

Now, one might wonder why the kiwi knows to run from you at all, given that there are no predators on its island. And that would be a good question. Many of these isolated, flightless birds (the dodo comes to mind) do in fact walk more or less right up to humans as if they were offering sandwiches (eighteenth-century British and Portuguese sailors famously and gladly and lavishly took them up on their offer; this is the true origin of the "club" sandwich, or so I'm told).

Nonetheless, we would seem to be confronted by an oxymoron, or, at best, a riddle. A bird is that creature which takes no joy in living but will not submit to death.

Do you have any Latin, editor? Do you know the term "Dies Irae"? Let me translate for you. It means in unmistakable terms that a day of wrath is coming. God's having a bad day and has been for some time. God is angry. And hasn't He a lot to be angry about! Look what has been made of His creation! A laughingstock. A public display. Humiliating. Just humiliating.

I take this opportunity to offer you, dear editor, the kiwi. May he serve you well.

Furtwangler
Rural Peru

A Sacrifice to Be Devoutly Desired

And the Lord God said, "I see how stiff-necked this people is. They have become depraved. My wrath will blaze up against them and consume them. Then I will make of you a great nation."

Moses frowned. "Let your blazing wrath die down for once. How do you propose to make a great nation out of a bunch of charred corpses?"

At which God put his finger to his lip and pondered mightily. And this is why his people were capable of bloody non sequiturs.

"I am wrathful and they are depraved. Someone must suffer for this."

"No argument. I have a proposition. Let us submit to a blood sacrifice all members of Congress."

"All?"

"All."

"The innocent with the guilty?"

"It won't be the first time for you, Lord, with all due respect, and so yes."

"But why them in particular, as the focus of my huge anger?"

"Because these member of Congress lead the people in their eternal grumbling. They take excessive joy in the destruction of little brown peoples, like the Egyptians, or Iraqis, to whom they refer as Dead People even as they live. They say, 'They live to die.' For from their view, they are always dead in potentia, when they will it, when it is expedient for Congress."

"That's my call."

"Exactly. Further, they boil a tiny lamb in its mother's milk. They wrong widows and orphans. They make sacrifices to false gods. I heard one curse his parents. Are they not then doomed? They sleep in. Or worse yet, they get up early in order to do things no one wants done."

And the Lord said, "I see. Well, show me how this might be done."

"It is very easily done," replied Moses, and he had God pluck up one Member by his worsted lapels. He wriggled and squealed and this gave the Lord much pleasure, for he was very unclean.

And the Lord asked, "Does this one have a name?"

Moses replied, "This one is Hoekstra of Michigan."

"He's very pink."

"Now what, my Lord?"

"Let me guide your hand."

Bringing the distinguished member from Michigan to the entrance of the meeting tent, Moses laid his hand on his gray head and slaughtered him before the Lord. He took some of the Honorable Representative's blood and dipping his fingers in the blood sprinkled it seven times before the Lord. From the body of the Distinguished Member he removed all the fat: the fatty membranes over the inner organs, and all the fat that adhered to them, as well as the two kidneys, with the fat on them near the loins, and the lobe of the liver, which he severed above the kidneys. The hide of the "Good Friend" and all his flesh, his head, legs, inner organs and offal, in short, the whole Honorable Representative, he took to a clean place outside the camp and burned in a wood fire.

Finally, the voice of the People from Michigan was only an ash heap. A sweet-smelling oblation to the Lord.

The Lord was very pleased.

And He said, "I feel good about this. Are there more like him?"

"Oh Lord, their numbers are legion. There is Gingrich unto Barr unto DeLay unto LaHood unto Ewing (who was sadly born without a brain). Slimy creatures more like frogs than what you meant by humans."

"But you say that this depraved, stiff-necked people are in fact elected by those they represent? My chosen people?"

"Yes, Lord."

"Then the people are not unlike their representatives?"

"That is likely, Lord, by implication." God's sense of consequence was sound this time.

And the Lord God Almighty did scrunch his brow most thoughtfully and deeply.

"Then I fail to see why we are not back where we began."

And Moses knew not how to reply.

"For this is a doomed people."

Moses sighed. "More or less. Sooner or later."

His Life Was So Sad (1)

BARITONE: Like Mozart, Camille Saint-Saëns was a child prodigy. Unlike Mozart, Saint-Saëns did not have a music-master for a father. Rather, he had to rise from the obscurity of the uncultivated rube, through the scorn and laughter of his young peers, in order to achieve his radiant position as one of France's premier Romantic composers. The person who almost single-handedly saved France from the Wagnerian madness.

TENOR: I hardly know anything about him. Is his music good? I only associate him with opposing and intriguing against the young Debussy. But I guess he was a sort of musical father to the pathologically shy Fauré. If so, that's one in his favor.

SOPRANO: His life was so sad!

CHORUS: Tell us about it.

TENOR: There's not much for me to say. He's not my favorite, as I said. I like this piece, this *Requiem.* The opening theme is magical. Those descending violins! And the organ. Very striking. And novel for the time, I believe.

BARITONE: Saint-Saëns wrote his *Requiem* when he was forty-three years old. He was still struggling against the intrigues of those musicians who wished to keep him from the sinecure of the *Institut.* His operas were not successful and opera was still the most important public music form in Europe. That's where composers made their fame and lots of money. Unfortunately, some of Saint-Saëns operas actually drove his impresarios into bankruptcy.

SOPRANO: It is true that he intrigued and he was intrigued against. One of his most bitter rivals was Cesar Franck. And his battles with Massenet were front page news. But there is something about music itself that allows it spontaneously to transcend the "merely human." Music's beauties strike quickly, forcefully, against what we might "think," against our will. And so Saint-Saëns's rivals (like Mozart's Salieri) were brought to their knees by the sudden revelation of musical insight. Those who really know cannot deny what is truly good. Saint-Saëns himself was humbled by others, including the monster Wagner. Beyond all that, he was another suffering human being. A fatuous ass in one moment, then an angel.

BARITONE: It's strange to imagine a time in which a serious musician, a composer, could be a celebrity. We certainly don't have anything like it now. Phillip Glass, perhaps, if you count him. After he wrote the theme song for the L.A. Olympics, he doesn't count for me. But hard as he tries to sell out to the Olympic Committee or whatever, there's always something recherché about him for people who really only want to listen to Garth Brooks.

TENOR: What about Leonard Bernstein?

BARITONE: A transitional figure. If it weren't for his vamping and jet-setting and his wretched Broadway music, no one would have cared about him. Of course there are ironies. Did you know that Saint-Saëns was the first composer of a film score? 1908. A film called *L'Assassinat du duc de Guise*.

TENOR: Well, like I said, I don't know much about it. I only know that he picked on Debussy endlessly and cruelly. From what I've read and heard, Saint-Saëns was just plain threatened by what Debussy was doing. He is said to have attended the first performance of *Pelléas et Mélisande* in spite of the sweltering Parisian summer. He said, "I've stayed in Paris to speak ill of *Pelléas*." Frankly, I don't think that this dogged and cruel pursuit of a young, obscure, and impoverished musician like Debussy reflects well on Saint-Saëns.

BARITONE: I thought you said you didn't know much about it?

TENOR: Of Camille Saint-Saëns I know next to nothing. Of Debussy I know quite a bit.

BARITONE: Well, he didn't do anything to Debussy that wasn't done to him earlier. Think of him as the child of a child abuser, destined to abuse in his turn. At least he didn't kill anybody. Really, there was nothing out of the ordinary about Saint-Saën's conduct. Vindictive, spiteful, small-minded behavior was part of Paris's art culture. Probably still is. Would you have preferred that art was again the privilege of the courts? Remember Haydn under Esterházy? Was he happy stuck out in the boonies his whole life?

SOPRANO: I think you two are missing the point. You're not seeing what was the real source of his need to work. He was the real thing. A musician. His whole being came out of music and music's relation to life. And his life was a human life. That is to say, he suffered.

CHORUS: What happened?

TENOR: Just a second. Pardon me for interrupting, but just listen to that. This *Dies Irae* is quite extraordinary. Complex. Transformative. Powerful and haunting. It's a thoroughly engaging musical and emotional experience.

BARITONE: A fan is born. A fan who has read too many liner notes.

TENOR: Pardon me?

BARITONE: *Perdone.* The story behind the *Requiem* is a good one. Want to hear it?

The Modern Prophet Speaks of the People Unto Death

And in that time . . .
        They were the People Unto Death and
        Their culture was Death's Culture,
        And you could know that they were the
                People Unto Death
        Because they always *chose* death,
        And to say that a people is what it chooses
                is not unfair.
        "We have made a covenant with Death,
        And with the netherworld we have made a pact."

They did not see the death they chose
        though it stood in their very faces.
        And if they kissed it
        they could not taste this kiss.
        For it was not the bombs
            the bombs
                they dropped on others
     that was the choice.
     The choice was in the positing
     of the others as the others and
     the wish that they should die first.
     That's all it was.
     You first, asshole.
     And in spite of that they
                        . . . were nice.

A very nice people.
Smiled a lot of smiles.
But every once in a while,
one of the dead people,
the dead people who had not chosen
        death for themselves,
but who had had it chosen for them
(for these were not the People Unto Death but
        Dead People
                a big distinction),
well, one of these dead would be
        marooned,
so to speak,
in among them.
A Dead Person among the People of Death.
He would wander in, bumbling down our powerful corridors,
tongue tripping over our unique way of saying things,
and ask, "Can I talk to you?"
What have you got to say?
We're busy.
We have big problems, you know.
Because we don't understand how things are related.
That things are related.
Relation is a HARD idea for us.
And our brains hurt from it.
"Pues, exacto, señor, la relación."
Okay.
        Well, okay, then. But not too loud!
"You're a very nice people, señor.
        Muy amable.
We Dead People like your smile.
We admire your freedoms.
We admire your shopping malls
        in spite of ourselves.

But your freedom is death for me
       in Santiago, por ejemplo,
a place you could not find with your fingertip on a map.
So, do not say, 'Hi, how's it going?'
Do not say 'Have a nice day.'
Because we're done with nice days."
And so that can be the beginning of it.
We call that death's integument.
Death's transmission. Or linkage.
      Or lineage.
Death's articulation.
Death's snaky body,
      that starts here and ends there.
The People Unto Death can learn from that.
As for myself,
              I am still foul with my ancient stains.
Like when Pharaoh would not wreck
Aaron's rod,
and the Lord sent frogs. A Plague of Frogs!
As if more than four or five in any one spot
Were not bad enough.
And the Pharaoh called in his magicians
to give an expert opinion
and the magicians said, "We can do that."
And so saying the magicians created even more frogs.
A frog for a frog, so to speak,
One magic frog for every frog of God.
And at that moment the Pharaoh knew
      he was in deep trouble.
And he looked at the magicians so that *they* knew,
it was a fucking stupid idiot thing to do,
because he hadn't called them in to create *more* frogs.
And the Pharaoh turned his back on the whole
      disgusting scene.

Implying to God, "You take care of it. This is your mess."
And the Pharaoh walked away, the scrunch of frogs
beneath each fateful footfall.
And heaps and heaps of frogs
were gathered up
and there was a great stink in the land,
which frankly bugged the Pharaoh
because he had some aesthetic principles,
        that guy,
and I believe at that moment with
the mounds of frogs moldering about
that the Pharaoh realized
that these "people" who were Moses' and
        wanted to "go"
                were a scary bunch.
He thought of his moron "magicians"
and
        "with friends like these etc."
he just shook his head.
Later, when it was gnats or flies or fleas or
        WHATEVER
and the Pharaoh saw the magicians coming
he'd think, essentially, oh boy, not this again,
but the magicians said, "This we can't do,"
for which the Pharaoh was relieved.
Further, the magicians said, "This is the finger of God."
And the Pharaoh was once again considerably
dumbfounded by these loony fucks
who called themselves magicians and he asked,
"The finger of God?"
"Yes, Pharaoh."
"Just the finger?"
"Yes."
"Fleas are the finger of God?"

"More or less."
And the Pharaoh said, "Let these magicians go.
I don't care if this God wants them or not.
But I hate the sight of them."
And then, as we know, God stepped in and
made Pharaoh obdurate and obstinate and like that,
and not really at all as he would have liked to be,
like light, or ironic,
      a playful Pharaoh
           a Pharaoh of subtle jests
maybe a little cynical at times,
quite modern, really,
but not a bad guy even if he "knew not Joseph"
as if who should remember a bureaucrat Jew
from four hundred years before,
and I believe he could have been the
first to help us with this people
who would cover the earth with their Big Ideas,
nasty as so many frogs, flies or fleas.
This, after all, being that people who could
look at a flowering prairie and say,
"I see corn and beans here at $2.10 a bushel,
and in the winter . . . well, look the other way,"
and so they did for decades on end
growing corn and looking the other way.
Of the land we need only say,
"The dickcissels have gone elsewhere,
and the crow and the starling roost over the world."
Amen.
At any rate,
      this Pharaoh was obliged to his contrarian posture
called "obdurate"
by this God
as if he didn't quite trust Pharaoh's commitment

to the role.
But what kind of drama is this,
        finally,
                in which the bad guy
may not choose to be good?
No wonder "they know not
        what they do."
And to the sad-sack Jews he said,
"That is your promised land
        like it or not
And you will replace those fun-loving Canaanites
        like it or not
however much you secretly wish to be like them,
however much you admire their bodies
        and their parties
                with the golden calves
                and Baal
                        and everything just
                                ECSTATIC like that."
But this is the very Idea of the nothing
        at the heart
                of the People Unto Death.
A shadow thrown against a rough wall,
        as if they would have been a people unto life
given even half a chance,
without all the smoting and
the wiping out of the errant tribes.
Just the endless *shame* of it.
But, as it was, the Great God to this People
said:
        "Blood will mark the houses where you are."
And thus has it ever been.

The Soul in Paraphrase (3)

To: Honeycomb@teenslut.com
From: Tom@english.nwfsu.edu
Subject: my surprise

You can't imagine how surprising your last was for me. I can't say
I've ever had a message quite like it before. It certainly wasn't what I
anticipated. My message to you, I assure you, was pure fan mail. I
simply wanted to rave about your site, about the transcendental intui-
tions about the love, truth, and beauty I received from it.

In short, the heavy vibes!

What I was afraid of, naturally, was that my enthusiasm was all the
usual, rather dumb self-delusion. I feared I would receive some sort of
tacky come-on. ("Oh, I'm so horny," "My pussy's so wet for you,"
"Call me on the Love Dial, only long-distance charges apply." That
sort of crap. By the way, in all the world of porn-dom, the one thing I
have never got is how phone sex with some strange, detached voice
works. I mean, you've got to know that your "partner" is painting her
toenails or washing dishes, or tending brats with their mouths taped
shut. And who knows what she actually looks like. Like a large, wet
towel, I imagine. A skin stuffed with porridge. But what's sexy about
it? You're a professional. Surely someone has explained it to you.)

At any rate, I expected anything but what I got. What did I get?

The only other surprise even modestly approaching this surprise
was the time I was surfing amateur sites and I found that one of my
neighbors had her own site! Her name is Leona, but her nom de whatever was Lexus, as if that was what she planned on buying with her ill-

got gains. And she had a little node called "Lusty Lexus" on a website for, how shall I say this, healthily plump girls. Remember Jabba the Hut in the old Star Wars? Before your time, probably. Or well after it if you're not kidding me with that seventy-something business. Well, imagine a potato sack full of Cream of Wheat approximately the size of a couch. In fact, they should have called this site the Ottoman Sex Site, because with these girls it was like having sex with overstuffed furniture.

I don't get it. Again. I just don't get it. There are definitely some sick twists out there. Nothing like the radiance I experience with you.

Anyway, as regards my neighbor's site, it was so sad. She claimed that she just wanted to find people who wanted to look at her. She just wanted the thrill of being looked at. Longingly. I guess she had trouble finding people willing to do that in the real world. And no wonder.

I don't mean to ramble on. I just want to put a closed bracket on this. After I found her site, I took to dropping off chocolate-covered cream puffs in her mailbox, addressed simply to Little Lotta Lexus. The best I could do for her.

I'm pretty sure it was her on this site. 95% sure.

Well, your predicament is nothing like that one. Although it is surprising. But let's look at it. You say you hear a kind of hissing? It sounds like numbers or sand? I think I know what this is. It is the sound of digital life. Actually, many people have remarked on this sound. Most people hear it if they have cheap CD players. You're listening to some music, a band is playing, a singer is singing, and suddenly you don't hear human beings or real music anymore. You hear something else. A sibilance. A wave washing over a beach. The sound of sand on sand. It's all the little "1's" and "0's" rolling over each other. The image of a human being dissolves into this indecipherable mess about as much like a human as road kill is to a raccoon. At any rate, this, I believe, is the hissing. If that's all we're talking about, I'd just say upgrade your system. Get a player that can adjust for digital jitter and that has an updated D/A converter and 20 bit capacity. That will take care of it.

But, unless I misunderstand you, you don't seem to be talking about your stereo system. You seem to be claiming that you are actually *inside* of whatever was making this noise.

I know this is going to sound strange, but I really have been thinking about it very seriously. Here are the three things I've come up with based upon the information you've given me. I wish I had a computer program that I could feed this info into and test my hypothesis.

Here are the three themes:

*you are lost in hyperspace;

*you are in the white slave trade;

*you are the victim of body snatching (or a really weird instance of metempsychosis gone awry).

How to make sense of this? Is it possible that at the moment of your death (at the age of seventy whatever), you were abducted into the white slave trade as it might exist in hyperspace, in a re-figured or purely digital topos available on or through the Ether? (I have an Ethernet card!)

I know this doesn't make much sense. Nevertheless, I think it's the case. I'm going to think about it in these terms just to see what sort of help you need.

Tom

The Seven Last Words of Christ (2)

3. *"Woman, behold thy son! Son, behold thy mother!"* (grave)

Statement

Like Mozart and Saint-Saëns, Haydn fell in love with one woman and then married another. In the cases of Herrs Mozart and Haydn, they fell in love with daughters of families into which they'd been taken, were then disappointed in their suites, and subsequently proposed to the younger *sisters* of the original object of their considerable affections. For Mozart this meant simply that his original love married someone else. But for Haydn, the original object of his regard actually joined the Order. When this young woman, Therese Keller, left for the nunnery, Haydn composed and performed music for her, including the poignant *Salve Regina*. Four years later, Haydn married the sister, Maria Anna. About her, we know from Griesinger that "she was bigoted, and was always inviting clergymen to dinner."

Argument

Frau Haydn was once the lover of a young painter, Ludwig Guttenbrun, who painted a well-known portrait of Haydn. There's something "wrong" with this portrait. Haydn is narrow, angular and severe. It's the sort of thing a cubist would do two centuries hence, but Guttenbrun is no cubist, he just has a problem with perspective. Haydn is "out of whack." A later self-portrait by Guttenbrun shows a jolly, rounded and superficial man perched in a window quite "in whack" from a painterly perspective. It's difficult not to wonder if he distorted the painting of Haydn for his own little reasons. It's difficult not to wonder if Frau Haydn is saying something to her husband through these portraits: in marrying me you have made a great mistake. She says, "The fact that I can't tell the difference between your genius and this painter's mediocrity shows that I am a very inappropriate mate for you. *My* sadness will consist in yearning after this incompetent painter endlessly and, for you, annoyingly." Because of her enduring affection for the *painter,* Frau Haydn clung to the portrait of her *husband* throughout his life. If Haydn or his wife ever saw the strangeness in her attachment to the painting, neither mentioned it. And while Haydn himself was not in love with his ill-educated and quarrelsome wife, the anger, irony, humor, and melancholy that this incident provoked was often expressed in his music. I think he thought of it not so much as a betrayal by his wife but as a fundamental betrayal by Life itself. He didn't get the woman he truly wanted, he settled for someone less, and then had to suffer for that as well. To lose and then lose within the loss. Listen to the "storm and stress" quartets (op. 20) and see if I'm not right.

Development

Haydn himself had a longtime lover, a lovely, olive-skinned Italian soprano named Luigia Polzelli. She was married to the court violinist Antonio Polzelli. Unlike David in his love for Bathsheba, Haydn was not able to send the inconvenient husband off to die with the shock troops in the next battle. Perhaps he thought that the situation between his wife and the painter made his relationship with "La Polzelli" unexceptional. There must have been a lot of "grin and bear it" especially for Señor Polzelli's son Antonio, whom Haydn raised "like his own son" (he was). In fact, the noble Haydn lived up to this duty very well. The young Polzelli eventually took his name father's place as violinist in the Esterházy orchestra.

Imagine this scene: Haydn and his wife face each other while standing before Guttenbrun's portrait of Haydn. Haydn's arm is around the shoulder of his son-who-is-not-his-son, Antonio. What do they say to each other, Haydn and his wife?

Restatement

Haydn spent the month before his departure for England in Vienna and frequently dined alone with Mozart. The two not only respected each other's work, they loved each other. Mozart called Haydn "Papa." Haydn never really stopped mourning Mozart's early death.

Wouldn't these two men have talked about the curious parallels and interdependencies not only of a musical but also of a personal nature between them? Wouldn't it have seemed remarkable to them that they'd both loved one sister but married another? Mozart's marriage to Constanze was, of course, largely happy. Mozart could only have sympathized with his older friend and bought the next bottle of wine.

"My wife is still sick most of the time, and is always in a foul humor, but I don't really care anymore—after all, this woe will pass away one day."

4. *"Father, why hast thou forsaken me?"* (largo)

Statement

Haydn's life, as seen from the vantage of a biographer, was fortunate, productive, lengthy, and often exciting. Imagine the vast creativity, the fame and financial rewards, and all in the context of princes, castles, and the king and queen of England! Every peasant's life should be so hard. And all of this dependent on the intuition and trust in intuition of a mediocre music teacher who observed a peasant urchin sawing at his arm with a stick.

But from a poet's perspective, a life is not its facts. A life is its metaphors, its displacements, especially those metaphors which speak to each other.

Argument

Prince Nicholas enjoyed not only music and opera, he also enjoyed theater and would frequently provide employment for traveling troupes of actors. In this way, Haydn would have become familiar with the works of Shakespeare, for example. In addition, there was also German marionette theater. The Prince loved the puppet operas so well, in fact, that he had a theater built specifically for the puppet performances. There was something about the little dolls belting out those opera tunes, I guess.

Development

As I've mentioned, although Haydn was always very loyal and grateful to the House of Esterházy for its kindness to him, as an artist he was by no means entirely free to follow his own heart. It should not be surprising to us, then, if the following scene once occurred between Prince and court composer.

"Haydn. I have a task for you."

"Yes, your highness."

"As you know, I have had a theater constructed for the marionette performances. I would like you to compose the music for an operatic version of Dido to be performed by the puppets."

"Puppets, my lord?"

"Yes. Puppets."

"And you want it to seem as if the puppets are singing?"

"Exactly. Is there something wrong with that?"

"What music is appropriate for a puppet singing of Dido?"

"Your music of course."

Restatement

On August 2, 1768, a great fire destroyed the lower part of Eisenstadt, including the building in which Haydn lived. Haydn lost his furniture and belongings and months of compositions.

5. *"I thirst."* (adagio)

Statement

Fire here becomes a leitmotif in Haydn's life. The flautist Franz Sigl went out shooting one night and set the roof of a house on fire.

Argument

Haydn wrote the music for the puppet opera "Dido" like a man condemned. But he could not, unfortunately, create his way to life. So why should he work? He was doomed. He became so depressed that no ideas came to him. He would not experience this sort of deep artistic despair again until he was nearly eighty years old.

Music for a puppet to sing!

Development

On July 17, 1776, another terrible holocaust ravaged the town destroying the town hall, the monastery, the brewery and the church. One hundred-four houses were lost. Haydn's house was again among them. And again, he lost reams of autograph scores.

Restatement

It's not clear how the following incident figures in all this, but on June 24, 1771, a brawl broke out between the cellist Xavier Martean and the oboist Zacharias Pohl at the Esterháza tavern. There had been a lot of beer drinking and dice-throwing. In the course of this fight the oboist lost an eye. The cellist later agreed to pay Pohl eight gulden per month as compensation for the lost eye. Somehow, the flautist Sigl managed not to set anything on fire during this tragic incident.

Not One Does What Is Right, Not Even One (1)

"Come on in!"

Two young men—one dark and attractive, neatly dressed and fit; the other portly with long stringy hair and dressed in jeans and ripped T-shirt—come into the living room of a very functional but also sterile-seeming townhouse in a new housing development on the outskirts of Austin, Texas. The portly man carries several digital cameras around his neck as well as a case of photographic equipment.

A young and very pretty woman looks through a short passageway from her kitchenette. Beyond the kitchenette is a sliding plate-glass door looking on a tiny backyard with a chain-link "Hurricane" fence.

"What's up, guys?"

"Not much, Michelle. How are you?" says the neater of the two.

"Hey, guys, would you mind takin' off your boots? I just cleaned the floors."

The two take off their boots.

"Where's Sandy?"

"Couldn't make it. Something about her daddy being sick. Out in the Amarillo area somewhere."

"Amarillo? Sick daddy or no sick daddy, I don't go to Amarillo."

"I hear you." The neater man is doing all the talking. His partner is busy unloading the cameras.

"Guess I'm on my own this month. Can't believe it's time to update the site already. How'd I make out last month, Mr. Numbers?"

"Hundred-twenty-thousand hits. About ten thousand made it specifically to your site. Then the usual cut of surfers, members and new members."

"Wow, come on! Tell me! How many new ones?"

"About a hundred."

She claps her hands and smiles as if to say "yippee."

"And so my total is what now?"

"Twelve hundred."

She frowns and stomps a bare foot. Feminine petulance. "Shoot, that means I also lost a few."

"A few."

"Still at twenty bucks a pop," she's doing a lot of math in her head, a math she has plenty of practice with. "That's $24,000 for the month and I take half."

"You got it."

She pumps her fist. "Bitchin'! That'll keep us in dog biscuits for awhile."

"Dog biscuits, caviar, whatever."

"Screw the caviar. Did you see what's in the driveway?" She drags Mr. Numbers by his sleeve back to the front door.

"That would be a Lexus."

"That is indeed a Lexus."

"What do your student friends think of that?"

"I just say I'm independently wealthy. Daddy's in oil or cattle or whatever."

"Don't you ever worry that one of them might happen to crawl over your site?"

"Crawl. I always think of snails when I hear that word. I think of something leaving this yucky, scummy trail behind. I guess they could chance upon it." Sucks her thumb and ponders the consequences. "Could create some comfort issues for me. Nothing I couldn't handle, though."

"Sure. You're a pro. And English majors are notoriously tolerant. They'd probably try to include you in some sort of diversity program."

She giggles. "Funny! Funny, Mr. Numbers! Well, let's get this over with. I got aerobics at eleven, lunch with Chad, then two classes in the

afternoon, and one tonight. Man, I thought I worked hard as an un-
dergraduate. Grad school is a straight bitch." She turns a can-you-
believe-it expression on the two. "I work my *ass* off!"

"I don't know why you think you're ever going to need a job. Not
everybody is willing to do what you do. Even when your body goes,
which will be a while with all the aerobics you do, there'll still be
work. Or just save some of this dough you're making now."

She winks. "Oh. Boys. I *do.* I *do.* And you know what? This isn't
always a real upbeat way to make a living. Chad freaks about it every
once in a while. And that's no damned fun."

"How is Chad?"

"Oh, fine. Fiancés are pretty predictable on the whole."

This remarkable young woman, this Michelle, radiates when she
speaks. She has an intellectual brightness. And she really is a remarkably beautiful woman. That's clear even through her loose workout
clothes. Then, without transition, she removes both her top and bottom sweats and is standing naked in the middle of the kitchen. Her
breasts are enormous. Heavy but perfectly round. Round as in circu-
lar. Round as with something outlined with a compass. You can only
just see the light line where the plastic surgeon inserted the silicon.

"Ready?"

"Ready," says the chubby, stringy man.

She goes to the backyard door and calls. "Murphy! Murph! Here
boy."

A large Irish setter comes bounding up to the door and in to the
kitchen.

"Oh damn. I just washed you and look at your feet. Just a minute.
I gotta clean his feet a little or he'll get these red clay paw prints all
over everything."

When the setter sees the two men, he gets suddenly agitated and
begins whining and pawing at the woman.

"Ow! Shit, Murph, you scratched my leg! Ooh, look how red it is
already. Damn it."

"Don't worry we'll just shoot from the other side."

She gets down to face level with the dog. "Oh, Murph, I know you didn't mean it. I know you're a good boy."

"I don't know about good, I just hope he's better than last time," says the camera man.

She glares at him, blue eyes flashing. "Oh like you could do better, Marky?" Back to the dog. "You were just excited, huh, Murphy-wurphy." She rubs the animal's ears and nuzzles the fur around his neck. "You're my little furry woodsman, aren't you?" She looks defiantly at Mark. "As for you, you know nothing about the wielding of wood. Fat techie voyeur. The word for you is 'difficulties.' If you tried, you'd have 'difficulties with wood,' Mr. Marky. *Little* difficulties. Maybe even tiny." As if in agreement, the dog lashes out with his muzzle and licks her mouth.

"Yuck! Murph. Cut it out." She wipes her face aggressively. "Okay. Time for work, honey. Time to earn our dog biscuits. Okay?" She waltzes to the refrigerator, bare buttocks shimmering, and pulls out a small tube of something.

"What's this, Murph? Do you know? Can you beg Mommy for it?"

Murphy whines. Wags his tail wildly. Barks once.

"That's right. Your favorite." She looks to the men. "He *loves* anchovy paste."

She looks around. "Okay, what do you guys think? Right here?" She frowns. "No, we need something really daring this month. Weren't we in the kitchen just a few months ago? I forget." She looks right at them. "I'm not going to lose one single member this month. Not one! We're going into the backyard. Public bestiality! www.twobackedbeast.com will be the talk of the web!"

Mr. Numbers laughs and rolls his head back. "You gotta be kidding. What if someone sees? You got neighbors, remember?"

"Yeah, I know I got neighbors, but what do I care? Besides, we don't have to go way outside. The sun is shining right up to the house and I'll just pull that shade so you can't see from the apartment complex next door and nobody will be the wiser . . . except my fans! And they'll just be the happier!"

"Whoakay. Whatever. That okay with you, Mark?"

"I don't give a fuck."

"He don't care."

"Well, let's do it then so I can get on with my day. 'Kay Murph?"

They walk out into the back, Murphy still whining in agitation, and she climbs onto a chaise lounge and spreads her long, Playboy-esque legs. Her quads are especially well-developed from thousands of weight room squats. She takes a bit of the anchovy paste and rubs it around her clitoris.

"He really only needs this as an incentive. It's kinda like a treat. Once he gets goin', he likes it for its own sake. I'm as good as anchovy paste. I guess that's a compliment. Is it, Murph?"

She grabs Murphy by his collar and places his head between her legs. He begins lapping. Mark begins snapping photos. Looking for good angles.

"D'jou guys see that that Carson Pirie anchor store at the South Side Mall was going out of business?"

"No."

"Gotta pay attention. I heard they had some unbelievable sales goin' down. I wonder if they've got those Coach bags marked down. I'd love to have one of those. But three hundred bucks! Give me a break. Ooh, Murph!" She strokes the top of the dog's head. "It's amazing how nice that cold little nose feels. And he always seems to get it right on my clit. Good boy!"

"I'll bet."

"You'll bet," she mocks. "What would you know about it? Okay, Murph, that's it. Get enough shots, Mark?"

"Oughta be a few good ones in there."

"Well, Zip disk 'em to me. I like to choose."

"Okay."

"All right, honey. Ready for what's next?"

"Ready? He's a fucking puddle."

"Shut up!" She fondles the dog's head. "He's my little sweetheart.

Plus he's more fun to take a walk with than you'd ever be."

She gets up and the dog leaps onto the chaise. He's trembling and whimpering. A long, thin, red erection has already come searching tentatively out of his shaggy foreskin.

"Calm down, honey. It's okay," she coos, as if to her child. "You know you like it. Just relax."

"I hope he doesn't like it as much as last time. He came like that and we didn't get a penetration shot."

She scrunches her brow and pulls back Murphy's ears. "Hmmm. What are we gonna do, Murph? The breeder told me you Irish setters were a little high-strung. Maybe I should have got something calmer. One of those Chocolate Labs. They're pretty. They look like logs to me. I'll bet they're calm. What do you think, Murph? Would you like a buddy? Then you could retire."

"They'd probably be out here goring each other all day thinking about when the next shoot was."

"Hey! Murphy is no faggot! Are you, Murphy? Okay. Let's try to get just a couple quick shots of me and him with his little peenee in my hand and a couple with his peenee up to my mouth. Got that trigger ready, Speedee? Mark? Ready? Be quick!"

"I'm ready. Don't worry. Just tell him to hold on. Tell him to replay the last quarter of the Citrus Bowl in his head or something. Sometimes a guy's got to take his mind off the matter at hand. I like to do the starting lineup for the '86 Mets. Gooden, Carter, Hernandez, Nails. . . ."

"Shut up, Mark. I thought you were a pro. Don't listen to him, Murph, he's a jerk and you're my puppy."

She reaches for his glossy erection and Murph gets a look of worried ecstasy on his face. She looks at Murph, thinking.

"You know, that expression they get on their faces just cracks me up. They really like it. I mean, they get very excited, but it also–don't you think?–half looks like they think you're gonna kill 'em. I mean, they really look crazed. Did you see that Great Dane on Allysa's site last month? That thing looked deranged! Happy but deranged. You know what I mean?"

She slowly strokes Murphy's cock. It's rigid now and very pretty in a sort of colorful, abstract way. But it's also not unlike a prop from some science-fiction movie. Something that would pop out of the alien's mouth. Mark is snapping rapidly.

"I wonder what this means to them? Do you think dogs think you love them when you do this? Are they as dumb as men? And what does this mean in terms of dominance stuff? Am I the Alpha dog? I oughtta read a dog book or something. Seriously, I really do think it means, and I've put a lot of thought into this, 'I can't help myself, I need this feeling, and you can kill me when it's done, I expect to die but that's okay.' I really think that's what's going on in their little dog heads. I mean, to judge by the expression on their face. You know, it's strange but kind of lovely." She's pensive. "I really think dogs have a very remarkable attitude toward sex. They're really committed to it. They see the death all around it, but they're totally committed."

"Maybe you've thought too much about it," says Mr. Numbers.

"Oh there's more where that came from. For instance, it's occurred to me that one of the things I do with him puts him in the most passive and vulnerable position he can be in. I've heard that when one male wolf lets another male wolf lick his dong that he's saying, 'I'm done. You win. You be the badder wolf. Take all them girl wolfies. I'm out of it.' Or is it the other way around? Maybe it's the one getting sucked that's the badder wolf. I forget. But, on the other hand, the thing he does to me is surely the most aggressive and powerful position."

"When he lasts that long."

"Mark. You know, I don't know why, but you really bug me. Too bad you're such a good photographer. 'Cause you really help me to hate men."

"He must get confused," says Mr. Numbers. "In dog land, you're not alpha today omega mañana."

"He can handle it, can'tcha boy?" Her slow rhythmic stroking has not faltered, nor has Mark's snapping. "And on the bad days we always have those new doggy serotonin boosters."

"Tell me, how is he around Chad?"

"Oh, generally okay. When things get tense, Chad just gets out the old jingle ball and pretty soon they're pals again. After all, Murphy and I only have this encounter once a month."

"Well, if he did it more often, maybe he'd feel more natural and calm about it. You know."

"True. Teeroo. But forget it. I'm not that into it, to tell you the truth. This is business as far as I'm concerned."

"Michelle!"

"Oh, crap, Murph, you did it again."

Murph had come all over the cushions of the chaise lounge.

"Oh, buddy, I'm sorry. I should have been paying more attention. This is my fault."

"He's not Mr. Longevity."

"Just see if you can get a few of me with my mouth up there while it's still kinda hard. Got it? Got it? God, this stuff smells! Reminds me of rotting mushrooms."

"Okay, Michelle, I got it or something. We'll have to see. They're not going to be ace shots though. You might lose a few subscribers. But you never know, one or two of them might be okay."

"All we got is a few anchovy shots and me playing with him. That's crummy. What are we gonna do about the penetration?"

The two men look at each other.

"We've gotta go," says Mr. Numbers.

"Damn it! You can't wait fifteen minutes?" She looks down. "I think I do need more dogs. Yeah, like there used to be three or four Rin Tin Tins, I heard. Dozens of Lassies. Why not two or three Murphys? Poor Murph!"

Murphy is at last mostly relaxed. He wags his tail, which thumps on the cushions. His cock is almost entirely back in its sheath.

"Forget the penetration, Michelle, the real question is what are you gonna do about that guy gawking at you from his Chevy?"

She turns and looks beyond the fence where a young man stares from his Chevy Malibu.

She turns her chest toward him and waves. "Hi sweetie! Bet he's whackin' it."

"Either that or throwing up."

"We call that full-frontal silicone. Nothin' else quite like it."

She looks at Murphy, apparently asleep already. "And besides, that guy can't possibly see that far. I'm just naked in my own backyard. That's all he cares about. He's just some kid."

"Shall I give him one of your cards with the site address?"

"Hey, you know, if he's eighteen. . . . I think that's where we're moving. I give head to a teenage boy while Murph does me from behind."

"If ol' Murph goes on like this, there'll be some timing problems."

She frowns once again and looks back to Murphy. "Poor baby. Such a good doggie. And I do love you. Not like this, believe it or not. But I love you." She turns to the men. "I really just love him as a pet. I might even keep him when I leave the site."

"That's some commitment. You really gonna leave your site?"

"Sure, I'll have to when I get a teaching gig. I guess we better go inside. I don't like the way that kid is hanging around."

Michelle and Mr. Numbers move back into the kitchen.

"We gotta go anyway, Michelle," says Mr. Numbers.

"Can you come back later this week to do the penetration stuff?" She's putting her blue sweats back on. "You know how my fans love those humpin' hounds. Something about those twitching hindquarters throws that little switch you guys got up in the old reptilian brain."

"Don't do nothin' for me."

"Really? You don't like this?"

"Not really. What about you?"

She thinks. "In general, no. But like I said, I do like Murph. He's sweet."

"Good lord."

"Well, if you don't like this stuff and I don't really like this stuff, who likes this stuff?"

"I don't know, but twelve hundred of them give you twenty bucks every month."

"Yeah. Twelve hundred." She looks up. "I'm sure they're all guys. This is what happens when you give reptiles access to digital culture. The Net has really changed things. You can hear Lizard Lounges all over America going bankrupt, turning to dust, blowing away. This is the New World Order, baby.

"But what about you, Mr. Webmaster, Mr. Overseer of Accounts, Mr. Compiler of Numbers Infinite as Grains of Sand? Where are you at? If you don't like this stuff, what do you like? You don't have a girlfriend that I've heard of, or a boyfriend (heaven forefend). That's worse than dogs in my mind. I can't even remember your name from time to time. You're just Mr. Numbers. Is it Harold? Greg? Ken? Here's what I think. I think you're just the most recent modern man. You have your own aesthetic. You like the music of bits. Bits on bits. Sand on sand. The sound of dry time. Like a universe of crickets rubbing their legs together. That's our webmaster."

Mr. Numbers looks at Michelle in some discomfort and uncertainty. He isn't used to revealing himself and he's not sure he trusts her to hear what he has to say now. He's thinking about what he should say. Mark, the photographer, is still out back casing equipment and mumbling to the spent dog. He seems to be having a heart-to-heart with Murphy. Fatherly advice, no doubt.

"It is in fact Greg," replies Mr. Numbers-Now-to-Be-Known-as-Greg. "You know, you're quite the thinker."

She folds her arms and frowns at him. "I am the Silicon-Boobed-Material-Grrrl-Who-Fucks-Dogs-(well, one very special dog)-for-Money, but I've also taken the requisite courses in feminist and cultural theory. Hello! We live in Austin! Body as site of power/knowledge. That stuff? If you roll a bag lady in this town you'll find a copy of *The Cyborg Manifesto* in her pocket."

Webmaster Greg smiles. "Well, if you really want to know, it's complicated with me. I like the money which you girls bring in. I have to upgrade my own equipment annually and that ain't cheap. So there's that. But I also like to think about what's going on. We're a lot alike, except I don't suck dog."

"Very funny. I'm sure you mean that in the most flattering way."

"Of course."

"So, what are you thinking today?"

"Actually, I concluded something. I concluded that women who like to fuck dogs or horses or whatever are actually much more intense in their moral sentiments than most people. But they're not aware that their intensity is in fact the intensity of moral sentiment. They think their intensity has something to do with sex, which it doesn't."

"Do tell." Michelle reclined against the kitchen counter and crossed her legs.

"Sure. Most people who wouldn't have anything to do with a dog, say, don't believe that sex is dirty or evil or nasty. These are so-called healthy people. I'm not sure they exist anymore. I sure haven't met one. Sex as 'normal function' people. They all died with the last fraction of hippy logic. The hippies were eaten by Lotus. The other not-inconsiderable group of people is the sex *is* dirty, filthy, evil group. Now, this group sub-divides into two. At least two. First, there's the more or less celibate group, especially women who think of sex, if they think of it at all, as marital duty. Sex as distasteful obligation. They think of it in the way anyone thinks about cleaning out gutters in the spring. Disgusting with all the rotting leaves and stuff but necessary for domestic harmony. These people are all over the damn place, but they're not worthy of consideration, not because they're wrong (in the long view, they're as right as anybody else) but because they're clueless about what it means to be alive right now. In this moment in time."

"I see."

"But the other sub-group here is those people who are convinced in a hyper-moral way of sex's essential dirty evilness but who will engage in it anyway. That's where things have always been a little more interesting." Greg raises his finger and lowers his brow. "Because *some* of this group actually see that there is a relationship between the evil and the pleasure. The more evil, the more pleasure.

And the evilest thing one can think to do is fuck with beasts. For that is strictly forbidden by the Lord in the earliest covenants with his people. The interesting question is, how did he and Moses or Aaron or whoever think to mention it? Was it the same as with don't lust after your neighbor's wife? 'Hmmm, now that you mention it, that's a hell of an idea!' I mean, after that injunction, do they ever look at old Wanda out sunbathing in the backyard without also thinking this other thought? 'Yeah, my neighbor's wife. What will that cost me?' This is David and Bathsheba, right?"

"So this is how you spend your time when you're out keeping Mark company and negotiating with the working girls. You generate your little philosophies?"

"Yeah, well, it gives me something to do. Like you said, it's Austin."

"Amazing what passes for profundity among webmasters. Ever hear of the Marquis de Sade? Genet? Artaud? Any of a large number of French guys?"

"What about them?"

"Never mind. I don't want to queer your deal."

"Sorry if I disappointed you with my trite notions. You asked me what I thought."

"And where do I fit in this scheme of yours?" She crosses her arms and scowls, obviously expecting the worst and prepared to chew his ass for it.

"You don't. You're obviously none of the above. You're post-all-that. You do it for the money. I wouldn't be surprised if you didn't even have sex with poor old Chad"—she flushes guiltily—"and not because you don't like it, or you like dogs better, but because it just never occurs to you. Or rarely. Not on your radar. In terms of my schema, it's like you don't exist."

Michelle is getting pissed. "Well, I like that! What do you mean 'don't exist'? What do you call these?" She lifts the baggy UT sweatshirt revealing her heavy boobs.

Greg has a disturbed look on his face, not because she has revealed her breasts to him, which he has obviously already seen, but because she has revealed to him the limits of her understanding of her own situation, and it strikes him as shocking and sad. But he continues on. "When I say, 'You don't exist,' I mean that you don't exist through any of the old human modalities and perplexities. You go beyond that. You really are 'of the moment,' and you can take some consolation in that. Because there is something worse than fucking a beast: fucking the dead. I mean, look at your gesture. You've revealed your 'breasts' to me but they're *prosthetic* breasts, my friend. They're exactly not real. Just as the sex you provide on the Internet is not sex. It's exactly not-human. It's a sex prosthesis. Admit it, sex has lost its body. Oh well, you might argue that the body was always a prosthesis. But it was God's prosthesis! I'm telling you, this is death we fuck with! Why am I the only one who sees this?"

Greg is getting carried away and he can see that he is upsetting Michelle, so he tries to calm himself. "Please, don't take me wrong. I like you, Michelle. I mean that in the very best, most old-fashioned sense. But it's as if you're dead, if you can understand not-human as the equivalent of dead for a human. And the saddest thing is that if you wanted to become human again, fuck poor Chad for example, inhabit your own body, you wouldn't know how. You forgot to leave bread crumbs."

Michelle's angry scowl turns to a quivering pout which is clearly about to generate tears. Greg feels some remorse for what he has said.

"Hey, don't take it so hard. I said we were a lot alike. I mean, what am I doing every day? Learning to play Haydn sonatas on the piano? Or am I feeding myself to my computer jones, losing myself in hyperlife, hanging out with lost souls like you? I'm a webmaster, for Christ's sake. I'm just more conscious of the situation, which makes me all the guiltier. All the more lost. In fact, I'm so lost that I'm capable of the cruelty of pointing out to you your lostness when I know for a fact that there's nothing you can do about it even if you wanted to. So just go on with the dog sucking, babe. Michelle?"

She is hanging her head, her face covered by her strong right hand.

Greg reaches his hand out to touch her shoulder, to which she reacts violently. "Don't touch me, you fucking sexist creep."

Suddenly, Mark thrusts his head into the room.

"Hey! Murphy says he's ready to go again."

Jezebel Shall Be Like Dung (2)

Death of Marilyn

When Marilyn learned that Robert had arrived in L.A., she shadowed her eyes, adorned her hair and looked down from her window. She danced about the room singing "I'm the First Lady" to the tune of "I Feel Pretty." For days she waited, drinking whiskey from a bottle and swallowing pills. At last she saw him beneath her window, but by then it was too late. For she was not that kind of girl anymore. As Robert entered her gate, she cried out, "Is all well, Bobby, murderer of your master?" Robert looked up to the window and wondered what this was all about. Whatever the case, murder and guilt were no laughing matter in the Kennedy clan. So he shouted up to the room, "Who is on my side up there? Anyone?" At this, two or three eunuchs looked down toward him. "Throw her down," he ordered. Marilyn was doubly perplexed by the presence of the strange eunuchs and the bloody command. They threw her down and some of her blood spurted against the wall and against the legs of Robert and his bodyguards. Robert strode over her body and, after eating and drinking, said, "Attend to that accursed woman and bury her; after all, she was a president's lover." But when they went to bury her, they found nothing of her but the skull, the feet, and the hands. They returned to Bobby, and when they told him, he said, "This is the sentence which the Lord pronounced through his servant Elijah the Tishbite: 'In the confines of Jezreel dogs shall eat the flesh of Marilyn. The corpse of Marilyn shall be like dung in the field in the confines of Jezreel, so that no one can say: This was Marilyn.'"

Murder Mystery (3): Clues

Hume had voice mail. Two messages. The first was the voice of a boy.

"I know what you want to know. You and your kind. I seen it all come down. Right from the beginning with that pasty-faced pussy. Ask the Cookie Ladies what they know. They know all about it. But don't take no baskets from them 'cause they'll destroy your life. When they start talking, wait a few minutes. They're sorta frothy. Then if you can listen real close, you'll hear all you need to know. They saw what they saw, and they know what they know. Mostly they know what people keep in their drawers. Tell your buddy Hot Cocoa or Rocky Raccoon or whatever his name is. He'll know what to make of it. This is definitely his kind of material. Just say, 'The Cookie Ladies have got the stuff from his drawers.' That's all you need to say. He can take it from there.

"'Nuther thing. You wanna talk to a certain LaCrema Pui Descansolo. That's a real name, I think. As real as any of these dumb names around here. Anyway, she saw this guy for a loser right from the beginning. The original 'fraidy cat. She knows he ain't natural. He's a fuckin' freak. But if you make an appointment with her, for God's sake keep it. She's become a little sensitive on this point all because of that pussy. Besides, I think you might kinda like her anyway. I know I do. Ask her about those special promotional pamphlets of hers. Yow! Don't worry. I gave her your number. She'll call you.

"Okay, that's all I can say. I'm afraid they might be listening so I gotta go now. I'll call later."

The second message was from the aforesaid Ms. Descansolo.

"Inspector Hume? Hello? This is LaCrema Pui Descansolo. I work at the Pontiac Academy of Beauty. I was given your number by some-one who wishes to remain anonymous. He said to tell you that the Cookie Ladies will vouch for me. Anyway, I believe I have some information that you want. It's yours if the price is right. I'm making a special deal for you because there is a personal, payback angle here. It's an ethnic thing, you wouldn't understand. But this has got to be private. I believe we're all being watched. So I'll meet you here at the Academy. It's not far from your station. We lock up at 5:30. Meet me here at 6:15. I'll leave the back door open. Go up the stairs on your right. There is a series of small rooms on either side of the hallway. I've got a little night light I like to use. It casts a pinkish glow. Bring lots of money and don't even fucking think about being late or blow-ing me off."

Who Cannot Weep May Learn from Thee (2)

MURDERER: You know what got me more than anything else about her?

PROPHET: No. What?

MURDERER: She used the word "wank."

PROPHET: Wank?

MURDERER: Right. You know what it means, don't you?

PROPHET: No.

MURDERER: Sure. A kid like you wouldn't. A snot-green kid like you.

PROPHET: Excuse me?

MURDERER: Forget it. Wank is English for jerk off in American . . . if you know what *that* means!

PROPHET: Sure I know. And?

MURDERER: And? And what? She used that word that just used to piss me off so much and I didn't even know what it was about at first, that word, wank, but *something* about that word . . . no kidding, so disgusting, and humiliating, but with a metallic sound. Like clank. A metallic humiliation. Now, what's that about? What's a metal sound got to do with jacking off? Or Yank. It had a vague sort of anti-American feel in her mouth.

PROPHET: Like I said, it's a new word for me.

MURDERER: And it wasn't just the word. The word itself I suppose I could have adjusted to. You know, made some adjustments. Although it's one of those words that just seems designed to light my fuse.

PROPHET: Your very short fuse.

MURDERER: Whatever. But here's how she'd use it. I'd be feeling kinda sexy, say, sorta amorous. And so I'd suggest we go get cozy.

PROPHET: Cozy?

MURDERER: Yeah.

PROPHET: That's what you called it?

MURDERER: That's what I called it. I wanted to be like genteel about it. What am I supposed to say? "Let's go do the ugly, bitch?" You know, I'm more sensitive than people allow. But let me get on with this, woudja? So, anyway, I'd say something like that and sometimes she would say, "I'm sorry, honey, but I'm not in the mood." And I guess I'd make some sorta disbelieving face. After all, the nerve of the bitch. I lay my feelings out like that, and she's "not in the mood." Well, fuck that, man!

PROPHET: Easy. It's over. It's in the past.

MURDERER: Sorry. But she'd like read all these emotions in my face like the clever British bitch she was and . . . laugh. Yeah, she'd give a little laugh and tilt her head and reach out her freckled hand to my face as if she were dealing with some sort of *child,* for Christ sake, and say, "Oh! Poor baby." I mean, you do *not* say that to a guy who's got a big hard dick in his pants. Or wants to have such. Underneath that little helmet they wear, a dick is thinking, "I'm going to fuck you or fuck you up, one or the other." So, you do *not* treat it like some puppy. You know what I mean?

PROPHET: *(Begins to speak)*

MURDERER: Just hold on. I'm not done here. No way. So then after she's said that she says, "Why don't you just go have a wank." Just like that! Excuse me? Have a what? Like it was the most natural thing in the world. Like she was saying, "If you're thirsty, why don't you go out into the kitchen and have a glass of fucking water." Can you believe that?

PROPHET: I'm not sure.

MURDERER: But that's Brits again. Tennyson and wanking. Right there in the same brain. Go figure.

PROPHET: It is strange, I suppose.

MURDERER: And that's not all. Sometimes we'd just be sitting there at the table after dinner or something and she'd say, "I think I'll go have a wank." Talk about confusing. I didn't even know women could wank. Shouldn't they have a different word for it? Okay, so I suggest maybe I should come along, you know? And sometimes she'd say yes but just as often she'd yawn and say, "Oh, I'm not up to that. I just feel a little tension. Then I think I'll take a nap. You can watch Gretchen." Gretchen was our kid.

PROPHET: Wow.

MURDERER: Yeah, she wanks and I watch the kid. Even a weak motherfucker like you, even a limp dick like you can see this as extreme. Maybe even cruel.

PROPHET: Well, just not something I've personally experienced.

MURDERER: And that brings me to *another* sore point. She was raising our daughter Gretchen to be a lesbian.

PROPHET: What? How do you know that? She was only two years old, right?

MURDERER: She was two going on sixteen from her mother's perspective.

PROPHET: I'm sorry, I'm still not following.

MURDERER: Well, think about it. *I* sure thought about it. What is she really telling me with this wanking business? She's saying, women don't need men. Look around you. Let's be honest. Women like each other more than they like us. And who can blame them? They smell better, they look better, they're nicer to each other. That's the future, pal. And what does it leave for us? Endless wanking. That's what she was training me for, preparing me for. And it's not like I could return the favor. Fuck a man? I tried to think about that and I'd start to puke. It's aesthetic. For me it comes down to this: men have assholes!

But when I figured this all out, that's when we had our first little incident.

PROPHET: You mean the beatings and the ambulances and the police and the restraining order?

MURDERER: You're missing something.

PROPHET: What?"

143

MURDERER: You forgot the lawyer. Oh that fucking lawyer of hers. Now that's another guy I'd like to whack. Not wank, mind you, but whack. Different. Hey, did you read in the paper about the old dude at the hospital the other day? Yeah, he was on a kidney dialysis machine, bored stiff probably, and he turned to his nurse and said, "I want a drink." And the guy wasn't talking water. He wanted a drink drink. But the nurse said, you know, you can't have extra fluids while you're on the machine or some shit like that. So they have a few words about it. He gets pretty hot. He wants a Goddamned Burgermeister or something and they don't even *make* that fucking beer anymore. Burgie, I think they called it.

PROPHET: I remember that beer! My dad used to drink it.

MURDERER: After a while, he gives up. He just sits there thinkin' his thoughts. He's very cooperative in a kind of ugly way. He gets up when the procedure's done. He goes home. He gets the ol' WW2 .32 out of the dresser drawer, goes back to the hospital and shoots that nurse three times in the chest. Then he shoots himself.

PROPHET: Good lord. That's so unfair. She couldn't have given him a beer if she had wanted to. They were in a hospital.

MURDERER: That's just like you. Out in left field. Do you see my point?

PROPHET: Umm, no. What is your point?

MURDERER: Well, fuck you if you're that stupid. *(Starts to smile)* You wanker. *(Laughs)* Wanker! *(Breaks down in laughter)*

Treachery (2)

Dear Editor:

In the October 26, 1999 issue of the *Proceeding of the National Academy of Sciences* one may discover the following treachery. Whereas one had thought that the Neanderthals (a brawny race of human and ape-like qualities) went extinct some 30,000 years ago (well beyond the historical perimeters and the smoky camp fires of modern human beings), the facts seem now to be somewhat different. Apparently, early estimations of the time of the Neanderthal extinction were off by some 6,000 years (oh, nice guess, fellas!), so that they could after all have been neighbors to human beings. Neanderthal skulls, dated precisely by University of Oxford accelerators, cast doubt and shed light on our previous assumptions. Now it is clear: Neanderthals coexisted with early modern humans in central Europe for several millennia.

Plenty of time, if you know what I mean!

Fred H. Smith, chairman of anthropology at Northern Illinois University, pins the old tail on the donkey when he notes, "There was probably a good deal of genetic exchange between Neanderthals and modern humans."

Oh, well and nicely said! Where was Moses when we needed him? "Thou shalt not fuck the Neanderthals over there, I don't care how much you like their brawny good looks."

Why the heck wasn't that "an abomination unto the Lord"? Huh? Was the Lord even paying attention?

Now, some folks may say, "Well, that clears up the football player issue. And pro wrestling." Perhaps so. Perhaps so. What I'd like to call to your attention is the "sorry fuck-up" issue. University administrators, to be quite clear about it. Provosts. Deans.

Base treachery is what it was. Goats and monkeys. Next time round, hands off the Neanderthals! All we're asking for is 6,000 years of forbearance. Take a shower. Hold your breath. But just stop it!

You people make me sick!

Ned Ansermet
Professor Emeritus
Department of Geology
NWFSU

The Soul in Paraphrase (4)

To: Honeycomb@teenslut.com
From: Tom@english.nwfsu.edu

Have I told you, dear Honeycomb, that marriage is sustained by the twin props of fatalism, on one side, and stoicism on the other? When these two dear friends fail, that is what we call divorce. (Assuming the poor bastard didn't go to jail for impaling his wife with a garden implement or smashing her against the garage door with the Taurus.) The odd thing is that one also survives divorce sustained by the twin props of fatalism and stoicism.

I know you operate under the bizarre and unsupportable notion that your experience is somehow more difficult, or hard, or painful, or *whatever*. But you have no monopoly on this. I know, you see folks walkin' around, drinkin' their grape Slurpees and you say, "Lord, why am I so different from that guy? Why am I uniquely cursed with this big pain? Where's *my* Slurpee?" But the truth is that if you stopped any one of them you'd get the same story. Every human life is fractured a million times over with betrayal, flawed birth, chemical error in the brain, toxicity (atrizine), toxicity (Jack Daniels), genetic defect (Neanderthals in the woodpile as my pal Ned Ansermet says), surgically removed body parts, surgically augmented body parts, more defect, defected defect. The guy with Lou Gherig's disease that you marry gets drunk and tries to kill you out of a sense of futile, irrefutable rage, but you escape and so he commits suicide and you're charged with his murder. Get it? That's what's behind the Slurpee. Without exception.

You are *not* alone. Wherever you are. No matter how dark. Others are with you. Can't you feel them?

Now, take me. I'm not even going to get into my present wife and her damned Chevy Nova or whatever that thing is that pulls up at 5:30 every evening and ruins my life. When I was a boy, I loved the little girl down the block. So I went to her father and asked for her hand in marriage.

He said, "Say, don't I know you? You're the boy from down the block, ain'tcha? You mow my lawn. Well, sure, you seem like a nice kid and I'd give you my freaky-deaky daughter with all my heart, but I guess you haven't been paying attention. She's already been married seven times. And each time on her wedding night her new husband dies before they can have intercourse. Do you know that big word, Son? But here's the thing, she says there's a demon killing them. That's the kind of hair-brained story you'd be getting for the rest of your life even if by some miracle you survived your wedding. Is that what you want? Wife a teller of psychotic whoppers? Meanwhile, all those seven families hate my personal guts for what happened to their sons. Police, of course, think she's offing them somehow. She doesn't even bother to cry anymore. That don't look good. And now folks what don't *like* their boys bring 'em here to marry and run off clapping their hands. But you. Why you want this?"

So I explained to him that my years in the lawn care business had taught me a thing or two. So I married her.

That night, Honeycomb, before climbing in bed with my new bride, I threw fish entrails on a hot brazier. And as my beloved complained about the stink, I fucked her up one side and down the other. What was it saved me? The magical fish entrails? Don't be goofy. I survived because *I* was the demon!

I killed her seven earlier husbands because she had been set aside for me since before the world existed. That's my opinion. Just as you, my dear Honeycomb, have been set aside for your loving Hank O'Hair since before the world existed. For if you are my walkin', talkin' Honeycomb, I am your ever lovin' Hank O'Hair.

Hank

Something Understood (2)

PROPHET: Sure.

MADMAN: Okay, you're out in the world. You're driving your car around town. You're looking at people. The people are "doing their thing," like we used to say. The things that make them who they are. It all seems congruent. There seems to be an "operating order of life" at work. Can you say that?

PROPHET: What?

MADMAN: "Operating order of life."

PROPHET: Operating order of life.

MADMAN: Very good. So you go to a 7-Eleven or the convenience store of your choice. Have you ever noticed that the franchise operations that proliferate in California all originated in, like, Ypsilanti, Michigan, or some other godforsaken backwater? It's like someone named John or Fred had this great idea. A great idea that was also a dumb, awful idea. For example, a place called Double Play where you can get hot dogs and donuts? People like hot dogs and they like donuts, so if you put them both in the same place they'll like your store twice as much as they would otherwise. The store takes off. Fred experiments with a new product called "Hum Doggie Dinger" which is essentially a hot dog going through the center of a donut. Then the "Doggie Doppel Dinger" in which the donut is in fact a meat product of who-the-hell-cares-what-kind and the hot dog is a seasoned pastry. People are wrapped around the freaking block to get the stuff. But there's still only one there in Ypsilanti. That's where the guy from Los Angeles gets in the picture. He buys the rights to market and franchise Double Play nationally. California first, of course. But later everywhere from Moscow to Bangkok. And just as soon as this "concept" hits the air of old California, it multiplies. It's viral. It really is. Not even the guy from L.A. knows prezactly why or how it works. All he knows is that one day he's in Palo Alto and there's a Double Play. He crosses the Bay. There's another in Hayward. Every two blocks in that place. He looks in his checking account. It's blossomed. The bank doesn't know how to count that high.

PROPHET: I'm not following.

MADMAN: Trust me. I'm on topic. So, as I was saying, you go into one of these places and there is the thing you want, a Slurpee, let's say, and the person behind the counter is, first, *there,* and she knows what to do, she knows she's supposed to give you the Slurpee and take a very particular and specific amount of money from you and you actually have the money in your pocket because someone who makes the pants knows that you'd like pants with pockets for your money and no one screws up with the numbers on the money either and she hands you the Slurpee which is purple and you smile like isn't it nice that someone knows that I'd like a cold purple drink as opposed to a cold drink of another color and further knows that it's not exactly a drink you want but a kind of un-creamy frozen mixture, more like snow, which gives you enormous amounts of spine-tingling pleasure (but who is responsible for that!?) and she smiles as you complete your transaction and you are both aware that you have participated successfully in a transaction with no effort or dissonance of any kind and you take your purple Slurpee outside, out into the warm, bright air and there are a few other humans around and it occurs to you that if you wanted you could engage any of them in an interaction—whether a transaction or some other sort of interaction, it's not crucial—you could speak with them or give them something, you understand their clothing and automobiles and so on.

In short, you get it. You're with it. You're in it. You're part of the flow, the operating order of life. Finally, you stick the Slurpee straw in your mouth and suck and it doesn't necessarily taste like "grape" but it doesn't taste like a window either. It tastes like what you expected, a purple Slurpee.

PROPHET: What?

The Binary God (2)

PROPHET: Okay, let's try another question. I think that last one went off route.

ALPHA: What, you didn't like our answers? I thought they were pretty good, given the topic. What do you want from a couple of working guys? What do we know from pretzels?

PROPHET: Let's just move on, shall we? The new question is, who is the most isolated human being in the world?

ALPHA: *(Confused look; he turns to* BETA*)* What do you think?

BETA: *(Looks back at* ALPHA, *confused, not sure how to answer)* Well, hell, kid, I won't speak for my friend here, but I was rather under the impression that you were.

ALPHA: *(Quickly nodding assent)* Yup.

PROPHET: *I* was! You think *I'm* the most isolated human being? In the whole world? In what sense?

BETA: No special sense, just the regular sense. Don't get all shocked on me. We talk among ourselves down at the Hall, you know. The subject has come up, let's say. You've come up. Call it a coincidence. I'm not saying we're right. But it is something we've thought. Said. Among ourselves.

ALPHA: Right. Sorry kid. We thought it was another trick question. Like that zinger with the pretzel.

BETA: Jeez, I'll never forget that one.

PROPHET: *(Trying to compose himself)* No, this is not a trick question, unless the trick's on me, I guess. But I don't think I am the most isolated person in the world, just for your information.

ALPHA: Whatever. We're not going to debate you on it.

BETA: Yeah, it's all the same to us. You asked a question, we answered. Hey, I've got other things to do this afternoon. I've got a job. They pay me real money to do what I do. Not these weird little coupons you give us which we're supposed to exchange for some sort of "merit." At the entrance to the Great Wringer. What is that? Some sort of Chinese fast food? Whatever. Let's get outta here. *(They get up)*

PROPHET: Look, please don't go.

ALPHA: Oh, *you're* not isolated! Not you. 'Fraid of being alone? *(Aside)* Poor fucking little loser.

PROPHET: Just stay a little longer.

BETA: You know, this talk about isolation does remind me of one little story. *(Turns to* ALPHA*)* You remember that guy who lived across from us? In the apartment across the alley?

ALPHA: In The City? When we were in public works? Getting junkers off the street?

BETA: Right. Back when I drove the truck and you did the rest.

ALPHA: Oh my sweet Lord, you aren't going to tell this snot-green kid about that guy are you?

BETA: Sure. Why not?

ALPHA: Why not overheat a tank of radium? Go ask those people in Japan. Big blue flash is why not. Poison the whole town is why not.

BETA: Oh, come on, it's just a story. Besides, he doesn't know if it really happened or not.

ALPHA: Yeah, but it did.

BETA: Big deal. Look, I'll take personal responsibility. My homeowner's insurance covers things like this, I think.

ALPHA: Oh, you think it's funny now. But I'm outta here. Leave you two girls to your own mutually assured destruction.

BETA: Fine. Clear out. Man, what a whiner. Just a damned story. Hardly in the fucking mood for it now.

(ALPHA *leaves*)

PROPHET: What's wrong with this story?

BETA: I'm not kiddin' you. It's not that big a deal. Just fuckin' words, kid. Honest.

PROPHET: Well, okay, let's hear it. It's about isolation, right?

BETA: Geez, and how! This was way back in the early seventies when me and Alpha were rooming together in The City. That was one weird time. Anything and everything, man. Happened. And happened. Well, we lived about five floors up in a flat that looked back on some other flats across an alley. Looked right in on their lives, so to speak.

In an apartment just over one but otherwise right across lived this guy. He lived all by himself. I think he had a nice job. He got up early and dressed in a suit and went out. Back at the same time each night. That's where this gets interesting. Every damned night without fail he came home at 5:45, went to his bedroom, took off his suit, then came back out in his boxers. He then took a handkerchief from a pile of clean laundered handkerchiefs and went to the window off his bedroom. Looking right out on this alley. And every night, come rain come shine, this poor son of a bitch would wank it for all to see.

PROPHET: Wank. There's that word again. You're not English, are you?

BETA: What? Hell no. Wank? You never heard that one?

PROPHET: Not until recently.

BETA: That figures. You're the kind of guy who will be on his death bed complaining about all the sex experiences you never had and someone will say, "Well, why didn't you just get some porn channels on satellite access," and you'll say, "What's that?" And everyone sort of groans and looks down because it's too damned late now, and you're embarrassed even when you're dying and so you say, "No, what's satellite access?" And the groans just get deeper and the looks more pained. Because you are the most painfully isolated fucker in the whole world.

PROPHET: What?

BETA: Look, let's just go back to he wanked and that's all you need to know. You'll figure it out. Anyway, Alpha and I would watch this guy every night. We came to feel like we'd be disappointing him if we didn't watch. Like we were the last thing between him and something sort of like interstellar remoteness. We felt responsible.

PROPHET: Okay, and then what?

BETA: Then he'd *come* on his handkerchief–this getting any clearer for you?–and fold it up oh so neatly, so unbelievably neatly, a little tri-corner affair, wipe himself like he was scrubbing tapioca pudding off the face of a toddler, and deposit the soggy cloth in the laundry basket. White wicker job, the hamper.

PROPHET: I get it, I get it.

BETA: Good boy. Anyhow, ol' Alph and I would roll around laughing about this poor guy. But one day it occurred to us, hey, doesn't this guy ever do anything else after work?

PROPHET: Never mind the guy. What about you two?

BETA: Shut up. No pals? we'd ask. No Guinness? No Bass Ale? No Anchor Steam down at The Grotto? I mean, he never missed a day. We started seeing this thing as very sad.

PROPHET: Yes. I believe it is sad.

BETA: But the clincher was one day he did bring someone home. Young kid like you. Nice looking, dressed in a suit. A young kid on the make, upward bound, career oriented, gonna make a killing soon as them damned Reagan eighties hit. Anyway, they're chatting and laughing like this is something that happens all the time. Yeah, the guy was a regular Mr. Hostess. So, he gets his friend a beer and sits him in the living room. We didn't even know he had beer. Hell, it was news to us that he had a fucking refrigerator. To us, he was just Mr. Show-and-Tell. We saw them both clear as could be. Then the guy went back to his room. And guess what?

PROPHET: Oh no, don't tell me.

ALPHA: You're told! Just nice and calm and, you know, we're watching him and his hanky in one window and his buddy in the other, sitting with his brew. And after a while, the kid's getting bored and starts walking around checking things out. He goes to the window and leans on it.

PROPHET: Uh-oh.

BETA: Don't worry. But what a picture for us! My fuckin' mouth was hanging open. The two windows at one time. Like a split-screen TV. The kid lookin' around, sipping his beer. The guy shootin' all over. That kid didn't have a clue what was happening just a few feet away, all he had to do was look out and maybe crane his skinny neck a little. Then the guy just folds up his little tri-corner handkerchief like always and walks away. Son of a bitch looked happy. Pretty soon he comes out all fresh in clean jeans and a white T-shirt. He pats the kid on the back and out they go.

PROPHET: Oh, my God. Can you imagine how he felt? I sometimes feel so sad after doing what he did, just in the ordinary way, but to do it in this way, who was he kidding? When he patted that kid on the shoulder, he must have been screaming with despair inside. He knew at that moment that he was interstellar. That lonely. My God.

BETA: Oh come on. Don't get screwy on me. He just didn't want to miss a day. Maybe he was trying to set some kind of record and he just couldn't miss a day even if it meant doing something a little sneaky like that. Maybe he was superstitious. Or maybe he liked the sneaky angle of it all. Maybe that finally gave the poor fuck a little real excitement or at least some different excitement beyond hoping some stupid morons like me and Alph were maybe watching.

PROPHET: You know, I don't feel so good.

BETA: What? You okay?

PROPHET: I'll be all right. Did anything else happen?

BETA: Nah. Alph wanted to brick in the window after that one. I convinced him to be reasonable and we just drew the curtain. Permanently. After that, we were afraid to look over there. After that, we made sure *we* were out at 5:45. We didn't even want to be tempted to look. But you know, I always wondered if he knew we stopped watching. And if he did know, if he knew why we stopped. And if he knew why, did he regret it. I've always wondered if we didn't make the guy even more alone by refusing to watch, just cause though we certainly had. What do you think?

PROPHET: I think I can't think about this anymore. It's getting to me. But thanks for telling me. Really.

BETA: No fuckin' sweat, kid.

PROPHET: You know, I really don't feel so good. I might need to lie down.

ALPHA: *(Returning, peeking in door)* You done yet?

BETA: Why you . . . ! I thought you were outta here. What are you hangin' around for?

ALPHA: I wanted to see if there were more questions.

BETA: There more questions, kid?

PROPHET: *(Doesn't reply; seems stunned)*

ALPHA: He okay?

BETA: Sure, he's fine. Aren't you, kid? Hey, kid, wake up! Is he in some kind of trance?

ALPHA: Hey, maybe it's one of those prophetic trances. Give him a little slap. Dang. I warned you about that story. Now what do we do?

Kyrie Eleison (Lord, Have Mercy)

The Book of Sam (1)

You *know* me. You know my name. You know it quite well. Practically beaten into your damned skull by this point. Mr. Numbers. No? The Modern Castrati? Hank O'Hair? Nothing yet? Murderer? Madman? How about Doeg the Edomite? Alph? Wolfy, Papa, Robert, or Caca de Puccini? Any of those? Okay, just plain simple Chad. Oh sure, you knew a guy named Chad once, huh. Installed stereos in cars. Got right under the dash. Well, I'm not that guy. Neither is he. I'm going to tell you a story–another story! as if I hadn't already told you plenty!– that you would surely know if you'd ever read a book. You know what your problem is? Too much TV! You ever think of turning that son of a bitch off? It's just like your mother said: "Go do your homework. That thing's gonna melt your brain." (I know, I know. If you came back in fifteen minutes, she'd be zoned in watching reruns of *Dallas* with her finger in her mouth. It's a crock from her but solid gold from me, buster.)

That's right, I'm not your mother and when I tell a story, brother, it stays told. It will be a little walnut of possibility right in the middle of your brain. So, here goes. This is the "Book of Sam." One *and* two. 'Cause they're *both* good. Ever hear of 'em? No it's not on cable, it's not on the Nostalgia Channel or Nickelodeon. You didn't watch it on the old tube with your father in 1962. And it's not on satellite or any sort of special access. It's in a book. A *book,* you fucking loser! In this country, we read 'em left to fucking right!

Let's start over. If you need to call me by name, you may call me The Modern Prophet. I do respond to that name. Or Chris-all-growed-up. That's a good one too.

I'm not the first one to marvel over a story in the Bible. I'm not the first one to try to retell it. For example, some people think a lot of the old story of Abraham and Isaac. A real test of faith. Who can understand old Abe etcetera. But think it through. All the way through. What was he sacrificing? A son, you say. C'mon! Isaac was an absurdity. Think about Abraham's wife, Sarah. Eighty something. And eighty something was really something back then. They didn't have workout centers in those days. No Jane Fonda videotapes either. You looked pretty nasty in your late twenties. Lucky if you had a damned tooth in your head. So when God said, "You'll have a son," naturally she chortled, guffawed, whatever. Your butcher has sides of beef that look healthier or more plausible for this feat. "Hey God, my man, have you checked out these withered loins? And ol' Abe, my husband, he hasn't visited these parts in years. I couldn't get him down there with promissory notes taped to my crotch, not that I'd want him down there. So you'll forgive me my little sardonic snicker, I hope, but *please!*"

Of course, as we know, God was not fooling around on this one. My point is that God's absurd request that Abraham "kill him a son" had as its earlier premise the idea that a woman half a century post-menopause, who never had sex, could suddenly conceive. It makes Mary's immaculate conception seem like something so common it deserves a federal program. Something parallel to teenage pregnancy. From this point of view, Ike was about as "real" as a Super Mario, or some other Nintendo being for which you get three lives at the beginning of each game. God's up there going, "How many more of these little Ikes have I got left?"

Anyway, it was all just some kind of joke. I'm still laughin' with Sarah on it. I mean, if you look at God and Abe with Sarah's eyes you have to say, "Fuckin' ridiculous, dopey losers. I mean really." I'm with her.

Don't get me wrong here. In dismissing this story, I don't mean to dismiss faith. Not wholly, anyway. For example, the freshness of being recalls us to faith. As Ivan puts it in *The Brothers Karamazov,* "Though I may not believe in the order of the universe, yet I love the sticky little leaves as they open in spring." Beyond the "sticky little leaves," of course, there is the vast mess of the human which makes anything like faith, or even cheerfulness, a willingness to go on with it, pull your socks on every morning, deal with the cold, horny feet, implausible. Imponderable. Absurd.

And it is scripture itself that first insists on this "incommensurability," as Kierkegaard put it, between the facts and what is asked of us. For I do not think that God asks us to be credulous. Let me put it to you: God does not ask us to be morons. Just the opposite. We choose that route ourselves. Write letters to the editor commanding people to the Bible and demanding that they right their ways. Morons. Someone's spraying me with something. My husband's head is loose. Morons. Their throats are open graves.

I would merely ask, as any non-moron might, as Job did, to speak with the Almighty. I wish to reason with God. So let us look at Samuel. I'll say what I have to say, and we'll see if God has any kind of explanation. Look, I'm willing to be fair about it. He can have all the time he needs to think it over. I won't rush him.

In 1 Samuel, we learn that the great judge Samuel had turned his role over to his sons, but that his sons were quite unlike him. Not only did they not follow God's law, they apparently screwed the women "serving at the entry of the meeting tent." What?, one wants to say, right there? In the dusty dirt outside the meeting tent?

But the people turned this difficulty into another. We need a king, they said. Other countries have kings and they're kicking ass. We think that's what we need. We're running out of women to serve at the entrance to the meeting tents. A king could put a stop to that business and pronto.

And old Samuel was as clear as he could be on this one. Okay, you want a king, here's what you get with a king:

1. He will make your sons work in his stable to take care of his horses and chariots *and* they will "run before the chariot," whatever that implies; it sounds like it implies a lot of run over sons if you ask me;

2. He will use your daughters as cooks (which, one admits, is better than what was going on with the girls in front of the meeting tents);
3. He will tax your crops and give the money to his eunuchs (this is plainly an expression of contempt although what the desireless eunuchs would want with all that cash is not explained);
4. He will make you yourselves slaves and if you complain to God about it, God will say essentially, "Hey, the king was your idea."

All of this stuff came to pass, by the way, at the end of the reign of Israel's mostly not very apt kings during that period called the Babylonian Captivity. Nebuchadnezzar. Now, *that* was a king!

And yet the people replied to this very clear warning by saying, "I think he's exaggerating. A king is a good deal for us. Kings are in all the Best Practices handbooks. It's a Total Quality Management concept. Kings are Excellent." Thus spaketh the people. (Whenever the Old Testament refers to "the people," it is as much as saying, "a large group of self-destructive dumb shits.")

The Human Condition (2)

It's just a painting, really. One of those brightly colored, geometric renderings, crude in the draftsmanship, that talented college students (majoring in psychology) produced in the 1970s when everyone was supposed to have hidden artistic talents, even psych majors. Their friends always liked these paintings very much and offered to hang them in their run-down student apartments and they did and they kept hanging the damned things decade after decade even after the point where they could afford to actually buy a real painting by a real artist. But a primary emotional bond had been formed with the piece– it was the work of a friend; it was part of their past–so up it went, frameless, a little dull now, the canvas scraped at the corners from twenty-plus years of sliding across the floors of U-Haul moving vans.

Anyway, the painting consisted of four things. Five if you count the floating head. Thing number one was big, blue, flat water. Thing number two was a diagonal horizon cutting upward from left to right across the canvas above which the sky was a pinkish gray. Thing number three was a mostly adequately rendered rowboat, tipping to the left near the horizon so that the viewer could actually seem to see the planks in the bottom of the boat. (Among half-comprehending amateur painters of the 1970s, a sort of twice-baked Cubism was the default style *du jour*. That's how you could tell it was Art. The effect on the observer, however, is that the painter–apparently all painters– lived in an off-kilter world of ever-dawning nausea. Actually, this is a perception that renders the 1970s with surprising accuracy.) It's not at all clear why it's tipping (beyond the influence of Picasso) because there are no waves or any other kind of movement, really, in the blue "water." It's more like someone has thumbtacked the boat to what is simply a geometrical image.

So that's three things. Thing number four is in the boat. It is definitely an animal. The artist insisted that it was a goose when he passed on his work. But the owner has never been able to see it as other than a dog. A dog in a boat. The painter suspected in his heart of hearts that it was the poorly (oh poorly) rendered bonnet on the goose that made it look like a dog.

Then, in the foreground, there is the human head. If we were asked to interpret it realistically, we'd say, "It's someone in the water, and we can only see his head. He's looking at the boat. Maybe he fell out or decided to go swimming."

What it really looks like, though, is a bright, childish marble on a field of blue.

The artist claims that it all came to him "in a dream." What he didn't know was that because of universal principles of economy, in order to have this dream, someone else had to live it. In this case, the owner of the painting.

This painting was found among the effects of the guy after his death by drowning. No one saw much significance in it at the time, but I thought you might find it suggestive.

His Life Was So Sad (2)

BARITONE: *Perdone.* The story behind the *Requiem* is a good one. Want to hear it? In the late 1870s Saint-Saëns was still struggling financially. But a wealthy friend decided to leave a substantial inheritance to him, enough money that he would be entirely free to compose in peace, with the proviso that Saint-Saëns write a *Requiem* for his benefactor. When the benefactor died in 1878 and Saint-Saëns learned of the condition, he immediately dropped everything and left for Switzerland. He checked into a hotel in Berne where he conceived and orchestrated the entire Mass in eight days.

TENOR: Was his haste about the money, or did he really have feelings for this guy?

SOPRANO: Now, please, excuse me. You two are missing the point with your gossipy chat.

CHORUS: And what is the point, pray tell?

SOPRANO: Like other human beings before and after him, Saint-Saens's marriage, to Marie Laure Émilie Truffot, was not to the person in whom he had the deepest emotional investment. *That* person was one Madame Viardot, who failed to requite his feelings. She returned to him a large stack of letters he had written her. Saint-Saëns carefully preserved these letters for the rest of his life. His *wife,* on the other hand, was much younger, very pretty and he was no sooner married to her than he commenced ignoring her and finding his true life in his work. He kept no letters or other mementos of this his real wife.

CHORUS: So far, sad but not that sad.

SOPRANO: Camille Saint-Saëns was a human being. He had a treasure of private hurt expressed in real-world decisions which were not necessarily admirable. Even when his children were born, he was the sort of father who–however instinctive his sympathy for children and passionate his love of his two boys–only occasionally saw them between concert tours and other demands on his time.

Nonetheless, he did love them deeply. Shortly after he had finished the *Requiem,* his family was visited by an "appalling tragedy" (as his biographers call it). His wife was in her room preparing to go out and his mother was dozing in the dining room. A servant had opened a window to let out steam from some washing she was doing. Little two-year-old André Saint-Saëns climbed to the window to look out. He lost his balance and fell four storeys, breaking his neck. A little later, Saint-Saëns returned from rehearsal to learn that his son was dead. He ran up the stairs and clasped the body of his little boy in the dismal dizziness of impotent grief.

CHORUS: Now you're really onto something sad, we believe.

TENOR: I believe this sadness is caught in the tremendous sadness of the "Oro Supplex." Crushed to dust! I'm starting to regret my own small-minded partisanship over Debussy. Boy is that silly. What am I thinking about? A hundred years after the fact and I'm still choosing sides! Still, this music and your story have made me feel his grief. I grieve anew for him and for my own mistakes.

CHORUS: What mistakes were these?

TENOR: I too have a tale to tell. For I once had a wife who was perhaps not the person I should have married.

Not One Does What Is Right, Not Even One (2)

"Oh hi, come on in! Glad you could make it. Any trouble finding the place?"

A young man with long blond hair and the build of a college quarterback enters with an Irish setter on a leash.

"I'm Karen and you must be Chad . . ."

"I'm Chad."

" . . . and this . . ."

"Is Murphy. Shake Murph. He shakes hands. When he feels like it."

"Guess he's not in a shaking mood today."

"Sorry. He's a friendly dog once he gets to know you."

"Well, come on in. I have some cookies and coffee and stuff first and some Science Diet treats for Murphy. I'm always very careful what I offer other people's dogs. Especially the special dogs I meet. Let's talk for a while and get to know each other."

This woman is about thirty, brunette, slim and athletic with small rather loose breasts the cleavage of which Chad can see plainly through her lycra jogging halter. The little condo is in a posh, professional section of Austin but is rather cheaply decorated with new-smelling synthetic carpets and mass-produced furniture. Blue-gray print on couch and chairs. Blue-gray curtains, drawn tight.

They sit at a small glass coffee table in the living room. The cookies are oatmeal, little ones from a big bag. Keebler. Murphy sits on the floor by the table and eyes the cookies, clearly preferring them to the Science Diet "treats" in front of him.

"You know, I think he really wants a cookie," Karen observes.

"He likes cookies. Especially oatmeal."

"Well, isn't that funny! He's very welcome to a cookie. You sweetie! Here." She looks to Chad in concern. "If you don't mind, of course."

"That's fine," says Chad.

They laugh as Murphy eats the cookie.

"Say, don't you have any dogs of your own?"

"No. They're kind of messy. I don't like all the hair on the furniture and carpet."

There is an awkward silence and then Karen turns to Chad and asks politely but seriously, "Now, Chad, I know we discussed this on e-mail, but I just want to be clear before we get started. You don't want to be involved in any of the action, right?"

"Right."

"And you don't charge a fee?"

"No, of course not. This is all for fun."

"Do you want *anything?*"

"I just want to watch."

"Okay! That's cool. You're gonna be Eyes, then. That's just fine, isn't it, Murphy?" She looks around, drums her fingers on the table. "Well, jeez, let's get going then. I'll put on some music and light some incense so we have a good mood. Excuse me."

Karen gets up and goes through the living room and into a back room. Chad looks at Murphy. Murphy takes another cookie delicately from the tray and chews it forlornly. A New Age version of Pachabel's Canon in D floats through the air. It sounds like it is being played by an ensemble of sensitive banjos.

When Karen returns, she is wearing white stockings, white panties and a white-satin brassiere.

"Okay boys! This way."

Chad gets up and signals to Murphy. Murphy gets up and follows the two into a bedroom made special for just such occasions. There is no furniture in the room, only cushions covered in bright, soft covers. Lots of printed flowers. There is one upholstered bench against the wall. Mirrors are everywhere and some top-flight video recording equipment is in the corner.

"Karen, I know I didn't say anything about this, but no videos, okay?"

"Oh, that's not for us. That's all about something else altogether that you don't need to know or worry about."

"'Cause Murph's already under contract."

"Under contract? Really? Murphy? What kind of contract?"

"Like you said, nothing to know or worry about."

"Hmmm. Okay. Whatever. He's that good, huh? Interesting."

Karen then sits on the ground and pats the cushion at her side. Chad indicates to Murphy that he should go to Karen and he does, slowly wagging his tail. He sits by her. Karen then lowers him to the ground and begins to pet him.

"He's clean, I hope?"

"I bathed him this morning."

"Mmmm. He does smell nice. But what I meant was, is he *clean?* You know, *clean?*"

"Well, yeah, sure."

"Okay, honey, you just relax and let me get this going."

Karen gently reaches for Murphy's penis and pulls back the foreskin. She lowers her head and sucks the dog's penis into her mouth. Soon Murphy is erect, although he shows no other reaction.

After a few minutes, Karen is satisfied and lifts herself quickly and removes her panties. She is trembling and when she crouches on all fours and spreads herself in Murph's direction, it is plain she is already very wet.

"Okay Murphy. Get up. Come on, honey."

Murphy gets up and sits looking at Karen. His little pink erection still lingers but is slowly receding. He shows no inclination to mount Karen.

"Uh oh. Chad, can you help a bit?"

"I'd really rather not."

"I know you'd rather not, but Murphy's not exactly gangbusters here and I think he could use some help. Please." She seems just a little irritated.

Chad crosses the room and takes Murphy by the collar, trying to lead him to Karen. Murphy growls and bares his teeth.

Karen turns and sits, appraising the situation. "Chad," she says, "I have a bad feeling here. I thought you said Murphy likes sex with girls?"

"He does. He loves it. I don't know what's up."

"Look. Is this dog your dog?"

"Of course."

"'Cause he sure doesn't act like it. Or if he is related to you, you're not the Alpha."

"He's mine. He's my fiancée's."

"Your fiancée's?"

"Yeah."

"So he's not really your dog."

"Well, not strictly speaking."

"Does she know you brought Murphy here?"

"No. But she wouldn't care."

"All right, that's it." Karen gets up. She walks straight to a coatrack and takes a bathrobe from one of the hooks. Chad notices only that she has a terrific ass. "I think you guys better go before this gets any worse. You don't care, and your fiancée may not care, but for some reason Murphy here cares."

Murphy stands and wags his tail a little. He clearly wants out of this scene.

"I'm sorry, Karen. This is very embarrassing."

Karen looks him in the eye as she pulls the robe tighter around her shoulders. "Just go away, Chad, and stay off the 'Twobackedbeast' site until you know what's what."

Isolation (5)

Dear Editor:

I am writing because I have had an extraordinary experience and, fast on the heels of this experience, I have encountered a problem that I need help with. Can you or your readers help me, please? This is a cry for help.

I was at the doctor's the other day for a routine checkup. He was examining my feet for what seemed to me a very long time. So I asked him what he was doing and he said that he had never in all his professional career seen skin tone, circulation, reflex and musculature so perfect in a woman of my age (I am forty-eight). I then looked at my feet and, once my attention had been called there, I realized that in fact my feet were the feet of a baby. Tears began to well in my eyes as I comprehended what he was telling me. I, of all the millions and billions of people born into this world, was eternal or immortal. All of my body parts were like those of an infant. I was dumbstruck. I considered pressing him for details, but decided that really nothing more needed to be said. Crying openly, I gathered my clothing and began to back out of his office, thanking him profusely. I didn't even put my shoes or clothes back on, but just backed out with my little white sheet wrapped around me. I said, simply, "Oh, thank you, doctor! Thank you!" He said only, "Where are you going?"

Now you might wonder just what sort of problem could possibly be associated with this wonderful news. Well, the fact is that my *understanding* of my condition, if not the condition itself, has made me hypersensitive and super-aware of the aging and the failing and the doom in those around me. Specifically, I began to notice—and I was amazed that it had never occurred to me before—that the gums of others were receding, swollen, reddish, painful to look upon. This is a sign, I believe.

I was speaking to a fourteen-year-old boy at a corner crosswalk the other day. I thought he was a nice boy. We chatted. Then when the light changed and we were about to part, he smiled. And I saw that his gums were bleeding, that the blood was actually running down his white teeth, that his gum-line was receding like the tide. I'm afraid I couldn't hide the worry and horror on my face. At the same time I had the most powerful prescient intuition, a true sixth sense experience, that this "nice" boy had recently raped his aunt's dog. (Please excuse me for having to say that so crudely.) I'm afraid I might have stared.

The boy said, "What's with you?"

My confusion is, I am eternal, yes, I have second sight, yes, but what is the nature of my responsibility to the rest of the world which conspicuously has none of these qualities? Oh Lord, do tell me, what should I have said to the boy, or any of the people I meet each day, whose bodies fall bloodily from them before my eyes, and whose awful histories blossom from their heads like cartoon balloons? Should I say to them, "You are rotting"? "You are hopelessly caught in illusion and suffering"? Does that capture it? Or is my duty simply to watch as generation after generation fails?

Any helpful suggestions you can offer me will be greatly appreciated.

Ms. Augustina de Calle
Chenoa

The Seven Last Words of Christ (3)

6. *"It is finished."* (Lento)

Statement

Haydn did his usual craftsmanlike work with the puppet opera. But he was surprised, at the first rehearsal, when he heard the voice of his lover, the olive-skinned La Polzelli, coming from one of the little wooden figures. He found it unbelievably moving. Even erotic.

He asked for the music back. He had some new ideas. This music for the little wooden heads would be the darkest, most tragic, most loving he ever wrote. In it he invented *late* Beethoven from whole cloth. Planetary crashing. The Hugest Love. He could feel the entire cosmos descending on the little carved bodies. It was too beautiful. Something about this thing was just occurring to him as totally *gorgeous.*

Argument

At the next rehearsal, Haydn was so moved by the big human voices, the implication of tears, God lingering, the enormous cosmic backdrop, that he wept in the audience. His musicians were aware of the strain he had been under (especially the tragic alternation of giant creativity followed by destructive and arbitrary fire consuming that creativity) and offered their support. "How can we help, Maestro Haydn?"

"I'd like to take one of the little puppets home with me."

"That will help?"

"Yes."

"Which one do you want?"

"That one. The female lead for which Polzelli sings."

"Okay, then."

Development

When Haydn and Polzelli arrived at the little suite of rooms that they used for their affair, he had the puppet under his coat. As she attempted to remove his clothing, she discovered the puppet.

She laughed, at first, recognizing "herself." It seemed somehow like a compliment.

"Why do you have this, Haydn? And why did you bring it?"

Haydn looked exhausted and confused. He'd been working late into every night on the new puppet music. He opened his mouth wide, gaping, and closed it, but he couldn't speak. Tears came to his eyes.

"Haydn, what's the matter?"

"I don't know," he squeaked.

"Here, give me the doll."

He pulled it back from her and clung hard.

"Haydn!"

Restatement

On November 24, 1779, a fire broke out in the Chinese Ballroom and spread to the opera hall and the marionette theater. Haydn lost many works in the fire, including all his works for the marionette operas, including the epic "Dido." It is said that among all the frenzy, Haydn sat on the Grand Staircase and watched the leaping flames without emotion. Dry-eyed.

All the little puppets perished in the blaze.

7. *"Father, into thy hands I commend my spirit."* (Largo il Terremoto)

This section is not in any conventional sonata form. It is one long, sustained hymnlike flow. It is a poignant and consoling and redeeming conclusion to a piece that has carried a deep religiosity in a music that aspired not to volcanic emotion (like the jejune Beethoven or the much worse Wagner, the two churlish titans who would entirely overwhelm Haydn for over one hundred years) but to simple "thoughtful speech."

In it is contained the elements or pieces of his life. A boy sawing on his arm. The sorrowful voices of the castrati. An eyeless oboist. Haydn's curious refusal ever to write a part for a clarinet into one of his symphonies, in spite of the fact that the Prince paid the salary of always one and sometimes two clarinetists. The affectionate praise of his beloved Mozart. The shock and disgust he felt when his wife said hello to him. The "pus sack" that burst in Prince Anton Esterházy's rib cage, killing him. The guilty joy of thinking the Prince had died a painful death. The phrase "I really don't care anymore." The endless flow of brilliant musical ideas, sixty years' worth. Over a thousand compositions. Each of them the result of the most serious and sincere concentration. Concentration. The idea that he was the Father of Harmony, and what that could mean. Beethoven's tears at the Vienna concert given in his name. Shaving every morning for so many years. Pulling on his socks, one morning after another. The cruel hideousness of his hard yellow toenails. The days when his enfeebled memory and the unstrung state of his nerves crushed him to earth and made him prey to the worst sort of depression. The stupid conclusion of music critics that his music was about "happiness." The curious idea that a soul could be paraphrased. What that meant.

Finally, with woodwinds and horns soaring, an angel approaches with the last question, the question meant for him alone, a question addressed to the most noble of human beings:

"Haydn, didn't you like clarinets?"

The Soul in Paraphrase (5)

To: Honeycomb@teenslut.com
From: Tom@english.nwfsu.edu

Dear Honeycomb:

Howdy!

Miss me?

I've been reading the Bible recently and came across the following passage in 1 Kings 12:10-11.

"My little finger is thicker than my father's body."

Isn't that a wonderful thought? It really inspires me. It's Rehoboam, son of King Solomon (who was himself the son of David and Bathsheba). Speaking of whom, how does the wisdom of Solomon come from the adultery of his parents and the murder (essentially) of Bathsheba's rightful husband? I mean, the poor dead son of a bitch that no one much remembers. His name was Uriah and he was a fucking hero! David was tupping his wife (and he already had three hundred concubines!) and then David tells Joab (who was really not much more than a hit man to David's Godfather) to put the poor guy right up front in the next available battle (and there was no shortage of those, let me tell you). So much for David the underdog, eh?

And there's more:

"My father beat you with whips, but I will beat you with scorpions."

Beat you with scorpions! I'd like to see how *that's* done! I mean, where did they get this stuff?

Funny you don't hear more about Rehoboam because he really

sounds like something else.

Before I get to the matter at hand, I thought you might like to know something about me. You've shared some of your background with me, so I ought to return the favor.

First, I am a person who has nominally survived many years of psychic turmoil (okay, illness) and a lot of very expensive treatment. I am now as normal as normal can be. I know this because I no longer receive bills from my psychiatrist.

I'm kidding, Honeycomb. Just kidding you.

In the morning, I wake from troubling dreams (last night I dreamed of television advertisements for the world's tiniest whistling teapots). That is a troubling dream, in my opinion, although the little teapots sold quite well. In the past, on the other hand, I dreamed that people found things in my brain. Little insectlike things or hybrid creatures which were like worm-fish. This may be why I was so struck by Rehoboam's imaginative use of scorpions. Because it's just this sort of flagellant insect/crustacean that people used to find in my brain while I was asleep.

Waking is not a lot better. This is so because of the apparently endless putting on of socks. The human condition: everyday I put on my socks. It is endless, meaningless, running out toward the horizon, this on-putting of the socks.

Then there is the weather. I seem to live in a place where, whatever the season, there is a promiscuous reason, a forceful argument, a mordant rationale, for not going outside. It is always life-threatening. Mostly, it is a place of cold northerly winds and snow flurries that never amount to anything pretty. It's just prohibitive. So I don't go outside unless it's to go to my classes. I love my students. They wear bathing suits to class. They're very interesting to me for this reason. And each one is different. Sometimes I just look at them, one at a time, and marvel at how unique they are. They try to cover over this endless variety by wearing the same kind of hats (like that baseball back hatward thing that the young Negroes invented), but it doesn't work. Still, I'll be darned if I know why this place is called Florida (never mind "Topiary"). Something's wrong.

As I believe I mentioned to you, I have a wife, although I rarely see her. Our house is large, multi-storied and intricate. I believe she hides from me in certain rooms that she thinks of as "hers." I long to see her, but when she approaches a feeling of panic seizes me. I run from her. I have certain hiding places myself. I would not say that my marriage is a happy marriage.

Now look! I'm crying again!

Let's get back to your situation. I have some theories about what has happened. The major question, as you have implied, is "where are you?" That I think I know. You are at teenslut.com. That's self-evident. What does it mean for a human to be "at" or even "in" a website? I leave that for the metaphysicians. Why *you?* At your age? With your particular disinclinations? It's hard to say.

But I want to try an experiment. I'm going to do something on my end and you tell me if you feel anything on your end. Okay? Here's a hint: I'm holding in my hand a can of Hungry Man Chunky Steakburger soup. Footnote: I've removed the label.

As I mentioned in my last, since you are Honeycomb to me, I think that henceforth I should be either "Hank O'Hair" or "Piece O'Bone" to you. I like them both. "Hank O'Hair" has the advantage of "Hank" for short. "Piece O'Bone," on the other hand, is very macho, don't you think? "My Dear Bone," you might say. It's up to you. You choose.

Oh, do you know that song? Jimmy Rogers, I think. You don't hear the Negroes with the baseball backs hatward singing that song. And don't you tell them about it or they'll put it in one of their silly mixes and ruin it for white people.

Okay! On with our little experiment. Please get right back to me with the results. One, two, THREE. . . .

Something Understood (3)

MADMAN: What do you mean "what?"?

PROPHET: It's very complicated, what you're talking about.

MADMAN: For a moron!

PROPHET: Okay, just go on.

MADMAN: What's the point? In Nehemiah it is said, when a faithful member of the covenant found guys like you, that he "took them to task and cursed them . . . had some of them beaten and their hair pulled out." And he expected that God would "Remember this in my favor."

PROPHET: Don't threaten me.

MADMAN: Okay, I'll just continue with this silly exercise. So we were talking about the incredible, miraculous everyday congruities of the "operating order of life." But what if I told you that that order, from the sociological perspective, from the point of view of the theoretical sociologist, that is, from the POV of my theory on the Human Ideologeme Project, *segun yo,* this congruity was unlikely, was nearly impossible, because of the truth that this "operating order" was in fact universally fractured.

PROPHET: Is it?

MADMAN: In spite of the fact that your Slurpee transaction went flawlessly and you had the benefit of the enjoyment of your Slurpee and might well expect to consume endless Slurpees quite happily in the future, that every participant to this great adventure lives conceptually in a world of utterly bewildering difference, the social world is an infernal machine. That it works is a fantastic paradox. This is what the phrase "in spite of the fact" refers to. My idea was to create a survey which would produce an exact description of all the forces in society, so that I could locate every idea in its right place.

PROPHET: Wow. I'm starting to get it. I mean, I just got a sort of glimpse of what you mean. Ah, wait, now it's gone. Shoot!

MADMAN: Jeez. Can you think this word?

PROPHET: What word?

MADMAN: The word I'm thinking.

PROPHET: But what is it?

MADMAN: Intersignification.

PROPHET: Ouch!

MADMAN: Let me continue. At first, I knew my project would dwarf Marx, but I thought it wouldn't be horribly complicated. It wouldn't be impossibly complicated. It wouldn't involve or threaten to involve physics, a physics that makes things like the second theory of relativity seem silly, safe and sane. But it did.

PROPHET: It did, huh?

MADMAN: And how. I created a simple but revealing survey instrument which presented the subject with a series of innocuous questions about the animal, plant and mineral worlds which—however they chose to respond—would oblige them to reveal within a few inches (centimeters, actually) their social "Position." I got the most spectacularly unpredictable answers. You can't imagine what people think about, for instance, cheese. Never mind eating it, producing it, etc. What I cared about was what they *thought* about cheese. My question took the form of "What do you think about the possibility of the existence of something like cheese?"

I thought at first that I would be able to make generalizations about classes of people. You know, white-collar workers think this, teachers think this, teenagers think this, etc. This was the influence of that damned simpleminded Marx. And I'd just gotten to the point where I thought I had a pretty accurate mapping involving 10,000 "affinity groups." I'd filled ten CD-ROMs with the details and precise derivations. But I'd already begun to suspect something was up. Something was wrong. For my conclusion was that each one of these 10,000 groups had only "murder in its eyes" for the other 9,999. But then I did a test reverse holistic regression analysis of just one of these groups and discovered that within this group (I believe it was med tech professionals) no one within this "group" had *in the last instance* anything *substantial* in common with the others. In fact, I found it impossible to avoid the fundamental conclusion that every member of this group had the clinical quantity "murder in the eye" for every other member of its own and every other group.

This was something I now understood. And so I put it at the top of that very short list: something understood: universal rage. Nebuchadnezzar! Revenge against the whole world, the whole of creation. At the social level, of course.

Murder Mystery (4): Evidence on a Videocassette

In the first cassette, a middle-aged woman with an intelligent face, a face that said, "I know what is happening, in spite of the facts," was sitting at a table covered by a red calico tablecloth. After a moment, she pulled the hem of the tablecloth up to her face and blew her nose on it. Then she laughed soundlessly and blushed, running her fingers through her hair. It was as if she'd been put up to this by the person behind the camera. That's were she kept her gaze fixed. Then she shook her head no, as if refusing some request. Again, no. She wouldn't do something. But the person behind the camera was patient and persistent. A man began to enter the frame from the left. She looked there with anxiety. She rose and the figure retreated. She stepped to the side of the table. She was wearing a long, full skirt. She was embarrassed. Biting her lip. Finally, she began to raise her skirt slowly. There was nothing of the striptease in this; she didn't pose. Her legs were heavy without being fat. Neither attractive nor unattractive. Her legs were functional, strong, human legs. And yet not without something erotic. As if this were exactly what you'd wanted to see all your life: something truly human. Here of all places. When the camera reached her pubis, you could see that the hair there was very long and dark and that someone had wrapped and woven the long braided strands with colorful bits of cloth and bright thread. It was pretty. The camera zoomed in. The wraps included small, square silver coins, paper clips, bells, metal buttons, knobs, tiny electronic pieces like transistors and computer chips, and frayed wire twist-ties for garbage bags. The woman laughed and jingled the mass of things with the fingers of her right hand. It looked like an elaborate and happy bird toy.

Hume was already uncomfortable. These were exactly the kinds of things he hated knowing about. People tying garbage and trinkets into their pubic hair. God. These were *private* things and although Hume was witnessing them alone, in a dark, locked room, he felt that they were being made *public* through him. Did he videotape his wife's bathrobe? Did he archive the world of things that fell from his nose? No! And why not? Because Hume wished to maintain order in the world. That was why not. A deep resentment flushed through him. Why was *he* responsible for watching this? For asking what it meant? And what *did* it mean? Were these people supposed to be dead too? Was Hume responsible for finding their murderers? In what sense was this even "evidence"? And evidence of what?

Why was he one of the chosen of the earth? One of those who must bear witness to the final, stunning truth: fair is foul? He felt this imponderable responsibility for explaining every human death in the history of the world. But why stop with humans? Weren't the deaths of little dogs, cats, birds, the beasts in the forests, weren't they all sad too? Didn't they all deserve some elemental explanation? Wasn't that what justice was about? For who should be satisfied with the nonsense of "all things which live must die"? A cop out!

Nevertheless, he watched on. Grandma. So it's a grandma now. But something is wrong with her. She's crying. Bewildered. She lives in a dirty dump. The place is in tatters. Cats. A cat licks the frosting from a corner of a half-eaten birthday cake. More grandma. More weeping. Her misery is loathsome. Somebody take her away! Put her in a cart! Don't they have curb-side pickup in this town?

It's beginning to seem as if this video is the weirdest synthesis of ersatz family video and the homemade pornographic stash.

Over on a dingy couch behind grandma, a woman is weeping. It is indeed the woman with the braided pubis from the previous scene. Every once in a while she raises her tear-streaked face to look at grandma at the table. The camera zooms in on her grief. There is apparently something very sad about grandma.

But Hume does not feel any sadness. He feels disgust and rage.

What was wrong with these people? Hume's repugnance was indisputable, monolithic, palpable, concrete, visible for all, and overwhelming in its sheer hugeness.

But then it occurred to him with a start. This was also exactly what the filmmaker thought. The filmmaker had no sympathy for granny. That was just his point. Hume felt that he was failing to look at this film properly, or professionally. He was letting his own subjective perspective dominate.

Then the film came to that part that Hume forever called "The Hamper." In his later years "The Hamper" became a sort of inscrutable religious text for Hume. He thought about it and what it was trying to imply. Endlessly, he thought about it. In its substance, it was simple: A large wicker clothes hamper for the family's dirty laundry is sitting in the backyard. In the suburban horror that is the "backyard." It rises like an ancient mystic ruin. It is timeless. Mute. Enigmatic. Suddenly, it twitches like a cocoon hanging from a twig. The twitches quicken. Something is going to burst forth! Something is going to have to burst forth! It is so *full!* Any moment! Some horror will spew forth from the depths of the hamper! This horror will answer all the questions that the detective, Hume, or any other detective or merely mortally curious person could have. Everything will be plain. Plain as this bright day in a suburban backyard with the blinding eye of God looking down on the bursting hamper.

The Life of Chris (3)

LAMONT LEINSDORF AND SONS

ATTORNEYS AT LAW

Dear Sir or Madman:

We are writing as representatives of Terry Gross and her nationally syndicated radio program *Fresh Air*. You recently published a book in which there was what appeared to be a transcript of a *Fresh Air* segment and your author, "Chris" (a.k.a. the Modern Prophet), designated Ms. Gross by name.

We would like to assert that although Ms. Gross has been the principal creator of *Fresh Air* for many years and has led hundreds of interviews, she has no recollection, and the program has no record, of the interview with Chris described in the pages of your recent book. Given the unusual nature of the conversation described, this is not something that Ms. Gross or the producers of the show would be likely to forget.

Further, it is legal copyright infringement to use Ms. Gross's name in conjunction with the show without her expressed written consent.

Further, there is cause for us to think that Ms. Gross may have been libeled in this fictitious segment. While the subject of the interview, Chris, reveals personal aspects about himself, we would contend that that is between himself and his therapist. However, when it comes to the character of Ms. Gross, your author should not feel nearly so free, and he should explicitly not feel above the retributive power of the law.

To come to the point, Chris states that he knows that Terry Gross has a pornographic website, that is, that she features herself nude on such a site. He knows no such thing because nothing could be further from the truth. Ms. Gross is a journalist of international stature. She is not a high-tech sex worker. I wonder if you or your author can imagine what pain and embarrassment this has caused Ms. Gross? Only the fact that, as far as we have been able to ascertain from the book's distributor, the book has sold less than two hundred copies has kept us from seeking a much more radical remedy than what we will describe for you here.

Further, Chris implies near the end of the interview that Ms. Gross has something to confess. She does not. He further implies, we would contend, through a subtle allusion to the New Testament, that Ms. Gross is a demon. We quote, Ms. Gross: "I know who you are–the Holy One of God." If you would cross-reference this with Mark 2:24, as we will ask the court to do, you will see that these are the exact words of a "man with an unclean spirit" or a "demoniac." The clear implication is that Ms. Gross has an "unclean spirit." She denies this claim and we are intent on seeking legal redress to clarify the matter.

If you would wish to avoid court proceedings, please inform us at your very earliest convenience that you will perform the following:

1. You will destroy all remaining copies of the work in question.
2. You will publicly apologize to Ms. Gross in a venue of our choosing and at your expense.
3. You will delete the passage in question from all future editions of the work or,
4. Seek our consent for the revised passage and agree to pay a fair fee for use of any copyrighted materials.

These stipulations seem to us reasonable and fair in view of the egregious infringements of *Fresh Air*'s copyright and Ms. Gross's personal privacy. Be advised, however, that if we are obliged to pursue this case, we will seek punitive awards and damages.

We will leave to you all considerations of the blasphemous quality of Chris the Modern Prophet's implied claim that he is a Messiah, assuming, of course, that you overlooked this bizarre claim in first publishing his book.

Yours very sincerely,

Lamont Leinsdorf

Who Cannot Weep May Learn from Thee (3)

PROPHET: What can you say about your past, your experiences growing up, that help to explain the kind of person you ended up being?

MURDERER: I thought you were a prophet.

PROPHET: I am a prophet.

MURDERER: Well, man, you're starting to sound like one of those social workers with whom I have had it right up to here. If you want the "understanding" of it, you are looking in the wrong place. Just like that girl from the social agency. The difference is that she was sexy, I mean her questions made her sexy. Asking me to talk about my past. *Revealing* myself, you see. Telling her how I liked my legs chubby. Like her legs were chubby. I always had this wonder, this fantasy, this certainty that she had her own secrets. And her secret was this: she had her own pornographic website and she lived in fear that someone would find out, especially that I would find out. And I would find out. But I would know it without even having to look at a computer because all I had to do was look in her eyes and I could practically see it. The cheap excitement of revealing her little plump body. Revealing to every damned body in the whole world in principle but to no one in the office who might get her ass fired. Then again, maybe that was the sexiest thing she could imagine. Getting fired for wiring her cunt to the Net. The humiliation. All the I'm-sorries. The eagerness for those abject apologies. The understanding that she was now so low that the janitor could oblige her to do it. Down with the dustpans and shit.

Speaking of which, you know who else has her own little, top-secret porn site, favorite to devotees and afficionados of a certain kink?

PROPHET: Who?

MURDERER: Terry Gross.

PROPHET: Terry Gross? The *Fresh Air* person?

MURDERER: None other.

PROPHET: I don't believe it.

MURDERER: You don't have to believe it. All you have to do is punch up the right address on your little computer. A top secret address. But I've got it and I'll share it with you 'cause you're a pal.

PROPHET: How do you know about this?

MURDERER: Well, after that *20/20* episode about me and my awfulness, which those pricks licked up like smutty candy, she talked to me and some other people involved. I don't know. It bored me to death, the whole thing. I hardly even paid attention. But my idiot lawyer thought the exposure might help me with my execution appeals. Maybe he thought the governor was a *Fresh Air* fan. He wanted to "humanize" me. What a crock of shit. It must have been a weak moment because I gave my consent. Anyway, in the studio with Ms. Gross and my two burly guards, I'm listening to her questions, her voice, and I start to get this erection. No, I didn't start nothin'. I *had* a full-fledged hammer in my pants. And I'm having, like, the most incredible flash in which I understood that she liked to bare it all, the pink, 2 on 1, the whole deal, and right out there in public digital life. I couldn't believe it.

PROPHET: I can't believe it either.

MURDERER: Well, if you want the proof of it, you ought to go on her show. You'll see what I mean.

PROPHET: Go on her show? How could I do that?

MURDERER: Come on. You can't be twelve years old forever, man. Get a life. Do something. She's got some of the most God-awful-boring wankers in the world on her show. You can get on. And you probably don't even have to kill anyone. Aren't you writing a book?

PROPHET: Yes.

MURDERER: Well, there you go. It's probably boring as hell. So she'll love it.

PROPHET: Hmmm.

MURDERER: But as far as that social worker babe goes, the truth is no one wanted to stay long on her ugly ass site anyway. Men are after those silicon-boobed babes. Hell yeah. Who wanted her ridiculous little fat belly? Funny to think on. They want to get to the professional sites where everyone looks like plastic. Like a bunch of deranged Barbie Dolls. Personally, I'd rather fuck a can of tuna fish. Give me the little fat-legged social worker any day.

So, anyway, I'd sometimes actually say to her, "Hey, what's your site address?" And she'd look at me like I'd lost my mind. And I had. But I'd just have to laugh 'cause I could see this was gonna get nowhere, but I knew the truth: www.sexysadiesocialworker.com. So then I would tell her whatever she wanted to know. It was the closest thing to sex I've had in the joint. I'd fetch up some gobbet from my past and it would feel like coming. Talk about dirty.

But talking with you is different. You do not give me the horn, as my wife used to say. So, don't tempt me in that direction. It's an aesthetic thing. You ain't got no website. Who'd wanna look up that robe you're wearing? Yuck. Your underwear is probably dirty. Don't tell me you're not wearing any. Those hairy ass legs? Man! I'm gonna throw up.

PROPHET: Will you tell me about your childhood or not?

MURDERER: Sure. What the hell. You'll just go on bugging me about it if I don't. What do you want to know?

PROPHET: How you came to be as you are.

MURDERER: One more time, I can tell you but this ain't where it's at. You're looking for cause and effect. Even you, a damn prophet. I'd expect more. I have my own logic for being what I am. And it has nothing to do with somebody did something to somebody else. Somebody ran over my mother and beat me with a claw hammer leaving me in the fifth grade and so when I had a child I tied her to the bed and wrapped her in feces. Give me a break. It's not like that. Maybe you'd feel better if I told it like that. I don't know. Fuck you.

PROPHET: Go on.

MURDERER: The first time I understood that murder was a good way to deal with things was when I was in grade school. I came home and my Grandpa was drunk and mad at me because I was supposed to do something or not supposed to do something. So I had to be punished. Man, I was sick of that shit. Same deal all the time. Down come the pants, out comes the old belt. Then he'd make me stand up straight with my damned jeans around my ankles and try to take a whack at my penis with that belt. After a while, I'd sometimes get an erection when he'd do that. Well, he'd just get simple then and hit me in the head with his fists. Anyway, one day after I did something or didn't do something, who the hell knows with that drunk son of a bitch, and he did his usual trick with his belt, I just got all kind of cold and calm. Philosophical, I call it. Like I could have sat down and written a great book or I could have done what I did. I got my Louisville Slugger Roger Maris bat and got up on a chair behind the kitchen door and waited for the old fart. Man, I caught that son of a bitch but good. Down he went crying and bleeding and moaning. And I just had to laugh to see what I could do. Then, you wanna talk about an erection. I had one. I had one for me, for you, for the whole world. It was like that. So I got down off my chair and I was sorta bouncing around and whack! I hit him in the side. It felt so good, like a double into the gap. Nothing feels better than that that I know of.

PROPHET: And then you killed him?

MURDERER: No! Murder was too good for that old fuck. I wanted him around to look at me for the rest of his life and know that I could kill him.

PROPHET: So, when did you first kill?

MURDERER: You know this. I already told everybody in and out of sight. Don't you believe what you read in the papers?

PROPHET: Just go on.

MURDERER: Okay, but I am not asking for any kind of forgiveness. Is that understood? I already did my confessing to the judge. If I tell you what I did, that doesn't change anything, right? 'Cause I like it just like it is, me against whatever dim bulb fuzz ball made this stinking world. You dig me?

PROPHET: Don't worry. I can't absolve you. That's not in my power.

MURDERER: I'm beginning to think you don't really have any power, which makes me wonder why I gotta go on talking but I guess I can wonder all I like 'cause I sure feel it. I gotta go on talking.

PROPHET: *(Nods)*

MURDERER: Okay. First one. Only one, really, before my wife and kid.

You know, there are things about being me that even I don't understand. I mean, you can't imagine how low I felt as a boy when my parents or my papa would punish me. The phrase "low self-esteem" don't get at it. Not at all. I used to have this nightmare where I would feel the blankets on me and think it was the slimy underside of a snail. My blanket was the snail walking over me. My mother would find me shivering in the cold with the blanket on the floor and she'd wonder, now what the hell? What's interesting to me is that arriving at that point led to the certainty that I was the one and true God. Let me be exact about this 'cause there's a lot of crazy guys out there who think they're God. I felt that I was the supreme law-giver. The God upon whom snails leave their slime. The God who in fact commands his people to beat his stiff prick with whatever is at hand. That God.

So one day I decided that it was time to beat on my mother. I was watching TV when I knew it was time. She wandered in front of me in her dirty robe, drinking her drink. I think I missed an 800 number for something. And I thought, "Well, there you go again," and I got up and chased her through the house. Because I was tired of her thinking her drunk ass could just walk between me and the TV. And she tried to protect herself with a knife and I said, "By your own knife will you be cut." That's how she knew me. And she tried to hit me with a frying pan and I said simply, "By your own frying pan will you be hit." And we ran through various rooms. I was very careful to take the implements with me, the knife and frying pan. She lost some teeth along the way. So I said, "By your lost teeth shall you be known." And she trailed some blood, so I said, "By your blood trailing through your own hallway, through infinite time and space, shall you be known."

Once I got her into the bedroom, I beat on her some more and tied her down to her damn bed. And she said, "I have stumbled upon one difficulty or another in the process of composing myself. No human body is perfection." And I did ponder what my mother said, for it was well said and deep. But finally I had to return to my own thought and. . . .

PROPHET: Enough.

MURDERER: What?

PROPHET: I said, enough. Enough of this. You're wasting my time.

MURDERER: What do you mean? I thought that this is what you wanted to hear.

PROPHET: The truth is enough. You don't need to tell me these lies. Are you trying to impress someone or punish yourself?

MURDERER: Oh you are one full-of-shit motherfucker. By your own full of shitness shall you be known. *(Laughs)*

PROPHET: How's this for full of shit: You didn't do these things. This is how your mother died, but you didn't do it.

MURDERER: Really?

PROPHET: It was someone else. Your stepfather.

MURDERER: Really?

PROPHET: I want you to tell me what *you* did.

MURDERER: You see, that's what I don't get. There's stuff going on all the time. It's a stream. I'm part of the stream. Who's to say where my part of it begins and ends?

PROPHET: Well put, but trite and beside the point. While this difficulty lasts, you will not want to be yourself. That's understandable. Predictable. But not good. What did *you* do?

MURDERER: I killed a guy. Old guy. He carried lots of money on him. I just waited. Then I thought that if I killed him I might not get caught. So I kicked him and stomped him till he died. That's what I did. That's all. Just maybe five minutes of awfulness and forever to rot in this damned jail as a consequence.

PROPHET: But in fact that's not why you're in jail. You did get away with that one. Your victim did die and there was no one to identify you.

MURDERER: You know, I hate a guy like you. Make all these little nice distinctions. Mr. Day-and-Night. Mr. Synchronize-Our-Clocks. That's not what the world's like. That's not what my Time is about. It's sure not God's time. This is what you don't get: Everything is messed up with everything. It's all one thing. One awful thing. One powerful thing. One ugly thing that gives you big pleasure. One horror that makes you want to go on and rippling on. Goodness.

Isolation (6)

Consider the two letters which follow. The first is a letter of complaint from Emperor Joseph II of the Austro-Hungarian Empire concerning the composing habits of one young Wolfgang Amadeus Mozart. The second is from an earthbound human being of the North American continent circa 1998.

Illustrious Editor:

While Herr Mozart is without question one of the greatest and most original of our composers and perhaps a genius, I have the following observations to make. First, Mozart possesses an astonishing richness of ideas; however, astonishment in itself is not a *musical* response to a musical experience. Astonishment is, in my mind, better reserved for social moments. For example, when a woman's bosom bursts forth from her dress and restraining undergarments, and one sees that the bosom is no longer a mere function of style and *couture* but is in fact not one thing at all but *two* shiny "breasts"! Then one can be said to be properly "astonished." Astonishment follows when the expected or confirmed is revealed to be something altogether unexpected. But the "unexpectedness" of an assault of musical ideas pushes the concept to an extreme so that one would better catch the experience with the word "annoying." For instance, when one is eating outdoors in the summer months the abundance and variety of flying and crawling insects is annoying.

Mozart does not allow the listener to breathe; for hardly will one reflect upon one beautiful idea than another still finer takes its place, crowding out the former, and so it goes until at last one remembers nothing at all!

Plus, singers have complained to me of all the notes that Mozart surrounds them with during their singing. Again, the idea of insects seems to me appropriate.

As a consequence, I have said to Mozart in very clear terms, "Well and good, young sir, but that is enough. That is enough of that. That is enough *notes!*"

In short, Mozart was asked by his Emperor to take some of his notes out. This conclusion is simple even for a person far less complex than the young maestro. But he has persisted. His music remains as edifying as plunging, dunking, or simply sticking one's head in a dictionary, a pot of barley soup, a beehive, or a snowstorm.

As for Herr Haydn's compositions, if you have not heard them, you have lost nothing, for he's just like Mozart.

His Majesty Joseph II

Dear Editor:

I was under the impression that laws had been passed limiting the volume of television commercials. It used to be that a program would be set at a comfortable level by the viewer then—wham!—the commercial would hit you like a humvee, whatever that is. Then there was a complaint and someone passed a law or at least that's how I remember it. But now it's the same damned thing.

I watch TV from five in the morning to close to midnight. That's nearly twenty hours per day. It doesn't matter what channel you watch. Commercials are twice as high as programs as far as I'm concerned. That's my opinion.

And they must be coordinating their commercials, because when I go from one channel to another they are on a commercial also. And it might be twice as loud as the other channel! So you go from comfortable volume x to 2x to x squared! I believe I have my math right. Isn't this a health hazard?

I know. I change channels and hit the mute button over 200 times a day, cursing each time, and I'm being very light on that count.

I was wondering if I complained to the FCC if that would do any good or if they would cut off my communications so I would have nothing at all to watch or listen to.

I guess I'll just hope that somebody else complains.

Duke Small
Rural Dubuque

The Modern Castrati (1)

To: Honeycomb@teenslut.com
From: Tom@english.nwfsu.edu

You know, for a long time I thought there was something wrong with me. I thought I was the only one walking around in despair, loneliness, mutilated, a modern castrati. (If I were a musician I'd write an opera called the "Modern Castrati.") I thought others led full, human, masculine lives. I thought only I huddled before my computer, boner in hand, digits flying on the screen and off. Digits flying around my head like I'd stuck my head in a hive of hyper-bees. I thought that only I was worthy of this contempt. But Honeycomb! There are ten thousand sex sites on the net! There are a thousand subscribers to each site. That's 10,000,000! We're a nation of dead people, eunuchs, people like you, cold Americans of the native soil on whom Arapahos look and shake their mangy dead heads.

So you'll take the soup can and like it!

The Binary God (3)

ALPHA: Look. I think he's coming out of it. Maybe you didn't entirely kill him.

BETA: How should I know a story could kill a guy?

ALPHA: More like you bored him to death. Hello! Kid? Modern Prophet? You home in there?

MODERN PROPHET: *(Waking)* I'm fine. I'm so sorry. I just started getting dizzy and next thing you know. . . . Or didn't know. I'll be okay.

ALPHA: Dizzy? You were out, man. It was a little scary. You want to go to the hospital?

PROPHET: No. Seriously. I'll be fine. Just let me sit up a bit. I have lots to do today. I don't have time to be sick.

BETA: No more interviews I hope. No more stories for you today.

PROPHET: I don't have that luxury. That's my job. My God, you know, I'm just like little Eutychus listening to Paul talk on and on.

ALPHA & BETA: Who? What?

PROPHET: Eutychus. A boy who fell unconscious while listening to Paul drone on about the sins of the flesh.

BETA: Which sins?

PROPHET: That's not the point. The point was that he was sitting in a third story window when he fell and he was dead when he landed.

ALPHA: Now we are getting close to the matter at hand.

BETA: So what happened?

PROPHET: Paul brought him back to life.

ALPHA & BETA: Just like us!

PROPHET: Sure. Not quite. Anyway, I'm under a time constraint.

ALPHA: Time constraint? Imagine, a kid like this under a time constraint. What is it? You got a contract? Are you a piece-rate prophet?

BETA: Or maybe there's some sort of cash prize attached? 'Cause we'd like to help if you could cut us in on the deal. If you get paid by the story, we'll tell more stories and you can kick back a bit of it to us. Get it?

PROPHET: *(Looks at* ALPHA *and* BETA *in fatigue, fear, but necessity)* Are you implying that you have more to say?

BETA: *(Looking at* ALPHA *in amusement)* More to say? More stories? Hell yeah! We're full of them, man! Stories Are Us!

ALPHA: I think we're like story sinkholes. Very deep.

PROPHET: *(Pulling himself up and becoming attentive)* Well, then, I'm obliged to listen.

BETA: Look, kid, is this a good idea? I don't want to go through that last scene again. You on your back on the floor.

PROPHET: I'm okay. Go on.

ALPHA: Okay, big mouth.

BETA: Okay, this one is funnier, I swear to God, this one is a fucking stitch and a threat to no one nowhere.

ALPHA: You're sure?

PROPHET: Look, I don't care one way or the other. I have to listen. So just go on.

BETA: All right, then. Alpha, do you think we need insurance on this one?

PROPHET: You don't need insurance.

BETA: I'm not talking to you right now, excuse me, pal, I mean Mr. Prophet. I'm talking to my lifelong buddy Alpha about just how far out we're sticking our skinny-ass necks.

ALPHA: I don't know. If you mean do we need to contact a lawyer, I hate those guys. Maybe just a disclaimer. "If this story fucks you up, don't blame me." Understood?

BETA: Good idea. You say it and I'll witness, then I'll say it and you witness.

ALPHA: Right.

PROPHET: This is *really* unnecessary. I understand what you mean and you don't have to worry about it. *I absolve you.*

BETA: Whoa! Did you hear that? That was awesome. Inspiring. Convincing. So authoritative. The way he said that. I really believed it. *I absolve you!*

ALPHA: Yeah. Absolve! Maybe we underestimated this skinny kid.

PROPHET: Please. I've got a little headache.

ALPHA: *(To* BETA*)* So what were you thinking about story-wise?

BETA: I was thinking about when we were delivering appliances in good old Iowa.

ALPHA: Don't tell me. The TV set and Grandma?

BETA: Right.

ALPHA: Oh God, I love that story. Let me tell it.

BETA: Be my guest.

ALPHA: Okay, Beta and I were working for some rum-ass lunatic joint in Davenport, Iowa, Crazy Eddie's or something.

BETA: Loony Leo's. It was Loony Leo's and there was nothing crazy or funny about that sumbitch Leo. He was all bottom line. He'd sell you a refrigerator by the pound if he could. And he'd fill it with rocks. And he'd make you think you were getting a good deal on the rocks.

ALPHA: That's right. Anyhow, all we did was deliver this shit—TVs, VCRs, and the like—to the charming folk of Iowa.

BETA: You know what I hated about that job? Discovering how dim and dingy the inside of everyone's life was. Just dark and boring.

ALPHA: Like your house, you mean?

BETA: Alpha, try hard, try very hard not to be a clever fuck.

ALPHA: So one day we were delivering a TV entertainment center thing to this old lady out by herself in the countryside, in some clapboard nightmare left by her farmer husband in 1967. Her kids decided to pitch in and buy her a new TV for Christmas. The one unusual thing was that they wanted to make sure they'd be there when the TV arrived. We thought they just wanted to be part of the surprise. Wanted to see the look of delight or whatever on her face. Didn't turn out that way, though, did it?

BETA: Boy, I'll say.

ALPHA: So, we get there and we're hauling the thing up to the house and the kids are holding open the door for us and suddenly there's Grandma.

"What's that?" she says.

"It's a new TV set, Mom. It's an entertainment center."

"But I like my old TV. I don't want this one."

"But, Mom, you don't get a picture anymore. It's just sound. Your TV is broken."

"I don't care. I like it. It's a console and I can put my potted plants and flowers on it."

"Mom, get out of the way."

"I don't *want* it!"

She was crying, poor old thing.

Meanwhile, this entertainment center is getting heavy. The oldest son comes up to me and says, "Hey, sorry. She can really be a pain in the ass sometimes."

So, a team of daughters-in-law move the poor old thing out of the way and we move the new set in, the old console out. But Grandma just keeps repeating, "I don't *want* it!" Over and over, Jesus, we just wanted out of there. Finally, one of them gives me a five spot and says, "Thanks a lot, fellas. We appreciate it."

BETA: You're leaving one thing out, Alph.

ALPHA: What's that?

BETA: We were standing at the door taking our five bucks, taking the pathetic scene in one last time. But Grandma is saying something different now. She says, "I can't see. I can't see." And I have to wonder, is she blind? No, she's not blind. Then I get it. There's one tiny window in this so-called living room. It looks out on her garden, some crab apple and pear trees and a rolling pasture beyond. Nice view even if it is like looking through a keyhole. The old TV console was low. She could put her plants on it and still see the damned world through that window. But *now,* it's floor to ceiling TV and entertainment.

ALPHA: Never forget that. Fucking sad, the way we live. Poor old woman just wanted to see some shitty trees. The little sticky leaves in the spring.

BETA: And what's next? The boys have got the new TV set cranked and they're watching the Blue-Grey Game. The wives are making snacks. And Grandma's wailing like someone on her way to the old nursing home out by the Amana Colony. If you can't pipe down while the TV's on, you've got to go. She wouldn't be the first grandma to get shipped out for this reason.

ALPHA: Now *you're* leaving out one thing, Mr. Sympathy. Mr. I-remember-it-all.

BETA: What?

ALPHA: You sat down with those fat heads and watched the second half of the fucking Blue-Grey Game is what. You ate their chips, drank their beers, placed a bet with the oldest boy, and around two o'clock the following morning were making out with one of the little chubby wives.

BETA: Oh, bullshit.

ALPHA: And that little bet lost my half of the five dollar tip.

BETA: But man, wasn't that Trinitron a good set! Beautiful picture, clear as a bell and way before cable.

ALPHA: Hey, shhhh, look here. Ol' Mr. Prophet.

BETA: Not dead again, I hope.

ALPHA: Nah. He's just asleep.

BETA: That's so cute. Little guy is snoozing.

ALPHA: Unless you bored him to death.

BETA: Fuck you.

ALPHA: Be just like you to bore someone to death.

Lacrimosa

The Book of Sam (2)

First Book of Sam

Chapter 9–An ass's tale
1. Once upon a time, a man named Saul lost his asses. 2. While looking for them, he met a prophet, Samuel, who told him not to worry, that his asses had been found. 3. Still, Saul never saw his asses again. 4. For the asses Samuel referred to were the people of Israel.

Chapter 10–A king is chosen
1. Saul himself realized the changes that had come over him when he was approached by a band of prophets dancing in a prophetic state. 2. Saul joined them, dancing. 3. He danced in a frenzy which was the Spirit of the Lord. 4. And when the people approached to congratulate their new king, he hid "among the baggage."

Chapter 13–Saul does not keep the Lord's command
1. And though Saul did defeat the Ammonites, did in fact soundly thrash them, did smote them with the sword of the Lord, still he was in his heart a keeper of asses and a hider among baggage. 2. For the Lord God had made it very clear that every living Ammonite thing was to be destroyed: man, woman, child, sheep, dog, crops, and shade trees. 3. And yet Saul brought back the best sheep for sacrifice. 4. And the spirit of the Lord entered Samuel as anger and he said, "You are King of the Asses. You really are." 5. And Saul said, "But I didn't know. I thought it might be okay if . . . after all, the sheep were going to die eventually. It's a minor infraction."

Chapter 14—Jonathan eats the forbidden honey

1. Saul's son Jonathan once routed the Philistines who were a people numerous as fleas, which was fortunate because there were ever so many occasions on which they were destroyed, defeated, smote and so on. And not one word about Philistine mothers, crying their Philistine tears. 2. Saul decreed that no one should eat before evening on pain of death. 3. But there was a piece of honeycomb on the ground, glowing, and Jonathan saw it, glowing, and Jonathan did not know how not to want to eat it, and he did not know how not to eat the delightfully sunny honeycomb, and so he did eat it, and his eyes were bright from this small taste of honey. 4. And when his father Saul discovered that Jonathan had eaten the honeycomb and that his eyes were radiant, he commanded his death in spite of the fact that he was his favorite and bravest and most competent son, wholly unlike what one might expect in the son of a chaser of asses, a hider among baggage.

Chapter 15—Saul's turn to be disobedient again

1. Amalek is attacked. 2. For some incredible blunder against the Lord's command, Saul is reproved. 3. The Lord is sorry he made Saul king. 4. This is not the first time that the Lord God has been sorry about having made something. 5. Samuel points out that the Lord made Saul king precisely because he knew Saul would mess things up and as a punishment to the people. 6. God remembers, but he is not happy about being reminded, and now he must wonder just how glad he is about having made *Samuel.* 7. Agag is "cut down."

Chapter 16—Saul's melancholy

1. Saul now and then realized that his position was untenable. 2. He was the fuck-up King of the Asses. 3. That is what he WAS. 4. In his bones. 5. His heart of hearts. 6. And his question was this: is the King of the Asses not an ass many times over? A transcendent ass? 7. And so he took a bag of grain and, without first removing the grain, pulled the bag down over his head. 8. A servant said, "Please! An evil

spirit from God is tormenting you." 9. And so a harpist was brought in to soothe the king. 10. The harpist's name was David. 11. This is how he enters the story.

Chapter 17—David and Goliath

1. David took a stone from the wadi, a stone the size, shape and color of a robin's egg, blue like that, and hurled it at Goliath with his slingshot, and it imbedded between Goliath's eyes. 2. For someone in the Vedic tradition, this blue robin's egg between the eyes of the monster Goliath is mystic. 3. It is a third eye. 4. Or perhaps Goliath becomes in this way a Cyclops. 5. David whacked Goliath's head from his body with Goliath's own enormous sword which the subtle harpist could barely raise. 6. As Goliath's head lolled to the side, the robin's egg fell from his forehead and rolled a short way down a slight incline. 7. Some days later, a small boy came by the place where Goliath had been slain. 8. He and his pals were looking for the spot of blood soaked into the rocky ground. 9. Because that was "awesome." 10. The boy happened to pick the robin's egg up off the ground and placed it on his tongue. 11. Instantly, his eyes banged open and his mouth gaped. 12. Fabulous scenes ran endlessly before his mind's eye. 13. His friends said, "Hey, Ichabod, snap out of it." 14. "What's up with Ichabod?" 15. But he did not snap out of it. 16. His mother was sad, but Ichabod was not. 17. For he liked the scenes he saw, which were colorful and radiant and kaleidoscopic. 18. Finally, someone fished the blue stone from his mouth, the stone which had embedded in Goliath's forehead, the stone which David had selected from the sacred water of the wadi, and Ichabod returned to this world. 19. Now, Ichabod was not happy. 20. And he said, "The glory is gone." 21. Hence his sad name. 22. And in truth he went on to live a short, nondescript, black-and-white sort of life there in that dusty little town.

Chapter 18—Saul and David

1. This is what we may claim to understand of this very strange story. 2. Saul's son, Jonathan, loved David even though David was a

threat to Jonathan becoming king. 3. But Saul understood this threat quite well, saw clearly what a good king of the asses David could make, and so, visited again by one of God's moods, Saul hurled disappointed spears at David in the dining room. 4. The spears merely struck the walls. 5. In a stunning piece of nonconsequential logic, Saul then offered his daughter Michal to David in marriage on the condition that David bring him one hundred Philistine foreskins. 6. Does this mean that David took the foreskins like Mohawks took scalps? And why cast this task in the form God had invented to express his covenant with the Jews? 7. David, ever the overachiever, promptly provided Saul with *two* hundred foreskins. 8. He "counted them out before the king." 9. Imagine the scene in which David "counted out" the two hundred foreskins. Were they dried? Fragile? Scented or spiced for courtesy's sake? Like delicate parchment? Could you write a story on them? Did he carry them in a box? In a pouch? How large a pouch, exactly? What was he trying to prove with the two hundred foreskins? Did he care nothing at all for what the Philistines must have gone through? Did rumors about what David was up to run through the Philistine troops? Did Philistine men flee, hands on their crotches, screaming, "Here comes David!"? 10. As we said, the story makes little sense, but there is something of the infinite in it.

Chapter 19—Persecution of David
1. Later, Saul returned to the strategy of trying to nail David to the wall with a spear. 2. We think David would have been good at Dodge Ball. 3. One day, Saul sent men to arrest David at Ramah, but David was with Samuel and his prophets. 4. The prophets were in a frenzy. 5. Soon, Saul's messengers joined in their frenzy. 6. Saul sent more messengers, which produced yet more frenzy. 7. Saul himself went. 8. Soon he too was in a prophetic frenzy. 9. It is our understanding that prophets were essentially storytellers. 10. Creators of whoppers. 11. This scene consists, then, of a growing crowd of men, milling awkwardly, each telling a different story. 12. It is a chaotic but rich scene. 13. David sits behind them all, with Samuel, smiling. 14. Murderous

Saul, possessed by evil spirits from the Lord, unable to control himself, becomes Comic. 15. Hear his groans like punctuation as he tells a funny little story about a country boy. 16. He's got good schtick, that Saul.

Chapter 20–David and Jonathan

1. In the Book of Sam, Jonathan frequently intervenes to save David. 2. Saul accuses Jonathan of stupidity for not seeing his self-interest. 3. But Jonathan is a real friend, and he truly admires David. 4. He is a "nice guy." 5. He may be the original "nice guy," certainly one of the first in the Old Testament to rise above script or screed. 6. The thought of Jonathan–who would do anything for his pal David even if it meant his own destruction–makes us smile. 7. We love Jonathan's simple virtue and wish the Old Testament were all about him: genesis of Jonathan, Jonathan and Eve, etc. 8. Jonathan dies rather obscurely, perfunctorily, and entirely without glory in 1 Samuel 31:2. 9. Nice guys are blank pages in history's book.

Chapter 22–Doeg the Edomite

1. Gath, Adullam, Mizpeh and Moab. 2. Gab, Judah, Hereth and Doeg. 3. Gibeah, Ahimelech, Ahitub, and Nob. Doeg the Edomite. 4. Doeg the Edomite killed all of the Lord's priests, eighty-five in all. 5. Doeg the Edomite "put the priestly city of Nob to the sword, including men and women, children and infants, and oxen, asses and sheep." 6. We could in all fairness call the Old Testament the Big Book of Drunken Doeg the Violent Edomite. 7. Doeg is another word for the universal force of fate.

Chapter 24–David spares Saul

1. David hid in a cave. 2. Saul entered the cave to pee. 3. David snuck up behind him and cut the end off of Saul's kingly mantle. 4. We are struck by David's generosity, of course, but more striking is Saul's delicacy. 5. Saul, killer of legions, must relieve himself out of the view of others. 6. Did all of his troops relieve themselves in caves?

7. Was it a long walk out of his way to the cave? 8. Did his men wonder why he couldn't piss on the rocky ground like everybody else? 9. Did Saul have a "shy bladder"?

Chapter 31–Death of Saul
1. Eventually, the Philistines got even with old Saul. 2. They caught him and his son Jonathan on Mount Gilboa. 3. They shot arrows through their abdomens. 4. Wounded, Saul fell on his own sword. 5. Given Saul's proclivity for trading in Philistine foreskins, which he had made damned near coin of the realm, you can hardly say the Philistines didn't have just cause.

Second Book of Sam

Chapter 1–David's first post-Saul act
1. David's first act after the death of Saul was to slaughter an Amalekite boy who brought him the news of Saul's death. 2. What would Jonathan have said to his best friend, David, had Jonathan not died ignominiously for his father's sins on Mount Gilboa? 3. We believe he would have said, "Let the poor Amalekite boy go, brother."

Chapter 2–Joab
1. Joab was David's go-to guy; Doeg the Edomite had nothing on old Joab. 2. When David really needed something done efficiently, he called on Joab. 3. For instance, he entrusted Joab with the murder of Bathsheba's husband. 4. Yet Joab himself had been cursed by David for murdering Abner, and in no uncertain terms. 5. David said, "May the men of Joab's family never be without one suffering from a discharge, or a leper, or one unmanly, one falling by the sword, or one in need of bread!" 6. But, as any modern Mafioso might conclude, Joab was useful.

Chapter 8–David's wars
1. There were a lot of them.

Chapter 11–David and Bathsheba

1. One afternoon after a nap, David walked on the roof of his palace. 2. From the roof he saw a woman bathing. She was very beautiful. 3. David sent some son-of-Joab to bring her to his rooms where he screwed her and left her "with child." 4. Uriah-the-cuckold, Bathsheba's husband, happily suffered, slept on the ground, in David's service. A real son of God. 5. Like Jonathan, Uriah would do anything for David. 6. So it was easy for Joab to place Uriah in the advance, the shock troops, the cannon fodder, in the next available battle. 7. And didn't he die. 8. We wonder if faithful Uriah–cuckold to the King of the Jews, murdered at the convenience of the Lord's anointed–had any thoughts, any suspicions, any intimations as he crouched with his little spear right at the leading tip of the ground troops. If they gave him a spear! 9. Did he say, "What am I doing here? Is David mad at me? I wish he'd just say something when he gets mad." 10. Uriah's poor thoughts are not important. 11. In the grand scheme of things, he is just another Philistine foreskin. 12. For these sins, the Lord ordained that David's "neighbor" would sleep in full view, in the open daylight, with all of David's wives and concubines. 13. Thus the immortal House of David and Joab: endlessly condemned adulterers and murderers. 14. In fact, the "neighbor" who would sleep with all of David's concubines was Absalom, David's son. 15. David had a lot of concubines, hundreds. 16. Poor Absalom was fucking them and fucking them. 17. He wanted to stop but he was seized by a spirit of the Lord. 18. At a certain point, he became confused about which concubines he had fucked and which not. 19. So he brought in a servant to keep them separate: unfucked ones here, fucked ones over there. 20. Stay in line and don't move until he's done. 21. And the servant said, "This is pretty work, even if it is the Lord's." 22. But on and on he went, weeping and fucking and weeping and fucking and just plain praying that the next concubine would be the last.

Chapter 12–Birth of Solomon

1. One of the great and enduring riddles of the Book of Sam: from

the murderous, deceitful and adulterous alliance of David and Bathsheba comes the wisdom of Solomon.

Chapter 24—The census
1. David asked Joab to count the people of Israel. 2. Even Joab knew this was wrong. 3. But David "numbered the people." 4. God was very angry. 5. We believe that what God really wants is that we should tear up our Social Security cards. 6. We believe He wants us to kill our TVs and computers. 7. He wants us to rip the cables from the wall. 8. Before the satellites can home in on us. 9. Before they tattoo the bar codes on our foreheads.

Appendices—Death of Joab
1. From his deathbed, David ordered his son, the new king, Solomon, to kill Joab, who had outlived his usefulness. 2. Clinging to the "horns" of the Lord's alter, Joab was cut down by representatives of the next generation of Kingly henchmen. 3. And when Solomon heard that Joab was dead, he was very glad. He felt splendid, unburdened and relaxed. 4. He went for a walk along the magnificent palatial gardens high up on the roofs of his father's palace. 5. It was spring, and each time he found a sticky little leaf, he was struck with the implausibility, perfection and freshness of Being. 6. And this incredible, holy feeling of happiness and tranquility came upon him. 7. He forgave the world; he forgave his father; he forgave himself. 8. He was just absolutely awash in clarity and bliss. 9. And he held one of the little leaves up to the light to see through it, to see there God's design. 10. But on the far side, in the distance, on the ground floor of his new kingdom, he saw a beautiful brown, young woman, scantily clad, practically a bikini for that time, sunning in God's gorgeous spring weather, there in old Palestine. 11. Solomon dropped his leaf and the hard-won clarity fell away from him in the same instant. 12. And he said to himself, "Gosh, who is that girl?"

The Human Condition (3)

"I am sorry. Please forgive me. I am willing to die."

So, he's talking to the two dogs, the basset hounds, in an empty, white room. They're sitting in plastic chairs, woefully mismatched. This one is purple and humped. That one blood-red and angular. The place has the feel of an impoverished church rectory. One of the dogs is mostly white (henceforth, "White Dog"), the other mostly black (henceforth, "Black Dog") although, to be quite accurate, they're both tricolor basset hounds, with regal ears, and very sharp, definitive cranial points. Championship stock. Or so he'd been told by the breeder back in Iowa. But that really was way back. 1975. The dogs look damned good, though, all things considered. Better than he looks in most ways.

White Dog gestures with his paw and speaks.

"You okay?"

"Me?" he says, a little startled, as if he were being awakened. "Sure. I'm fine. Why not?"

"So how was it out there?"

"In the water?"

"Yeah."

He looks around, a little afraid of his emotions, not wanting to make eye contact with White Dog. He'd had a serious soft spot for White Dog, back then. He was always such a baby for him. Even when he was fully grown, he kept his puppy ways. Although you could hardly see that in this moment. No. In this moment he seemed transformed. He was a cop, or an inquisitor. A therapist at the very best.

At last he pulls himself together to speak, his eyes misting up. He's a human being, after all.

"I'll tell you the truth. It was scary." He nods his head, leans forward over his knees, clasps his hands together. "Being out there, alone, isolated on that huge ocean, seeing you guys in the boat, barking, worried for me. I really thought I was going to die."

"Oh, you died," says White Dog. Real emphatic, his two long ears bouncing with the emphasis.

"What do you mean?"

"You died."

"I don't get it. What are you trying to say?"

White Dog frowns in frustration and maybe a little annoyance. Black Dog then leans forward. It appears that Black Dog's role will be to clarify things should they get confused. That may be his role because he's the angrier of the two and willing to put things in very blunt terms.

"There's nothing complicated about what he said. It was two short words. You died."

He tries to smile. "You must be joking."

Black Dog again, "Hey, numb nuts, we're dogs! We have no idea about joking. We don't know what it is. We are known to be happy— under the right circumstances, I might add—and we can be playful, but we never joke. When you used to make little jokes with us and laugh, and we'd run around with our tongues hanging out? Remember that? Yeah, well, we didn't get it. We weren't laughing. *You* were projecting. It's called anthropomorphizing. You used to do that a lot and it was pretty stupid. Like thinking we were worried about your ass in the water. That's a good example of what I'm talking about. But we are not capable of jokes. See?"

White Dog: "Look. We don't mean to upset you so early in our conversation. But we will be frank with you. *That* we can do. *That* we must do. In fact, it is required of us where willing and doing are one." He looks to Black Dog and they nod at each other. They really seem to know what they're about.

White Dog slips back in his chair. He looks pensive. "Tell us what it was like out there."

"What do you mean?"

"Nothing complicated. Just tell us what you saw, what it felt like, what you thought. You know: 'What it was like.' "

"Well, like I said, it was scary. . . ."

Black Dog, a little impatiently, "Oh come on, man, you can do a little better than that. You went to college. You're a bright boy. You were even in graduate school, as I recall. You must have *some* powers of observation and expression."

"Sure I do. I do. I'm trying. Give me a minute. When I say it was scary, I mean there was terror in some of the things I saw and felt."

The dogs look at each other and nod, almost as if they're taking some grim satisfaction in this.

White Dog: "Tell us about it."

"Well, first, I felt the enormous depth of the ocean. This water was deep. It was also very dark. Amazingly dark. Dark like dreams. Dark like space itself. Then I thought of the living things which must be below me. Fish. There's something about fish. Something I've always mistrusted and feared. I think it's the idea that they are breathing underwater. I've never really believed that. I've always felt that the very idea of fish was some sort of trick being played on me. What I have suspected is that fish are alive in such a way that they can't be distinguished from dead things."

"So, they're not at all like dogs." Black Dog. Icily.

"Of course they're not."

"You didn't always act like 'of course not.' "

He's a little alarmed by this. By the implications.

"What are you implying?"

White Dog intercedes: "Nothing. He's implying nothing. Just go on. You're doing very well." He gives Black Dog the dog equivalent of a dirty look.

"Okay. So, the water, the depth of it, the black of it, the fish of it. And of course all this is literalizing my worst old anxiety: isolation. No warmth. No human contact. The Cold Boy. I used to think the right metaphor for it was being caught by your sleeve off the most distant jagged star. When it came time for it, the feeling was right but the metaphor was wetter."

He smiles. He has charmed at least himself with his talk. But not the dogs. Well, they had told him. Dogs don't do humor. They're grim like Moses and Aaron with some stiff-necked covenant breaker. What they're considering could be awful, just as justice is awful. But they also seem to know that that's all we've got, grim justice, between us and the wild beasts.

White Dog again, kindly: "What else would you like to tell us about your experience?"

"Well, I told you about the terror. Or the first part of it, at least. Because then the second part was the non-neurotic part of the terror. The anyone-would-feel-that-way-in-that-circumstance part of the terror. I thought I was going to die. And I was afraid."

He thinks he notices Black Dog smile a bit, but he could be seeing things. He is a little dizzy with the strangeness of this, although even the strangeness is strange and so not quite recognizable as strangeness.

"Well, next, I saw you guys out in the boat. And I tried to figure how I could get to you and the boat. And I knew you guys must be afraid and worried for me. And I saw you both there, my two lovely basset hounds, and I realized how much I loved you two guys."

"Oh come off it!" screams Black Dog.

White Dog: "Calm yourself."

"I am not going to sit here and listen to this tired, mealy-mouthed crap from this fucking. . . ."

White Dog, sternly, the Alpha Male: "I said calm yourself. WE'RE NOT DONE."

Meanwhile, he doesn't know what's going on. He looks at the two dogs, his own pets, and thinks that this experience could be almost as scary as drowning in the middle of the deep, black, starless sea.

White Dog: "Sorry. You know how he is. He was *your dog,* after all. Always a little ornery streak. Never knew when a little snap might come your way. I took a few of those on my own hindquarters."

He smiles. "That's right. You were the sweetie. He did have his moods."

Black Dog scowls as if to say, "Fuck off, the both of yuz."

White Dog: "Where were we? You were thinking about us. About how much you loved us. That's nice of you, considering. But may I ask you, did you have pets?"

He's perplexed. "What kind of question is that?"

"Just a question. Answer it, please."

"Of course I had pets. I had you guys. Dogs. And I had some birds."

"Birds!" Black Dog mutters contemptuously.

"And how did you treat your pets. Let's start with the birds."

"Very well. I loved them. I took pretty nice care of them."

White Dog lifts a tablet of paper from beside him. "Let's see. Did you once have a parakeet. A 'Hank'?"

"Yes."

"And how did he die?"

"Well, it *was* sad. We went away one Christmas, and while we were gone there was an awful arctic cold snap and our heat went down and the house froze up and when the neighbor boy came over to feed him, he was dead."

"Frozen straight up, still sitting on his perch. His feet frozen to the perch. Isn't that about right?"

"Yes. I mean, it was really cold. The toilet bowl was one solid block, and it cracked the porcelain right through."

"I see."

White Dog flips through a few pages on his note pad.

"And a hamster? A 'Mr. Teddy'?"

"That was my daughter's pet. A typical story. Got out of his cage and ran down the heat vent. That one was grisly and smelly but not as sad. He had this little clear, plastic ball that we'd put him inside and he'd run around the house in it. My daughter loved that. But after an hour or so in his little bubble, you could sort of see the filth–the pee and the pellets–sort of centrifuging universally in there. After a while, you could hardly see the little guy through the grime."

"Yes. Very loving. And you had a lovebird named 'Hot Shot'?"

"He died of natural causes, I believe."

"Hmmm, yes, lucky for him. But you never hit him so hard in the head ('thwocked' him, as you used to put it), for the awful sin of nipping you, that he nearly died in your wife's hands?"

"God, I felt so horrible about that." He looks down between his feet. "But you say 'nipped.' Good Lord! That little bird could put the death grip on you. It was unbelievable. Not to mention painful. I lost my temper."

Suddenly Black Dog seems to break down or through. "Oh I see. 'I lost my temper with a little bird.' As if that justifies something. And dogs? What about dogs? Ever have any dogs? A couple of dopey basset hounds that were stupid enough to care about your lame graduate-student ass? Who were stupid enough to think you cared about them? Ever have any of those? Huh? What happened to them?"

He was intimidated. These memories hurt. Plus it looked like he might get bit.

"You know what happened. We had to move back to California. We had a little baby girl. We couldn't afford a place for you guys, with room for you to run. I'm sorry about how that worked out. I loved you guys. I'll never forget the look in your eyes when that farmer packed you onto his pickup truck." As he's saying this, he's clearly being distracted by another thought. If he had left the dogs behind way back when, well then how were they with him later, in the boat? Confusing. But his thought is broken by a violent eruption from Black Dog.

"Fuck you! Fuck you, man! You cringing shithead! Do you know what old Farmer Pfister was like? That alcoholic son of a bitch. I ought to eat your ass." And he was nearly down on four legs, now, just like a dog. And that is nearly it for him, his "lame ass" eaten eternally by his own former pet basset hound, were it not for the restraining presence of White Dog.

"I'm sorry." He was actually crying now. "I'm sorry."

"Now, now. Here." White Dog hands him a Kleenex. There's a little muddy paw print on the Kleenex. "One more question and then we're done."

He's still half-sobbing, but he looks up. "Okay."

"How did you fall out of the boat?"

"You know, I've never really had a chance to think about it."

"Well, this is your chance, my friend."

"It was so shocking to be in that cold water. I didn't have much time to figure it out. I guess I just lost my balance. Caught a wave the wrong way. Slipped."

White Dog bends far forward. As far as he can. He peers into the man's eyes. The man sees nothing but infinite black in the dog's eyes.

"Tell me," White Dog nearly whispers, "did it ever occur to you that you might have been pushed?"

"Pushed?"

"Pushed."

"Pushed by whom? I was the only person on the boat. And you two guys, of course."

At that moment, between the master and his pets, there is an amazing exchange, an exact flow, a reciprocal balancing. With each moment that his eyes acknowledge the horror of what the dog suggests, the eyes of the dog fill and reflect brilliantly an exactly, appositely measured . . . glee. As his eyes become the vessels of a consciousness of the nadir, the dog's eyes fill with an electric and luminous joy.

Finally, White Dog says, "Okay. That's it. He's got it. Got it all."

And then, suddenly, as if it's midnight New Year's Eve of the millennium, the two dogs leap in the air, join paws, dance in a tight circle, howl in doggy mirth, their nails clicking on the floor, their bony dog elbows occasionally banging hard when they slip, but they don't care, pain means nothing, they're celebrating something that has been a long, long time coming.

Not One Does What Is Right, Not Even One (3)

Chad! Chad! What is going on? What are you doing? Where do you take Murphy? Are you thinking? You say you're going to the park, but you are not going to the park. Something's wrong. Chad. Chad? Chad!

His Life Was So Sad (3)

TENOR: I too once had a wife who was perhaps not the person I should have married.

CHORUS: Perhaps be damned!

TENOR: What? What did they say?

BARITONE: I think "perhaps," my friend, they said that if this is now to be a confessional that you just go ahead and confess, tell things as they were, without extenuation. You know, "perhaps" be damned. Think of them as really first-rate editors.

TENOR: Well, I don't want to hurt anybody's feelings. My ex-wife is still alive, you know.

BARITONE: Do you imagine that the discovery that your emotional attachment to her was not what it should have been will be a surprise to your *ex*-wife!?

TENOR: I suppose not. But no one likes stuff rubbed in their face. So I won't go into the gory details. . . .

CHORUS: Like hell you won't!

TENOR: . . . but the facts are basically these. When I was very young and studying music at the university, I met the most astonishingly brilliant young woman. I came from a very ordinary background, not unlike what you describe for Saint-Saëns, and I had never before met a woman whose desirability was largely in her intelligence. For me, her mind just flashed. I wanted it as my own. And I think, in fact, that she did want me, too. I wasn't without my own brightness at the time, if I may say so.

BARITONE: Sir, your brightness precedes you as shadows do for ordinary mortals.

TENOR: Thanks, even if you are kidding. But frankly I was so fundamentally clueless about what one did to actually have a relationship with a woman—other than listen together to Ida Presti and Alexander Lagoya play guitar duets—that I did nothing. Other than love her in my heart.

CHORUS: Awwww!

TENOR: They're mocking me!

BARITONE: Just get to the point and they'll be happy.

TENOR: I remember she said to me, "When are we going to stop messing around?"

BARITONE: By which she meant what?

TENOR: Well, obviously she meant, "When are we going to fuck?"

CHORUS: That's better!

BARITONE: But you didn't?

TENOR: No, I didn't. And now, of course, I'd like to go back to that moment and seize it, but I can't. Because that's how it is with time. All I can do is mourn.

SOPRANO: I'm starting to see the shape of this. You are a human, aren't you? Yours was and is a human life.

TENOR: Exactly. So when just a few years later I did marry, it seems to me like it was just to the first person who wanted me. Who was she really? I don't know. Why did she want me? No idea. Who did she think I was? Milkman or a bus driver maybe. Again, it's all pretty obscure for me. The weird confusion of human motivations.

Just a few years into the marriage I began to look at it and see it and its laws as arbitrary. Marriage wasn't anything that I was "in." Rather, it was an alien reality opposed to me. I treated it cynically. I thought it was an unjust limitation on my individuality, on my right to sup freely, to taste at nature's table, in short to do what I now had every inclination to do: seduce and have sex with other women.

CHORUS: Yeah! Tell us more!

TENOR: Well, look, I'm *not* going to go into a lot of detail here, these people are still *around*, for Christ's sake. Let's just say that while I was married I liked to have two or three little things going on here and there. And this went on for years. And I always felt it was my "right" to have these relations as compensation for my disappointment—and grief!—at not having had the one I truly loved.

CHORUS: Whatever happened to her, by the way?

TENOR: I lost touch with her. The irony is that she did end up marrying a singer, a tenor, a guy who has been far more successful than I've been. He's on all sorts of CDs, singing with Placido, singing with Fischer-Dieskau in the seventies. On Deutsche Grammophon. Leontyne too. He's big. Personally, I think he's conventional and predictable. You'll say that's jealousy. I say it's God's own truth.

SOPRANO: [*Obviously emotionally affected*] Please. Please. Stop. I can't take this. You're hurting me.

CHORUS: What's up with her?

TENOR: I don't know.

CHORUS: Sopranos are pussies! Hahaha! Go on with your story. We're lovin' it.

TENOR: Well, the long and short of it is that finally I paid ten-fold in horror and prolonged suffering for every moment of stolen bliss I had in those years. The D word. Divorce. I lost my house, car, wife, and money. Everyone I respected hated me. I lived in a hovel, mostly drunk, and so sunk in debt that I needed to add another $500 on my credit card every month just to pay the rent and buy groceries. And beer. But I don't remember anyone feeling sorry for me. On the other hand, I was still getting laid nearly every night. Go figure. Impoverished, drunken, and fucked up, but still sexy as hell.

Eventually, I had to come back to the question of commitment to other people. Hedonism didn't work. Stoicism didn't work. Tragic removal from the world didn't work. But when Marriage again confronted me in its imponderable LAW, I still had no idea, really, where it came from. It still seemed arbitrary and stifling. But, boy, was it REAL. It was now a bona fide, don't-fuck-with-me actuality.

BARITONE: You did a good job the second time round. I've met your present wife. She's a nice person. Lawyer, right?

TENOR: Oh yeah.

BARITONE: And I take it you've learned your lesson.

TENOR: Well. . . .

BARITONE: Well what?

TENOR: Well, I *am* a tenor.

CHORUS: HE IS A TENOR! HE IS A HELL OF A TENOR!

SOPRANO: [*Faintly but forcefully*] I should like to know how a woman's voice interrupts this orgy of male self-absorption. Would it be too much to ask of you two if I suggested that we return to the matter at hand?

[*Saint-Saëns's* Requiem *begins to spill out softly. First Movement.*]

TENOR: What was that?

SOPRANO: Saint-Saëns.

BARITONE: Right. Saint-Saëns. [*In a sort of reverie from which he pulls himself*] As I was saying, the *Requiem* was written before the death of his son, André.

TENOR: Shades of Mozart, then! It would appear that writing a requiem is a dangerous thing to do. Ask not for whom you write a requiem, you write it for yourself.

SOPRANO: And the story isn't done.

CHORUS: We're always glad for more.

SOPRANO: Yes, unhappily, Madame Saint-Saëns's grief and sense of guilt over the death of the boy cast her into such despair that she was unable to continue nursing her second infant son. Six months later, he too died.

TENOR: Good God. Enough. Don't tell me anymore.

CHORUS: No! Don't stop. This is the kind of stuff we like.

SOPRANO: But there is more and you will hear it. You won't avoid it. Not this time.

TENOR: Oh, like I've been good at avoiding things in my life.

BARITONE: She's brutal with you. And you've already told us your secret story. Is there more we don't know about? Do you think she's punishing you for what you did to your first wife? Your irresponsibility?

TENOR: What irresponsibility?

BARITONE: My God. Listen to the woodwinds of this Agnus Dei! Truly, whoever has ear ought to hear.

SOPRANO: [*Perhaps in fact a little vengefully*] After these two deaths, as Saint-Saëns himself put it, his "gaiety was notably restrained." He was devastated. The marriage itself, always the most emotionally superficial part of his domestic life, limped on for three more years. Then in July 1881, while the couple was on holiday, he simply left. Vanished. His wife complained, "He left me . . . and not very kindly, but through some whim that has never been explained to me." Or something to that effect. Can you imagine? As a woman, it hurts me even to think about her feelings in that moment. "Shall we go hiking today, dear? Dear?"

BARITONE: Yes. I know this story. He blamed her for the death of the first son. Still, it doesn't reflect well on Saint-Saëns. Nonetheless, Marie lived a long if somewhat dry life. She attended Saint-Saëns's funeral in 1921. The sad old lady died with her memories in 1950, in her ninety-fifth year.

TENOR: That's very strange to think. That's the year in which I was born. It doesn't seem possible. The two of us alive on this green earth and breathing air at the same time. The past lasts longer than you think.

SOPRANO: Whatever that means.

BARITONE: Is this about when Saint-Saëns began visiting Morocco in order to indulge in Gide-like orgies with Arab boys?

CHORUS: No wonder he didn't have much use for a wife.

SOPRANO: What you've said is probably not true. Just more gossip. Even so, it is part of the very human life of a rare man who only knew how to comfort himself through art.

TENOR: [*Laughs; others, including* CHORUS, *turn on him in stern reproach*] *Perdone,* but I just remembered something that Mussorgsky said about him: "You'll deceive no one with your pretty tunes, M. de

Saint-Saëns. You're just about as important as a woman politely handing round bags of jujubes to her friends."

SOPRANO: You've learned nothing, have you? Ever the partisan.

BARITONE: Did they really have jujubes in France in the nineteenth century?

TENOR: I know. Another strange one, eh? I used to eat those at the movies when I was a kid.

CHORUS: Hush! Listen! "Lux Aeterna!"

The Soul in Paraphrase (6)

To: Honeycomb@teenslut.com
From: pieceobone@aol.com

Very disappointed not to have received a reply from you after my
last re. Hungry Man Chunky Steakburger experiment. Although,
strangely, *I heard my computer itself moan last night! It moaned!*

Anyway, I've been thinking about your situation. Have you ever
read that story by Edgar Allen Poe about the guy who is hypnotized at
the moment of death? Monsieur Valdemar? And his mind lingered
behind after his body died? Super creepy.

"I'm dead," he said. Wow!

So, imagine that your worthless, dry-ass, seventy-whatever-year-
old, can't-reply-to-pen-pals cunt was inhabited by a new tele-operative infrastructure so that, essentially, your nervous system and mental circuitry was taken over by a ghost-bot, a sort of dematerialized
robot using your "hardware" for other purposes. Humans immersed
in cyberspace experience telepresence as if they were interacting with
physical objects personally since the ghost-bot imbedded in your cor-
tex sends back stimuli for the five senses. Honeycomb, this has been
very one-sided. We haven't even begun to look into what *I* might get
out of this.

Interaction with synthetic objects in cyberspace is actually initi-
ated and some genius maintains a certain kind of presence/process in
that world, which is an actual world as you well know, and you are
obliged to perform certain lucrative tasks that regular humans wouldn't.
Like with the soup can. To fuck someone with a soup can in fantasy is

one thing. To fuck a statistical anomaly, a digital holograph is better. But to fuck such a tele-operative constellation with the Hungry Man Chunky Steakburger product who is really a human being re-deployed cybernetically is . . . about as good as good gets. (Short, of course, of finding a real human being who has the same cathected longings for Chunky Steakburger that I have.)

Anyway, I think you get the picture. You've been waylaid by hackers, cybermonkeys, who have essentially reconstituted you as a seventy-whatever "teenslut" and sold your ass into hyper-sex slavery. And can't you just hear their little adolescent computer nerd baseball-backhatward asses laughing their asses off?! (When an ass laughs his ass off, he becomes the nullity he was all along. Just thought you might like to know that.) There's also undeniably an element of necrophilia and grave robbing here, but that's too deep for me. For me, mere word processing is profound. Even when I type, I feel that I am forcing myself to do something that is horribly wrong simply because it must be done. In the face of all this, what can your personal pain be worth?

So trala-fucking-la with your private pain.

Let's go on with our little experiments. The kids will want to know that we've put their little hyper-toys to interesting use. Do you know about the powerful kitchen products made by Kitchen Aid?

Something Understood (4)

PROPHET: Frightening.

MADMAN: Frightening!? That's what you make of this? Listen, what I'd discovered–through mere questionnaires, mind you–was that there was in fact a hole at the heart of Being. I discovered that the Real was dependent on its impossibility. I had, in short, discovered the sociological equivalent of a Black Hole. Which explains why the only people who have really understood my project have been physicists. Physicists and a handful of incarcerated computer hackers doing time in federal pens for pathological (not to mention sociopathic) virus manipulation and body snatching.

What passes for "order" on any given day is nothing other than the random but ephemeral viral (viral! consider that word!) redundancy which washes over us from moment to moment. Social life is a grand tautology, if you know that big word, little prophet man. I think what people fear is not that my theory is true (which it is beyond any question) but that once *my theory becomes viral* (and that's just a matter of time) it will create a moment which will wash quickly over the entire field (moving ecstatically from node to node, doing nothing more complicated than communicating) and make it impossible to be succeeded by another virus. Because it is the virus of viruses, the ubervirus, the ultimate metanarrative, it will send not only hard drives crashing, it will freeze, lock, virally corrupt, and then utterly displace human consciousness as such. Because my viral turn is the turn of absolute self-awareness. It is paralyzing, no, it is more than that.

Through this thought I AM BECOME DEATH.

Contrition (2)

Then, quite miraculously, the consort organized. Constanze, Salieri and Süssmayer stood like a chorus over poor Puchberg who was on all fours beneath them. Each of the chorus members had a timpani mallet with which each was pummeling Puchberg on his poor head, kidney and ass, rhythmically, as if it were the *Dies Irae* and they were a wrathful God's instrument playing a score marked "furioso." To the side was the nameless official to the court of the Emperor, not far away, really, but far enough that he seemed impotent. Before them all, the maestro, was Papageno.

He directed the group vigorously. They sang:

Constanze: "I am sorry . . ."

Süssmayer: " . . . please forgive me . . ."

Salieri: " . . . let me die . . ."

Official: " . . . what's this about? . . ."

Building in a powerful crescendo! Incredible counterpoint, fugal, like Mozart himself after his discovery of *The Well-Tempered Clavier.* All of their stories came together to make a moral universe.

"I am sorry . . ."

" . . . please forgive me . . ."

" . . . let me die . . ."

" . . . what's this about? . . ."

Then all together: "WHAT'S THIS ABOUT!?"

And sustained, powerfully, the mallets fell repeatedly on Puchberg's all-too-human tympanum.

Finally, Papageno signaled FINI!

He shouted, leaped in the air, twirled and rushed to embrace all his players, providing his own universal applause. And then he looked to poor Puchberg, beaten near to death beneath his feet. Beaten thoroughly and bloodily. No bogus stage bludgeoning. The real thing. Papageno looked down. Puchberg was quivering, trying to lift himself. And Papageno kneeled and took his chin. "What now, old mole? Do you understand at last?" Puchberg nodded his head and smiled. Papageno smiled in return and kissed him tenderly on both cheeks. "Now, my dear companion, you must do it all again." A look of terror from Puchberg. "Oh, no, not that. Not the beating. That will come in its own time. You must return to your business world, to your caca. You must do *that* again. For again will come a time when you can exchange shit for beauty. It is foretold. Again you will fail. Again we will beat you. You will fail and be beaten into what can only appear as eternity to you. We have the strength for it if you do. But, dear sweet soul, there will always be the chance that you could for one time in all world history make the right choice. And when you do, the heavens will open, and history will be done. The little drums will sound, and the choir of boys will bleat its beautiful song. We will lift you up, shit-meister, as we will all be lifted by you." Puchberg looked bewildered but then seemed to understand something dimly and smiled one last time. The real smile this time. The smile of understanding.

"Yes, smile, dear old mole. Smile."

Murder Mystery (5): No Solution in Sight

By the time Hume arrived home, it was nearly midnight. Grenda was already in bed. He made some tea and toast with honey and sat in his quiet home. He always felt tired at the end of a long cop day, but this was a tired beyond tired. This was a weariness beyond anything he could blame on his damned ten-year cold bug. He'd broken through mere human exhaustion into a metaphysical dimension, like punching through a wormhole in outer space. This was the tiredness unto death. Tedium vitae. That funny phrase. It kept intruding in his mind. Like a little worm was running around up there singing it in this chamber and that. But what the hell did it mean? Sounded like Latin, whatever Latin sounded like.

He crawled into bed beside his formerly-buff, presently roundly-ursine wife. She groaned darkly. By God, that was good. She sounded just like something tucked away in the old den for the winter. A few decades back in the gym and she'd be the girl he'd married. Tie her to the Stairmaster for nine months to get things started. But don't give in to her bawling! Hume laughed at the spectacle of his wife-the-land-mass on a Stairmaster and stared deadly into the dark.

He continued staring blankly, stupidly and sleeplessly into this dark until the phone rang urgently, a little crazily, as if phones too were capable of panic attacks—at 3:07 A.M. Grenda roared from her sleep, leaping straight to her knees like any wild beast might.

"Easy, dear," said Hume, "it's just the phone."

"My God! My God! The phone again!" She was panting. "I think it's trying to kill me. I really do. I think it's trying to give me a heart attack."

Hume had his hand cupped over the mouthpiece. He was in control. "Just lie back down. Everything's okay."

Grenda obeyed, whimpering. "I didn't even know you had come home. I waited up as long as I could."

"Everything's fine, dear. I'm going to talk to the person on the phone now, okay? Okay." He turned back to the phone.

"Hello. Yeah, sure, no problem. I'm on my way."

He hung up.

Grenda was sobbing at his side, her face in her hands.

"Now what the hell is this all about?" he thought. He hated it when Grenda made boo-hoo.

"Well, what's wrong?" he asked.

He wasn't exactly patient with this question.

"I don't know," she said, between sobs, "I just feel like you're so far from me. Like we hardly know each other anymore."

Oh Christ. This one again. The old you're-so-far-away. Brother. *Well, how close do you dare get to a big brown bear? They're dangerous, darling.*

"Can't you say something? Can't you hold me? Can't you at least touch me? Just for a little while? Then you can go to your job."

I left my ten-foot pole at work, love. Look, I'm the fucking monkey without the mommy. I didn't even get the cloth doll. I'm the monkey in box C. It's a bare, plastic world. And now that poor little monkey don't wanna touch the big fat bear.

Hume lowered himself from the bed and began putting on his pants.

"Why won't you say anything? Don't you love me anymore?" Grenda got out of bed and put on her robe, the one that Hume always thought had clumps of oatmeal clinging to the terry cloth. He could see her out of the corner of his eye, moving like a huge shadow. She went on, "Do I disgust you? That's how it seems. It's like I make you sick to your stomach!"

Hume swung his head around at that word. Disgust. Because that *was* the word, he realized. But he didn't think *she* knew that that was the word. Yes, she did disgust him. Disgust him and disappoint him. The great big animal pores in her skin. Her smell of flesh. But touch her? Above and beyond. Explain it all? Why bother?, she'd already figured it out. And he wouldn't deny it any longer. He just wouldn't. Not this time. In making this choice, he felt as if he'd done something for the first time in all human history. He felt almost moral.

Grenda crouched on the floor beside the bed. In the dark she really did look like a big, round hump. Hume tried to imagine her as a human, as the person, a girl, he'd married—but he couldn't. It was too hard. Too hard and a very long time ago. In somebody else's life.

"I've got to go see what happened," he said. There'd be time for this later. While his wife remained out of sight behind the bed, Hume went to her dresser and removed his gun guiltily, as if he were borrowing her vibrator for the use of a girlfriend. He felt he'd need a gun today. To protect himself from dead boys among pigs, to protect himself from ursine wives. To protect himself from his own bloody self. And just how was that done with a gun? But he'd show them, the killers. They were keeping their distance today. The killers were well behind the scene, as if they were the world's hidden truth. But he, Detective Hume, wasn't fooled. How could you have all this death and not have killers? Someone would be held responsible.

Then he went out of the room and downstairs, but even when he was out on the street he thought he could feel their whole house rising and falling like shoulders sobbing.

I Want to Make People Weep

"He doesn't keep us waiting. He gets on with it . . ."

D'Annunzio, of the Turkish slippers and sour ideas . . .

the lithe girls kiss the olive oil from his forehead . . . the sweat brought by creditors from whom he has purchased a cellar of wine fit for a poet . . . the best, Mouton Rothschild . . . he jingled ancient coins in his pocket to renew their patina from the heat of his body . . . everyone played the fool to D'Annunzio's poet, except Puccini, who trumped his "poet" with his own "composer of operas" . . . incomparable . . . Puccini, the center to every periphery, lived life like a fire, consuming what came before him . . . a bounder . . .

Giacomo Antonio Domenico Michele Secundo Maria . . .

"And the stars shone and the earth was perfumed / the gate to the garden creaked / and a footstep rustled the sand on the path . . ."

I had no money and smoked only the butts of Tuscan cigars—at least that way people could smell me . . .

I took a girl behind the bathroom and let her take a few puffs on my cigar . . . these memories come to me like the fragrant suggestion of that smoke . . .

Sant'Ambrogio by Giusti, after all . . .

one night, when I was a child, my eyelids froze together . . . later, I jumped up and down at the joy of being able to see . . .

And then there was . . .

Elvira

a grand pain in the ass, she made la dolce vita a pig's life . . . but what a chest! . . . and could she cook! . . . spaghetti alla

239

puttanesca . . .

the Hotel Aurora at Fiesole . . .

the truth is, Puccini never wrote a proper requiem because Puccini wanted nothing to do with death . . . even that says too much . . . to want to have nothing to do with something, you at least have to recognize it . . . give it credence . . . allow it standing . . . when death entered Puccini's life, it was merely a nuisance . . . annoying . . . Puccini's attitude was that of a self-centered infant . . . that's what most art is about, playing in the face of a raging world, doing exactly what you want, without importance, making things out of flowers or caca or whatever presents itself in the moment . . .

just ask Puccini . . .

and as for death, it is the material for sentimental pleasures in opera . . . it's what you put at the ending . . . it is most appropriate for naive young girls . . . they die best . . . it is in fact a species of pleasure . . .

but, really, that requiem, three little half-hearted movements for old Verdi, a sort of public obligation, certainly nothing personal . . .

half a liter of wine, a square of Gorgonzola and a cheroot . . .

he met Elvira at the home of Narciso Gernignani, a friend, a schoolmate, now a prosperous merchant . . .

one may owe some burden of loyalty to a friend, but to a merchant? never! forget it! . . . he didn't even sell things you could eat . . . all durables . . . *serbarla a ricordo de lire* . . .

Puccini noticed Narciso's wife, Elvira . . . he noticed her full indulgent mouth and the hardening of her nipples whenever he kissed her hand . . .

"Fragrant, she entered and fell into my arms . . . "

Les Villi a thicket of blots . . .

roast beef with mushrooms and asparagus, Roquefort, wild strawberries and a Havana

cigar . . .

they went to see the Buffalo Bill Circus . . .

240

Leoncavallo's upturned, waxed moustaches . . .

Porchizia, root here, my love . . . the sheets with certain suspicious
spots . . .

"Oh sweet kisses, oh sweet abandon . . ."

Quaglia alla cacciatora, quail served with garlic, onions, spices and
red wine . . .

the constant need of fresh subjects . . .

as if music wouldn't come on its own terms . . .
and it wouldn't . . .

a musical biography of Buddha? . . .

an exciting idea! . . .
artistic sensualism . . .

Puccini argued that Buddha's large, pale-brown nipples drove
men mad . . .

he looked to Elvira, who blushed and left the room . . .

but he couldn't find the right librettist . . .
wild boar cooked with tomatoes and herbs, served with cheese . . .
"Not suspecting his diabetic condition, they joked about his frequent urination which was gaily ascribed to exhibitionist pride in his
organ . . ."

well, he *was* proud of his organ . . .
"the weariness which comes with sunset stirs the imagination . . . "

he'd wear his big Stetson hat indoors . . .

every municipal band in the country
played tunes from *La Bohème* . . . it was like Sousa . . . he grew to hate
his own creations . . . he hated the world which made him . . .

caca de Puccini . . .

post-bronchial depression
treated with chains of Abdullah cigarettes . . .

Remember the game of oyster? passing the mollusk from my mouth
to the mouth of the young girl . . . sucking the tongue she so gener-
ously introduced into my mouth . . .

"As I trembling unloosed her veils and disclosed her beauty . . ."

Puccini's "Requiem" is three short, if gorgeous, choral movements on the death of Verdi . . . it was as if that were all the time he had for death . . .

"I always loved women with a pronounced scent . . . clad from head to foot except for a hint of the incomparable ivory of her breast . . . then I'd have to seek the source of the aroma . . . and I searched very many women, but low though I was willing to go, I never found it . . . that is the great sadness of my life . . ."

cut prosciutto into thin strips, gather truffles, combine with the tagliatelle . . .

the best truffles are born when lightning strikes oak trees . . .

it was a frankly magnificent erection, I remember it well . . .

Climbing the stairs, I found the door open and my women waiting for me, ready for me, embracing me . . . "Giacomo, you never took a bubble-bath before?" . . . moments later, I entered the bathtub, full of lavender scented foam . . . how many women were there? . . . many . . . enough . . . I floated in the tub in the middle of a garden, next to a fabulous plum tree . . .

and in that time, people really enjoyed perfume! . . . it had nothing to do with "smelling" . . . I'm telling you, nothing to do with smelling at all! . . .

but in the end, it was a pig's life . . . because Elvira could not understand that life was about being large, it was about pale brown nipples, Buddha's or her own, erections magnificent or otherwise, smoked trout and Ruffino . . . a melody that makes men weep . . . tears the heart out of the fuckers . . .

"Oh vanished forever is that dream of love, fled is that hour . . ."

no, Christ, fuck it . . . Elvira! . . . deranged by menopause, the simple bourgeois . . . Madame *Pomme de terre* . . . hounded Doria, the simple little servant, into suicide with her mad claims that she'd been shtupping Puccini in the gazebo, in the basement, behind the root stocks . . . wherever . . . but for just that once she was wrong . . . Doria died a virgin . . . and Elvira was found liable and given jail time . . . Puccini wandered, grumbling, what the hell? . . . women are morons . . .

and then his damned jaw and throat . . . quick as that . . . a billion cigarettes paved the way . . . carve it away, then . . . carve my jaw away . . . what good is it to me? . . . the radium necklace . . . the radium needles inserted directly into the tumor under local anaesthetic . . . screw it . . . bury me in that fast little Fiat . . . and keep the wolf hence, would you, I'm talking about her! . . . and see if the little girls, the flower girls, the waitresses and geishas and chorus girls, can come . . . can they sing? I'd like them to sing . . . something even more beautiful than anything I ever wrote . . . and please not one damned thing from that fucking *La Bohème* . . .

      but the girls, the little flower girls, they don't remember me? . . . all married to durable goods merchants? . . . none of them remember? . . . their sweet little tongues! . . . unbelievable . . . they don't even remember the mollusks!? . . .

 "I still want to make people weep; therein lies everything . . ."

      the crackle of dead leaves . . .

 "And desperately I die . . ."

      my Butterfly! . . .

the white patches in his hair showed plainly through the dye . . .

 Toscanini: "Here the opera ends, because at this point the Maestro died . . ."

     "And never before have I loved life so much . . ."

     It is said that his fingers moved over the coverlet as if he were playing the piano.

Who Cannot Weep May Learn from Thee (4)

MURDERER: That's where Nebuchadnezzar comes in.

PROPHET: Nebuchadnezzar?

MURDERER: It's what we had in common.

PROPHET: Which was . . . ?

MURDERER: We "took revenge on the whole world."

PROPHET: You would call slaughtering your own wife and child taking revenge on the world?

MURDERER: In small.

PROPHET: In small? What do you mean?

MURDERER: C'mon, man. I thought you were educated. "In small." It's an expression.

PROPHET: Forget the pretensions. You slaughtered your wife and child because of your wife's insult to your infantile sexual ego.

MURDERER: Talk about pretensions.

PROPHET: *(Exasperated)* Just get on with it. This is getting old. I've got more interesting people to talk to.

MURDERER: *(As if seized by divine compulsion)* I gave them fair warning. I said, do not disobey a single one of my orders. Fulfill them exactly as I have commanded, and do it without delay. But if you resist, I will show you no quarter but deliver you to slaughter. What I say I will accomplish by my power.

PROPHET: But she didn't obey.

MURDERER: No. She did not obey. And so I did my thing, or the first part of it. That's where the court orders came in. The injunctions. All the ceasing and desisting. The restraining. The court mandates. The abrogations of basic rights. The annulments. The searches and seizures. The random testing. The protective custody. The legal retribution. In short, the insults and humiliations directed at me by the British bitch through the instrumentality of the court.

PROPHET: *(Look of stunned incredulity)*

MURDERER: Okay, moron, I'll start over. If you and me and Nebuchudnezzar want revenge against the whole world, you must start at home. We're serious about the *whole* world, right? That implies your family as well as everybody else's. So you show you're serious about his. You're not messin' around. Okay, so, once you are on task you take things one at a time. First, you call in sick. You got other things to do today. You cash out your savings and any retirement money you can get your hands on. You gas the SUV up. You don't forget the gun. You wait near what used to be your home (that you are *still* paying for) for your wife to arrive with your daughter. You walk calmly toward them. Your daughter is still in the child seat. It's the kind of child seat that requires that she look backward. (Maybe she even saw your vehicle parked down the block. Maybe she even said, "Hey, Mommy, I see Daddy's car!") The British bitch is anxious, her adrenaline is sure enough going, but she knows she's got that restraining order. That you-can't-touch-me piece of paper. And you've been good about visitation. Always brought the Littlest Lesbian back on time. You continue approaching and she starts into the logical argument the premise of which is, "I don't want to have to hurt you." With her pieces of paper, with her prick lawyer. But the gun says, "No more talk." Bam! Down she goes. Awkwardly. Not a good fall. For some reason you feel contempt for the ungainly way she falls. She's put on some weight you think. Another insult: women are supposed to lose weight during divorces! But when she falls it's real sack-of-potatoes time. And you know how they say that the fact of the murder itself as opposed to the idea of killing, the desire to kill, is always shocking and tends to return you to reality. Forget that. You think, "I hope that hurt a lot. I'd like to do it again. Into infinity." Then you look inside at your child, strapped in her child seat. Does shooting her seem excessive? She's so small. Forget it, you blast her and get the fuck out of there.

On the way out of town, going down the coast, tearing through the magnificent conifers, big as you, you use your cellular phone to call a buddy back at work. "I took care of that problem I was telling you about." "What problem?" "You don't need to know details. Just be cool and I'll see you around."

Jezebel Shall Be Like Dung (3)

I have never had an orgasm. It is a point of personal pride with me, and it shows to just what extent I am God's boy after all. Do you know the story of Jezebel? Thrown to her death. Fed to dogs. Spread on the fields. Well, here's a riddle that I have puzzled over for many years: the eunuchs took the side of the Lord against Jezebel, killer of eight hundred prophets, child killers in their own turn. Who was in the right?

The Seven Last Words of Christ (4)

Something Understood . . . "Suddenly afraid, half waking, half sleeping, and greatly dismayed, a woman sat weeping. . . ."

Three days after his death, Haydn's grave was disturbed by two well-known men of Vienna—Johann Nepomuk (!) Peter and Josep Karl Rosenbaum—who severed Haydn's head from his torso for the purpose of studying his skull. The two were advocates of phrenology and sought to relate the shape of Haydn's skull to theories about genius. If the shape of genius was to be found anywhere, it would be found formed in the skull of Joseph Haydn. This skull-theft was a more or less open secret in Vienna.

Except to Prince Nicholas Esterházy. The Prince brought Haydn's sarcophagus to his castle for the performance of a requiem in 1820. Haydn's body had been resting in place and missing its head for twenty years. To the Prince's horror, when the sarcophagus was opened, he found only Haydn's wig. Imagine that. They cut his head off and left the wig behind. Is the wig a metaphor? It makes me physically ill to think of that wig. Resting there wrongly for years.

Even in the days after the Great Revolutions (which Vienna only just escaped; on the day Haydn died, his building was struck by Napoleonic cannon fire), an angry Prince imagined that he could accomplish what he wanted to accomplish, especially when his magisterial wrath was focused on a little phrenologist. He demanded the return of the skull. He got a skull promptly, but it was the cranium of a man no more than twenty years of age.

The Prince protested once more, maybe now beginning to suspect a limit to his *puissance* in this new bourgeois era. He then received a more appropriately aged skull with which, as far as we know, he was content. (That was finally the fatal flaw with those princes: they were no smarter than anyone else, maybe less so, as the peasant-genius Haydn demonstrated for nearly a century.)

Still, it wasn't Haydn's skull. No, that truest skull stayed far from his body for more than one hundred years. It was returned to his sarcophagus at Eisenstadt in 1952, where it still keeps its secrets about genius quite to itself.

In the year Haydn died, 1809, one Georg Wilhelm Friedrich Hegel had only recently finished writing *The Phenomenology of Spirit.* Napoleon's troops passed his window at Jena, on their way east, in all probability carrying with them the cannon ball that would rock old Haydn's home.

According to Hegel, the fundamental argument of phrenology to humans is: "your reality is a bone."

Who Cannot Weep May Learn from Thee (5)

MURDERER: *(Puts his hand on Prophet's knee)* Hey, what's the matter? You're shaking. Are those real tears, buddy?

PROPHET: What do you think? Your story.

MURDERER: Oh, come on. It's just a story, man. Only some little words. You must hear this stuff all the time, in your job. And how do you know that I really did it?

PROPHET: But you did do it.

MURDERER: Yeah, well, so what?

PROPHET: Yeah, well, it was pretty awful even just to have to imagine, that's so what.

MURDERER: Oh, grow up. You're the one who wanted this little conversation. Remember? Practically dragged me out of my cell.

PROPHET: Fine, we're done now and I'm leaving.

MURDERER: Wait a minute. Don't go mad or anything. Don't we get a cool down or debriefing or some sort of closure? Cup of coffee? They'll bring it if we ask for it. To tell you the truth, they're really pretty decent to me here. Starbucks too. Decaf, light and dark brew. They even have an espresso machine. I'm all alone here, you know. Just these cold stone walls.

PROPHET: *(Appealed to against his will)* I'm sorry. It's true. I did ask you to tell me the story.

MURDERER: That's right. It's almost like your fault.

PROPHET: But I've got to go. Sorry. *(Extends his hand)*

MURDERER: Me too. Sorry. For all the good that does. There's no end to sorry once you get started. Sorry can go pretty deep. Sorry you did something, sorry your dad beat the shit out of you, sorry you were born, sorry for the sorry-ass earth.

PROPHET: Don't say that.

MURDERER: *(Laughing)* Still the good boy prophet. Funny. Well, at least I know what a prophet is now. But, hey, what's your name, your *real* name?

PROPHET: I don't know if I'm supposed to tell you.

MURDERER: Oh big deal. Come on. My name's Thomas.

PROPHET: Okay. I'm Chris.

MURDERER: Chris. Good to meet you, Chris. Take care.

PROPHET: Yeah. Same to you.

MURDERER: Bye now.

PROPHET: Bye.

Isolation (7)

Dear Editor:

I am writing this letter from a local motel room which I have rented because I have reason to fear for my life. Because of my enemies, I have to change motels and rooms randomly every day. But they should not make the mistake of being cocky: I am well-armed. Ever hear of a "tank buster"?

But on with my story.

Just a few short days ago, I was sitting in my own home watching television. I was relaxing after a long day of hard work. Suddenly, I became aware that the guidance systems generated by a network of twenty-four military satellites had provided coordinates to Stealth fighter-bombers and Apache helicopters and that these enormously destructive weapons had discreetly focused laser guidance devices on my own home zeroing in on me through my digital cable pickup. This is something that they can do to virtually any home in America at their pleasure. And this capacity is present because of our own insistence that we have fiber-optic cable connections for TV, computer and telephone. Please, folks, before it's too late, pause now in reading this letter, go into the living room and rip the TV cable from the wall. Do not forget any upstairs or secondary sets you may have.

Now, my own home is a brick home and I selected it from a vast market of housing options precisely because an older brick home can withstand a lot. But we are talking laser-guided cruise missiles here!

I promise you it was a very eerie feeling to know so certainly that my own government had brought these modern crosshairs on my own home. If others are sitting in their homes and feel an extraordinary searing, tingling, as if their blood is being boiled from inside their veins, I suggest you do as I have done. Your life and the lives of your loved ones are more important than your possessions. Move out and check in. Our little town has many affordable lodging options. You can disconnect the motel cable system on the TV with a Crescent wrench. Frankly, given the resources and ethical thinking at work in those wrathful and unconstitutional forces to which I am calling your attention, it is a matter of little difference to them if they have to take out a whole wing of a Motor Lodge, torching the good parents of Springfield and boiling their immature offspring in the motel pool, so long as they get their mark. Just ask the people of Iraq.

One further word of strategic advice, when planning your move to your next motel, do not make reservations ahead of time. But do be aware that if you live in a college town, as I do, you may have difficulty finding an empty room on weekends featuring homecoming, parents' day, a football game, high school tournaments, or the rare political inauguration. Plan accordingly. And don't be shy about using threats with that out-of-town girls volleyball team if you really need the room. There are pressures on you they wouldn't understand.

For personal reasons, I would like to return to my house some day. Lord knows what I will find there. I shiver to think about it. I will continue to read the pages of your newspaper daily to see if there have been any mysterious bombings.

In fact, the purpose of this letter is to signal to you, "heads up," please do cover all home bombings as I am eagerly awaiting information. If my home is bombed, I would like to know about it so that I can get on with my life.

Thank you,

Marty Monday
Champaign-Urbana

How Sex Lost Its Body

Hi, my name is Chad. I'm a bounder.

[Long pause]

Go on.

That's it. That's all I have to say.

That's it?

Yep.

You have to speak, you know.

You're not going to pull that willed-where-willing-and-doing-are-one crap on me, are you?

How do you know about that?

Ha!

So you're really not going to talk?

What you know you know. That's it. Henceforth etc.

You're being cryptic.

No. I'm being allusive. Don't you know Shakespeare? Iago? No wonder you didn't get the Dante. I always loved that guy, Iago, his pose. "What you know you know." Awesome. Totally controlled.

That's right. I forgot you and Michelle were English majors. So you're not going to say anything about the time you took Murphy to that woman in order to watch them perform an unnatural act?

Oh jeez, that time. That one was so embarrassing. But that was like hardly the first time I'd taken Murph on one of our little walks. I think he just hit the wall. I guess even dogs can get confused and depressed. You could kind of see it in his eyes: "What is this person to me?" Very moral, really. Especially for a dog. I would have been moved by it, I think, if I didn't like that scene so much. And that woman, what the hell was her name? She was fucking hot. I wanted to see that dog stuff all over her boobies.

Hmmm. What do you like about bestiality?

Oh no. Like I said, I'm not talking. Total silence. I'm like the grave, my friend.

[*Pause*]

Unless what you wanna know is how Michelle got started in her little cottage industry.

Sure. You can tell me that.

As I recall, check with her on this, it was the first night we slept together. We got it on big time. Fell asleep around three in the morning. Then just before dawn, she woke up with a start, screamed and started pushing me out of the bed. I turned on the bedside light. She was looking at me in bewilderment like she didn't know who I was. This of course did make a certain amount of sense. It was, after all, our first night together. I figured a little first time anxiety was coming out. So I just said, "It's okay, honey, relax, it's me, Chad." Which was really a funny thing for me to say, come to think of it, because I don't even know if I'd told her my name, or my right name, at that point. So she said, quite appropriately, "Chad?" She didn't remember who she was sleeping with. I was humiliated, although for no good reason. Was I supposed to explain to her who I was? Then she said, "How did a dog get in my bed?" "What?" And she looked at me very hard. "You're not a dog, are you?"

"No."

"I thought you were a dog."

"A dog?"

She fell back over onto her side, trying to remember what she'd experienced, that faraway look in her eyes. I just let her calm down and figure it out on her own.

"I must have been dreaming," she said.

"Guess so."

"But it was so real."

She paused, looking straight up, confused again.

"And so erotic."

"Huh?" I asked her, "say what?"

"The dog was fucking me so beautifully. It felt incredible. He was so kind and gentle and considerate and emotionally engaged."

"The dog? The bow-wow dog was emotionally engaged?"

I had no idea what to say. She just lay there, staring up, and kinda smiling.

What your girlfriend experienced is called a "bed trick," if I'm not mistaken. There are hundreds of tales ranging across time and place in which you go to bed with someone you think you know, and when you wake up, you discover that it was someone else—another man, a brother is a very popular option, or another woman, or a god, or a snake, or an alien, or your mother or father.

But a dog?

Well, it's the first time I've heard of a plain domestic dog in one of these, but like I said the animal option is not unusual.

Okay.

It was really a very spiritual moment for her I suspect.

[*Laughing*] Oh, sure was, doc, sure was!

Why are you laughing?

Some people are too much, that's why. Anyway, that's just the beginning of my story. The next week I came over again and what do you know, she's bought a puppy. An Irish setter. The famous Mr. Murphy. So I said, "I didn't know you had a puppy."

"I didn't. I bought him from a breeder this week."

I looked at her. "Am I supposed to feel jealous?"

"Jealous? Why should my buying a puppy make you jealous?"

"Well, don't you remember your dream last time? Is that what this is about?"

"Oh. I forgot about that," she says. "How embarrassing. Gee, I don't think there's a relation."

Anyway, I let it slide. Our relationship developed well. We got along, liked each other, had something to share because we were literature majors, after all, but also the sex was incredible. The strange thing here is that at the same time I had the clearest presentiment that I ought to kill the dog, the dog as a young rake, but it was also me who took the next step in Michelle's development as, how shall I say, fancier of dogs.

You know, according to Michelle, she doesn't even like dogs.

How would you know that? Have you interviewed her, too?

Not exactly. She says she does it for the money.

Oh, sure, I believe that. It's only that bounder old Chad that really likes the weird shit. Everybody else in this world is just right as rain. Okay, listen, about six months into the thing, we're high on something, coke I think, and doing a little bondage. Nothing outrageous, just some old cloth karate belts around the wrist and ankles. I've got her tied up. And Murphy wanders into the room. That's when it occurs to me. So I get him up there and try to stick his nose in her crotch. But you know what?, he's not interested. Michelle is blindfolded, so she's not quite sure what's going on. I run to the kitchen and grab a jar of peanut butter. Spread a little messily on her cunt and *now* I've got ol' Murph's attention. He's lappin' it up and Michelle is screaming and moaning at the same time. Murph would finish one serving and look up for the next. I'll never forget that look in his eyes. It was, "Hey, I didn't think you even liked me, but this is all right!" He really loved that peanut butter. Seemed pretty oblivious to the rest of it. Believe me, Michelle was not.

After that, she wouldn't even speak to me for a while. We went two-three weeks without talking. But by the time we got back in touch, she already had found a sponsor site and was into the online sex with animals scene big time. When we did get back together, she gave me a hug and a kiss. "I forgive you." "Okay, so, hey, why didn't you return my calls then?" Shrug. "I've been busy." You know, there's something about when women shrug that I just hate. It really makes me crazy. It's like, shrugging is not something women should do.

As for "busy," I guess so! She and Murph were making buckets of money. Let's be honest, Michelle is a fucking good-looking woman, and the breast enhancements haven't hurt a damned thing, and in his own way Murph is an awesome dog. Check out that coat. And like most setters, he is hung okay. Better than me, I'd say, pound for pound, and I don't particularly like to say that. Some guys out there (but it wasn't just guys, let me say) couldn't stay away from Michelle's scene. I don't know how they explained those credit-card bills, but they must have been huge. They were like mollusks on that site. Schlupp, I'm stuck here and I'm not leavin' unless I'm pried off.

So, the bottom line is, this whole bestiality thing was your doing?

How do you conclude that? I had a role. I'd call myself a bit player.

Then came the dog abduction and abuse, right? You snatching Murph away for various escapades?

Our little walks? Yeah. God that was funny. Murph loved going for walks, but after a while when I got the leash he'd fight like hell. I had to drag him out. Michelle didn't know what was going on.

And because of that, you and Michelle are no longer together, right?

She took it the wrong way, really. It still hurts me to think about.

Treachery affects some people that way. But what about you, did it also affect you negatively?

I guess so. I live alone. I work on my master's thesis. I'm doing an analysis of C. P. Snow's *Strangers and Brothers* series. A low-tech approach theoretically. Beyond that, I try to cultivate Iago's silence, not very well obviously. But I feel that I have learned a lot about life, even if what I've learned comes under the heading "tragic knowledge." One very interesting and unexpected thing is that I'm starting to understand my father. He was a very quiet, uncommunicative, withdrawn man, and I always interpreted his silence to mean in some awful way that he didn't love me. This famous taciturnity of men in marriage feels like lack of caring to the others in the family. Especially to wives, who accept their husbands' self-absorption as a final, long burden which they must suffer without comment. So marriage becomes a forced yoking of two people without comments. From the father's perspective, however, this silence is in fact—and this is the substance of my insight—the *kindest* and most *polite* but personally *resigned* consequence of his profound sense of disappointment in and betrayal by the wife, marriage, family, children, human relations in general, and life universally. This is a disappointment and sense of betrayal—a *knowledge* of failure—which he comes to think of as impenetrable to words, inexpressible, and uncorrectable by anything he might try to do. This all becomes, finally, the sadness which is his life's most conspicuous Truth. The simplest form this Truth takes is silence. What it means is that though he may be married, and he may have children, he will die alone.

Chad! That's so deep! Especially for a dog kidnapper, molester, abuser. I have to say that your reputation doesn't entirely do you justice.

Oh, I know. I'm more than Chad dog-sex-voyeur. We're all more than we are. On the other hand, I did those things. They're concrete in a way my "truths" can't be.

Well, it was a pleasure to meet you anyway. May I shake your hand?

Whoa! No one's wanted to do that in a while. Aren't you afraid of what might come off?

Don't get me wrong. I think your conduct is disgusting and reprehensible. But I'm impressed with your self-awareness of your utterly flawed humanity.

But we're not done are we?

Yes. You can return to the depths of your Iago-like inscrutability.

You're not leaving, are you?

Yes. I've got to run along. You're not the only guy on today's list.

Look, man, don't leave yet. I don't want to be alone. I'm not as brave as my father. Besides, there's other stuff I could tell you.

Jesus, you're becoming a regular Chatty Cathy. There's a difference between Chatty Cathy and Iago, you know.

Don't rub it in.

Okay. What do you want to talk about?

I haven't told you about *my* site.

You have a site.

Oh yeah. Fucking hell yeah.

What is it?

My site is a real-time video feed. I rent a loft downtown with three video cameras in a line hookup to a collaborative site called www.sevenjewels.com. I'm on live from about nine in the morning to dinner time. Working hours, more or less. It's called "Chad's Rich Inner Life." I do two things. I lift weights and I masturbate.

You are a pumped guy.

Everything gets archived too. DVD so it's real compact. Sometimes I watch my own archives while I'm masturbating. My clients love that one. Some of them tell me that they video themselves masturbating or having sex while watching the video feed of me masturbating while watching a DVD of myself masturbating or being blown by a temp worker.

Don't tell me they have temp workers for this stuff.

Welcome to the 21st century.

Wow.

So what do you think?

Vertiginous. I don't know whether to be aroused or nauseous.

Well, don't get either right now. I'm not in the mood.

Does Michelle know about this adventure?

Yeah. She checks it out all the time. She's not threatened, though. There are thousands of sites like mine. People want it, but they get lost in the options. Actually, my venture into online sex has kinda brought me and Michelle back together. My site is more cutting edge. The erotic content is actually part of the formal features of the site *and* the emerging technology of the Net. Hers is more straight ahead. For her, the computer is just a modern dirty magazine. She's capable of being culturally punky in some ways. Especially if you request and pay for punk. I'm still a fan of her work. Frankly, I believe sites like ours are reinventing the species.

The human species?

Of course.

Is that a good thing?

We'll see.

God.

God?

I'm a little overwhelmed.

Buck up, kiddo. The bottom line is good. Michelle and I are no longer engaged in the old-fashioned sense, perhaps, but in some very unexpected ways we are closer than we have ever been.

And Murphy? Is he doing okay?

Actually, that too is a complicated story. I don't know how he is and neither does Michelle. He's gone.

Gone? Did you lose him? Did he run away? Hit by a car? Stolen by another woman? What?

I'd put it this way: Murph is off doing his own thing. I suspect he has his own site by now. That dog is capable of it. I search for it, but there's just so much out there. Sometimes I think every American fat, skinny, and indifferent has a site. In one sense or another. We're each one lost in his or her own site of his or her choosing. I think it goes back to our nation's founding principles. The only problem is it just gets so darned dark. As for Murph, I'll find him eventually. How many dog sites can there be, after all? I got a tip the other day that he was involved in that Dogs Against Sadness movement. Dogs Against the Sexual Abuse of Dogs. Something like that. I'll have to warm up the old search engine and see.

Look, there's one more question I was supposed to ask but I didn't quite have the heart for. Did you ever fuck a dog yourself?

Do you have to ask that?

I tried to avoid it and if you'd let me out of here earlier we might have, but now I must.

What is this "must" stuff? I don't get it but you're right. I can feel the little sucker of awful compulsion moving up like poison through my veins. Lord. Yes, I did. I fucked a little schnauzer-type dog one afternoon. It was my aunt's dog. Name of Diane, or Deedee. I did it right on my aunt's crinoline sofa. With the doilies. I was fourteen and my aunt was supposed to be "watching" me. Watch this, you old hag. She was "viewing," as she used to say, reruns of Lawrence Welk in her little television room. Couldn't have the old box in the living room like regular people. That black-and-white world, those sounds. Pure despair. At the same time, I found Welk's music weirdly erotic in the way things have to be erotic to want to fuck your aunt's schnauzer-type dog.

Go on.

I can only remember the look of lostness, dog accumulation of horror, shaky pain, faint wet pushing sounds from her mouth, abject belligerence, as if she would nip me if she weren't so sad, the thought of having any old thing for dinner afterwards, sitting with little girls on the porch, standing still, leaning slightly and warmly, a certain kind of shock setting in, the idea of armchairs as places of comfort, sparks in her cerebellum, the intense desire to run away, run away, run away, and never stop. I didn't come though. At one point she gave me this little grieving look back over her shoulder and I realized I had hurt her feelings. Plus the smell. It was like. . . .

Stop. [Bows his head into his lap]

Huh?

[Puts his hands to his head] I can't take this anymore. I don't care what I'm supposed to do. This I can't take.

Wait a minute. Hold on. I heard this about you. You're not going to start . . . oh yes you are . . . crying on me. Yep. You are. Too late. Okay, that's it, get outta here. We're done. I know I'm done. What you know you know. From this point hence and so on. I'm outta here.

Isolation (8)

Dear Editor:

I have been deeply troubled by a number of things–thought-things, ideas, you might call them–which I hope you or your staff can help me with.

First, I have found myself thinking deeply and obsessively about certain passages from the Bible. I admit I have found myself frightened by these passages. The Bible terrifies me.

The Bible says (actually it is Himself speaking in Genesis), "Thus my covenant shall be in your flesh as an everlasting pact." He was speaking, of course, of his desire that boys be circumcised. I have two questions with regard to these lines. First, just how "everlasting" did he imagine the penis to be? I'm quite familiar with my own penis. My personal penis was circumcised at my mother's request and for no reason having anything to do with a contract with God. She merely wished that I should look like the other boys in this most boyish of worlds. Thus question number one point two: with whom, then, is my covenant? The other boys? But nothing about this weird "pact" seems to me "everlasting," especially at my sixty-something age. And why the penis?, especially since God is interested in something eternal or at least somewhat durable, which any woman I have ever been with may tell you mine is not.

Okay. Let's move on. Question two: For some reason when I see the word "circumcised," I read "circumscribed." Written around. Have other readers expressed this confusion? For me, this passage is about God surrounding us with his language, and carving that language in our very flesh. I see God as a small, peculiar, infinitely particular Asian man, with the little flowing goatee and celestial robe, the whole bit, holding in His hand what is essentially an Exacto knife, carving with great patience some obscure script into the flesh of some poor lost soul's penis. The script runs around it like runes in an obelisk. (I have begun asking my wife to search my penis for these "runes," but she has looked only once, and refused ever since. Editor, my wife has not been home in four days. Some vague complaint in her note about no longer wishing to indulge "male self-absorption.") So, how is this a question? Did God mean to carve some sort of message in our flesh? And if He did, what was the message?

In another "related" passage in the Good Book of Terror, it reads, "You shall not boil a kid in its mother's milk." And my thought is: was this something that needed to be said? Or was this the first time such a thing had been suggested? Once suggested, did people not wonder what it would taste like to boil a kid in its mother's milk? Did God, in short, not create a new temptation, mischievously? Did people not imagine that the milky sauce would be more piquant *because of God's prohibition?* Is God's law not the negative spice of life? Should Martha Stewart produce a cookbook called *Cooking with God*?

One might well ask the same question with regard to the prohibition against sexual relations with animals. *Was this something that needed to be said way back then?!* Or just what was going on out in Zion? Paul had it right in Romans 7: "When the commandment came, sin became alive."

Finally, I have been heart-struck by Esau's complaint to old Isaac, "Have you only that one blessing, Father?" I think of that line and poor Esau's terrible grief and I begin to weep.

Lack. A moment lost. Let me give you an example.

Last night I was listening to Bruckner's *Ninth Symphony,* the second movement, the great scherzo, the scherzo after which no scherzos are needed. So convinced am I by Bruckner's scherzo that I went through all of Mahler's symphonies, re-recording them to CD but deleting the scherzos. (In Symphonies 2-7, if you're curious.) I was also reading

Dostoevsky's *Brothers Karamazov* as I listened. And with a flash it occurred to me with real force that I was almost certainly the only person listening to just this music and reading just this novel in the whole of our little town. I imagined my neighbors watching the Animal Channel on their TVs. Or communally enjoying *Judge Judy*. Thousands of them apart yet together. None of them was alone as I was alone. In fact, I quickly concluded, I was probably beyond all probability the only creature in this country, on this planet, in this galaxy reading Dostoevsky while listening to Bruckner *at that moment.*

And I thought again, as think I must, of old Esau. "Only one blessing, Father?"

Do you see?

Furthermore, it struck me, as I recorded a maimed Mahler to CD, that our commitment to the madness of the magic of digital binaries, those 0s and 1s, is like old King Saul's decision to kill young David. Yes. For we are told that "an evil spirit from the Lord came upon Saul." That's what our commitment to computers and machines and bureaucracies is like. A madness. An evil spirit. Because these machines are all infernal machines. We will follow this madness in spite of the obvious as if it were our fate, just as death is our fate, for some old, obscure sin none of us remembers.

Because of computers (and bureaucracies) there are no human beings left who can produce what either Bruckner or Dostoevsky created. There was something that was a human capacity that is no longer a human capacity. Think about that! Then ask your Lord, only one blessing? All to Bruckner? Nothing to me? I am fated by you to be caught up in the circuits of this Big Machine, a puny ghost-bot in the electronic stew? Lost in a digital snowstorm wide as consciousness? Dostoevsky's clerks to the Czar's bureaucracy had it better. At least they could feel their own mutilation!

Well, these were my accelerated thoughts that long, dismal, Dostoevskian evening.

Tragically, my thinking that night on this subject was hardly done. It was pulled forcefully along by Bruckner's energetic "joke." For it occurred to me that, as much as I listen to Bruckner, I believe I am missing things. In fact, I fear I'm missing the whole of it! The notes run by, scampering like tiny insects. So, I thought, I will have to proceed one bar at a time. I even looked for *legato* passages to study. I put a phrase of Bruckner's Ninth on repeat and recorded it to another blank CD. I had seventy minutes of this one phrase. I've listened to it now maybe a dozen times. And do you know what, sir? I am still convinced that there is something there that I am not quite getting. A tickle. An ineluctable squiggle of the true import . . . of just this one phrase! Never mind that the damn thing goes on then bar after damnable bar, each bar with its own abysmal secret to conceal from me. It's like wanting to swallow the ocean. Or if I could just make time stop, then perhaps I could hear in the hemi-demi-quavers the understanding (hear that word, Mr. Editor, *under*-standing; I want to be this music's Atlas) that I seek.

That I seek! I can't even write a coherent sentence let alone understand the ugly German, Bruckner.

And on what can I blame our tawdry, fallen state? I will tell you so that you know: Windows 98. Mariah Carey.

Basta,

Mister Krips

(PS: should this be over your maximum word limit for letters to the editor, please feel free to edit.)

Requiescant in Pace

The Human Condition (4)

This time he stepped out of his boat deliberately. He was in a small rowboat on Fancy Bluff Creek. For some reason, he was living in Georgia now. He was trying to salvage a piece of his dock which had been busted up by a recent storm. The marshy creek bed was at low tide. He stepped out, careful to make sure that the muddy creek would support him. But within two steps he plunged to mid-chest in a sinkhole. His pet cocker spaniel Goldie was along for the ride. She came right over to the edge of the boat and looked down on him, her wavy, regal ears flapping gently in a mild offshore breeze. She didn't bark. In fact, she didn't seem agitated at all. She would occasionally lift her brown nose, sniffing the air, reaching toward him, but that was about it. She just kept her gentle brown eyes fixed on her master, sunk to his neck in mud. Oddly, her calm seemed to insist on his calm. He was quite relaxed about the whole thing, dying though he might be. After a while, he began to think that Goldie was judging him. Evaluating him. And it struck him: his dog was God. Dogod. Do good. Had he? He couldn't say for sure if he had or not, to tell the truth. He looked into the limpid brown depths of her eyes. Goldie? Girl? Is that you in there? Can I make my peace with you? I'm sorry for all I've done. Do you forgive me, girl? And she bent down and touched her cold nose to his. Oh, if Michelangelo could have seen that scene!

In a tributary of the Fancy Bluff Creek, in a saltwater marsh in southwestern Georgia he was saved. He felt it. The salvation. Thank you, Goldie. Thank you very much, girl. He looked around him at the forest and the water and he smelled the gorgeous rot of his sinkhole and he was a little ecstatic at the sticky freshness of it all. He began to cry.

That's when the Coast Guard rescuers got to him. They got him out of the creek and into an ambulance. Ordinarily, they would have taken him to the hospital for a quick checkup and then sent him home. But he kept babbling about how fresh and beautiful everything looked, even the jowly doctor and the downright homely med tech. Then he described how his cocker spaniel, Goldie, had redeemed him. So they decided to keep him overnight for observation.

He never exactly said that his dog hadn't redeemed him, but he seemed otherwise okay, even better than okay, so they sent him home where his wife and little girl and Goldie greeted him happily.

Every night thereafter, he would sit on his front porch alone with Goldie and give her a doggie treat and scratch her behind the ears and maybe sip at a beer, and together they would watch the sunset, gloriously.

The Modern Castrati (2)

May I speak with Dr. Ditto, please?

( )

Yes, this is Tom X. I'm a former patient.

( )

I'm not sure how long it's been. Less than a year.

( )

Great. Yes, I'll hold.

( )

Dr. Ditto, hi, this is Tom X., your patient from a while ago.

( )

Well, I'm doing okay except for a couple of things which I thought I'd talk to you about if it was convenient. Do you have a minute?

( )

Sure, we can make an appointment, but I'm having some experiences, very interesting experiences, sort of right now, maybe too interesting as experiences go, if you follow me.

( )

Great. Thanks. I really appreciate it. Thank you *very* much. I don't know exactly how to begin this so I'll just blurt it out: I spent last night with Clara Schumann. Née Clara Weick.

( )

Oh, I'm so glad that you know who she was.

( )

That's a very good and astute question. It's just the right question, under the circumstances. Of course, I'm not sure how to explain it to your satisfaction or my own. But I do have a theory. I believe that what has happened, essentially, is that the Net, you know, the Web, called by some the really very revealing name of "Ether-net," has become so vast and the holes in this Net, created by our myriad crisscrossing communications and investigations and perusals and just plain looking, that this Web or Ether-net or what-you-will has begun catching the souls of the dead as if they were bugs in a spider's web and holding them in our realm.

Now, I know this sounds a little mad which is in part why I called you rather than my department's technical support staff, most of whom I would suspect of being in on a scam like this. But this instance with Clara Schumann is not my only evidence that something is going on out there. A little earlier this year I began an online relationship with a woman called Honeycomb. I thought at first she was an amateur porn personality at a site called "Teenslut," but as things developed I learned that in fact she was, or would have been, a seventy-something housewife from the Cleveland area. Shades of Abraham's Sarah, right?!

( )

Well, doctor, it's in the Bible. Genesis.

( )

No I'm not lording my "eccentric" knowledge over you again. And besides, what's eccentric about the Bible?

( )

I agree. So, as I say, "would have been," she would have been seventy-something if it weren't for the fact that she claimed to be dead.

( )

Dead as in toten, muerte, defunctis.

( )

So as we puzzled this out together I was able to deduce that she had been inadvertently captured by the World Wide Web, scooped up like a hapless dolphin in a tuna net, and discovered in the electronic/spiritual ambience by some webmaster prodigy at Teenslut and marketed to unsuspecting guys like me as fresh teen meat. Those guys must have been laughing their butts off when they weren't scared to death by the implications of what they were doing.

( )

How do I know? Tests. Certain tests.

( )

I don't want to go into any detail.

( )

Yes, my reluctance is shame based.

( )

No, I think you're wrong there, this time. I say it's "shame based" because they were shameful. My tests. What I did. I will only say this, the tests involved kitchen appliances.

( )

No, of course not, smaller than that.

( )

Right. We'd better get back to Mrs. Schumann. What's scary about this metempsychotic situation I'm describing. . . . By the way, don't you think that's a clever word for this situation? "Metempsychotic"? Of course you get it. You know about metempsychosis, right? Anyway, what's scary about this situation is that it seems to be "progressing," as if it were a disease. But if what we're talking about is essentially a *mechanical* circumstance involving computers, the Internet and the spirits of the deceased, how can it be progressing? But progressing it is. It has gone from being something of a weird curiosity on the Net, to being something equally weirdly tactile, and now the whole thing is falling out of this Ether and into my lap. Literally. Clara Schumann was in my lap. I mean, what could be next? Actually, I'm afraid to think that thought. Maybe "next" is *me* getting sucked into the binary Ether! Maybe this machine has a reverse!

( )

I know she died a long time ago. I've been thinking about that little logistical problem. I can't resolve it yet, I'm sorry to say. Maybe the Net reaches further than any of us can imagine. How do we know exactly what it is we do, what realities we mess with when we invent these toys. Maybe we're reaching across some fucking space/time continuum thing.

( )

No, that's not technical language and I'm sorry I forgot your little rule about the f-word. May I continue?

( )

Yes, I know you are not an opportunity for me to act out hostilities. I'm sorry. Again.

( )

Thank you. The one thing that I have learned is that toward the end of their life together Robert and Clara Schumann would join with friends to play at table turning. This was largely Robert's weird enthusiasm. Prelude to his total mental breakdown, perhaps. Reflective of his own cerebral "haunting." But table turning is, I think, the analogue version of the "digital" phenomenon I'm experiencing: the invocation of the dead. The making-present of ghosts. So perhaps her own earlier participation in such demonic activities made her especially vulnerable to these Net eccentricities. I don't know. I'm speculating here. I just teach composition and introductory literature classes for not-very-bright students at a "direction" university in dear old venereal Florida. I don't think that the legislators who fund us annually are even clear about where exactly we are. Northwest Florida State

University. I think Northwest Florida is in Alabama. Teaching stupid kids in a stupid place that has only a marginal existence in the Official Mind means that I function in a sort of cognitive Bermuda Triangle. I mean, I look in the eyes of these kids that can't even put their hats on right and all I can think of is *The Shining*. There are certain rooms at the university, in my own hallway, that we all *know* not to go into.

( )

Come on, everyone knows what the Official Mind is.

( )

Well, maybe they ought to let you out more.

( )

Sorry. Back to the Clara situation. Fact: I was on the computer last night, surfing websites. Fact: I clicked on the GO button. And boy didn't I went. Suddenly, sites were flickering past me one after another. Scrolling. Sexy Sadie and her progeny. Twobackedbeast and those barking multitudes. Teenslut. And all the little nooks (so to speak) and crannies (so to speak) on each of those matrixes. Just flashing by like a deck of cards flipped in my hands. Out of control. Or like a slot machine, perhaps. And when it came to rest, the scrolling and streaming of these sites, there she was, Clara Schumann. In my lap. Corporeal. A jackpot spilling over.

( )

Yes, I did take advantage of the situation. You know me too well.

( )

Do?

( )

Well, first you need to know that as soon as I felt the pressure of her body on my lap a giant erection, a prodigious thing really, like a fast-forward time-lapse image of the construction of a skyscraper, ripped unbidden from the pitchy depths of my trousers, tore through that fabric, tore through the crinoline of her dress (the fabric was probably pretty old and maybe even rotten), and that damned penis just went straight up into her, banged against her cervix, and shot about a bucket of this pure spunk, I mean about the purest spunk I've ever produced, agate quality really . . . huh?

( )

Sorry. But that's what happened. I thought it was interesting that I could go from limp to hard to shooting in one instant. I mean one *instant.* Nanosecond, whatever that is. And Clara Schumann to thank for it.

( )

Next? I made her play the piano, of course. Couldn't have been easy for her with all the crying she was doing and she hadn't practiced since the 1890s. But she pulled it off. What a pro. But she was famous for her error-free playing under emotional duress. I had her play her own piano sonata in G minor and then her husband's F minor sonata. His first. Believe me, I was in tears by the end of that one. His earliest works were the most utterly engaging, and when I say engaging I mean sunk like the sweetest claw in your too-human heart.

( )

Thank you. With each succeeding work it's as if his genius is being slowly drained, one idea at a time, as the bugs chewed and swallowed his brain. Even with these bug caverns in his head, his last works were better than the whole Wagnerian corpus. And I use that word advisedly.

( )

More? Oh, yes, there was more. Basically there was: Fucking. Piano. Fucking. Piano. Fucking. Piano. All night.

( )

No, I'm ashamed to say, I never did try to find out what she knew. She would have had a hard time telling me much of anything anyway, what with all the sobbing and pleading and begging for mercy. But to tell you the truth, I was completely focused on this incredible opportunity that modern technology run amuck of a preternatural geist-stream had provided me. All my life, I've worshipped the very idea, the very possibility of a mutuality like that of Robert and Clara Schumann. To me their music was like watching them make love. And in some ways that's exactly what Robert's early piano work was: sublimated desire for young Clara, the passion diverted by the cruel intervention of Clara's father, old man Friedrich Weick, who had forbidden their marriage and for a desperate two plus years kept them in separate cities. Hence, for example Schumann's "Kinderszenen" is Robert creating these make-believe music-babies with Clara. The real babies would follow in time, soon enough, eight of them, practically falling out of fecund Clara's womb.

( )

Of course I did eventually stop, and it wasn't her tears and pleas for mercy or claims of anguishing pain that did it. (I don't know. Maybe it did hurt. What kind of wringer do you put your hand in when you fall through time and space and electronic fate?) I was mounting her for what must have been the eighth time that night, right after she'd played Liszt's "Paganinni Etudes" (which should have signaled something to me about how febrile and enervated and just generally spent the evening had become) when I remembered something that should have been obvious to me from the beginning. But when it struck home, it struck with a depressing bang.

It was this: Robert Schumann's little "wound." The guy had syphilis! I was having sex with a syphilitic's wife! And then I actually saw it, the little inflamed gash like a telltale, ghastly vagina on the tip of our penis.

( )

Did I say "our" penis?

( )

Oh. That's really weird. Anyway, I withdrew from my virtuoso, spritelike, digital love slave in horror and—poof!—she was gone. As I've considered this since, I have wondered if the whole strange experience weren't just a complicated plot to infect me. Do you think that's plausible? Should I seek treatment? I wonder what the Schumanns had against me. Or is this some elaborate prank by the tech support staff? I think I may have run afoul of the university's "appropriate use" policy. They're tying to get me fired! Those support staff techies wear baseball hats backwards, and they have this unbelievable hatred for me that I have never understood. I think they've trapped me into this awful thing I've done to poor Clara, this sinful thing I've done with the machines provided by the university.

( )

Sure, you can send me back to your secretary.

( )

Twice weekly? Is that necessary?

( )

Well, that's not much of an alternative.

( )

Those were the little blue ones, right?

The Voices

*For the first 5-10 minutes he spoke with horrifying haste of
what the voices, or else the doctors, had whispered to him, he
confused the two.*

–Johannes Brahms

AaAaAaAbAbAbBaBaBa.

–Robert Schumann

Most people claim that they don't see enough "connectedness" in life.
Things don't make sense, they complain. Their lives have no mean-
ing or coherence, they lament. But there are some persons, of whom
I am one, for whom the world makes *too much* sense. There are too
many "connections." They're everywhere. The coherence is nearly
blinding. In fact, I must spend considerable energy *not* noticing things.
What?
    With the apparent exception of the sponges, there is no phylum of
the animal kingdom that is not liable to sporozoon infection.
What?
    For instance, I was reading the early aesthetic criticism of Robert
Schumann and I noticed how often he favored the idea of the "masculine" in art. Then, there it was, suddenly, the recollection that the
Irish poet William Butler Yeats received shots which contained the
desiccated gonads of monkeys taken in serum. One assumes that Yeats
wanted his poetry to be bigger, more enduring, more massive in its
consequences, and just generally more athletic. Like a monkey. And

can you picture all the poor ball-less monkeys lazing about, torpid, because of this poet's craze?

AbAb, *What*?

Extraordinarily delicate, weakly refracting, but very actively motile. The little beasts produce an indolent swelling about the size of a lentil.

Beasts? Where?

I should like to know how a woman's voice ever interrupts this orgy of male self-absorption.

BaBaBa Claaara?

What did Robert say? Do you think he's hungry?

He thinks the chocolates are poisoned.

Of course they are. And the wine is urine, which is why it goes in the chamber pot.

As I had the sad duty to report to you yesterday, Robert's condition grows worse by the day. On the one hand, his poor head is stretched full of the music provided by the "voices." On the other, he is himself practically speechless. At one point, as I described, he was capable only of stammering AaAaAaAbAbAbBaBaBa. The stuttering of a child, I thought. Devastating.

You can imagine, then, with what amazement I woke last night with the realization that Robert was in fact trying to communicate to us from his Voiceless Land of the Voices. Abegg! Clara, Abegg! The Abegg variations! His fondness for organizing music around acronyms. The mythical Countess Abegg has become, in his sad condition, AbAbAb, or something like it.

I went immediately to my piano and began to hunt out the tune. Three penetrating A flat invitations in thundering chords! But what of Ba? Rapid movement from B major to A minor? Daring but ugly. I tried other combinations, up an octave/down an octave, various creative transpositions and re-articulations. I can't say, though, that I've found much of anything that compares with his old style. Still there are many unanswered questions. Should I imagine that the blocks of three reflect the fact that he intends a minuet or something in 3/4 time? And how should I understand tempo? He repeated his little Ab run very quickly, as if he were stuttering. Does that mean prestissimo? Faster still?

But the most chilling possibility here is this: didn't certain Jewish/Christian sects during the time of the apostles call God "Abab"? I'm quite sure that they did. Should we imagine, then, that Robert is calling to God in his deranged babbling? Should we imagine that in order to call God we must Babble (!), of all things? Is that our lesson?

Oh, Clara, there is so much to consider.

Yours, Brahms

Who is there?

We have communicated briefly the investigations we have been engaged upon during the past few months *what the hell* in the meantime we have continued our investigation and have come more and more to the conviction *Liszt fucks someone every night of his life and he's clean* that there are two kinds of spirochaetes, the one coarse and darkly staining, the other much more delicate in structure *I spend one or two, okay two women times two nights is four, four occasions with a couple trollops a long time ago* most patients are not willing to submit themselves to the procedure (it is invasive) and so we aspirate some of the fluid *I'm pretty sure that one woman was the same woman twice* of the gland by means of a well-fitting syringe of medium size, obtaining in this way a few drops of juice mixed with a little blood *a trollop I didn't even want to be with!* S. pallida is an extremely delicate object with a long, threadlike body which is twisted spirally and pointed at either end *and look at me!* we will now give a short description of one of the cases we have examined *Just look at me!*

AbAbAbBaBaBa

The first stage of syphilis infection is the chancre. It is the painless sore or sores that are round or flat. One might well call them "little wounds." These sores will go away without treatment, but the bacterium is still in the victim.

In the second stage, rashes may appear anywhere on the body. It need look no more threatening than heat rash. The palms of the hand or soles of the feet may turn scaly. Hair may fall out in patches. Even those symptoms last only two to six weeks at which point they too will disappear and, again, even in the absence of treatment.

After these symptoms, the disease will go into a latent or hidden stage. At this point, the carrier is no longer contagious.

Be it noted and noted well, however: even in "latency" the spirochete is busy burrowing into the carriers tissues.

Please! Stop! Please!

Very disturbing incident. R. and I took our customary evening walk down by the river. We came upon a beggar, a homeless person, a very rare sight in Dusseldorf. Horribly, he approached us and spoke directly to Robert. "Oh Jesus, man, the worms are eating our brains," he said, looking with the wide eyes of a drowned man directly into Robert's eyes. Even when we quickly reversed our direction he followed, repeating his awful sentence. R. very disturbed. Took to his study for the remainder of the evening, sitting in his armchair, trembling.

When at last he emerged from his room, he looked at me very clearly and calmly and asked, "Why do so many artists fail to realize that they've outlived themselves? That's one mistake I won't make."

Now it was my turn to retreat in despair.

Remom of Abwit.

Case A–R. S., male, age 25. Previously healthy. Infected at end of July, 1837. At the end of August small moist nodules about the size of a pea on the skin of the penis. Soon after, painless swelling of the inguinal gland.

September–Typical primary sore of about the size of a bean on the skin of the penis. Primary sore of about the size of a hazel nut extirpated. Followed with mercury treatment.

Kreeeee!

The central biographical fact in the life of Robert Schumann was, of course, his relationship with Clara Weick. And the central fact in his relationship with his dear Clara was her father, and Schumann's own piano teacher, Friedrich Weick.

Weick had raised his daughter from the earliest possible age to be a piano virtuoso such as the world had never seen. His efforts in fact were so successful that he himself became famous for the instructional method he developed for his child. Clara's virtuoso playing made her renowned even in a time when the likes of Franz Liszt, Anton Rubenstein, and Sigismond Thalberg were competing for concert stages all over Europe and Russia.

One might like to praise Weick for having the sense of fairness and the confidence in his daughter to allow her to aspire to heights normally reserved only for men, and there is, in fact, something liberated in his attitude. (He was more liberated by half, in fact, than her often jealous future husband, Schumann, who felt she ought "to recognize motherhood as her primary vocation.") But Herr Weick also suffered from the chauvinist assumption that he had in a very concrete sense created Clara—she was his creature, she was nothing without him—and that he owned her productive capacities and, indeed, her professional and personal life. She was, in short, a sort of factory for him. A player piano. An automaton. Her performances were freaks of nature and he was her impresario.

Until she met Robert Schumann, young Clara never wished to be anything more than her father's touring marvel. But then Schumann did come into her life, at first as a fellow music student and lodger in her father's house, but eventually as her suitor. They were mutually enraptured by each the other's skills, her delicate, expressive play, his bottomless creativity. There is nothing strange about Clara's admiration for the great composer, but it's worth observing that for Schumann's part the qualities he was most "enraptured" with were those pianistic techniques taught her by her father.

As it is famously known, when Clara and Robert declared their love and asked for old man Weick's cold benediction, he took it very badly. He admired young Schumann, but Clara was business. He understood in an instant that the boy Schumann was now asserting his rights as a man—or manager, the two got easily confused by Weick. He was a competitor. And Weick knew how to deal with competition.

In the legal declaration which Weick was ultimately obliged to create in order to protect his rights, Weick wrote that Schumann was "socially inept, badly brought up and egotistical; he neither spoke clearly nor wrote legibly; he had injured his hand through his own stupidity; he had lied about his income; he wanted to exploit Clara for financial gain; and he was a shoddy musician, a mediocre journalist, and a drunkard to boot."

Aargh! AbAb!

Actually, Weick's declaration was as right as it was wrong in nearly equal portions. Let's look at his charges one at a time.

"Socially inept . . . neither spoke clearly nor wrote legibly"—I group these charges together although they're separated by the crime of "egotism" to which we'll return in due course. The fact is that virtually everyone who ever met or knew Robert Schumann commented on his withdrawn nature, his tendency to despondency, and his often disturbing inability, both before and after the major onslaught of his disease, to articulate his thoughts. What astonished people was just how fluid Schumann could be when writing or composing music. As for his handwriting, forget it; Clara couldn't even read his love letters. She was always having to ask her confidential maid, Nana, for help deciphering his script. How seductive could that have been? "Is this word 'smoke,' Nana?" "I think it's probably 'stroke,' dear heart." "Oh."

"Egotistical"—Schumann was an Artist of the Romantic era, and he was prototypical of the type. Here we're obliged to throw ourselves on the mercy of the court. Personally, I think the grand assumption of "artistic egotism" in the pejorative needs to be revisited. After all, who/what was it that surrounded Schumann, true type of the genius that he certainly was? I'll tell you. Regular human-type beings. Normal folk. The dull folk with the bellies and the reindeer on their sweatshirts. The same ones who made dear Flaubert want to jump into a grave feet first. Even if they didn't have sweatshirts with reindeers back then, they were the same lumpen-folk. It shouldn't be hard to believe me. Look around. They're still with us and more than with us. That's them, with the bag of potato chips. Over there. Look! Right over there!

Who? *Who?*

"He had injured his own hand through his own stupidity"—Guilty again, as charged, but *providentially* guilty, my friends, for by injuring his own hand he created the need for Clara to be his (much more capable) hands as his first great interpreter. What stupid thing did he do exactly? Well, the long and short of it is that he stuck his right hand into a machine called a "chiroplast." Schumann called it a "cigar mechanism," which doesn't make it sound much safer. It was designed to strengthen the fingers. Ultimately, however, it permanently damaged tendons in his right hand. By June of 1832, the middle finger was "completely stiff."

One Professor Krull prescribed the following treatment which was probably just as stupid as the procedure that caused the problem in the first place: "The patient was to obtain the carcass of a freshly slaughtered animal and insert his hand into its entrails, thereby absorbing healing warmth from a repellant mixture of blood, intestinal slime, and fecal matter."

Schumann found the treatment "invigorating," although he worried that in among all of the "absorbing" that "some of the animal nature will seep into my own."

One early biographer claimed that "the stiffness in the middle finger of Schumann's right hand came about as a psychosomatic reaction to guilt over excessive masturbation."

AbAbAbAaAaAaBaBaBa

"He lied about his income"—Well, those are strong words for what he did. He was merely projecting the income that would come to him when he began publishing all of the compositions he would surely write. And he wasn't wrong, he did write them, he was paid, and well, although Weick would be technically in the right to complain that it was mere youthful hubris to claim those expectations as present "income."

"He wanted to exploit Clara"—No. No, no, no, Herr Weick. You could hardly be expected to know, curmudgeon, miser and pre-Freudian that you were, but that is called "projection." That sin is on your head, my friend.

"He was a shoddy musician"—Please!

"A mediocre journalist"—And this from a man who wrote a review of a Chopin concert that Chopin himself called "stupid." And what was most stupid was Weick's clumsy efforts to mimic *Schumann's* journalistic style!

The constellation of emotions among these people was very strange. In the abstract, we might describe it in this way: a man loves a woman in large part for qualities drilled into her by her father. That delicacy of touch is a technical delicacy prescribed by her father's system. The father, in turn, officially loathes the man but unconsciously imitates his style (badly). Here the woman is but a mediator for mutual male self-absorption. They deceive themselves in thinking the woman has anything to do with it.

"And a drunkard to boot"—This, unhappily, was a large boot. During Schumann's youth, and especially during those years when he and Clara were kept apart, Schumann was such a regular at a local pub that he never had to ask for a fresh beer. It was understood that when Robert Schumann's glass was empty it needed to be full. His most common diary entry at this time was "drank a frightful amount" (this phrase is repeated like a dirge: "another day, drank a frightful amount"). No wonder he suffered a frequent "numbing of spirit." With all that beer he was lucky he could feel his feet! Here, as any father would understand, is Weick's strongest and most sufficient argument against the marriage. Schumann was a *bierhund* and marriages to *bierhunds* are often unhappy things. And for whatever reason, the marriage of Robert and Clara Schumann in fact proved to be an unhappy thing.

No! Ahbeanabab!

The raw truth of the situation was, in his own words, that Schumann was "a ruin pointing forward." But the source of his ruin wasn't really beer. The source of his ruin was a woman he called La Faneuse. Something about a discovery in a cellar. He "suffered the consequences in

1837."

"Oh, my poor Robert!"

Klärchen?!

The only cure for his tragic condition that Schumann ever sought was in his titanic study of counterpoint in Bach. This, needless to say, had little effect on his advancing physical ruin except that by it he discovered a "beautiful melancholy," a high forest current which roaringly flowed strong and full of thoughts. He discovered the language of prophets that poured from his poor head. God cleansed and sanctified his lips. God made it clear that He had known him from before the time he was born, and before he was conceived. But then the bugs opened up the bags in his head and let it all pour out in some wild misconceived celebration. His musical language was described as bizarre, excessive, eccentric, capricious, and arbitrary. In truth, he wanted only to contain the whole of the world. Its everything. This would be the ultimate gesture of self-annihilation: becoming World. To become World he had to become eclectic, he had to be the God of eccentric sequences, the waltzes, polonaises, the familiar tunes, the infinity of contrast, the putting of the small beside the great so that when viewed together a kind of laughter resulted which contained pain and greatness. This was Schumann's art of improvisation, making it up as he went along. Intuition worked in those days, hardwired into God-Brow.

Ab, yes, be Gob!

Lived experience is a constellation of fragments awaiting the transfiguring touch of the poet.

Why, ab, yes.

Charting the expanses of a complete moral universe.

How beautifully the angels are singing to me!

But as much as he fabulously filled the bag with invention, the bugs let it out the buggy bottom. Finally, he was just soggy.

"Robert, sometimes your music actually frightens me and I wonder: Is it true that the creator of such things is going to be my husband?"

Clara, I do not deserve your love.

Of course, ironies abound in old Weick's otherwise simply dead-on accurate and legally compelling evaluation of Schumann's drinking habits. Consider the following: Weick claimed he was separating the lovers because Schumann was a drunk. Because Weick kept him from his loved one, Schumann drank. Because he drank, he suffered "violent congestion of the blood, unspeakable fear, a numbing of spirit." His doctor advised him, "Find yourself a woman . . . she'll cure you in a flash." Doctor! That's some prescription!

So, should we say that Schumann's death from syphilis proved old Weick right? Or should we say that if it hadn't been for Weick's ugly stubbornness, Schumann would never have contacted syphilis? If he'd had his Klärchen, he never would have sought comfort (under doctor's orders) from Caritas or La Faneuse or who-the-hell-else.

But wait. This irony is not done. If Weick were going to keep the lovers apart, it is very good that he did it with a singleness of purpose, with a systematic approach that prefigured Metternich, that reflected his own approach to the piano, because he was so successful for so long (two to three years!) that Schumann's disease had time to move from its genital to its latent stage.

Neither Clara nor any of her children with Robert ever had syphilis.

Unworthy!

According to Schumann, Weick eyed him "like a cocked pistol." The threat in that look kept him away and kept his dear daughter safe. Safe from the Schumann scourge. You see, Robert, he was ultimately saving her from you. From your miserable touch! You contaminate what you contact! You and the contagious bugs in your brain! Take him to an asylum!

Ab! AbAb! Ayeuummm!

The final stage of syphilis is called "tertiary syphilis." This is the most terrible stage of the disease. Victims may develop problems with hearing or sight, brain damage, paralysis, insanity, and eventually death. This is so because the spirochete is degenerating tissues of bodily organs. That is, the vital organs of the victim, muscle, bone and brain, are being slowly eaten.

It's death one tiny bacterial bite at a time.

Oh!

"Often indignant and sullen, his expression vacant and squinting, his face and limbs twitching uncontrollably, frequently coughing up phlegm, unable to control his bladder and confined to bed due to the edema in his feet."

Oh!

My breath is abhorred by my wife; I am loathsome to the men of my family. The young children, too, despise me; when I appear, they speak against me. All my intimate friends hold me in horror; those whom I loved have turned against me! My bones cleave to my skin, and I have escaped with my flesh between my teeth.

J-oh-b!

Oddly, for a long time Schumann considered the symptoms of his disease as the necessary burden of his "poetic nature." He suffered from:

1. anxiety about certain objects like keys, things made of metal, medicines (they were all poison), and tall buildings;
2. an intense burning feeling in the back of his head;
3. auditory disturbances.

It is this last, the auditory hallucinations, which we remember most poignantly. It was a horrible condition which deprived him of peace and sleep but it was at times wondrous. What began as piercing, monotonous tones became "entire compositions in splendid harmonization, played by a distant wind band."

One night he rose from bed to write down a theme, a melody, "dictated by the angels." It was a gift from Franz Schubert. The next morning he rose and composed a set of variations on this angelic theme. The *Geiservariationen*.

Have you heard them?

Oh. Ooooh.

By the next day, the angels had become demons, tigers and hyenas singing a hideous music and threatening to throw him into hell.

Schumann understood as well as we do (even if his obtuse biographers don't) that this "devilish music" was simply the music of Wagner, Liszt, and Berlioz, for which the Schumanns had a very strong contempt. Clara described the playing of Franz Liszt as "no longer music, but like demonic boozing and bluster . . . a diabolical buzzing and banging."

Once during this last period of his illness, Schumann went searching through the house for a gun. Clara was very frightened.

"But Robert, we don't own a gun."

"I will find a gun."

"And what will you do with it once you find it?"

"I will defend myself and my family. I will kill them before they kill me."

"Robert, who?"

He paused then counted them off, flicking a finger forward emphatically for each marked man, "Wagner, Liszt, and Berlioz."

"But Robert, they are not here, and you don't know where they are, and why would you want to kill fellow musicians?"

"Has it occurred to you, Clara, as not even a little strange that all the sweet musicians that we love, our Davidsbündler comrades, are all dead? Schubert dead. Mendelssohn dead. Chopin dead. And who is living? The New Music barbarians! Wagner and Liszt! And they're interbreeding! Wagner will have spawn with Liszt's daughter!"

"Spawn, Robert?"

"It appears that they will live forever. And so now it's my turn to die. But they won't get me so easily. I will fight back!"

"Oh, Robert! We hardly know Wagner, and Liszt, in spite of his awful playing and hideous compositions, has—even I will admit—been unfailingly kind and friendly. He's just a bit bohemian. That's all. He's from Hungary or some place, dear. Maybe he's even a Gypsy."

Perhaps because he couldn't kill Wagner or Liszt, Schumann later tried to kill himself by throwing himself in the Rhine. He was saved by fishermen and taken to a sanatorium at Endenich, an estate just outside of Bonn, where he was put under the care of Dr. Franz Richart.

No one, of course, referred to "the voices" or Schumann's grand conspiratorial theory about Liszt after he was confined, but we consider the following observation by Dr. Richart to be very interesting.

"He [Schumann] played the piano in a wild and crazy manner for almost two hours, hollering all the while, and threatening his attendant with a chair."

But clearly, this is the very essence of the Lisztian style! Right down to the chair! Possession! A case of demonic possession as certain as the residence in his brain of the syphilitic bugs.

Gack!

There's more! Schumann's one pleasure during his last years at Endenich was to walk with Brahms or an attendant to visit the Beethoven statue, the memorial sculpture in Bonn. For him, this was like returning to the true well-spring of his own artistic inspiration. It was enormously calming. It was one last thing forever free of contamination.

Or so he thought.

But even here there is a subtle cruelty: the statue had been paid for with a 10,000f contribution from Franz Liszt! Even the memory of the great man was tainted by the rascal with the sprightly fingers. Liszt! He who gave virtuosity a bad name.

Oooh!

It is said that the tragedy of Schumann's last years "exercises its fullest and most devastating impact if we recognize it for what it was: the story of a richly layered personality in decay."

That is well said. One pictures these "layers" coming slowly unbound, undermined by the persistent, voracious nibbling of the spirochetes. Leaking out his ears, so to speak. But what is not quite grasped here is that the famous voices, the music by a "distant wind band," the tune delivered by angels, is all the music Schumann would have written but didn't, but couldn't, and it all poured from him in waking and sleeping like a springtime Rhenish shower, cascading from his head and falling onto his shoulders.

"Robert."

Yes.

"Robert, are you there?"

Yes. Who is it?

"We're not done yet."

Who is it? I know that voice!

"Yes, you know me. It's Franz, Robert."

Liszt?

"Yes. And say, can you turn down the music? It's a little loud. There's a piercing quality about these angel voices. I can't hear yourself thinking."

And it is indeed Franz Liszt, or a perfect image of him, which has popped into Robert's beleaguered brain like a bubble bursting. It is even a young Liszt, the one sought by every woman in Europe, with his chiseled features, trite as any star of Italian opera, long blond hair, exotic cloak and the dark ring with the ivory skull on his right hand.

"I'm sorry to say that it is my unhappy duty to report to you that . . . we're not done yet."

Not done?

"Not done, dear boy. There's one more story to tell."

Oh please, no, please, no, please. ObObOb.

"Oh come on now. ObObOb. You sound like some funny little furry thing trying to play a bassoon. After all you've been through, one more little story won't matter. I heard it myself from the lips of a worm."

Oh. Warm. Harm.

"You have no doubt already heard that Clara, your dear Clara, and that young Johannes Brahms, the 'genius' you discovered just before your collapse, that they have become a sort of couple, I guess you'd call it, in your absence. Brahms has taken your place. I think that's how the worm put it. Let me tell you, by the way, that a conversation with a worm is no sweet matter. One must lean right down and cock the ear over his little lips. And the breath!"

Warm worm.

"I'm sorry. Did you say something? You haven't heard this one, have you?"

No.

Good.

No. Good.

"Well, my apologies. I thought that if I was hearing it from a damned worm everyone knew it. I'm usually the last to know such things. You're quite sure? Because he, Herr Brahms, stays in your house, watches your children, uses the 'du' form with Mrs. Schumann like any good Beidermeir husband. Clara has been told in no uncertain terms by Frau Lesser that she 'makes herself cheap,' fat lot she cares. She's a regular Lola Montez, if you know what I mean. But she hasn't been reported dancing on any tables that I know of. Or swallowing off glasses of champagne with young Russian officers. I wouldn't think of her as a proper harlot just yet. Oh Clara, Clara, Clara, when will these young women learn? 'In the evening you can do with me what you will.' That's what they say. And I would a lot! Lord!"

No.

"You don't believe me? Nor should you. It's all gossip and lies. Just ask the worms. That's what worms are for. Especially when they're in our brains. That's why we like them, and tolerate their peculiarities. They keep us good company. No, young Brahms's fate will be quite different. Your case has so frightened him that he's afraid to masturbate let alone have sex with a woman. Sad. The passionate, romantic involvements of his life will all be unfulfilled, I fear. Not that, let me add from my own experience, fulfillment of this type is always fulfilling. Otherwise gluttony would be no sin. Still, one keeps at it. Doggedly. Ever hopeful. Looking for a break into the beyond. Am I right?"

Oh God.

"Let me ask, though, if this troubles you at all, my little story? For example, this letter that Clara wrote to you. Did you read it?"

Please stop.

"Does that mean 'no'? If it means 'yes,' I think you did not read it very carefully, for it says, I quote, 'Brahms has had a splendid idea, a surprise for you, my Robert. He has interwoven my old theme with yours—already I can see you smile.' She wrote this right to you! Oh, that's bold!

"Smile, grimace, cry in pain, what's the difference, eh? But oh sweet surprise! And she calls me devilish! What kind of kinky perversity does she describe, after all? Does she imagine that you would not remember that for years before your marriage that you and Clara made love exactly through your music? That in your 'Kinderszenen' you actually conceived little music babies with her? You're not supposed to remember that! The unholy whore! And Brahms, with his 'interesting young face,' 'his beautiful hands.' It's grotesque! And he handles things, sir, he takes your music secretly from your drawers and puts his jejune fingers to them. Manipulating them. Intertwining the parts, for God's sake. Oh, his nerve is great, the blagard! They are odious; they have done abominable things, yet they are not at all ashamed (see them smiling happily, sitting together on the piano bench?), they know not how to blush. Don't you think that this is far worse than anything having to do with his penis? Although he's got a penis, and as long as he does there's always the possibility that . . .

"Robert. Hey Robert! Wake up. I'm not done with you yet, wake up!"

I hear it, the angelic music of the bugs. Ethereal worms. A wonderfully peaceful, holy theme. After all.

Oh Zion! Awake, awake! And all you wild beasts of the field, come and eat! Cry out full-throated and unsparingly! Be not a dumb dog that cannot bark. Rise up in splendor! What else is this music that flies along like clouds swept? We will not be silent.

Oh Zion! I have often written to you in invisible ink, and between the lines runs a secret writing which will come to light later on.

I must end now. For it is already growing dark. But there will be someone else along shortly to take my place. For I would not leave you alone. I would not abandon those I love.

Pace. Abab.

The Life of Chris (4)

Magdalen's Members Only!

"Please send me e-mails. I want to know if you like me!" . . .
Magdalen

• **Welcome! Welcome! Welcome!**

Hi, my name is Magdalen and thank you for joining my site!

The first thing members usually want to know is how and why I started this site. Well, I'm a happily married homemaker and I live with my husband and two kids in the Ozarks. (That's in southern Missouri and Arkansas, generally speaking, guys, and that's as much of the cat as I'm letting out of that dangerous bag! That's the first thing the experienced girls tell you about running a site. Don't tell 'em where you live!) Now, I adore my husband, I truly do, but that doesn't mean that all of the guys you'll see on my site are my husband. Not hardly! And here's why: I love cock!

The rest of the story:

One day my husband was fucking me in the doggy position, and he started slapping my butt rhythmically and saying things like, "You whore. You slut. You housewife slut. You'd fuck anybody, wouldn't you?" And I was so intrigued and excited by what he said that I pulled away from him and turned. I looked right at him. And I think he thought I was maybe angry or something. Not hardly! I said, "What did you say?" And he said, "I'm sorry. I got carried away." And I said, "No really, it's okay. Just tell me what you said." "I called you a slut. A housewife slut." "And you said I'd fuck anybody." "Yeah." And my only thought then was, "How did he know?"

Well, that little conversation was followed by a longer conversation, and the next thing you know I was sucking off the teenage boy who lived next door. And he wasn't the last. Not hardly! Our front door began to look like the dessert line at the high-school cafeteria. Cupcakes, anyone? Slurpees?

Anyway, that's how this got started. The pictures came a little later because I wanted to be able to remember what we did. Of course, once we were taking the pictures it was only natural that we should want to share them with others. And what better way to share pictures with the whole world than over the Internet?

Two more things before I let you go to explore the rest of the site. First, the most guys I've ever fucked at one time is eight. (The limit there has less to do with me and more to do with finding guys ready for that kind of action.) Second, I really am a slut.

I'm a slut! The real deal! And I love it!

And just what is a slut, you ask? Well, come on, boys, it's what's inside that counts.

• ABOUT ME
• BORN DEAD

I was born in the Ozarks. That's in southern Missouri and Arkansas, generally speaking, and that's all I'll say on that because much as I'd like to suck off every one of you, there's two or three of you out there making a list of girls that even I want to stay off. And getting on that list all starts the day you discover the location of my front porch.

When I was little, we had a lot of money and a big new house in the country. My Daddy made all his money by betting on football games. We were a pretty typical family for our part of the world, I think.

Daddy married Mommy, who was the daughter of a Little Rock cattle king, but after living with her for twenty years he decided he was in love with his niece and sister-in-law, Heddie. She was the daughter to Daddy's half-brother, Uncle Arnie, and had married *her* uncle (Uncle Phil), who was in what they called "private practice." That's how they said it. "Private practice." Then they'd all laugh except me because I didn't get it. I *still* don't get it. (Hey guys, if one of you gets this old family joke, could you please e-mail me? I'd appreciate it. Maybe I'll send you a little something on the old e.love as a thank you.) Anyway, on a journey to Kansas City, Daddy lodged with Uncle Phil, fell in love with Heddie, and proposed marriage to her. She said yes, of course, sweet and compliant thing that she was and is. Eager to please, as they say. But Mommy had to hightail it out of the picture because from Daddy's new point of view she just didn't have a place anymore. She went back to her daddy's ranch in Little Rock. I don't know what she's doing there, but knowing her as I do I suspect she's still thinking about it and one of these days we'll find out what she's been thinking.

With Mommy out of the way, Heddie came to live with Daddy as his wife. Don't ask me about my Uncles Arnie or Phil, cuz I don't have a clue. I suspect they were pissed at the time and maybe they're still pissed. Beats me. But maybe they had something to do with Daddy's little accident in the Camaro (when he peeks out of his coma, he mumbles something about a Ford truck and a winding road). The good thing about the coma is that he doesn't miss his legs nearly as

much as he would otherwise. And Heddie actually seems quite okay with the whole thing. She's a very upbeat person generally.

Heddie was always okay with me. When I was little, she taught me how to dance.

Click on the jpeg at the left and see the first picture ever taken of my tits. I think I'm about thirteen. Not bad, huh? Daddy was a good photographer.

• ASK ME!

Dear Magdalen:

First off, I want you to know I really dig your site. It's hot. I love your chubby-ass little body. I can only imagine what that feels like to have next to me. Like jumping in a bowl of cream of wheat, I suspect. Kind of soft and warm all over. I like Cream of Wheat best when my Mom makes it with milk instead of water. I have a friend and his wife makes it with water and it looks like all gray and pasty. And you can smell the chlorine. Then I enjoy a pat of butter there. And Aunt Jemima's syrup. Then it's ready for the big dive. I'm just in there, you know, like I'm in you, or would like to be. Simmering in my cream of wheat while that stuff just sorta caresses me.

I'll bet you hear this from a lot of your members.

While I'm on the subject of being in you, I say a big vote "yes," I vote "yes" for your update called "What Goes In Must Come Out." You are so imaginative! Not *a* banana like those other morons on the Web, but the whole bunch! And an aluminum baseball bat! Could you please give more details on the bats you use? Like, was it a Mark Grace signed bat (he's my favorite)? Was it a 32-ounce bat? These things matter. They're important to your members who are also base-ball fans. For example, if it was a Greg Maddux signed bat, that would be a big turnoff because a) he's a fucking traitor to the Cubs, b) he's a pitcher, and c) I think he's cross-eyed.

If I had a Mark Grace bat in my hand and I happened to meet Greg Maddux, I'd beat him over the head with it till I saw all his awesome brains on the sidewalk or the shiny floor of the airport if that's where I happened to run into the son of a bitch.

What I'm trying to say is, if I knew that the aluminum bat you used was signed by Maddux, I'd probably have to quit your site. And that would really make me mad because I paid $9.95 and that's a lot of money.

If I had had a Mark Grace bat, a lot of the stuff that has happened to me in my life would *not* have happened, I guaran-Goddamn-tee.

Anyway, if I had you at my house (especially if my mom and uncle were out), let's say you were looking for a friend's house and your car got stuck in the snow and you didn't know where she lived and you couldn't get your car out of the snow and you thought I might be able to help or might know where your friend lived so I said, "Come in! You must be freezing, you poor thing!" Then you saw my weight bench in the living room and the stack of sexy XXX videos over by the VCR, and you said, "Ooh, why don't you just fuck me or something?" This is what I'd do to you.

First, I'd tie you upside down with your legs wrapped around the bar of my bench press and your big fat cunt sticking right up in the air gasping like a big old fish or something. Then I'd line your cunt with a ten-gallon plastic garbage liner so I could have a way of getting any of my mom's stuff out of you. Then I think, you know, I'd be cool as hell with you hanging there, your head by the floor, your legs around the bar of my Joe Weider bench press.

Your cunt, red,

Ugh!!

Anyway, then I'd, you know, like, experiment. I'd do the sort of things my ex-wife would never let me do. And that's why I'm glad she's gone. First, I'd try to put a bottle of cold PowerAde in you. Then I think I'd see if a bag of Mom's baking flour would fit. Then, let me see, I'd come out of the kitchen and take the potted plant with all the dead leaves and see if that went. Meanwhile, you're like in fucking ecstasy down there because you've never met anyone with such a good imagination and who really knew how to turn you on. Then, I think the canister vac, starting with the floor attachments and the whole hose and, finally, the canister itself.

You know something that's funny? There are, that I know of, no commandments that say you can't put things inside a woman! Any thing! What's God going to say? "You're going to hell because you put a vacuum cleaner inside that poor girl"? And I would just say, "Okay, you show me where that's prohibited. Because I looked and looked in all those boring lists of things you're not supposed to do according to God, in those awful boring books like Leviathan or something and there's nothing, *nothing*, on this subject at all. So, as far as I'm concerned, I can drive my Chevy Celebrity in there and park it and you've got nothing to say on the subject and should just keep your judgements to yourself."

I mean, I think I'd be completely within my rights to say that to God if he pulled some Moses-style crap on me.

Man I hate big shots. Like what happened at my last job when I got a little carried away with the fork lift.

So, finally, if I could get that vacuum in there, I'd try to put the TV in next. I'd unplug it first, of course, although you have to wonder what it would be like to put it in with a show on. Donnie and Marie, for example. You could see them sitting there together talking to some fucking dummy and sliding in and out of your big cunt. I suppose it's dangerous, but think if it's not!

And then after the TV I think I'd just have to stop and sit at the foot of the weight bench and cry. I'd cry because it's sad. Cunts aren't big enough to hold everything you want them to hold. The things you put in the cunt don't say everything you feel or want to feel or even say about yourself or the whole big world. I mean, I'm sitting there crying and you're just hanging there a little heavy from all the things I put in you, sighing, asking for more. And you don't even care if I'm sad, you whore!

And I turn to you and say, "That's enough, woman! You cavern! You bottomless pit! Sometimes you just make me sick like I'm gonna puke." That's when I head for the kitchen appliances. The stuff Mom uses with turkeys.

Is this turning you on?

Okay, gotta go. Looking forward to your next update. Just what are you planning to do with the high-school wrestling team and a case of Coke in non-returnable bottles! (What difference does it make if they're returnable or not? I guess I'll find out.)

Your best fan,

Joe's Desire

Dear Joe's Desire:

I've turned your electronic fingerprint over to the authorities. I'll see your sorry ass in hyper-court. But in the meantime, don't forget to keep your membership current! Just because you're an asshole doesn't mean I don't need your money.

Sincerely,

Ms. Magdalen (to you!)

Dear Magdalen:

We surfed onto your site while touring random porn rings and we were reading your e-mail and we have to ask just what the hell is going on? But we don't know whether we should ask what's going on on your site, or what's going on out there in the brains of those people who visit your site. We mean, we're normal guys who like the idea that we can see pretty girls naked and no one's the wiser. But this "Joe's Desire" character is what our mothers would call a "caution." He's a straight caution. He wants to do what with what? A vacuum cleaner!? And you condone this shit? Your fat ass ugly body condones this shit? If we could get our hands on that little pencil-necked son of a bitch, we'd show him what to do with his vacuum cleaner, because it's guys like him that are going to get carried away, gonna get all revved up, and next thing you know there's a law and our deal—the deal of normal guys—is totally queered and it's bye-bye tits. Bye-bye pretty girls that we could never see naked otherwise. So long master-fully sculpted jugs.

So, what we say is that you should get your site, you should get your chubby ass and really not masterfully sculpted jugs the hell off the Web if you're going to attract and encourage scumbags like Mr. Joe's Desire with his vacuum cleaner of the canister variety.

Sincerely,

Amerigo Vespucci and Company

Dear Amerigo and all:

I'm with you on that one, Amerigo. Someone's got a loose circuit out there. As for my jugs, I like 'em, my husband likes 'em, and my fans gobble them up. So go fuck your various selves.

Maggie Mae

• MAGDALEN'S LIVE VIDEO FEED

Hey guys, check this out. We've got a video camera streaming live images 24-7 from our basement Love Den! There's not always action there, of course, but check it often and you might get lucky. I keep pretty busy! I love the site and I love my members! All sixteen of you! Hey, you know, if it weren't for customers like Joe's Desire we could maybe have a party. Call it a reunion! Right in the old Love Den. Let me think on it. Sixteen! Sweet!

[Live video feed, 16:23:17 $\Omega \approx \varsigma \sqrt{\int} \dagger \hat{} \Sigma$, 1-24-00, www.housewifesluts.com/magdalen.]

Video: blank, black screen.

Audio: [*Distinct drunken male voice*] "Nigger! Hey nigger! Get your black ass up here! Son of a bitch! Hahaha! I'm gonna get my gun! I'm warning you! Nigger, Goddamn it, answer me! Last time, I swear, last time Tracy, that I let a nigger fuck you. I've learned my lesson! And you took the last bottle of Jack too. That's just not fair! Goddamn it, get up here you slut. Nigger! Hey! I'm goin' coon huntin'! Haha! [*Light streams in from door being opened at top of stairs; suddenly, series of loud banging sounds of a body falling down the stairs*] Oooh. [*More moaning*] Nigger!"

• **ASK ME! UPDATE**

Dear Magdalen:

Have you ever noticed how often the Bible refers to the Philistines, the Babylonians, the worshippers of Baal, the Gentiles generally understood, getting it on? I mean, one gets the very distinct impression that for about five hundred years the non-Jewish community was rubbing itself raw in endless orgies. For that's the word they used. Orgies. Even as late as 1 Peter 4, written some sixty years after the death of Christ, they're still going on about it.

"For the time that has passed is sufficient for doing what the Gentiles like to do: living in debauchery, evil desires, drunkenness, orgies, carousing and wanton idolatry."

Nowadays, that's the idolatry of the pussycam, as you very well know.

And it's not surprising that they got so worked up about it because you get the idea that they imagined the typical Jew guy kind of stopped in his tracks looking over to where the Gentiles live and hearing this soft moaning and you can't blame the typical Jewish guy for wondering what was behind that moan. All the sucking and flowing of juices.

You just can't blame him. Because what did he have? Unleavened bread. That's crackers, if you want to know. Dry soda crackers and a hot-tempered God who every so often regretted that he'd made this hard-hearted and stiff-necked people at all. But Christ it must have been hard to please the guy living on soda crackers and no sex with the cute Gentile chicks even when they called you over and said, "Hey, don't be a hermit. Drop by for a drink. And bring the wife." I mean, who wouldn't be resentful about living under such a regime? You'd be "stiff-necked" too.

Personally, I like to think of all those Baal-crazy people getting it on. It seems so perfect, *centuries* of Bacchus and Baal and swollen clitorises. My my. But then I think, as think we must, of five hundred years of erections . . . gone! Where are they? What did they count for? Where is that pleasure they enjoyed now? Incredibly sad, I'd say. I know how they felt. An erection just seems so *historical* in the moment in which you have it. But what would you know about that? [Ha! You'd be surprised!]

It is then we turn in full seriousness to Peter's admonition "not to spend what remains of one's life in the flesh on human desires."

So, I know where he's coming from, that holy Peter. I been there, Magdalen or Slut or whatever that drunken tattooed asshole with the semi-erect penis floating on the periphery of your photo shoots is calling you these days.

I'm a serious guy, a very serious guy, and a few years back I put in a whole lot of time refining myself. I learned to play the piano. I'm off the beer and whiskey. And finally I'm playing Haydn's "Seven Last Words" in its piano format.

Know that music, Magdalen?

Thought not.

Anyway, it occurred to me that even music is not immune to the failures and fatalities of the Gentile erection. The reason for this is that the gorgeous childlike piety of Haydn's unspeakably beautiful music contains its own failure. The subtlety here is that just as I grew to mistrust orgies because I couldn't say where they were, those erections of yesteryear, so I had the same problem with this music, those notes, which vaporized before me in that instant, no better than a fading erection, or better but participating in the same failure.

They have a term in music: decay. The decay of a musical tone. That's where the oscillations, the frequency of the note's sound waves falls apart audibly until it is no more. It's a lovely thing to listen to in itself. And full of truth. In fact, one way of thinking about music, which is note after note, is that it is an anxious response to this decay. The decay gets covered over by the next note, as if we hadn't the courage just to listen to one note and understand it deeply, right into the ground. Nothing, Magdalen, nothing speaks more directly to the pathos of lost time. Not even five hundred years of fading Gentile erections.

By the way, Magdalen, did I tell you that I'm coming over? I need to talk to you. So, see you soon.

Compassionately yours,

The Modern Prophet

_____

Dear Modern Prophet:

Hey nonny-nonny, dude! Catch me if you can! I'll keep the midnight candle burning! Mags

_____

Dear Magdalen:

I found your site by a miracle. I barely know how to use the computer, and yet your site was opened for me miraculously. And when I saw it, I knew why. You have been provided to me because I am unhappy, desperate and in need. I don't know where else to turn. I've caused unspeakable suffering to others, people that I ought to love and care for. And I don't know what to do about my own huge guilt.

Can you please help me? If I confess to you, friend to Jesus, teacher of the apostles, if I tell you exactly what I did, will you offer me forgiveness?

I was a good little girl. I was such a good little girl. But I was never good enough that I could keep my parents together. You know when they talk about the black box on airline crashes? My father had a black box. The box was a dark recess, fathoms below, with all the secrets that could have helped ease our pain if he or it could only have been obliged to speak. But we can't find the black box, Magdalen, that's the problem. They send the little submarines out that can withstand great pressures, with the little mechanical arms and grasping hands, but they can't find it because it's so deep. It's also very depressing to be so far underwater. And I think of the little prosthetic, mechanical, grasping hands and I just want to cry.

So, in its absence, all I can say is that my father made so much money that he didn't need my mother or us so he left us. He had a lawyer who he seemed to like a lot and he gave a lot of money to this lawyer so that he didn't have to give any at all to us.

I grew up with my mother and sister. When I think about my mother, the temptation of words is so scary that I cry instead. Please don't ask me to think about her now. And my sister, so hard to explain. But it's like when you hear about people living in a town in Idaho. You hear they have a lovely house in the country, they have a garden, they can see the mountains, but it's all very far away and mostly unimaginable. That's my sister.

So when I grew up I was sort of a mess wondering about the black box at the bottom of the ocean, weeping when I looked at my mother, and wondering about what kind of people lived in Idaho. That was my inner life. That's when I met Stavros.

Stavros is Greek. Even when he is thousands of miles away from his Greek family, they are with him like a parade. I look at him and he's walking across the room and I see in his wake this happy, colorful band of people waving flags and carrying blankets and children and if he turns, they go, "Hey, he's turning!" and they too turn, hugging each other and laughing like they are on some sort of comical carnival ride that is whipping them about like a long tail. And this is just him walking across the room. And of course his contentment and happiness and confidence in his place in the family depress me terribly and I am always crying. So Stavros of course consoles me and asks what is wrong.

"What do you want?" he asks.

And right up to that moment I have no idea what I want, Magdalen, but then my mouth opens and I say, "I want a baby." And then it's all clear, "I want a baby." And I smile and Stavros smiles, because there's nothing easier for him.

I wanted a family, too, Magdalen. Was that wrong? I wanted the happy, colorful, little people trailing behind me with the banners and good sense of fun.

And Stavros with a wide sweep of his arms says, "Darling, why didn't you say so? You and the baby should join the crowd." And you could see the little Greek people with this sneaky look in their eyes gesturing to me. "Come on! It's fun!" they say.

That's how we got little Angela. And oh when I had Angela, I knew I at last had someone who could be in my parade, who would follow me around the house, as she did as soon as she could walk!, waving whatever toy she might have in her hand. But then something very strange happened inside of me. I only wanted Angela in *my* parade. I didn't want her with the dirty Greeks. You know how democratic babies are. She didn't care which or how many parades she was in as long as there were a lot of them. But I had this very strong, nasty feeling that I didn't want her in their parade. I thought she might catch something. Or I thought they might let her drink a Coca-Cola, which is bad for her teeth.

But there is worse to tell. Then when I looked at Stavros, who would be standing smiling at our side, I heard a voice say to me, "You don't need this character." And I didn't need him anymore, and I resented the little parade of happy, dirty Greeks who trailed behind him and I resented having them around the house all the time, my house, so I found myself saying things like, "If you (blank) (you fill in the blank, Magdalen: 'spill coffee,' 'speak,' 'act like this is your home,' 'ever try to touch me again'), I'll kill you." And then I realized that *I* had a little black box, that I had been involved in an airline crash at sea, and that my black box was speaking its secrets, divulging its nasty black soul to poor Stavros. I was like one of those dolls with a string that you pull and out comes, "You make me sick to look at you." "I can't stand being in the same room with you."

He'd stand still and look at me in pain and confusion when I said these things, but you should have seen the parade. All the little aunts and uncles and cousins hunched their shoulders and the pretty banners drooped and their arms hung down and old ladies with veils over their heads and large crooked noses tried to look around to Stavros's front side as if they would ask him, "What's going on? What did she say? Can you explain this American saying, 'I'm going to kill you'? That does not translate well into Greek." "No, no. In Greek that means, 'I'm going to kill you.' But no Greek says such a thing unless they're going to kill you!" "But that's what she said!" "Then why don't she kill him?" "Crazy American!"

And that, Magdalen, would make me laugh because it was so funny to see the happy parade get confused and sad because I recognized that sadness as my own and it was very strange to see Stavros' little pack of supporters looking like *me* of all things.

So, it was inevitable, I said, "I'm moving out and taking Angela. This is my lawyer. He has the biggest lawyer house in town. It's brick. Each brick is a successful divorce. Good luck."

That's what I said.

But when I moved into my own new apartment with Angela, she came over to my knee and put her little hands one on each knee and looked at me very inquiringly in the eye as if to say, "I'm listening but I can't hear you. Say something to me, Mommy, so that I know you're here." And I would shout, "I love you." And she'd say, "What?" And

I'd say, "I love you, you little creep!" And she'd say, "You'll have to speak up, Mommy."

And that is why I need to be forgiven, Magdalen, friend to Jesus. I need to be forgiven by the lowest of the low. Forgive me. Cleanse me of my sins.

Please.

Constance

Dear Constance:

Whatever!

Sincerely,

Magdalen

• **ABOUT ME!**
• **STILL HUMAN**

Which brings us up to the Millennium! And hasn't it been quiet around here recently! Not hardly! It's been crazy!

You guys may recall that my big number one rule is "don't tell 'em where you live." Well, I never have, you know. But somehow one of my sneaky fans figured it out and, what do you know, there he was at my front door. (Those of you who read my e-mails may remember one from a certain Mr. Modern Prophet, a guy who actually threatened to come over. But I said to myself, "Not to worry. He'll never find me. No way." Well, *way!* He did find me. And how! Those of you who happened to be watching the live basement video stream at just the right moment last week know exactly what I'm talking about!

But I wanna tell you the whole story, from the beginning and not leave out a single awesome detail. And that all begins with a knock on the door.

Knock knock.

I opened the door and there was this wild and not a little scary lookin' guy. It was mostly his eyes that frightened me. I looked at them and in each eye I saw a tiny world on fire. It was our little blue world all up in smoke. He also had something written on his forehead. To me it looked like a bar code, if that makes sense. Then, of all things, he pointed to it, to the message on his forehead.

"Woman!" he said, "what's this say?"

I backed away, really shaking and afraid. "I don't know."

"What do you mean you don't know? Just read it."

"I can't read it."

"Why not?"

"It's not in words."

Now, he was getting a little frustration on top of his fury.

"Doesn't it say, 'Behold, the Modern Prophet'?"

"Not exactly. It doesn't say anything."

All of a sudden it looked like he was going to start crying or something. "Well, does it say, 'Death, Destroyer of Worlds' or something along those lines?"

"No. No, sir, it doesn't say that either."

"How about, 'Hi, my name's Chris'?"

"Nope."

"Well, what does it say?"

"Honest to God, it doesn't say anything. It's like a bar code sort of thing."

"Bar code!"

"That's right. Hey, check it out for yourself, if you don't believe me. There's a mirror right there."

So he looked in this mirror we've got in the entryway.

"Christ," he said, "I really thought it was going to say 'Behold, the

Modern Prophet.' I'd been given assurances. I don't get it." He rubbed at it then like a mother would rub at a smudge on a kid's face, but not even spit helped to loosen it. "Boy, it's really on there. It's like a tattoo or something. I hope it's going to come off eventually. It looks ridiculous."

Can you guys believe the weirdness of this scene? The things you don't expect in this life-online, this digital life of ours. But, you know, in that moment I was starting to feel sorry for him. He looked the opposite of what he had looked. Gone the worlds ablaze, one in each eye. Gone the fierceness of the redeemer. Now he was just a boy, a lost boy, who had wandered into something way over his head. I actually thought he was going to cry.

Where is Net Nanny when you need it?!

"Look," I said, taking him by his shaky hand, "why don't you come in and have a seat and we'll sort this out. Would you like some milk and cookies?" I led him over to our couch.

"Now," I said, "what's all this about? What is a Modern Prophet, anyway?"

He was really disappointed about something, the poor kid. "It was going to be so perfect," he explained. "I couldn't believe the perfectness of how it was supposed to be. I was given assurances. Here it was the site of Magdalen and I was the Modern Prophet. I was going to show you and the whole world the End of the Age. The Seven Seals."

"Seals? Like in the circus?"

"Not that kind of seal."

"Oh."

" . . . and then the destruction of Babylon, reduced to ashes by the angelic hackers . . ."

"Angelic hackers?"

" . . . and the meaning of the Beast and the Harlot . . ."

"That scene's over at Twobackedbeast.com. I'm not into that. Forget it if that's what you're after. The harlot part you've got right, although I prefer simple 'slut.' "

" . . . and then you'd be so wowed and grateful that you'd bathe my feet in precious oils and dry them with your hair."

"Kinky! I've got some of that Body Shop foot-massage lotion if that's what we're talking about here. I don't know about 'precious,' though. Does $4.95 count as precious? But I need to tell you something before we get too carried away. My real name isn't Magdalen. It's just Tracy."

I touched his knee.

"Tracy?"

"Tracy. Yup. Tracy. Sorry."

"Geez, that doesn't make any sense at all. Tracy."

"Well, forget it, just go on."

"If your name had been Magdalen, and the writing on my forehead had come out as I was led to believe it would . . ."

"Led to believe, dear? By whom?" I gently inquired.

" . . . I don't want to go into it. A Voice. But my idea was that I could announce to you the End of the Age."

"Oh that. These days, Ages don't last long. We have to update our software every three months."

"I had this great speech all worked out. It's ruined now. It was so clear before, and now it doesn't make any sense at all. What am I doing here?"

I giggled. "I think I get it. Your name is 'Chris,' right? Well, you're sure as heck a bringer of confusion. So maybe you are the Anti-Chris!"

Oh, but that brought a scowl back to his little face, and you could kinda see those tiny globes in his eyes kindle for a second like an almost hot charcoal briquette.

"Get it? You did say your name was Chris?"

"I get it. It's not funny."

"I laughed! I'm sorry. Go ahead. Tell me more. This is really very interesting. Tell me what you were going to do to me. Were you going to rape me? Tie me up? Stick things in me? That's a theme on my site, you know. We have a little contest here called "What Goes In Must Come Out." It's a sort of guessing game. Winners get something wet on the ol' e.love."

"I have no idea what you're talking about. I was going to tell you about our final devolution and the End of the Age."

"Oh well, go ahead. I'm bored to tears hearing about it already."

"Devolution is how we've all devolved."

"Duh! Just what do you mean by it, devaluation, or whatever you said?"

"It means going backward."

"So? Give me an example."

"Okay. Give me an area of life and I'll give you an example."

"Area of life?"

"Yeah, like food."

"Okay, food."

"The truth is that people who live in Third World countries eat better than we do, *when they eat,* because their soil is not depleted, they don't use chemicals, and their food is fresh and not processed. For us, we might as well be eating the vinyl siding on our crappy houses."

"Oh, you've got something against houses too?"

"If a house is made of bricks and is full of the character of design, it's human. If it's a flimsy vinyl box, it's an abomination unto the Lord, a mendacity, and deserving of plagues of frogs. Deserving of the Lord saying, 'I wish I hadn't made them.' Meaning human beings."

"Aren't we full of ourselves! People make bricks, just like people make vinyl. Right? What's the difference? You don't find bricks out lying around in the woods."

"You're starting to sound like my father."

"Well, then, I think I'd like your father."

"My point is that we've been building houses out of bricks for centuries. There's beauty in it. Craft. Vinyl is something that if it burns and you breathe it, you get cancer."

"I don't think you know what you're talking about."

"Yes, I do." He was getting kind of arrogant and snotty on me. "Try another one."

"Music."

"Right. It used to be that we sang, joined community choirs, and played the piano. Then we had radio, records and now the CD. Or worse yet, MP3. No one makes their own music. When I listen to a CD, I can't tell if it's music or insects rubbing their legs together. Ever listen to a real piano? And I won't even go into the difference between Mozart and Fat Daddy Cool or Chubby Whatever."

"Give me a break! I like my CD player. It sounds nice to me." But he did have a point: I had never heard a real piano.

"Don't you get what I'm saying at all? This is why I've come to you. I was supposed to reveal to you, Magdalen, all of this stuff about the fallen condition of the world and you would repent. Before it was too late. I was going to save you before your human body was utterly sucked up into the Digital Domain. I was going to show you The Way."

"Well, if The Way means I have to listen to boring classical music, forget it."

He put his head in his hands and moaned. "I know. I've failed. I'm a terrible fraud. I *am* a false prophet."

There he went with the almost-boohoo thing again. "Don't be sad, little friend. Maybe you can still save me. I'll give you another chance. What about sex?" I think I probably leered at him just a little.

"Sex? Oh, please don't make me speak of that. Don't you see? We used to be humans. We had loving sex with our human bodies, with people we loved. Now our primary libidinal cathexis is with machines. Cars, power tools, computers, Kitchen Aids, audiophile equipment. All day long we're having sex with machines and the monsters we're breeding are terrifying, terrifying to God himself. They are not human."

Well, guys, you can imagine what I made of this line of crapola. Bizarre! You meet all kinds in this biz. The poor fucked-up goofball. I just stared at him for a while, wondering what to do. I couldn't wait for my husband to meet him, as he surely would if I could get the guy to stay another fifteen minutes. And what do you make of that gobbledy-gook about rabbinical labyrinth catheters or whatever he said? Please, write in! Help me. Maybe we should have another contest. Like always, winner gets something wet on e.love!

Anyway, this had gone on long enough. So I said, "Honey, here, take this." I pulled out a tit for him. "Go ahead take it. With your lips, goofball. Your human lips, if you insist. That tit is one hundred percent fat human tit. Purest tit on the Web. That good enough for you?" And boy didn't he just come over and suckle on down like my own little baby boy! Little sweetie!

After a while, I think he fell asleep there, drooling on my chest, so I scooped him up—and he couldn't have weighed much at all, he was, like, so airy, like he'd turned himself into pure thought with all his crazy thinking—and took him down in the basement.

"Where are we?" he asked.

"Just down in the old Love Den, dear. It's nice and quiet here."

"What's that music?"

"Hmmm?"

"The music."

"I don't know. I bought some CDs at Wal-Mart for background music."

"It's Chopin. The *Marche Funèbre*."

"I think it's pretty."

Then I shushed him, got him all snuggled back in, and pulled my skirt up, spreading my legs.

And didn't you boys just dig it!

"Honey," I said, touching his cheek, "can you turn your head a little this way? That's it."

"Why?"

"Oh, never you mind. Just do me the favor. It's not too much to ask you to turn your head a little given what I'm doing for you." 'Cause I do believe that it was the first time he'd had a tit in his mouth. Can't say the obverse for the tit, though. No, that's a "been around" tit if ever there was one.

Then I heard a noise upstairs. My husband was home.

"Tracy? Where are you?" he hollered.

"I'm down here, dear. We have a guest. Get a beer and come down."

Marche Funèbre

What miserable rogues fill the marketplace while that beautiful soul burns out!

                                                        —Delacroix

1.

The soldiers of the Czar have come to the home of Mikolaj Chopin and his wife Justyna, an apartment at the Saxon Palace in the Saxon Gardens in Warsaw, Poland. The Russian imperialists had ruled in Warsaw and Poland since the defeat of Napoleon in 1812. Mikolaj Chopin was actually considered by most Poles to be a collaborator with the Russians. He taught at their lyceum, presented his child prodigy Frédéric at the Russian palace, and refrained from participating in the periodic "uprisings" against the Russian status quo.

So he was surprised, in the winter of 1830, when the soldiers arrived at his door. He of course opened it for them anyway, surprised or not.

"What can I do for you?" he asked.

Four grim, crimson-coated soldiers stood before him. "We have orders to burn the bed of your son."

"What? Burn his bed?" He called to his wife. "Justyna, the Russians have come to burn Frycek's bed."

Justyna Chopin came to her husband's side looking over his shoulder, her hands on his arm. Chopin's parents had a long, successful, mutually caring marriage, something their son would never have.

"What? Has the world gone mad? Why would they want to do such a thing? The boy no longer even lives here. And where will he sleep when he returns to us?"

The officer in charge replied, "We have our orders. We are to burn his bed. Please step aside."

They stepped aside, of course, and the soldiers entered and climbed the stairs to the bedroom where Chopin spent his youth. Justyna and her husband followed, confused but persisting in their complaints.

"I tell you, the boy has done nothing wrong. Nothing to deserve that his bed should be burned. And he has left the country. He is a musician. The Czar himself loves Frycek. Please, explain to us what you are doing and why."

At the top of the stairs, the officer stopped, although his men continued forward, into the bedroom. They didn't even need to ask where the room was, or which was the bed in question. But the officer paused and explained their purpose for a last time.

"Madame, sir, we do not know why we have been required to do this thing. We have orders to burn the bed of Frédéric Chopin. It is that simple as far as we are concerned. We do not press beyond that fact. And we will burn his bed. You would be well advised not to interfere or to ask too many questions. I do not wish to be obliged to include your name in my written report."

The parents of Chopin paled. Mikolaj turned to his wife and said, "Did you hear that, dear? There is to be a written report about the burning of Frycek's bed! It is beyond question an important matter."

The soldiers lifted the bed and were carrying it down the narrow wooden stairs when the officer returned to them. "No," he said to them, "there is no requirement that we burn the blankets or the pillows. Throw them to the floor."

The soldiers hesitated and looked at him with some concern.

"Don't worry. I'll take full responsibility for the decision." He turned to the Chopins and nodded as if in fact he wished them to understand that he understood their position and truly cared for them. They could be his own parents.

"And the bed is small enough that we can simply throw it from that balcony window to the street. Don't bother with the stairs."

So, they threw Chopin's bed from the balcony over the narrow Warsaw street. It landed awkwardly with the legs at the foot of the bed striking first and causing the bed to buckle and break with a loud snapping of tearing wood and ripping pegs.

The soldiers rapidly and noisily descended to the street, their boots thudding as the boots of soldiers do when descending wooden stairs. Some kerosene was thrown on the bed and the sad, broken thing was ignited. It blazed quickly, the flames climbing the crazily tilted headboard. A crowd gathered and muttered stormily. Perhaps Chopin's bed would be the cause of the next uprising.

"The filthy Russians have gone too far this time . . . they're burning our beds . . . even Chopin! . . . Serves him right, the dirty collaborator. . . . But why would the Russians do this if the Chopins are with them? . . . I'm going home to see if they're burning anything at my house."

2.

Frédéric Chopin, as is well known, had tuberculosis from a very young age and was sick and feverish off and on his entire life. Most troubling for both Chopin and his friends was, naturally, his intense cough, a cough through which, he once complained, he would "cough up my soul." But Chopin's cough was also, oddly, a part of his charm for the women in Paris society, especially for the great George Sand. This was, after all, the era of Romanticism, and genius was thought to be coterminous with "consumption," as it was then called. Consumption was the "fever of the Romantics." According to Dr. Jean-Claude Davila, "thinness and a pale face were an extreme distinction: women loved thin and fragile men, considering it symbols of virility." According to the "cult of consumption," the disease gave its victims "an exalted inner life" as a sort of compensation for their ravaged bodies.

The most notorious period in Chopin's famed relationship with the novelist and ur-feminist George Sand was the winter of 1838 that the two spent with Sand's children on the Spanish island of Majorca. Sand sought an idyllic retreat from the intense life of Paris. She also argued that the southern climate would be good for the delicate Chopin's health. The reality of Majorca, however, was anything but salutary. First, upon their arrival in Palma, they discovered that there were no hotels. And as soon as the word about Chopin's condition spread, there were no private rooms available to them either. Ultimately, the beleaguered family was obliged to live above a barrel maker's shop while waiting for rooms in an abandoned medieval Carthusian monastery at Valldemosa. Once in the monastery, the very walls sweated with an antique decay. A fine place for a tubercular man to take a cure!

While the near-indestructible Sand and her children enjoyed the romantic ruins of the monastery and even enjoyed the daily deluges of rain to which they were subjected during their stay, Chopin found that the infectious walls of the monastery leaked all-too-familiar anxieties about death.

As Sand wrote in her *Story of My Life,* "He became completely demoralized. . . . For him the cloister was full of terrors and phantoms, even when he felt well. . . . I would find him at ten o'clock at night, pale at his piano, with haunted eyes, and hair standing on end. . . . He then made an effort to laugh, and he played sublime things he had just composed or, better said, the terrible or heart-rending ideas that had captured him, despite himself, in that hour of solitude, sadness, and fear."

In general, that winter "death seemed to hover over our heads to seize one of us." So, Sand decided to cut short their stay, and on February 11, 1839, they left the monastery with all of their belongings, including the Pleyel piano that had only just arrived after several months en route from France. It was none too soon. Chopin was suffering "a frightening expectoration of blood."

When they boarded the ship, *El Mallorquin,* bound for Barcelona, the piano had to be shipped above deck. (They would have preferred to simply sell it, but the good people of Palma believed that the tubercular Chopin had infected the instrument and they would not offer to buy it.) It was strapped to the deck and covered over in canvas. Chopin would not leave the piano's side, despite the "basins full of blood" he was spitting up. It even appears that at one point he asked to be strapped to the piano. A strange idea, perhaps, but not when compared with the alternative: being transported below deck with a herd of pigs being shipped to the mainland.

But the horror of this trip did not end in Majorca. Sand writes, "When we left the hotel in Barcelona, the manager wished to make us pay for the bed in which Chopin had slept, under the pretext that it had been infected, and that the police regulations obliged him to burn it."

Sand had no choice but to pay for the bed they would burn, and try though she did to hurry her loved ones from the scene, they witnessed the peasants—who seemed, oddly, to be the same dark little men they had seen in Majorca—bring the detested bed into the street before the hotel and set it ablaze. As their carriage pulled away, headed for the ship that would finally return them to France, Chopin stared out the back window at the conflagration. Humiliated. Appalled. Ashamed to live.

The peasants danced about the bizarre pyre.

3.

The great Frédéric Chopin, virtuoso pianist and consummate composer of the romantic style, had just settled back in his seat on the train bound for Paris. It was the fall of 1846. He was humming to himself the melody he had created for one of Mickiewicz's ballads. At just that moment, a delegation of farmers arrived at the home of the great French writer, she of the beautiful soul and fat ass, Madame George Sand, in rural Nohant. We will not disappoint you: she was smoking a cigar when she came to the front door, summoned by her maid.

"What do they want?" asked Madame Sand.

"Excuse me, Madame, but they say they have come to take Chopin's bed."

The cigar dropped from her mouth. "Damn! His what?"

"His bed, Madame."

The spokes-farmer for this delegation tried to clarify the situation. "In fact, if you will, we don't want to take the bed. We are here because we are obliged to burn it."

"Well," Sand replied, "that is some clarification." There was a despairing look of recognition in her face. This again. Familiar and awful. It was really the farmers themselves who were most confused about what exactly they were doing. For Sand, it was awful life-business as usual.

"Our apologies, Madame Sand, but we must take M. Chopin's bed and burn it. We would prefer to burn it outside and away from the house. But burn it we will. It occurs to us as in the nature of a sad and strange necessity."

Sand stared at this mopish delegation sternly. She retrieved her cigar and puffed aggressively. "You farmers never really liked the poor, suffering, angelic man, did you?" No response.

Sand was nonplussed. "Sad and strange it is; you are right about that. Listen, Mssr. Chopin is a sick man. He needs a bed. He spends a lot of time in it. Just where is he to sleep when he returns?"

The farmers looked one at the next, as if mulling this question over as a group. "Excuse us, but you could perhaps afford to buy him another bed."

"Why? So that you could come back and ask permission to burn it too?"

"Again, our apologies, but we do not ask permission. We will take and burn the bed. If it's not clear to us which of the beds is Chopin's, we will have no choice but to burn all of the beds in the house."

"Oh, a fine idea! I'll be the first French woman driven into poverty through the burning of beds! Sad and strange indeed!"

Just then, the farmer who functioned as some sort of spokesman put out his hand and gently touched Sand's wrist. "Madame . . ." he said, "si vous plait."

Sand sighed deeply. "Oh, of course, come in." And she moved aside.

The farmers walked through the house carefully, quietly, apologetically, with a certain melancholy. It was as if they were coming to move the corpse of Chopin and not his bed. Four of them lifted the bed at its corners and in a stark procession moved gravely out of the house and into the yard, beneath a group of fruit trees. They set the bed down with extreme care. The maid came running after them to take the blankets and sheets from the bed before they ignited it. The farmers kept her firmly away, a burly farmer's forearm across her chest.

"Gentlemen, Madame Sand had this quilt made as a gift for Chopin. There can't be a need to burn it, too."

The farmers discussed the issue. The quizzical, rough expressions on their farmer faces. The throwing of hands in the air. The dolor of the wrinkles, and graying beards. These were not young impetuous farmers but the oldest, wisest men in the area. They did what they did with all due deliberation.

"Our profound regrets, mademoiselle, but you must inform Madame Sand that since we are unclear on the fate of the blankets, but we know that we may not delay in our chore, we have no choice but to burn them with the bed. We would not wish to make a mistake here. The consequences would be grievous for the entire agricultural region."

This rather stunned the poor young woman. Her bewilderment leapt to yet higher levels. "Oh, my God, what can you mean? Agriculture? Are you afraid your pigs will catch his disease?"

The farmers sighed and returned to their awful business. How could they expect this young maid to understand what big, strong French farmers could not. It was a necessity and a mystery and therefore a solemn obligation. That was all there was to say about it.

A small fire of sticks and newsprint, Sand's own journal *La Revue Independente,* was started beneath the bed, but it did not grow quickly because the air could not circulate well with the blankets hanging down on both sides. Eventually, though, with much flapping of arms, the fire did blaze and catch the mattress and soon the poor small bed with its fiery headboard looked like a comet scorching through the yard. The farmers had to cover their faces from the heat.

Already, George Sand had gone to her desk and was beginning a letter to Chopin.

Dear Chopinet:

I have most disturbing news for you. . . .

And at just that moment, Chopin sat bolt upright in his seat, as if his intestines had been connected to an electric current. He sensed that something had happened, something awful. He was very receptive to such psychic presentiments, especially where Sand was concerned. He recalled the time the peasants had burned his bed in Spain. He saw it burning, floating in space, a universal emblem of some depressing kind. But then the tune for the *ballade* returned, winding about the burning bed in a pleasing and blissful way. Chopin thought, "The sky is beautiful and my heart is sad." In his mind the *note bleue* resonated and there he was in the azure of transparent night. And nothing else mattered.

4.

At the end of his life, back in Paris, impoverished after the Revolution of 1848, permanently estranged from the "vampire" Sand, surrounded strangely by "Scotchwomen" who were "so good, but so boring, so help me God," Chopin retreated to die to an apartment in the Passy hills overlooking the Seine. He was now "an arch-delicate insect" that could be touched only very carefully lest a dry wing should snap off.

His death scene has been recounted by many, including a majority who were not there at all. The "mucosities" in his lungs made him feel as if he were suffocating. It had been a short life, surely, but hugely productive from a musical standpoint. It had also been a sad life in many ways—the tumultuous burlesque of the relationship with the omnivorous George Sand was at the top of that list—but not so oddly, perhaps, in those last moments Chopin's thoughts turned to the happy things, the little jewels in the pig shit of life. In particular, he recalled that when he lived with Sand at Nohant they spent many evenings with the children creating their own puppet theater. They had one hundred twenty puppets, all dressed by Sand. *Le Théatre des marionettes de Nohant* was a little world over which they were Gods intensely glad of what they had created. Chopin's part was to improvise at the piano while the young people performed different scenes together with comical dances.

At first, Chopin was most struck by how ridiculous his own deathbed agony made him feel. The Scotswomen were sniveling around and offering to pay for everything. The musicians were trying to figure out the most appropriate last things for the immortal one to hear as he passed through the Great Wringer. Something from Mozart's *Requiem*? Of course, a fine choice but a bit on the obvious side. "Hymn to the Virgin" by Stradella? An air by Pergolesi? A psalm by Marcello? Yes, yes, fine, but sing something, quickly, his belly is swelling with death. He is more than a candidate for the next world, he is half-inaugurated! In the end, it hardly mattered what they played for no sooner would they begin than Chopin would suffer a loud coughing fit and interrupt the tableau.

Dying people make for a very poorish audience.

And then, naturally, every aristocratic lady to whom Chopin had once given piano lessons was there determined to be witnessed by the rest of the *haut monde* achieving a successful faint beside Chopin's bed. The one "Lady" who was not allowed near his deathbed was the highest of them all, Madame Sand. Her apparition, cigar at mouth, enveloped in purling smoke, was felt at every window looking in on the last pathetic moments of her dear, vulnerable Chopinet.

But of course the only thing Chopin himself wished for, as he had wished all his life, was simply not to be disturbed. He said, "God shows a man a rare favor when He reveals to him the moment of the approach of death; this grace he shows me. Do not disturb me."

When at last he died, his heart was cut from his body, placed in alcohol, and given to his sister, Ludwika, who smuggled it back to Warsaw hidden beneath her dress. She feared that the filthy Russian czarists would confiscate the great heart. The body was interred at Pére Lachaise. It is said that women still like to faint before his headstone.

But the deathbed itself had to be burned, *bien sûr*. And the musicians, artists, ladies and benefactors lifted it high upon their shoulders and passed through the front door into the courtyard, the lugubrious opening chords of Chopin's own *Marche Funèbre* from the B-flat minor sonata echoing behind them. They moved through the Parisian suburb of Chaillot, on the Passy hills overlooking both the city and the Seine. On a long hillside they paused and set the bed afire, still raised high on their shoulders. Then with an enormous shrug they sent it down the hill over which it seemed almost to flow, brightly, like lava, on unearthly wheels, flames arcing back.

"*Bon voyage,* Chopinet," they cried. "*Au revoir* you who first made us completely human, through your universal tears. *Bonne chance.* Your triumph is the beginning of our long failure."

Mahler's Last Symphony

Here's a little secret. Every one of Mahler's symphonies is his last symphony. The urgency in his music is the certainty that he has to finish this massive statement before it is too late. "Hurry up, Gustave. It's that time." And so in each symphony he expresses his essential love for life and being, the green freshness deep in things, and he expresses his contempt and horror at life's baseness and brutality. (Disgust is not too strong a word for it.) Then he says, "Goodbye." Fare thee well, world. See you, smelly, violent, stupid world. Adios, brilliant, ethereal, sweet world. That's what the Mahlerian pathos is about from the first symphony to the last. Never did he make a symphony for the heck of it or because he had a "career goal."

But, you might protest, what great composer hasn't composed against the discovery of mutability? Musicians are always saying, "Listen to this note! Ah! It's gone! Do you see how it is with time? Do you get it now? You numbskull!"

We marvel at the sand paintings of Tibetan monks. We say, "How incredible and strange it is that they are willing to put so much care and art into the creation of something that they will sweep away! Oh! They are revealing to us the fragility of human action and human time!" But our astonishment at the works of the monks only underscores our failure to perceive that our own music carries this same grim message.

Each musical note begins decaying in the moment it is created. At least with the sand painting you've got this colorful pile of very durable sand when you're done. What's left in the wake of a really poignant largo?

Infinite longing. That's what's left.

The 1967 Columbia Records recording of *The Nine Symphonies of Gustav Mahler* (conducted by Leonard Bernstein) contains the final, awkward Mahlerian farewell. On a bonus disc called *Gustav Mahler Remembered,* a musician with the New York philharmonic, Herbert Borodkin, violist, speaks of his experience under Mahler's baton during the 1910 season. Borodkin is being interviewed by William Malloch and the two are studying an old New York Symphony program.

Borodkin: "There was a big let-down in the Philharmonic for a year or two after Mahler's death."

Malloch: "It's funny, in the basses there's a bassist named Mahler."

Borodkin: "Mahler. He died long ago. Fine bass player. I knew the family very well. My goodness. You know, come to think of it. There's very few of us left. All the rest are gone. I don't see anybody else here."

Malloch: "Isn't that strange."

Borodkin: "All these people are gone now."

The Human Condition (5)

This time, the last time, there's no boat. He's been sitting in his recliner with a headache for two days. His dog has been dead for several years. Still, he wonders where it is. He's worried about it. Poochy. Has Poochy eaten yet? Don't want to forget to feed him. Dog gets grouchy. He gets up, opens a can of minestrone soup, puts it in a bowl and puts the bowl on the floor. Where the hell is that dog? So, he gets back in the recliner. After two days, a recliner feels just like a boat. He pushes back horizontal. Feels the tide. He feels like an Indian floating out to the Happy Hunting Ground. The gentle rise and fall of the tide. The pleasant floating. The pleasant knowing that it's all over, all the baloney of life. He would call himself happy if it weren't for the damned headache. The red-hot railroad spike into the center of his head. But after a while, really, what's the difference between this pain and the sunset? The ineffable, kindly red radiance of Mr. Sun just sort of spread all warm and hazy around him as he floats toward the horizon in his old green recliner with the red-hot railroad spike in his forehead.

His hand dangles over the side.

It's wet.

Must be the water. Or the minestrone.

But he looks and sees that it's good old Poochy who has returned from his two-day walk around the block and is licking his hand.

He grins and greets him. "Poochy! You're home!"

Poochy replies, "I always loved you."

His head feels so heavy and burnt-brilliant and smoky and he can't keep it out over the edge because it's like dangling the globe out there and it's making his neck sore, so he reclines back again and thinks,

"I'm so blessed. I'm so blessed. I'm so blissfully blessed. Thank you for this, Poochy."

Of course, from another point of view, two days floating in the recliner, talking to the dead family dog and leaving bowls of minestrone soup on the floor get him to the emergency room at the hospital. That's where it gets him. Never mind his assurances that his headache that feels like a burnt-umber sunset is really rather remarkably pretty. Never mind that. No one calls him "blessed."

And at the hospital, they don't call it a pretty sunset. They call it a "vascular incident." They call it an "inner cranial aneurysm." His brain is leaking and what's coming out is Poochy, boats, sunsets, and all sorts of stuff including repeated appearances of cans of minestrone soup and just how did *that* became so important in his life? And by the way, that sunset he was so pleased with is called "blood pressure 200 over 120" by those who know. Not volcanic, but enough to crack the foundation of that little house of cards he calls his mind.

What doesn't leave, though, is this beautiful little feeling about a dog, a boat, a sunset, and a superb sense of forgiveness.

SELECTED DALKEY ARCHIVE PAPERBACKS

FOR A FULL LIST OF PUBLICATIONS, VISIT:
www.dalkeyarchive.com

SELECTED DALKEY ARCHIVE PAPERBACKS

FOR A FULL LIST OF PUBLICATIONS, VISIT:
www.dalkeyarchive.com